A FORMIDABLE FORTUNE

Anne

All good wishes

Vera

2. 8. 07

Vera Morrill

About the Author

Vera Morrill was born in Yorkshire and has always had an interest in writing and in the theatre. A secretary in her early years she soon moved on to writing and performing and also teaching English and Drama.
She has written and broadcast six short stories for BBC Radio Solent and is an accomplished poet having been published in numerous anthologies.
She now lives on the beautiful Isle of Wight.

for Ian,
with love.

A Formidable Fortune
by Vera Morrill

© Vera Morrill 2005

ISBN 1 873295 96 0

First Edition November 2005
Published by Cross Publishing
Chale, Isle of Wight
Layout and cover design by Fiona Crouch

Prologue

In the mid-morning sunlight, the domes and minarets of the Palace of Jaishalpur glowed like mother-of-pearl. Glittering in his suit of gold, Niaz, the young Maharajah, stood at the head of the front portico's marble stairs and surveyed the courtyard below. The officials of his household, his Palace guards, the royal elephants, resplendent in ceremonial trappings, all awaited his signal.

Half turning he drew forward the woman standing, as protocol decreed, one pace behind him. She was, he thought, like a tiny bird of paradise in her shimmering sari of blue-green and silver. She was nervous, he knew. Felt the tension in her body, noted the over-bright glistening of her eyes.

For her sake everything must be perfect. All possible sources of embarrassment and distress had been considered and eradicated. Most important of all the royal tigers had been moved outside the environs of the Palace, so that no unwelcome roars should distress this particular guest. Now he smiled down at his grandmother and squeezed her hand reassuringly. 'All will be well', his eyes said.

She had told him everything. He knew that their guest had every reason to hate his father, perhaps even to hate Niaz himself. But as the Rani smiled back, her tension easing, the cream Rolls was already gliding into the courtyard, the elephants had begun to make their obeisance and for the first time Niaz too, felt a flicker of nervousness...

It was a mistake to come back on my own, Helen thought. 'You need a few days alone with the Rani', he'd said, 'the children and I will join you later'. But the children would have provided a distraction and I need my husband's strong right arm now more than I've ever needed it. What shall I say? What shall I do?

So many memories of this place. Mostly bad. Unhappiness and unspeakable cruelty. And that night...Oh God, that terrible, terrible night. Only the Rani's love saved my sanity and only her courage and wisdom secured my escape.

And there she is!

With a quick movement Helen was out of the car and locked in the Rani's loving embrace. And as the watershed of their tears flooded over them, the young Maharajah moved forward to greet his guest.

Chapter One

Helen did not recognise the image confronting her in the mirror. Could this exotic oriental figure really be her? The pearls glowed with a life of their own and from the top of her lightly veiled hair to delicate gold sandalled feet she exuded glamour.

She was ready and the deep-throated voice of the conch shells indicated that it was time to go. Gently swaying, the palanquin carried her through the vaulted corridors towards Jai. Carefully she obeyed her instructions throughout the service as wave after wave of incomprehensible language flowed around her. Then she and Jai were borne aloft into the great Durbar room and for the first time she was able to observe him fully. Resplendent in white silk trousers, gold flared brocade jacket with diamond buttons and studded collar, an emerald encrusted sword at his side, he was magnificent. His white and gold turban bore a huge clip of diamonds and pearls and his eyes glittered with pride.

Now the British would see that a mere Indian was capable of taking from them a much desired prize, Helen's Indian garments serving to underline the fact that she was now entirely his and must bend to his will.

The awning of a second wedding pavilion afforded some slight protection as, covertly, Helen tried to take in the scene around her. The nobles sat in rows, their ceremonial swords across their knees, each jewelled hilt tied with a ribbon of golden gauze, signifying that its owner came in peace. Now a seemingly endless stream of princes and nobles came before Jai, each offering a token of a single gold coin, symbol of their allegiance. The room was a kaleidoscope of brilliant colours, which with each movement of its occupants, splintered and reformed. The bandoliers of precious stones worn by the Princes caught and spilled light in all directions, the feathers of their aigrettes fluttering softly as heads were bowed and raised. The air of the great Durbar room redolent with the aroma of perfume and spices.

Just as Helen was beginning to wonder how long she could remain immobile, eyes downcast, she was startled into awareness by a very English voice

"Prince Romesh, Your Highness, I bring to you and your bride the felicitations of his Majesty the King, and of the Bombay Regiment."

"Thank you Colonel. My dear, may I present to you Colonel Endicott of the Cavalry Regiment. He and I are well-known opponents - on the polo-field." The slight hesitation before completing the sentence, was enough indication to Helen of Jai's antipathy towards the man standing in front of them.

She inclined her head in acknowledgement of the introduction and in that movement her eyes met those of the young adjutant standing two paces behind his superior. It was Walter! Unbelievably, after all these years, here at her wedding, here in India. Grown beyond recognition physically, but his eyes she would always

5

recognise. This was undoubtedly the boy who had cared for her like an older brother and made life bearable when her mother was dying. How could she not speak to him? A whispered aside to Jai produced the response she had hoped for. A message would be given to the Colonel and a meeting arranged - but most certainly not today. As the Colonel turned to leave and Walter came to attention their eyes locked. Illogically she felt a wave of relief flood her being. In the past, Walter had proved himself to be a tower of strength. To know that he was close at hand was somehow very satisfying.

By the time Jai came to her after dining with the Princes, Helen was rested and wearing her gown and robe of palest pink mousseline de soie. Any fears she might have had receded in the wake of Jai's gentle caresses. Gradually he stimulated her senses until she started to long for closer physical contact; she wanted to shed all her inhibitions and beg him to enter her. When all was over and they lay, bodies intertwined, she was suffused with contentment. As the tiger's roar startled them both into awareness, they were able to laugh together and her happiness was complete.

In the orderly peace of her prayer room the Rani's mind was in turmoil. Two days ago she had begged her wicked son not to proceed with his plan but he had now done just as he had intended.

The ritual she had been forced to witness had been merely one of betrothal, not marriage. The priests would never dare disobey Romesh's commands or divulge what they knew. Ashok and other family members, well aware of Romesh's vicious streak, would never flout his wishes. As for herself and Almeera, her attendant of many years, they too knew what the penalty for disclosure would be.

Helen, the Princes and nobles and, most importantly, the British, believed a wedding had taken place. Romesh could now keep the girl without interference from any quarter. If he wished to dispose of Helen, something her mind recoiled from with horror, then he could do so at any time.

The wedding which had taken place in England had no validity here, the betrothal was immaterial and with plans for an independent India already well advanced, the British would soon be leaving their shores.

Knowing that Romesh would never consider allowing a child who was not wholly Indian to inherit their throne, she could only believe that the whole episode with Helen was a mere dalliance on his part, an opportunity in a small way to vent his hatred of the British on a Briton. His vanity was such that he would also wish to see what handsome specimens he could produce from his union with this beautiful girl.

Doubtless his mind was already leaping ahead to a further marriage. Should no heir be forthcoming from that then he could, as was his prerogative, nominate a male child of his choosing. With a son already in the zenana, born of his liaison with Metta, daughter of an Sirdar, the choice was obvious.

Walter's alarm at learning of Helen's intended Indian marriage had been considerable. He knew a great deal about Prince Romesh -Jai. Information which had been unavailable to the Foreign Office had been discovered by regimental scouts and on Walter's desk for over a year. Jai's marriage to the Princess Mumtaz and his subsequent 'cooling off' period had been well documented, as had the existence of Metta and the small boy in the zenana. The sexual perversions encouraged, indeed instigated, by Jai's father were also recorded and from palace spies he learned that screams from the tiger's compound and blood-stained remnants later recovered, coincided exactly with the disappearance of those who had attempted to thwart the wishes of the Maharajah Elect.

How could the beautiful and gentle creature he remembered ever have contemplated union with such a man? No doubt she had been flattered by his attentions, seduced by his status and wealth, beguiled into believing that the urbane exterior represented the real man. In this case, nothing could be further from the truth. His sojourn in India had already taught him that the vast culture difference between Indians and British could not easily be bridged. Here, he suspected, the problem ran even deeper. This man and his father hated the British so much that any apparent liaison with a Briton must be regarded as having an ulterior motive.

It was imperative that he gain access to the palace and speak to Helen as soon as possible.

Betty's Journal

Saturday

I begged Prince Romesh, Jai, that as Helen's only English female friend here in India, I should be allowed to attend the wedding. To no avail! After a great deal of talk about custom and tradition it was obvious I was wasting my time.

Helen looked divine. I know it was a tremendous ordeal for her - it's so awful when you don't understand what is being said - but I've no doubt she managed to remain splendidly regal the whole time. She seemed so happy after her wedding night, but is now full of anxiety again, not having seen Jai for two whole days.

Another strange thing! Last night whilst I was with Helen, Ila brought in a gold tray on which was a tiny crystal goblet of what appeared to be water. When Helen asked what it was, the girl said it was a gift from Prince Romesh. Pressed further the girl said it contained crushed diamonds and after many gestures and much misunderstanding on the part of the three of us, we finally realised that Ila was telling us it was an aphrodisiac Not very tactful of our Prince, sending that after an apparently blissful wedding night!

This adds to my worries about Helen's marriage. When she first came to the salon I thought, along with the other girls, that she was too proud to talk to us and when she did open her mouth she sounded almost as posh as our customers. We soon learned she was just shy and unsure in her new surroundings and her beautiful manners and way of speaking were the result of her unusual upbringing. I now know her to be a romantic and a dreamer and how that relates to her princely husband, who is abrupt to the point of rudeness and so sullen, I can't imagine. Never does he show her affection. Just taking her arm or her hand wouldn't kill him and I'm sure she would find it reassuring. Even allowing for the difference in culture and his own royal upbringing I find this unforgivable. After all, she is a young woman in a strange land and with the exception of yours truly, surrounded by strangers.

Helen's meeting with Walter has now been confirmed for ten days from now (can't think why the delay). They are to meet in one of the palace's main sitting rooms and Ila and I are to remain present.

Tuesday a.m.

Great excitement - Jai's wedding present has just arrived. What appeared to be a small set of drawers of carved ivory is in fact a jewellery casket, about four feet high. Its drawers are all velvet-lined and divided into sections. Inside the top drawer was a doe-skin pouch and inside that, the largest diamond I have ever seen. It is a drop pendant for Helen to wear either on her forehead when she is dressed Indian style, or around her neck when in European garments. Hard on the heels of this came a further gift. Bearers carried in a magnificent circular leopard skin rug, made from the skins of no fewer than ten animals! Accompanying the gifts was a message from Jai saying he would be joining her for dinner this evening. Everything in the garden is rosy and Helen is all smiles again.

Friday

Zizi has kept me awake for the third time this week, with his incessant roaring. The sound seems to bounce off these marble walls and is quite deafening. They tell me he is calling for a mate. Thank goodness all the men around here don't make quite so much noise when they feel playful!

Helen is obviously in a state of bliss. Jai has now stayed with her several times, leaving in the early hours. It seems to me a most bizarre way to run a marriage, but then I've never mixed with royalty before.

We have started our tennis lessons with Herr von Pieter, whose English is somewhat fractured, but we manage. He's about 30 and typically German, short-cropped blonde hair and steely blue-grey eyes. Tall and athletic of course. Helen and I have adapted our English blouses and skirts and Pieter as we call him has provided us with suitable shoes. Our lessons are arranged for nine in the morning, before it gets too hot. Ila accompanies us and sits at the side of the court. (It seems we, that is Helen, must always have a chaperone).

Two more discoveries today - a music room complete with a Steinway grand piano, inlaid with gold leaf and a dais for performing soloists and for those not so much interested in culture as body-building, a gymnasium with weight lifting equipment, boxing ring - the lot!

I must place on record my own gift to Helen of a silk shawl. Purchased in England, I spent the sea journey on the applique work of embroidery and beads. Amongst so many exotic offerings I feared it would prove very mundane, but, (though I sez it myself) it has been much admired and is certainly unique. (Perhaps I should go into business on my own.)

Helen had spent the morning in a reverie. Laughing when Betty asked what was occupying her thoughts, she answered, "Memories, just childhood memories." Her mind leap-frogged from one incident to another; Walter arranging for lambs to be brought into the farmhouse on the day of her mother's funeral; Walter formally asking Prinny, Miss Pringle their governess and surrogate mother, if she and Rosa might be excused from their lessons for an hour one day in April and leading them through a leafy tunnel into an amethyst lake of bluebells; Walter bringing Prinny snowdrops in January and the Spring's first primroses; the four of them picnicking on a golden carpet of buttercups; the swing he'd made to hang from the boughs of the apple tree - and the day she had declared herself too old for such childish pastimes. Their arguments... She, anxious to protect all living creatures, horrified at the thought of a hunted fox, cornered and distraught. He, endlessly and patiently, telling her of the fox's night of slaughter on the farm, even taking her to see the dead bloodied chickens, so that she'd turned away shuddering at the sight.

Only now in retrospect did she wonder at the infrequency of his visits during those years before she left for London. Busy at the time with her studies, outings to Northern cities and visits to the Manor, she and Rosa had found so much with which to occupy themselves that they had not missed the gradual tailing off of Walter's visits. Had not even, she ruefully admitted, remarked upon their absence. No doubt during that period the difference in their ages had become more marked. Walter's background had made it necessary that he grow up quickly and by the time she was a gawky fourteen year old, he was a young man of nineteen, albeit rather lanky and ungainly in appearance. Probably he felt himself much too grown up for the company of two silly girls. Taking himself off to the farm at Featherstone, 'to broaden his knowledge of farming' had somehow brought an end to their close companionship and the informality of their relationship.

From that time, his infrequent visits had taken the form of 'elevenses' in the cottage kitchen, always accompanied by Rosa's incessant chatter and Prinny's constant fussing with tea and cake. Since then, each of them had experienced major changes in their lifestyles, an uprooting of everything familiar. He, to a life in barracks and the strictures of army life both in Britain and overseas. And she to London and her amazing good fortune there. Retrospectively, the knowledge of her success was still difficult to accept. Everything had happened with such rapidity. How often she had longed for an adult, caring voice to suggest and advise her on how to deal with a particular situation. How she would have welcomed Walter's presence on so many occasions. Now, miles away from home they were two adults meeting in the most bizarre of circumstances. No longer could he discount her as too childish a companion. Not only was she married, with all that that entailed, she was now a Princess of the Rajputs, the princely lords of India. How wonderful Jai had been on that first night, sensing her nervousness and knowing her innocence. How quickly all her doubts and anxieties had been erased by his gentle expertise. And what an amazing quirk of fate had brought together the boy who had been her mainstay during those early difficult years and the handsome, lordly Jai, now her husband. According to Rosa, Walter had been in India for some time which would mean he and Jai would have so much to talk about. It was going to be a wonderful afternoon.

Betty's Journal

Quite obviously, Helen had been down 'Memory Lane' all morning and was both nervous and excited when we adjourned to the appointed reception room for Walter's visit. After much deliberation, she had donned one of the Aston dresses in pale green lawn. To an outsider she appeared cool and composed, but I have now learned to recognise the signs of agitation and the twisting of her rings and occasional fingering of the tendrils over her ears belied her composure.

Ila attempted to make herself invisible by taking her sewing to the farthest corner of the room and I ostentatiously surrounded myself with writing materials in order to make it obvious that I was there for the sole purpose of writing letters.

Walter was not quite what I had expected from Helen's description. Her brief glimpse at the great durbar had been insufficient for her to erase the remembered picture of a youth grown beyond his strength. Now, large and blonde, Walter at no time appeared clumsy, or indeed out of place in our elegant surroundings. Clearly, Walter has found his niche in the army and with maturity has come self-confidence.

Conversation was at first stilted then, as incidents were laughingly remembered, the formality slipped away and by the time tea had been served we, (for I was repeatedly drawn into their reminiscences) were relaxed and chatting happily together. No doubt Walter had been briefed with regard to protocol and the duration of his visit and at 4.30 p.m.exactly, in spite of Helen's protestations, he rose to leave. As he formally proffered his hand, Helen brushed it aside and throwing her arms around him reached up to kiss his cheek, exclaiming, "Dear Walter, it has been so wonderful to see you. Do promise you will come again and very soon."

It was at that moment I became aware of Jai's presence and simultaneously, heard the swish of Ila's sari as she rose and made her salaam. (Indians, we have learned, move almost soundlessly on their sandalled feet, particularly the males, who unlike the females wear no tinkling anklets to announce their approach). My own eyes were lowered immediately and I felt rather than saw the effect of his presence on the room's occupants, as if a black cloud had suddenly plunged us into its shade.

Helen's euphoric state seemed to have made her immune to the changed atmosphere. As I raised my head I saw her smilingly present Walter to Jai and, amazingly, she seemed unaware that the men's stiff little nods fulfilled merely the minimum of courtesy permitted. Only when their footsteps receded down the corridors in opposing directions did her smile fade as she commented "How rude of Jai to go so quickly, I wanted him to get to know Walter properly. Ah well, perhaps another time ...."

My own feeling was that there would never be 'another time'.

Zizi's roars almost drowned Helen's screams. Almost, but not quite. From the moment Jai crashed into her room, madness had reigned. She had half expected him, half thought he might apologise for his unreasonable behaviour of the afternoon, but as he moved towards the bed mouthing expletives in English and Hindustani, she shrank away from the ferocity of his attack.

"So my virginal English rose is just another whore. Couldn't wait to get him here and let him start fondling and kissing you, could you, you bitch? Who knows what you would have been up to if those other two dolts had not been present. Perhaps I have been too gentle with you and you prefer things a little rougher!" Her night-dress split from neck to hem as he pulled her towards him and her first screams rent the air as he struck her on the side of the jaw. Then, pulling her from the bed, he dragged her screaming to the mirrored dressing-room.

"Please Jai, please..."

"Begging for it now are we?" With one movement Jai shrugged off his outer robe and stood before her, his erect organ thrusting forward his loincloth. Helen gasped with pain as grasping her wrist he flung her face downwards.

"Got a taste for farm labourers have you? This should be just to your liking." Savagely he thrust himself into her from above and behind, as she had seen the farm animals copulate. She screamed as her unwilling flesh refused to open to his onslaught but his own multiple reflections seemed to fuel his excitement and the savage thrusting continued until at last he collapsed exhausted across her naked back.

Ila, cowering on the verandah, at first covered her ears, tried to shut out her mistress's agony, then when Zizi's roaring and the screaming stopped simultaneously, she became even more alarmed, listening intently for the departure of her royal master.

With the soft closing the door, she ran to the bedroom and from there to the dressing room, gasping with horror at the sight confronting her. Stopping only to throw a soft blanket over her mistress, she ran to the zenana, past the eunuch guards and straight to the Rani's ante-chamber, in which Almeera slept. A rapid interchange and the older woman moved unhesitatingly to the Rani's room. Touching the arm of her sleeping mistress she said only "Highness - it has happened." Instantly the Rani was awake and slipping into the proffered robe.

11

Moving to the door of the zenana she issued a swift order to the eunuchs, two of whom followed the three women back to Helen's suite.

Helen lay on the floor shaking violently. Pupils dilated and her face grey with shock, she was incapable of speech. The women wrapped her in the blanket and a further command brought the eunuchs who carried her gently to the zenana. There, in the Rani's own bathroom the semen and blood-stained remnants of her nightdress were removed and her injuries examined. Jai's first blow had left a spreading bruise along the left jawline. Her arms and knees were scored and bruised and the left wrist either broken or severely sprained. Her right side had suffered most from the dragging action along the floor and a large bleeding abrasion on her hip had spread into a bruise some ten inches in diameter. Even whilst they were assessing her injuries, Almeera was busy preparing a sedative and whilst the taut constriction of Helen's throat made swallowing difficult, Almeera was at last satisfied that the girl had absorbed sufficient to be beneficial. Gently they lowered her into a warm bath, where she was carefully cleansed. Then salve was applied to her bruised body, a loose robe of finest lawn wrapped around her and finally she was placed between sweet scented linen sheets. Now Almeera bandaged the swollen wrist and when at this point Helen's mouth tried for the first time to shape a word, the Rani gently placed a forefinger on her lips.

"No words are necessary dear Helen. You are now quite safe with me in the zenana. No-one, (the words were stressed), no-one can harm you here. My eunuchs are always on guard. They will be watching over you all night. It is now most important that you rest, for it is in rest that the mind and body heal. Sleep soundly, Helen, you are quite safe."

A little colour had now filtered back into Helen's face, the pupils had returned to normal and, as Almeera's sedative took effect, Helen still holding the Rani's hand, fell asleep.

Now the full horror of the past hour seemed to strike the Rani and the tears streamed down her face. She made no sound. Her restraint had been learned in a hard school where no allowance was made for childhood tantrums or hysteria. Almeera turned her attention to her mistress, the mistress she had served since they were children together, and took control. The Rani was given a sleeping draught and returned to her bed, Ila was despatched with two other girls to Helen's rooms; she to cull together whatever Helen's requirements might be for the next few days, they to remove all traces of the night's events.Two hours after the drama had started to unfold, only the eunuchs remained watchful and alert as all the occupants of the zenana finally slept.

Chapter Two

Friday

Helen has not told me what happened last night and I very much doubt if she will ever tell me or anyone else. That she was injured by his not-so-Royal Highness is obvious but the pain in her eyes runs deeper than that.

No-one seems to know Jai's whereabouts or if they know they are not saying. Few seem to care. When he's around they obey him, but I suspect that they do not respect him as they do the Rani. In any event he is definitely not in the Palace.

I sat with Helen this afternoon. The Rani's doctor had visited her this morning and said the wrist was badly sprained, not broken. As soon as she feels strong enough she is to sit in the gardens. Meanwhile she is mildly sedated and her bruises are painted regularly to reduce the discolouration.

I know there are women in London who are regularly beaten by their husbands but they are of a coarser metal than Helen who, until yesterday, had never been struck in her life. I've no doubt that her body will heal quickly enough, like me she is young and healthy, but I fear the repair of the mental damage suffered will take much longer.

A week has elapsed. Helen and I have spent long days in the gardens. There is a huge library in the Palace (naturally!) and I have passed my time reading some of the classics. How's that for a not very literate Cockney sparrow? Helen doesn't read. She sits for long periods, staring at the fountains, showing no interest in anything.

Walter knew exactly where Jai was. His palace spies had informed him of Helen's injuries and that she was now closely confined within the zenana. But, if it came to a confrontation between the Rani and her evil son, for how long could the Rani hold out? His anxiety for Helen's safe-keeping was matched only by his desire to see some curb put upon the activities of Prince Romesh.

There was something else, something which had been eating away at the back of his mind since he and the Colonel had attended the palace wedding. Why had the members of the Rajput not been invited to attend the ceremony? That Romesh might wish to exclude the British was understandable, but traditionally, his peers should have been present. Helen had not mentioned any conversion to Hinduism and whilst Romesh could bend many rules, the marriage of a non-Hindu in a Hindi ceremony was most unusual.

On that occasion one of his spies had reported a strange conversation between a Sirdar and the senior priest. In the process of handing over money towards temple funds, the Sirdar had issued what was clearly a threat. "The beast devours those who divulge the secrets of his master". Just what had taken place during the wedding ceremony? Walter was still hopeful that the priest's greed might eventually overcome his fears and for a further substantial sum (towards temple funds!) he would unravel the mystery.

As to Jai's whereabouts, Walter was aware that two hours after raping Helen, his Rolls Royce had slipped quietly through the palace's golden arch en route for the home of his wife, Princess Mumtaz. Two other cars followed containing the Prince's requirements for a protracted absence and his escort of armed guards...

Walter decided that his first move must be to contact Betty. Her mail would not be under such scrutiny as that of Helen and from her he might be able to ascertain whether Helen was yet in a fit state to learn all the unpleasant information he had about Jai.

Betty's Journal

Something happened yesterday which aroused even in Helen a slight flicker of curiosity. Two young women appeared at the far side of the zenana gardens during Helen's resting period. One was Alisha whom we haven't met since our arrival. The other girl we have never seen before. Tall and slender with that rather provocative swaying movement of the hips which men find so attractive, she glanced in our direction several times and clearly found in us a great source of amusement. The Rani confirmed that one was indeed Alisha and that the other girl Metta was the daughter of one of the Sirdars, then changed the subject rather too quickly. She has been a tower of strength, bringing a variety of objects to rouse Helen from her apathy... an exotic bloom, unusual pieces of material and embroidery and today, best of all, a baby marmoset, which produced from Helen the first smile since Tuesday night.

Arrangements have been made for Helen to see the Rani's doctor on Friday. She told me, in Helen's presence, that she wished Helen to have an examination to ensure there was no internal damage. If Helen wished I could be present. All this confirms my own thoughts that the episode went far beyond a few heavy blows. I keep hoping that Walter will make contact with me. If I addressed a letter to him at the barracks it would be so noticeable, the Sirdars would be informed and know who had 'spilled the beans' to the British about their lord and master.

Friday

I didn't think anything worse could happen and it has. Helen is pregnant! We, that is Helen, the Rani and I are all stunned. Suddenly everything is different. I am convinced that Helen had almost reached the decision that she would leave for England very soon, but now....

She has at last started to talk and now puts forward endless reasons why she should remain in India. Jai was mad with jealousy, which was a sort of compliment showing just how much he cared for her. (Not much evidence of that during his attack, I thought.) He has a right to see his own son ruling the province, etc., etc.

14

I did point out that with an independent India and a central government already in the pipeline any actual ruling would be drastically reduced, but she still imagines a situation where her child will be able to act as a power for good in the area. In that of course she is taking the Rani as a role model. Although we have never left the Palace since our arrival, the Sirdars and our own attendants have told us just how much she is loved throughout the province. Much of her personal fortune (and she was a Princess in her own right before her marriage), has been spent on improving conditions for the people. Wells have been sunk and roads or tracks of a sort now exist to most of the villages. A yoke of oxen and a plough have been provided in many areas with a team of two doctors visiting regularly hitherto inaccessible places.

Helen is ridiculously romantic about things - I'm working hard to make her see sense and persuade her that what Jai has done once, he could do again. Twice the Rani has seemed on the point of making some major statement and then clearly thought better of it. This I can't understand. She is I think, a woman of great integrity, yet I feel there is here a strong undercurrent of intrigue and she and Helen are slap bang in the middle of it.

The news of Helen's pregnancy has been sent to Jai with all possible speed. It's my belief that, with equal speed, he will be here to try and patch things up. Helen seems to have entered that 'sleepy' stage of early pregnancy. Each day a chaise longue is placed in her favourite arbor in the zenana. Adjacent is a lotus-shaped pool, the water fed into it by means of a small waterfall. The sound of the water splashing into the pool beneath, the heavy scent of the flowers and the pleasant warmth, make it an idyllic place. Often Helen feels sick on rising but Almeera is dosing her with some herbal remedy which keeps the sickness well under control.

Surprise! Surprise! Our royal Prince is hotfoot on his way home. That news brought a pronounced flush to Helen's cheeks. Clearly she has not yet decided how she should react, but the mere thought of seeing him again after that dreadful night must be very disconcerting indeed.

A letter from Walter! I replied immediately telling him the dread news that Helen is pregnant and that she was definitely in no state to cope with further unpleasantness. I am inquisitive by nature and this has made me very curious indeed. What more unsavoury news is waiting in the wings? Is this what the Rani keeps trying to summon enough courage to tell us?

He is here, the monstrous Sir, whom I could never again bring myself to trust about anything. How can Helen be such a fool? His performance was exactly as expected, the anguish of a jealous husband, etc., etc., finally telling Helen how clever she was to become pregnant. All very nauseating and so predictable! Unnecessary too! Helen had already convinced herself that, for the sake of the child, she should agree to a reconciliation. Slowly, but gradually, they are becoming a couple again.

Invitations arrived today for Sir, Helen, Ashok and me to attend the 19th Cavalry's Regimental Ball in two weeks' time. Surprisingly, our Lord and Master says we are all to go. Obviously he's out to prove to Helen that his repentance is complete and she may see her English friend again without any repercussion.

Helen is at last starting to look and sound like her old self, although I feel her gentle composure has now acquired a hard edge that wasn't there before. And who can blame her?

Sunday a.m.

What a wonderful evening. Leaving the Palace made me realise just how long we'd been here without going outside its walls and very conscious indeed about returning to it. Helen and I are probably being held in the most beautiful, luxurious prison in the world!

The Barracks are about ten miles from here and quite a large township has developed around them. We travelled in two silver Rolls Royces and were met at the outskirts of the town by a troop of cavalry. In their scarlet and gold with flashing white cockades, the young men on their matched black horses looked very impressive indeed.

Col. Endicott and his wife Rita received us, together with half a dozen senior officers and their wives. I spotted Walter almost immediately and when we had shed our cloaks and were seated he came up to greet us, bowed low to Jai, then again over Helen's hand and mine. Pleasantries were exchanged and he then returned to his friends. All very civilised. When he later came to ask me to dance he advised me to keep smiling no matter what we discussed. So, we grinned inanely throughout a series of waltzes, whilst covering as much of the news as we could. No, I told him, Helen was no longer contemplating returning to England. Yes, as he could see, she was well and now determined to have the baby here. No, and here I missed my footing and stumbled, she was not aware of another wife. It had been recognised as a possibility - in the distant future - but now? Yes, of course the wedding ceremony had been in Hindi and no, she had not been converted. Could she have been duped? There had been the customary exchange of tokens etc., but not understanding the language, this could just as easily have been a betrothal ceremony as a wedding. Suddenly, I knew beyond any doubt that this was precisely what had happened.

The Rani's unease was now explained. She had tried to stop Jai to no avail and had then been forced to attend the ceremony. There was yet more Walter said, but insufficient time to tell it. Still smiling, he returned me to my seat.

Walter did not dance with Helen of course. That would have been stretching Jai's goodwill a little too far! She was permitted to dance with Jai, Ashok and Col. Endicott. Jai then said that as she was rather unwell it would be advisable for her to sit and watch. Everyone was too polite to ask what was wrong. People are so prissy about pregnancy as if it was something to be ashamed of - which, come to think of it, in this instance it may well be.

*Sir actually invited me to dance and proceeded to tell me how pretty I looked.
Now I know him for the liar he is! I am five feet three inches tall and about half
a stone overweight. On a good day my appearance might be described as
interesting and even, on a very good day, as handsome. Pretty?...never, ever.*

Daphne Craybourne to her brother, The Hon. Robert Craybourne in Australia.

27 St.James's Avenue
Kensington

Dearest Rob,

I don't know how much news you get in your far-flung corner of the Empire,
but here there is actually talk of war. Our M.P.brother James tells me the Germans
have increased both their army conscription numbers and the production of army
supplies. Taxes there have rocketed and our Government feels everything points
towards preparation for war - probably next year. Do come home. I would hate to
think you were on the other side of the world should a war break out in Europe.
On second thoughts if you are here you will probably be sent away to fight and I
hate the thought of that even more. Stay where you are!

Our own 'war' with the Government continues apace. The Suffragettes' arson
campaign about which Wiggie (my former teacher and now a dear friend) and I
have never been happy, has resulted in a number of our members being
imprisoned. Whilst in jail several of them resorted to hunger strikes and after a
time were force-fed.

You cannot begin to imagine what an assault this is on one's personal dignity. It
is, they tell us, a totally degrading experience and yet some of our stalwarts
continue to do it, despite the fact that Eleanor Mountjoy (you remember - Sir
Roger's second daughter), almost died in the process. There has been tremendous
public outcry and authorities are clearly at their wits' end as to how to cope with
offenders. James tells me a special committee has been formed, which could result
in legislation.

Loved your story about the village priest who said both his parents were convicts
sent out to Australia on prison ships. So... it would appear that criminality is not in
the genes!

The news about mother is not good. She has at last admitted that she has a
problem and no longer goes to great lengths to conceal the tremor in her hand,
except when strangers are present. She's also taken to wearing a glove and manages
to turn even that into a rather elegant mannerism. She and Prinny spend quite a
lot of time together these days. They visit the tenants, walk in the gardens and
even attended a suffrage rally recently at a park in Leeds. These seems to be much
less 'county' visiting now, probably because more and more offspring (like us!)
have removed themselves from the eternal round of socialising.

Now to the saga of our home-grown Indian princess. You will have received my
account of the U.K.wedding shindig, well, now come very strange rumblings from

the Orient. I know brother James went to great lengths to find out what he could about Jai, (the princeling). In spite of that something has gone very wrong and, here's the rub, James absolutely refuses to say what. Right in the middle of all this is, of all people, Walter. (You remember - Hislop's farm?). He joined the army a few years ago, the cavalry of course, he was always good with horses, and has done well. He's now an N.C.O. with the Bombay regiment. What I do know is that James feels the Foreign Office let him down badly by only referring to their central records, without talking to 'our man in the field' , in this case, Walter. He apparently has some very unsavoury information about Jai. I will absolutely refrain from saying 'I told you so', but you will recall my suspicions about his very 'civilised' manner, which belied his glowering looks and barely concealed arrogance.

You can imagine that Walter is as upset as James is about all this. He was always fond of the Calloway girls and spent a great deal of time with them just prior to their mother's death. It's all very intriguing. I've even asked Wiggie to employ all her feminine guile to get James to talk, alas to no avail.

The other sister, Rosa, fares well at Oxford, I hear. I gather she's very talented academically - but don't build up any mental pictures of a blue-stocking. She, like her sister, is quite a stunner and much more vivacious. Knowing she won't be able to take a degree and will probably be wasted in some humdrum backwater job makes my heckles rise. Sadly for her she was probably born a few years too early. I'm convinced in years to come there will be women lawyers, barristers and, who knows, even judges.

As you will have gathered the James/Wiggie relationship is still very much 'on'. The more I see and know of Wiggie, the greater my respect. I can think of no finer person to help James move with the times and at the same time preserve what is best at Craybourne.

So you know all about 'diggers', 'billabongs' and opals. Do keep on digging for the latter whenever you're off duty. I shall ignore all the superstitions and be most happy to wear the biggest opal you can find. Just make sure that in the process of searching you keep a sharp look-out for any 'bities' which might creep up on you.

Wiggie (sorry, Muriel) sends regards and from me,

   All love, as ever,

    Daphne

Betty's Journal

My tennis lessons continue, without Helen of course. Pieter (I refuse to call him Herr Pieter, it's so formal) has become a good friend. It is a release to be able to laugh at some of the strange things that happen here.

For example, a man from Asprey's has been again. This one was asked over to grade pearls and was anticipating the sort of quantity one would require for a necklace the size of Helen's. He was first shown into a room where there were some twenty large tea chests, all full of pearls, then (perspiring profusely), he was taken out onto a balcony where pearls had been spread out like a carpet. The poor man fainted!

Pieter and I went together to see Zizi. The keeper told us that Jai visits him regularly and often feeds him - inside the cage! Apparently tigers have a great sense of loyalty and are not nearly so dangerous as we imagine. Zizi regards Jai as a sort of parent, or leader of the pack, because Jai cared for him as a cub. Zizi's keeper was quite adamant that there is little danger unless the tiger smells fear; this they react to almost immediately. (Zizi could probably smell mine from quite a distance!). Obviously this is where Jai's supreme confidence/arrogance protects him.

There is a child in the zenana! Absolutely unheard of. Helen and I saw Alisha's friend walking through the verandah at the end of the gardens holding a small child by the hand. The Rani says it is a member of a Sirdar's family, as is the girl, Metta, but her eyes were evasive and I feel this is all part of the other unpleasant news which Walter didn't have time to divulge.

Helen, at three months, still sleeps a great deal, but her skin has an added lustre and the gaunt look of a few weeks ago has gone. As yet there has been no suggestion that we move out of the zenana and Jai seems content to make purely social visits here. His conversation now centres on the baby Helen is carrying and what he intends doing and buying for the little 'Prince'. Already he has ordered from Rolls Royce a child's car, the cost of which would probably house, clothe and feed a family here for the rest of their lives.

Today we were told that the Maharajah was losing ground. Harsh as it may seem, everyone has been expecting his death for so long that such comments have little or no impact.

Something unpleasant has happened. Helen, asleep by the pool, was aroused by a whimpering sound and found wrapped in a blanket beside her an Indian baby of just a few weeks. The baby was covered in sores and clearly on the point of death. No-one knew anything about it - of course! But it had what I assume was the desired effect of giving Helen a nasty shock. Jai is now insisting that Helen should return to her own quarters. Could it be that he is aware that the zenana girl has some axe to grind and sees her as a threat to Helen? I desperately need to talk to Walter about Metta and the child, but fear it is too dangerous to send a letter through the palace system.

The Rani has capitulated and Helen will be moved back into her own suite tomorrow.

Today was a festival day. We were told this morning that we would be travelling in one of the howdahs and went to the pilkhanna where we watched the elephant kneel on command and then practised climbing in. I told Jai at the outset that I thought it was a dangerous exercise for Helen in her condition but he answered brusquely that there was no more danger than riding in a car and the mahout would ensure we were perfectly safe. When Jai is at his most authoritative, there is no arguing with him.

From early in the morning we had heard the deep tones of the conch shells and the higher pitched notes of the shenai. When we reached the front entrance of the Palace the procession was assembled. First the Palace guard, then the three magnificently caparisoned elephants for Jai, the Rani, Helen and me. Behind us were some thirty or more elephants in full regalia and bringing up the rear a collection of people all wearing garlands of flowers. Inside the howdah was like sitting in a golden tent, the tasselled edging of the brocade swinging as we rode along, the movement rather like sailing. We loved it. We were outside the Palace and there was so much to see.

The procession moved out under the Golden Arch and through the surrounding villages scattered around the perimeter of the Palace. People waved and clapped and threw flowers and Jai and the Rani threw out handfuls of coins. By the time we returned we were exhausted and Helen, feeling somewhat sickly from the continuous motion, was sent straight to bed.

Wednesday

What a dreadful day! As planned Helen was moved back into her own rooms. At mid-morning we sent her outside to rest by the pool and I went back to the zenana to oversee the transfer of her jewellery. Ila meanwhile had received a rather vague message to attend one of the Sirdar's offices some distance from their suite, so only the guards remained on duty. When Helen's screams ripped through the tranquil air of the zenana and we started to run in her direction, my first reaction was.. ..Jai! It was soon apparent that this was not his handiwork.

The guards were not at their post. Later we found out they were chasing off one of the monkeys which often get into the Palace. Clearly this particular animal had been used as a decoy. We found Helen huddled on the chaise longue, her back to the pool. And it was there we saw the cause of her distress. The pool was full of blood, or so it appeared. And floating in it, the small pale form of a foetus. Her pains started almost before we could get her into the bedroom. The Doctor was summoned but the outcome was inevitable and within a few hours the miscarriage was all over. (Investigations later showed the 'blood' to have been produced with vegetable dye and that the 'foetus' was a skinned monkey).

I have read about people being in a 'towering rage' and never quite appreciated the expression. Seeing Jai, who seemed to have suddenly grown six inches, turning all his fury on Ila, the guards and even me for leaving Helen unattended, made me realise its full meaning. Fury we saw in plenty, but not one caring gesture, not one term of endearment for Helen, who lay sickly pale, her eyes encircled by patches dark as bruises. We were relieved when he left. Able at last to attend to our women's work of comfort and healing.

The Rani who had been at the bedside of her husband, arrived taut and outraged at what had occurred. Her visit was brief. More than anything, she said, Helen needed rest. I have my own views about that. What I feel Helen needs more than anything is someone who loves and cares for her enough to consider her well-being first and foremost in all situations. The self-centred Jai could never fill that role.

Ila now sleeps on a chaise longue in Helen's room and I have taken over the dressing room. The guards are in no doubt about their master's wishes and will, I feel, stay at their posts should a whole horde of marauding monkeys appear on the scene - or anything else for that matter.

After a troubled night in which it seemed to me that Helen's screams and Zizi's roars were once again intermingled, we were aroused early by Almeera, her usual bland expression showing signs of anguish. Her mistress was with the Maharajah whose condition was deteriorating rapidly, but asked that we be ready to receive her within the hour on a matter of the gravest importance.

As I made my salaam to the Rani her face told me that we were at last to hear the truth. The first horror I hadn't expected. During the night Alisha had disappeared from her bed. This morning she had been found dead in Zizi's cage. The Rani's eyes signalled me that there were other more gruesome details, details which could not be given because of Helen's state of health. Taking Helen's hand, she said "I ask your forgiveness now Helen for having played a part, however reluctantly, in what has gone before. There is so much I have wanted to tell you, but knew my own life to be in peril if I did so. Alisha has, I fear, died because Romesh knows that she and Metta plotted together and yesterday caused your miscarriage. There is more appalling news, Helen. This is the worst possible time for you to hear it, but I have no choice, it must be so.

"Metta is, as I told you, the daughter of a Sirdar. What I could not tell you is that she is also the mother of Jai's son, the boy Niaz, almost three years old. Because of her social standing, she and Jai are not married and unlikely ever to be so. My son already has a wife, the Princess Mumtaz, and it was to her home he went following his attack on you. She no longer pleases him. Mumtaz has had several miscarriages and because of this Jai has lost interest in her.

"And as if all that were not sufficient pain for you to hear dear Helen, I have to tell you that your wedding ceremony here in the Palace was a sham, a farce. It was merely a Hindi betrothal with no binding contract attached."

There was a stunned silence as the Rani paused and we tried to take in all that she had told us. Helen was the first to speak.

"Am I still married to Jai under English law...and is that recognised here?"

"As Jai already had a wife prior to the English ceremony, I am not sure about the legal position in your country, but you are certainly not bound to him in any way under the Hindi religion or under Indian law."

"My child …?"

"No my dear, there is no possibility that he would ever have ruled Jaishalpar. Jai would have never permitted it because of his mixed blood. Metta was obviously afraid that this might happen. Clearly, she did not know Jai as well as she thought.

I am afraid he desired the liaison with you merely to see what beautiful children he and you could together produce and also, indirectly, to wreak some revenge on a member of a race he hates so much."

"And Metta's child, Niaz ?"

"If Jai does not have children by Mumtaz or any other wife, then he is empowered to nominate his successor. I think it is obvious he would choose his own flesh and blood."

"Highness, you said this was a bad time for me to hear this, but that it had to be.. is there something else...?"

"My dear, Alisha's cruel end has made me realise what danger you, and I for that matter, could be in. My son removes from his orbit all those who question or refuse to agree to his wishes. And there is another factor. My husband is on the point of death. What little control I have been able to exercise over Jai has been because I was seen as the Maharajah's agent. Once he is gone, my authority will be drastically reduced.

"I must be brutally frank, Helen. If you were to conceive again and then miscarry, Jai would want you removed as quickly as possible...by whatever means he thought fit...we cannot wait or plan for such an unhappy situation. Our plans must be laid now. Jai will never consent to your leaving the Palace under normal circumstances, but during the funeral ceremony he and his guards will be totally occupied and that is when we must leave - all of us. You to the Regimental Barracks and me to my own Palace in Narawaz. I shall never return here whilst Jai remains in control.

"Throughout his life my husband has consistently done everything wrong. Perhaps on this single occasion he will oblige me by dying at a time convenient to us, that is within the next forty-eight hours. A ship sails for England on Thursday; if we can only get you and Betty onto that then I would feel you were safe at last. I have made contact with your friend at the Barracks. There will be many troops on board going on leave and Walter and his Sergeant are to act as your personal escorts. If you should miss the ship then it will mean remaining in close confinement at the Barracks until the next ship arrives in about four weeks' time.

"I will talk to you again with more detailed plans for leaving the Palace. Please make sure your jewellery is packed and ready to go". Here, the Rani's raised hand prevented Helen's interruption. *"Yes, my dear, the jewellery is yours, it was given to you personally. I regret you will be able to take nothing else so regard that as your security for the future. You are after all more than entitled to it after all the unpleasantness you have suffered. Col. Endicot's wife will ensure you have clothes and other requirements for the journey."*

And, turning to me, *"These are for you my dear. You have been and will, I know, continue to be a good friend to Helen. These are your security - I know you will make good use of them."* With these words she handed me a draw-string pochette of soft leather.

"Almeera and I are concerned for your health dear Helen. She has prepared herbal remedies which you should take each day, these will ensure more rapid healing and give you strength for what follows Hopefully the sea crossing will assist your convalescence... but regretfully, there are many hurdles to overcome before that."

With this, the small regal lady we had both grown to love and respect, once again embraced Helen and, escorted by her faithful Almeera, left us.

In an attempt to distract Helen, however temporarily, from all we had just heard, I emptied the contents of the pochette onto her bedcover. Like a brilliant multi-coloured collection of children's sweets they rolled in all directions. At least thirty jewels, an assortment of emeralds, rubies, sapphires and diamonds, six of them as large as marbles. Speechlessly, I collected and returned them to the purse, then taking Helen's hand sat beside her to try and make sense of all that the Rani had said.

In the privacy of her prayer room, the Rani allowed herself the luxury of tears. She recalled her own black moments of despair when she, a Princess of Damrasheer had first seen her husband-to-be, the Maharajah of Jaishalpar. At just twelve years of age she had become Second Highness to a bridegroom of forty-five, whose face and obesity already displayed the hallmarks of a dissipated, indolent existence.

Well-versed by her concubine tutors in the arts of love, she was nevertheless totally unprepared for the assault upon her immature body by a balding man, his erect organ almost obscured by the sagging layers of abdominal flesh.

During those early months there had been few things for which she could give thanks to her gods but an oft-repeated puja had been one of relief that as Second Highness she was not visited so often by her husband as a First and only Highness would have been. To have been the sole recipient of her husband's lust and perversions would have tested to the limits the spirit of a much loved daughter of the House of Damrasheer.

Nevertheless by the time she was fifteen, she had experienced two miscarriages and been safely delivered of a baby girl, who within hours of her birth had 'disappeared'. Never had she forgiven her husband for this, vacillating between sadness at being deprived of joy in a daughter of her own flesh and thankfulness that at least no child of hers would be exposed to the horrors of her own existence.

In her sixteenth year her first son Han, had been born, followed two years later by Romesh. Her delight in her two tiny sons was short-lived. A fall from a pony on his fourth birthday had broken Han's neck and resulted in the deaths of those six body-servants, grooms and tutors responsible for his well-being.

From that day all her love had been focussed on Romesh and her pent-up joy and youthfulness only able to find full rein in his company. Then, on Romesh's fifth birthday, the Maharajah had announced that the boy would in future spend his days in his father's company, observing protocol and matters of state, learning how to hunt and shoot. Her protestations that the child was too young were duly quashed and her son was lost to her. Now the evil spawned during those early years had reached maturation and been laid at the door of this young innocent from England.

Surely the gods would understand that her husband's death was necessary in order to ensure Helen's safety? Surely they had observed his life of wickedness and the evil now inherent in his son? The Rani dried her tears and sank to her knees....

Helen's self-esteem was at its lowest ebb. In the hours following her miscarriage, weakened from loss of blood, she vacillated between awareness and a semi-conscious stupor. Images of past events surfaced to torment her with reminders of how she had been deceived, used and abused.

On occasions, the horror of Alisha's death roused her shuddering with terror, her face and body sheened with perspiration. But at last the sedative from Almeera began to take effect and through the welter of self-recrimination at her own stupidity, she began to focus more positively.

One thing's for certain, I'm no longer the innocent of six months ago, I shall just have to steel myself and begin again. There must be a niche for me somewhere. Thanks to the Rani I suppose I'm rich, very rich, beyond most people's wildest dreams. No doubt that will present more problems. Still, I've learned my lessons the hard way and nobody's going to make a fool out of me again. But first things first, I must rest and prepare for the next ordeal - our escape.

At two a.m. the beating of the great drums echoed throughout the Palace corridors, the conch shells took up the sound and Zizi roared his own accompaniment. The Maharani's prayers were answered and her husband drew his final breath. Now funeral arrangements prepared some weeks ago were put into practice and the vast Palace household galvanised into action.

Helen would not have been welcome at the funeral. Invitations to Col. Endicott and his deputy were issued merely because protocol demanded it. But Helen, female and British, would have been a source of irritation and embarrassment at the cremation of a man who had constantly denigrated her sex and hated her compatriots.

The question of her attendance did not arise. Anticipating that she would remain confined to bed for several days, Jai had not even considered the possibility of her attempting to leave the Palace. Had he done so, then he was secure in the knowledge that his guards had their orders and would never allow her passage through the Golden Arch.

By mid-morning, Helen and Betty in full funeral robes, their faces slightly darkened by cosmetics and wearing the face veils of women in purdah, were already in the home of the Rani's personal mahout. As Helen sipped the stimulant which Almeera had provided for her, she tried to stem the tears which came flooding back when she thought of the Rani. How meticulously she had worked out their method of escape. Ashok's wives should have travelled in the third howdah, but had been confined protesting, to their chambers in the zenana. Two women in purdah would nevertheless travel in the procession and at the funeral site would be taken to the temporary zenana, from whence they would conveniently disappear amongst the crowds.

Only during Helen's final embrace had the Rani's composure faltered and it was Betty who, at a signal from Almeera, had gently separated them and then escorted Helen through the rear corridors to the pilkhanna where the mahout awaited them. Almeera's final instruction had been that they must retain the funeral cloaks and once in the safety of the British Barracks, examine closely their weighted borders.

It was time. The elephant knelt at the mahout's command. Together Betty and the mahout assisted Helen into her seat. Betty followed and the curtain of the howdah was closed. The elephant rose on command and purposefully moved forward to take its place in the funeral procession. At the front entrance, the body of the Maharajah lay banked with flowers on a wheeled conveyance drawn by the ruler's own elephant. Jai followed in the royal golden howdah, next the Rani escorted by Ashok, and then the third elephant bearing the concealed Helen and Betty. Completing the procession were the Sirdars, members of the royal household and other mourners.

Outside Shalpari town, three miles from the Barracks, great crowds gathered around the site of the funeral pyre. Two hundred yards from the pyre the lead elephant stopped and Palace guards unhooked the conveyance and hauled their ruler's body along the final stages of its journey. Jai, the Rani and Ashok also alighted, their elephants moved away and they walked to their appointed places beside the body. Meanwhile the following elephant had moved towards the temporary zenana and set down its occupants. Temporarily blinded as they stepped out of the shadowy curtained enclosure, they hesitated. Then strong hands clasped their arms and they were swiftly guided to the closed carriage standing a short distance away. As the Rani had anticipated all attention was focussed on the activities at the heart of the crowds. Only Almeera and the trusted eunuch guards were aware of the speedy transfer of the two girls from Indian imprisonment to British safekeeping.

At the moment when His Royal Highness the Maharajah of Jaishalpar raised the burning brand which would assign his father's body to the flames, Helen, faint from nervous tension, was already inside the Regimental Barracks and secure in the knowledge that, unless she wished otherwise, she would never again have to set eyes upon the man she had called 'husband'.

Several hours were to elapse before Jai found the messages left for him by his mother. The zenana was empty - empty that is, except for Ashok's wives locked inside one of the innermost chambers. His mother's bedchamber held a portrait of the two of them, painted when he was a small boy. The artist had captured all the innocence of childhood in the sweet smile reflected in and around the child's eyes. His small hand was held securely in one of hers and her other hand rested lightly, protectively, on his shoulder. It was a picture of trust and perfect unison. He knew that his mother had greatly treasured it. Now the exquisite painting had been torn from its frame and the whole section showing the child, had been cut into ribbons. The unspoken message was quite clear. 'You have violated my trust, nothing of the child I knew remains in you'. He recalled their last conversation. His suggestion that she should join her husband on the funeral pyre had been rejected with scorn. Had she cared for his dead father, suttee might have been a consideration in spite of the new thinking which condemned it. But her contempt for the Maharajah ... Her unfinished sentence had spoken volumes and he knew that her intention to remove herself from Jaishalpar after the funeral was the most for which he could hope. From the zenana he went to Helen's room. Here too, his mother had left symbols for him to read. On one of the bed's pillows lay a perfect lily, newly opened, its stem snapped in two and scattered over the bed were the blood-red petals of a poinsettia. So his mother believed Helen had not only lost her maidenhood but was broken in spirit. Mentally, he rose to his own defence. Her miscarriage could not be laid at his door, even though he must concede that his liaisons with both Metta and Alisha had played a large part in bringing it about.

Brusquely he moved towards the verandah. His mother had thought to punish him in some way by the day's events. In fact, by removing herself and the English girl from the Palace she had done him a favour. Now there was no need to worry about losing face with his contemporaries. Politeness would require that no questions be asked of him. The episode was a closed book.

But his son. What of his son? Finding Metta and the child ensconced in her father's household he relaxed. He was now in sole control. No longer must he suffer his mother's interference in matters of state and, with regard to matrimony - well, he would in due course survey the field again and see what was on offer. In any event, this sturdy little boy would ensure the succession. He must see to it that the child was well tutored in the handling of their British 'masters'.

**

Pride of the Orient' at sea

"Wake up Helen! Can I get you anything - a drink perhaps?" Betty smiled down at her friend, comfortably stretched full-length on the wooden deckchair.

"Thank you, a drink would be nice, but not for a moment. I seem to have slept for hours..."

"Yes you have, it's almost lunchtime, but for heaven's sake don't feel guilty. That's exactly what we, the Rani, Walter, Almeera, all of us wanted. It's the quickest way for you to regain your strength and you have to admit here on deck, surrounded by sea and sunshine, is the ideal spot for recuperating!"

"It's wonderful and when I'm awake, which I admit isn't too often, I tell myself how fortunate I am. At the same time..." Helen hesitated.

"Yes?"

"At the same time I'm just beginning to realise what a stupid romantic young fool I've been. Gullible, self-indulgent and indolent!"

"Surely you're being too hard on yourself? How could you possibly have known?"
Betty pulled up another chair and drew it close to her friend.

"There were things which puzzled me, but I was just too lazy to dig out the truth. Instead I just sat back and let things ride, blinded by a silly young girl's ideas of knights in shining armour and true love. Well my knight proved himself a liar, a cheat and far, far worse, a cruel vicious individual who allowed nothing to get in the way of his own desires."

"Well I'll certainly go along with that description of our former lord and master, but don't forget you were by no means the only one he deceived."

"I'm still baffled as to the real reasons for his deception. His mother says that as a small boy he was indoctrinated to detest the British. She believes that because I was so well-known as a model, taking me to India and going through a sham marriage was his way of humiliating the British, by displaying the fact that in India he, rather than them, was in control, especially as part of the ceremony was witnessed by some of the military personnel. Why oh why didn't I realise? Clearly Walter was in no doubt as to his reputation."

"That's not quite the same!" Betty protested. "Walter was in India, where Jai was well-known. The Jai you, and the rest of us, knew was the Oxford undergraduate, who was always charming, generous and polite."

"Just occasionally I did see a darker side, but I thought, again like a silly schoolgirl, that once we were married that would disappear..."

"Well you're by no means the first to have made the mistake of thinking that and I very much doubt you'll be the last." Betty was reassuring.

"But there were other signs which should have alarmed me." Realising that for Helen this was the catharsis of coming to terms with events, Betty waited for her to continue.

"I had a feeling that James and his mother didn't like him...There was just something...unstated. That's why I think Lady Elizabeth insisted that she couldn't give her approval unless I had an English companion. And Betty, I give thanks every day that as a result of that you were with me during the past weeks. Whatever would I have done without you?"

Seeing Helen was in danger of becoming emotional , Betty's reply was brusque.

"You would have coped! You're a strong girl and in any event, the Rani would have looked after you. But, Helen, you can't live your life on the basis of 'if onlys', it's time to put the past behind you and think positively about the future. You've had a rotten experience but on the credit side you and I have seen and done things girls of our age can only dream of. We've travelled half way across the world and lived in a palace which looked like something out of a fairytale. These are things no-one can take away from us."

"Yes and you may be surprised to learn that I have been thinking quite positively about what I should do next. If the Rani is right then that ceremony in India was in no way legally binding and I'm sure that in the circumstances I could have the English marriage annulled."

Betty smiled "Good! I'm in full agreement with all of that."

"The next thing I've decided is that I'm no longer going to be an easy target for liars and cheats, whether male or female. People are going to find that the new Helen is a more shrewd and astute version of the old one. I shall be on the lookout for those whose aim is to deceive. Because it's occurred to me... there could be fortune hunters!"

Betty sighed, "I wondered when you'd come round to that."

"It's obvious even to me, who's proved herself pretty much of a simpleton in the ways of the world so far, that the jewels I've brought out of India are worth a great deal of money. When I think of the thousands of young women who lose their virtue to rakes and philanderers and have nothing to show for it, except perhaps an unwanted pregnancy, I know I am very, very fortunate. And how about this for positive thinking? My work as a model taught me a great deal about materials, but look at the wealth of new fabrics we've seen in India! I knew nothing about jewels and their settings, or about fine porcelain and furniture but the Rani has taught me well and as for food, I think I can now hold my own with the most exotic of cuisines."

Betty laughed, "I couldn't agree more. I can now recognise an Aubusson carpet, or a piece of Limoges at ten paces and, my own particular favourites, the beading and decoration I've seen on some of the saris has left me drooling with envy!"

"So, we're agreed that we are now quite knowledgeable on a variety of subjects and we now have a great deal of money - don't forget your own little treasure trove!"

"As if I could! I wake up in the night thinking of those beautiful gems and how many doors they could open for me." Betty gave a small sigh of pleasure.

"It would be great if we could open some of those doors together..." Helen hesitated.

"I never imagined it any other way," smiled Betty. "Now what about that drink, or lunch, or both!"

"Now don't scold me, I'm not really hungry. Have your lunch and bring me back a drink when you've finished." Helen laughed. "All this self-analysis has left me quite exhausted. I might just be ready for another sleep."

"Expect me back in an hour and I'll probably be ready for a snooze myself!" With that Betty smilingly turned and made her way to the upper deck.

For the first time sleep eluded Helen. Soon she would be back in England. Waiting for her would be her sister Rosa, with much to tell about her new life in Oxford. Also to greet her would be James and Daphne, siblings whose realisation that their own father was Helen's grandfather could have resulted in hatred. Instead the relationship was now producing nothing but support and goodwill. And Muriel Wigmore, Wiggie to everyone. Daphne's former teacher, now a fellow suffragette and dear friend and, if the letters from home were true, fast becoming a close friend of James too!

A period of rest at Eynsford House, home of James and Daphne's aunt, and then back home to her beloved Yorkshire and Craybourne Manor. There Prinny would be waiting and Lady Elizabeth, quietly watchful and caring, both anxious to cosset and protect her. And Walter... Walter who with the Rani had so carefully planned their escape from India, Walter who had always seemed to be on hand when she most needed him, Walter who though not much more than a boy himself had comforted her and held her hand at Mam's funeral. As the memory of those early years came flooding back, Helen closed her eyes, remembering...

Chapter Three

I know you said, Mam, that we shouldn't come here until the spring flowers were out and I'm really sorry to disobey you. They did try to stop me... all of them. Said I was too young to attend a funeral, especially my own mother's. But Mam, I had to be here, had to stay with you until the end. Walter told me that if I bite my lips or my tongue really hard it will help to stop the tears, so I'm doing that now.

There are lots of people here. From the Manor and the village, even Mrs. Hinton, who was never one of your favourite people. Lady Elizabeth and Mr. James have been very kind to us, just like you said, but James's sister looks at me as if she hates me. I can't think why she should. I've only seen her a few times when she was home from school.

Rosa's alright, she's with Mrs. Dennison at the farm. They've brought some lambs right into the kitchen for us to feed. Afterwards... well, later on... we're going with Miss Pringle to our new home. Mam, I hate it already without you, but I will try to be brave and I promise I'll do what you asked and look after Rosa - always. I love you Mam. Goodnight and God bless...

Rags of mist drifted over the Craybourne cemetery revealing a dozen or so mourners. Lady Elizabeth Craybourne, elegant in black velvet, accompanied by her three children, James, the young Lord of the Manor, and Robert and Daphne, the two irreverently referred to by members of the staff as the 'Dishonourables'. As class dictated, distanced by a few feet was Lettice Pringle, formerly of the village Dame School, gaunt frame swathed in a thick woollen cloak, no-nonsense velour hat securely anchored to thick folds of greying hair. Mrs. Waring, the Manor cook, and friends from the staff stood tearful and red-eyed alongside the deceased's neighbour,a white faced Flora Hinton. The principal mourner, Helen Calloway, the small girl fighting back her tears, held the hand of Walter, the boy from Hislop's, the Manor Farm.

Eyes fixed on the coffin, oblivious to the sonorous words of the committal, Walter shuffled his feet...

What sort of a God would take Mary Calloway from her little girls? Why, with all the wicked people in the world, would he take someone so kind and gentle? Life had really dealt her a raw deal. As if losing both her parents as a youngster wasn't enough, she'd finished up with a rotten husband whom she and the whole village had been glad to see the back of. And then after all her struggles to build a new life, she's struck down by something the doctors can't cure. It was so cruel, so unfair...

Flora Hinton knew she had killed Mary Calloway. Desperately she tried to control the violence of her trembling...

Dear God, what have I done? I know I said, Lord, that I was sick and fed up of my Bert being such a stupid moonstruck fool over this woman. That I was tired of hearing him droning on about what a struggle she was having, never giving a thought to how hard my life was, what with five of us to feed and always trying to make ends meet. But I never meant, ever, that she should be struck down like this. I know I asked you to get her out of my life, but not dead. I didn't want her dead and those two girls motherless. I'll surely burn in Hellfire for my evil thoughts. Forgive me, forgive me...

The Hon. Daphne Craybourne, head slightly bowed, watched through lowered lids as her mother scattered the handful of moist earth on the coffin...

Whatever are we doing here at the funeral of this Mary person? Some sort of half-sister Mama said, which means Papa, who I don't remember, must have had an affair with a servant and this woman was their child. Very odd, everyone here seems to have idolised Papa. What's that saying about idols and feet of clay? Goodness, Mama, who never cries, is crying! It's all so embarrassing and just to cap it all, I do believe the Heavens are about to open...

Surreptitiously, her brother Robert, also stole a quick look at the sky...

Careful, mustn't appear not to be listening to the dear Rector. Pompous ass! Oh God, it's going to rain and we'll be soaked. Queer collection of mourners, hard to believe that whey-faced woman is Flora Hinton. Always thought of her as one of those rosy-cheeked peasant types. And that must be Walter Heaton from the farm, grown out of all recognition. Not a bad looking lad now, in spite of those ghastly clothes. Poor little Helen, she's trying so hard not to fall apart. Life was hard for her family before this, but those two little girls really are in dire straits now. It's unbelievable! Mama is really starting to make a fool of herself over this stupid business. If she's not careful she's going to tell the whole world about Papa's little indiscretion...

As dark spots of rain started to fall from the leaden sky James took his mother's arm...

Mother's so pale and drawn. I only hope I can get her to the carriage before it pours. I think we've done the right thing. At least we were able to ease Mary's passing. So much unhappiness in her short life, Papa would have been distressed at that. Mama's right, our main task now will be to make sure the little girls, Helen and Rosa, are kept happy and fulfilled. Whatever the circumstances, their mother was half Craybourne, which makes them blood relatives...

Lettice Pringle's eyes darted from one face to another...

Well they say God moves in mysterious ways. Thank heavens he's ensured Craybourne is in the hands of the child who seems to have inherited his parents' better qualities. Young Robert's supercilious manner and effeminate appearance are hardly likely to endear him to the tenants and as for that peevish arrogant child, she should have been spanked hard, years ago...

With a gesture of annoyance, Miss Pringle almost wrenched the button from the wrist of her glove. Turning from the graveside she set out for Hislop's farm, knowing Walter was a short distance ahead with Helen, but sensitive to the fact that in his company the child now seemed more composed.

Contemplating the task ahead of her, she shivered and tried to subdue a wave of panic. At Lady Elizabeth's request she was to be both teacher and surrogate mother to Helen and Rosa. For the first time she would not only be teaching children but living with them, caring for them. Their education was not a problem, the love of books inherited from her own father meant there was much she could teach them. Their other needs were more complex. Menstruation for instance! How to explain this when the time was ripe? But explain she must. Not for them her own experience when the sight of blood on her underwear had convinced her she was bleeding to death! Her aim must be fairness and firmness at all times, showing affection without ever being maudlin.

This "showing affection" aspect unnerved her most of all. Her own undemonstrative nature was rooted in a childhood where any show of affection was seen as an admission of weakness. But others, and certainly these children, would have different expectations. This was a wonderful opportunity for her and she would seize it with both hands.

One thing was certain she was going to need a lot of support and with a silent message to her Maker 'I hope you're listening God', she tapped on the farmhouse door.

"Come along in, you look chilled to the bone." Annie Dennison's welcome was genuine. Physically and mentally as different as chalk from cheese, the past weeks had seen a growing rapport between the two women. Privately Lettice admonished herself often that she was too skinny and prissy by half. In Annie's ample presence she mellowed, sensing the generosity of spirit underlying the brusque 'Take me as you find me' veneer.

"The tea's mashed and there's a nice bit of parkin just out of the oven. Hurry and take off that wet coat and come over by the fire. You're drenched, it must be fair chucking it down." As Lettice shrugged off her wet coat, Annie bustled between table and hob.

"Well you girls have a lovely job." Lettice smiled down at the children. For a moment Rosa's eyes swung in her direction, taking in the dark clothes, aware of their significance. Then without comment she turned back to the large wicker basket where two new-born lambs were suckling from twists of rag soaked in milk. Grateful for the thoughtfulness which had prompted this diversion for the bereft children and all too aware of Rosa's rejection, Lettice seated herself at the large scrubbed table feeling herself in need of moral and physical sustenance and all too ready to partake of Annie's 'stay-bit'.

"There are some more babies out in the barn need feeding. How about you girls giving me a hand?" The burly form of John Dennison smiled down at them all from the kitchen door. Speedily Helen and Rosa were buttoned into thick cardigans and, scarves draped over heads and shoulders, half running and half walking, scurrying across the farmyard in an attempt to keep up with John Dennison's huge strides.

Brushing crumbs of parkin from the bib of her apron, Annie beamed with pride.

"He's a lovely man. Got no learning, 'cept what he knows about animals, which would fill a book. But he's a kind soul. No children of our own, more's the pity. Suppose I shouldn't say it under the circumstances but it's been a treat having Helen and Rosa here. We've all enjoyed it, him and me and Walter of course. We've right spoiled them I'm sure, but who can blame us? Poor little loves, what must they be feeling? I just hope we haven't made your job any the harder, Letty. . . Now tell me all about this morning. Was the whole family there?"

"Well, yes... Lady Elizabeth, the two boys and Daphne."

"Ah, Miss High and Mighty! And who else?"

"Your Walter of course. Now he has the makings of a fine young man, unlike ..." Lettice Pringle stopped abruptly. Whatever her feelings about the young Hon. Robert, she did not approve of gossip.

"Say no more Letty, I've got your drift. Her Ladyship will have to watch that young man, there's something not quite..." Lettice resolutely bit into her parkin and no response forthcoming, Annie continued unabated.

"But you're right about Walter. He's a good lad. When her Ladyship first asked if we could spare him to give Mary a hand, John thought the boy might be offended, think it was woman's work. No such thing! Doted on Mary he did. Would turn his hand to anything to help her and when he first realised how badly she was and no chance of getting better, he really grieved. But as I said to him, 'Someone's got to look out for those bairns and they know you now as well as anyone, so you'd best he strong for their sakes'".

"And strong he's been. Struggling to behave like a man this morning, but a credit to you Annie. How long has he been here now?"

Neatly the question was ignored….."You know Letty…?"

"Yes?"

"This business about Mary has been a bit queer all round don't you think? I mean.. well I know the squires round these parts usually keep a bit of an eye on tenants, but there was no need for Lady Craybourne to do all this."

"No…"

Once again Letty felt they were moving into the sort of area she would do well to avoid.

"Let me tell you what I've heard. Putting two and two together from what I've seen for myself and from what you've been asked to do I'd say it sounds like more than mere gossip."

"But it's not our..." Letty carefully replaced her cup into its saucer, her embarrassment now obvious.

"Hear me out - you don't have to say whether you agree or not. They say that Lord Craybourne's first wife was one of those whingeing women, always lying around saying she felt ill. He used to spend a lot of time riding and hunting at his sister's over at Melton Hall especially when she had guests there. Well. ." Annie paused for dramatic effect, "apparently he became more than friendly with his sister's personal maid, Sarah."

In spite of her good intentions Letty was now listening carefully. This could be the missing link she had wondered about; the reason why Elizabeth Craybourne was so concerned for Mary's children.

"When they found Sarah was in the family way, Lady Melton arranged for her to marry one of the footmen and made it worth his while by setting them up in a little business."

"So Sarah had Lord Craybourne's baby?"

"Yes and what's more, in spite of the circumstances, by all accounts those three were as happy as sandboys in their little village shop.

"And the baby was..?"

"Mary, of course. It was a hard birth though and Sarah couldn't have any more, but she and her husband both loved the child to pieces and were proud enough to burst when she did well at school."

"I knew she was at the school until her parents died…"

"Amy Jessop says that was the most terrible time, with so many of the village taken. The problem then was what should happen to the girl."

"So someone suggested she work at the Manor? Surely not Oliver Craybourne?"

"That we'll never know. Though it's possible he might have thought that having his daughter under his own roof he'd at least be able to keep an eye on her. What I do wonder is whether at that time Elizabeth,his second wife, had any inkling as to who Mary really was. There'd been no children from his first marriage, but by the time young Mary moved in there were three little ones in the nursery."

"Yes..." For a moment Letty's mentally pictured those three as she had just seen them. James, young Lord Craybourne, unfailingly polite and considerate, Robert, all 'waff and puffen' as they said here in Yorkshire, which meant lacking in substance and Daphne, a rude self-opinionated child still in her teens.

"So they're all related. I mean Helen and Rosa are…?" Letty hesitated, working out the relationship.

"Well if it's right and it certainly has the ring of truth as far as I'm concerned, then those two little loves in the barn are his late Lordship's granddaughters!"

Before Letty could comment the door burst open. A breathless Walter first, carrying a smiling Rosa, then John carrying Helen. They brought with them a flurry of rain and the room was at once filled with activity as Annie bustled about finding towels. Whilst their tête à tête had been brought to an abrupt end, Letty had little doubt that Annie would make sure the subject was re-opened in the very near future.

"We won Miss Pringle! Walter and me. We had a race and we beat Mr. Dennison and Helen."

John Dennison laughed. "Not surprising eh Annie? Walter's legs are a sight younger than mine. And I was handicapped. Look at this big girl I was carrying!".

34

"I'm not so big". Helen protested amidst more laughter. The light-hearted atmosphere was maintained until Letty knew she could no longer procrastinate. It was time to leave for their new home, Orchard Cottage. Only a few hundred yards into the Manor grounds, but suddenly it seemed miles away.

There was much kissing from Annie and assurances from John that he would always be glad of extra help from two small pairs of hands. Walter said he'd be round to see the children during his lunch break the next day and then they were on their way.

In later years Helen's memories of her mother's death and those first days with Prinny became a fusion of the senses. The smell of the lambs' woollen coats in the heat of the farmhouse fire, mingled with that of Annie's baking and a suspicion of moth balls from Prinny's black dress; the fascination of Annie's plump fingers almost obliterating her wedding ring and John's calloused hands with their ripple of dark hairs; Prinny's eyes watchful and wary, the feel of Rosa's moist little hand curled inside her own and the gnawing realisation that they would never see Mam again...

Lettice Pringle was only too aware of her good fortune. A spinster of fifty-five years with little capital, she was now blessed with the security of which most women of her age and class could only dream.

Orchard Cottage, her new home, faced south across the kitchen gardens to the Manor with, a few hundred yards away, Hislop's Farm and its outbuildings. To ensure that Miss Pringle's energies were not dissipated on household duties, Lady Craybourne had arranged that their laundry be dealt with in the Manor kitchens and that Walter be spared from the farm when necessary, to deal with heavier chores. The abundance of dairy and kitchen produce surrounding them meant they would never be short of supplies.

Contrary to received opinion in Craybourne, Lettice had never needed nor wanted a man in her life. The product of an indecisive literary father and a mother whose highest aspiration was gentility, she had emerged at an early age as the masculine element of the family. Her two sisters, mere carbon copies of their mother, came to rely on her, both to balance their unsteady finances and to deal with those problems which did not relate directly to dress, social climbing or related trivialities. That her father, banished so often to the summer house with his pipe and books, chose to endure the chill of November frosts, rather than her mother's constant harangues, was not surprising. His sudden death from pneumonia as a result of this, causing the merest ripple of disturbance in the household, and his absence thereafter, were barely noted.

Children Lettice loved and the Dame School had been a dream fulfilled, when the overtly feminine domain proved, as it had done for her father, too much for her. That there were 'spoiled' children she was well aware and equally convinced that these were the result of irresponsible parents. She had always been convinced

35

that given such a child for three months, nay a month even, she could eradicate the problem! Until now... Suddenly she felt frightened.

Not that Helen and Rosa were spoiled. Far from it. They were pleasant, bright little girls, well-mannered and nicely spoken. What Annie Dennison said does make sense she thought. Personal maids are always well-spoken, have to be. Sarah would have passed that on to Mary, who in turn taught her own little ones. But... and it was a big but. How can I, with my inexperience of close human contact, unused to displaying affection and certainly unaccustomed to receiving it, fill even in part the void in their lives? Why, I can't even remember the last time any one kissed me!

Step by step the obstacles were overcome. Often by common sense, sometimes by a flash of inspiration. As on that first evening at the cottage when Helen addressed her as Miss Pringle and Letty realised that even her name would act as a barrier.

"Shall I tell you a secret?" Lettice asked. Solemnly, the girls nodded their heads. "When I was teaching, the children had their own name for me. They thought I didn't know but I did and I rather liked it. I wondered if that's the name you might care to use...?"

So without more ado, she became Prinny and the children loved it, feeling themselves both privileged and slightly naughty to be using such a familiar mode of address. It was good for them to feel naughty she decided. They were almost overwhelmed by their new surroundings and an anxiety to please. The girls' shared bedroom was very superior to the room they had had at Piggotts Lane. Their truckle beds had given way to solid mahogany bedsteads and the small marble-topped wash-stand with its pretty bowl and ewer were a delight. Only the small outhouse had flagstones, elsewhere all was carpets or linoleum. Furniture was an amalgamation of the better items Mary had managed to keep and Prinny's own pieces, supplemented here and there by furnishings from the Manor. Looking around her on that first evening Prinny felt more than satisfied that the total effect was both cosy and welcoming.

It was during those first uneasy hours that a further milestone was achieved. The children fed and washed, Prinny heard their prayers then tucked them into their beds and said goodnight. As she turned to the door a small tremulous voice asked, "Aren't you going to kiss us good-night? Mrs. Dennison always did."

Prinny reacted quickly,

"How naughty of me, I almost forgot..." The taste of Rosa's tears and the tension evident in Helen's slight frame were to remain with Prinny for a very long time.

Chapter Four

Helen could not rid herself of the feeling of having done something wrong, of having been disloyal to Mam. It was all to do with the speed with which everything had occurred and their lives had changed. No-one was to blame. Everyone was kind. Almost too kind. Trying to take their minds off what had happened. Sometimes it seemed to her that Mam had never existed.

Only Walter seemed to understand. Knew that she resented too much happiness so soon. Needed to talk about Mam. The three of them would walk in the Manor fields and once Rosa was absorbed in making daisy chains or gathering wild flowers for Prinny, Helen would ask her questions.

"Didn't Mam love the flower book, Walter?"

"I reckon Lady Elizabeth knew how much your Mam enjoyed the Manor flowers. That book meant she could still enjoy seeing them even when she was in bed and right poorly."

"You came with so many presents. The dolls' house and the nighties for Mam and all that lovely food!"

"Well, it was Christmas Eve. It was so bitter I thought I'd never feel my fingers again. But your little cottage was always cosy."

"That's because you cut all those logs for us. But what about the goose? Tell me about the goose!"

"It was your Mam who told me what to do with that. Even so I felt right pleased with missen when it was ready to eat."

"It looked so lovely, all brown and shining and you looked so funny in Mam's pinny."

"Thank you very much young lady!"

For a few precious moments Helen was transported back to Christmas in Piggott's Lane, cherishing memories of their happiness as Walter brought to the table the flaming aromatic pudding into which Mrs. Waring had packed silver coins and trinkets. Such conversations helped her to remember Mam. Frail, but smiling and apparently happy. Not as she had looked that last time... reminiscing helped Helen assuage her sense of guilt at their new-found contentment.

Because they were content. A comfortable routine had been established. Of the two reception rooms, Prinny had selected the larger to serve as both dining and schoolroom. At the rear of the room the window looked north across the Manor lawns and under this a long table served as a desk for the three of them. Prinny's books lined the wall and in pride of place was a splendid circular globe sent over from the Manor schoolroom. Their dining table, placed under the side window which faced the clusters of fruit trees from which the cottage derived its name, afforded glimpses of the kitchen gardens and hothouses.

Lessons followed breakfast, then before lunch there was a half hour's break, usually spent at the farm. Afternoon lessons were informal and of a more practical nature; the study of flora and fauna, French oral exercises and experiments with cookery in the Manor kitchen under Mrs. Waring's supervision. One afternoon was sacrosanct. Every Thursday at 4.00p.m. the two small girls were delivered to the Manor drawing room to take tea with Elizabeth Craybourne. At first they were overawed by the size of the room and the procession of good things borne in by the Butler and the maid, the nerve-wracking complexities of managing cups and saucers and plates of food. Gradually in the warmth of Elizabeth's understanding and kindness they relaxed and soon began to look forward to their weekly visits.

They told her of their studies. Already as they chattered enthusiastically about the books and poems they were reading there was evidence of Prinny's love of literature and Elizabeth knew she had chosen well. She in turn told them of her own activities. Visits to London and the theatres there were a source of interest. Her exquisite clothes often provoked discussion. Where were they purchased? Who made them? Helen was particularly interested in the different textures of the materials used, the subtle blending of unusual shades.

Their lives now filled with new and pleasant experiences Helen and Rosa blossomed, enjoying the daily stimulus of Prinny's lessons, the sophistication of the Manor and the down-to-earth approach of Hislop's Farm and their daily contact with Walter. In an atmosphere both caring and serene they were content.

Contentment was not so obvious in Craybourne Manor during the school holidays, when even the mild tempered James found it difficult to be civil towards his unco-operative sister. In the Servants' Hall, Haig the Butler and Mrs. Waring the Cook, well out of earshot of the other servants, muttered dire threats as to how such a wilful child should be dealt with and how her father would turn in his grave if he but knew the dance she was leading her mother.

Robert, already entrenched in the hedonistic lifestyle which was to be his undoing, smiled at her antics and turned his back on the situation. Frequently his mother wished she was in a position to do the same.

"I'm not going visiting - it's pre-historic driving around leaving cards and drinking all that tea." Daphne pouted her disapproval.

"Everyone does it. It's a way of meeting one's friends."

"They're not my friends, they're yours. There'll be no-one there under thirty, except for those horsey types who expect me to be madly interested in their stables and paddocks. You're behind the times, Mama, people are doing this less and less."

"And you Daphne are both ungrateful and unsociable. Very well you may stay at home today, but tomorrow you will accompany me to Leeds; there are one or two school items we need to replace before your return."

"Must I go back? I hate it there. I've no friends and the teachers are always picking on me."

"My dear girl, has it not occurred to you that the fault might just lie in yourself? If you maintain this antagonistic approach towards any and everybody then I'm not surprised no-one is rushing to be your friend, nor that the teachers are displeased with you. Yes, you are most certainly returning to Kent and during your remaining days here I insist upon a greater civility when dealing with the servants. At breakfast this morning you were less than polite to Jane. At the age of two you were taught to say 'Please' and 'Thank you' and now is not the time to forget such niceties. Several members of our staff have been in this house since before you were born and you would do well to remember that good breeding is not a matter of station, but rather of good manners and behaviour."

Following this and a succession of similar incidents, it was with a sigh of relief that at the end of each holiday Elizabeth saw Daphne and Robert depart for their respective boarding schools.

James, down from Oxford the previous year with his Law Degree, was currently learning how to run both the Estate and the family holdings in the county. It had been, she reflected, a godsend having him here during the trauma of Mary's illness and death. As she would have expected he had been totally supportive with regard to the provision for the little girls. No criticism of his father's behaviour had been forthcoming and from an acceptance of the situation he had swiftly moved to the practicalities.

He it was who had talked with her until at last Prinny's name had presented itself as the ideal solution. James had suggested Orchard Cottage and personally supervised its cleaning and refurbishing. Together they had formulated plans to ensure Oliver's grandchildren remained within the orbit of the Manor where, whatever James's future plans might be, she would be on hand to give Prinny practical and moral support.

Hislop's and Walter in particular, proved an unexpectedly rich source of both. Prinny, amazed at the boy's intelligent appraisal of the girls' different needs, his self-effacement and total dependability, never ceased extolling his virtues to Annie.

"I wouldn't trust these girls with just anyone, you know, Annie. Walter is really quite a remarkable boy. Is he ambitious?"

"I think so but I wouldn't say his ambition has anything to do with farming! Don't get me wrong, he always gives of his best here, but sad as we'll be to see him go I suspect that with another few years under his belt he'll leave us. Wouldn't be surprised to see him join the army."

"Surely not! He's such a quiet lad, I can't imagine him ever wanting to inflict harm on anyone."

"He wants to travel Letty. How do you think he's ever going to manage that on a farm labourer's salary! Not only would the army train him but he'd probably get to see something of the world."

So in Walter's company Helen continued to ask her questions and to enjoy reminiscing. Nevertheless, two years were to elapse before she was able to tell even him about the terrible night when Bert Hinton came to the cottage, the night she first wondered if Mam was going to die...

"It started with Rosa's tears and ended with Mam's. Rosa and I were alone in the cottage waiting for Mam to come home. I knew the early darkness was because of the rain, but Rosa didn't - she was after all, only six. I tried to keep her occupied. We laid the table and I got out Mam's clothes because I knew that she would be wet through. It had to be her best things, she didn't have any others. Soon we had everything ready, the towels were warm and the fire was blazing and we waited...

"When Rosa started to get tearful I suggested a game. We'd both look out for Mam and if Rosa saw her first she'd win my best green ribbon and if I won then I would have the drawing Rosa had done that morning. You know how the windows go all steamy? We had to wipe large patches clear so that we could see out. The rain was falling in great sheets, all silver-grey, and the grass was crumpled and flattened. Do you know what a 'quagmire' is Walter? Mam used to call it that when the cart-track was just covered with deep mud. That's what it was like that afternoon.

"I saw her almost at once. She looked so small, dwarfed I suppose by those huge trees. I knew those dry clothes were going to be needed because her cloak was so wet it clung to her. She was clutching a parcel very tightly as if she was afraid the wind would tear it out of her hands and I guessed that it contained her sewing. Very precious it was too. I was only eight you know, but even then I knew it was the only way Mam could earn any money.

"Rosa opened the door and quickly we drew Mam into the warm. I helped take off her wet things and told Rosa to rub her hair dry whilst I mashed the tea. Mam tried not to smile when she saw the 'doorsteps' of bread I'd cut, then started to unpack her parcel saying she'd brought a treat for us from the Manor. The wet knot was a bit difficult to undo because it was so wet I suppose. First she took out her sewing, that was always wrapped in soft flannel to keep it safe. Then inside another layer of paper there were two pots of jam and a huge piece of the yellowest cake you ever saw.

"'It's blackcurrant jam, as only Mrs. Waring can make it, and you can see from the colour of the cake that it contains lots and lots of eggs.'

"' How many do you think Mam?.'

"'Oh, a dozen at least.' We all laughed at Rosa's expression of amazement. Then as Rosa and I helped ourselves to the bread and jam I suddenly noticed Mam wasn't eating. When I asked why she said,

"'Cook made me eat some bread and soup before I left, told me it would help keep the damp out of my bones!' Rosa laughed, but it was then I realised Mam hadn't eaten much at all lately. I noticed how thin and pale her hands were. So pale they were almost transparent against the brown of the teapot. I saw that her face too was pale and drawn, the sockets of her eyes almost purple and her whole body seemed to have shrunk. In that moment I knew that Mam wasn't just tired, she was ill, seriously ill.

"There was no-one I could talk to, nothing I could do. That evening seemed like any other except that I now had this dreadful feeling that something awful was going to happen.

"It was 'All-over wash and clean nightie night'. Rosa and I toasted ourselves in front of the fire before we put on our nighties. I think I'll always remember sitting in that amber glow, the warmth of the fire on our skin and Mam smiling at us and saying as she always did,

"'Your hair shines just like the copper at the Manor.'

"As usual Rosa giggled when her long hair became entangled in her nightie's buttons and then at last we were in bed and Rosa was soon breathing deeply. Lying there I wondered why Mam hadn't been to the doctor. It would cost money of course, but at least he would give her some medicine and perhaps that would make her better. I heard Mam putting things away and getting undressed and then footsteps, the heavy footsteps of a man.

"I couldn't think who would be calling so late and in such awful weather. I went to the window and looked down. The downstairs curtains were still open and the light was all spilling out. I could see Mr. Hinton from next door but one, peering in, his face pressed to the glass. I heard Mam cry out and then the swish of the curtains being drawn. The footsteps went away and I could hear Mam crying. I just didn't know whether to go down to her or not.

"Nothing was ever said about Mr. Hinton and why he would want to look in on Mam, but the next day she did tell me if she was out I was to make sure that both doors were always locked. I could feel Mam was frightened and it made me afraid too. I wish we'd known you then, Walter. I mean really known you like we do now. Then I could have told you all about it and you would have known what to do..."

Two other people had good reason to remember that evening. Another pair of eyes had watched Mary's approach up Piggotts Lane. In the first cottage Bert Hinton had been standing at the window for half an hour or more, making inane comments about the weather, comments to which his wife Flora did not even bother to respond.

"It's fair chucking it down - yon path'll be a mudlark for days after this lot." The big man's head inclined slightly towards the other occupant of the room. Flora, head bent over her work, made no reply and turning back to the window he continued, "Send the young 'uns to school t'field way tomorrow, it'll be mucky still, but nowt like yon path."

So she was on her way home, his precious Mary! Flora, keeping her eyes glued to her crochet work, knew that she would quickly be made aware of Mary's approach by Bert himself. And so it was! His sudden stillness and the absence of comment told her all she needed to know. A flood of anger and frustration blurred her vision to such an extent that the fine hook missed its point of entry, becoming entangled in the delicate work. Hearing her angry exclamation, Bert was all solicitude, assuming that the tear-stained cheeks were the outcome of the mishap, rather than its root cause.

What was there about that woman? She herself had put twelve years into her marriage with Bert, the "best" years, most would argue. A complete innocent at sixteen, she had happily entrusted herself to the burly six foot labourer and, if the marriage rites on her wedding night had both shocked and repelled her, she had certainly concealed the fact from her lover.

Gradually she had come to accept the rough and tumble, the gruntings and groanings of the marital bed as an inescapable wifely duty, determinedly playing her part with a growing lack of enthusiasm. That these unattractive skirmishes should have resulted in three strapping children never ceased to amaze her. True, a fourth child lay in a small cold grave in the churchyard, but to rear three out of four children was more than most women could hope for.

Though singularly unimaginative both in and out of bed, Bert was by nature unselfish. The ease with which he could shed this trait during copulation astonished Flora. Taking his pattern from the animals he tended, his sexual approaches were totally and implacably selfish. Intercourse must be instigated by the male and once aroused, conclusion was reached very quickly indeed.

In those early days Flora had tried murmuring endearments, deliberately prolonging kisses, but Bert seemed not only startled by such overtures, but somewhat annoyed that the task in hand should be even marginally delayed. Perhaps he had been afraid that his masculinity was insufficient to cope with another five or ten minutes' delay? Eventually she had resigned herself to the speed with which her nightdress would be raised, his maleness thrust at her and his stertorous grunts give way to gulped draughts of satisfaction. Then, his face beaded with sweat, he would say, "That was right good luv, just what I needed", and completely oblivious to any needs she might have, turn on his side. Within seconds he was asleep.

For the past twelve months Flora had known of his obsession with Mary, Bert possessing neither the wit nor the intelligence to cover his obvious interest in her comings and goings. There had been offers last winter to chop logs for Mary, to clear her path of snow, Bert's "After all luv, she's got no man to be doing the heavy work for her, like you 'ave", effectively putting paid to any complaints Flora might have lodged.

Then there had been the nights when he had muttered that he was just going to 'stretch his legs', not reappearing for an hour or more. Flora allowed another wave of self-pity to engulf her. It wasn't as if she had let herself go. She'd put on a bit of weight of course, but that was only to be expected after carrying four bairns... She'd always been, well to be honest, 'round', not like that skinny piece next door but one. Men were supposed to prefer their females a bit fleshy, at least that's what she'd always believed. In a perverse way the fact that she had never seen Mary by so much as a word or gesture encourage Bert was a further source of irritation. There was no way that her Bert would be good enough for Mary Calloway, she was always on her dignity that one. Distant, cold even. Hadn't she already sent Jim Calloway on his way? A bit of a devil perhaps, but as good-looking and well set-up a man as any woman would give her eye-teeth for.

She always had to be different! Flora's own bairns had sensible names, Thomas, Sidney and Annie, unlike the high-faluting ones Mary had bestowed on her girls.

Helen, named after some Greek Queen so she said, and Rosa. Flora's Annie had once called across the gardens to 'Rosie' and been told in no uncertain terms that the child's name was 'Rosa' and was not to be shortened or lengthened in any way. Annie, who was five, did occasionally play with Mary's girls, but the boys always regarded the Calloways as 'too prissie and stuck-up' for words. And now her Bert was acting like some love-sick animal and all on account of a woman who would hardly give him the time of day.

At this thought she almost choked with emotion, causing Bert to exclaim,

"I've never known so much fuss and palaver about a bit of crochet! I'm going to make sure t' hens are safe and dry and t' fences and gates still standing."

Pulling on his jacket he stumped out of the house, leaving Flora in a temper which she sought to expiate on the kitchen range, the results of this being so devastating that a sleep-saturated Sidney emerged from the loft bedroom, asking what all the noise was about. Even he was astonished at the torrent of abuse with which he was greeted and beat a hasty retreat to the safety of the bed he shared with his brother.

Flora's temper was now well under control, her self-pity having given way to an icy resolve. Putting away her crochet, she carefully banked up the fire then prepared herself for bed. She would pretend to be asleep when he returned, knowing only too well how Bert would feel after one of these abortive sorties into the night. Why should she be used as a vessel, a release for his frustration at not being able to touch Mary Calloway? Or had he touched her? Hearing his footsteps on the flagstone path, she hastily turned towards the wall and feigned sleep.

Chapter Five

The hamlet of Craybourne was sited to the north and east of the Manor and consisted of the row of cottages known as Piggotts Lane in which Mary and her children had lived, and a second, larger cluster, nestling in the hollow just over the brow of the hill. Dominating the hamlet was the church which effectively kept a foot in both strata of local society. It had not always been so. For years the church had been used solely by the Craybourne family and their employees. Now, whilst a private family chapel was retained for the Craybourne family's use, the church was open to all who wished to attend, there being for the first time a few inhabitants of Craybourne who were not occupied in some capacity in or around the Manor.

The private approach to the church was from the rear of the Manor. On fine days this meant a pleasant walk through immaculate gardens and parkland, but when the weather was considered unsuitable for the 'gentry' to be exposed to its rigours, the carriage would draw up to the front entrance and take the circuitous route around the Manor to the east, depositing its occupants at the lych gate.

This 'church drive' through avenues lined with poplars had been constructed by an earlier Lord Craybourne for the convenience of his house guests and Helen's mother had many occasions to be grateful for his foresight, providing as it did a short cut from the estate to Piggotts Lane, glimpsed beyond.

To the north-west of the Manor were the stables and coach house and beyond those the farms and the dairy, whilst linking all these main arteries of Craybourne were the huge kitchen gardens situated on the north west fascia of the Manor. In this section of the building were housed the kitchens, the Butler's pantry and that focal point of all such establishments, the Servants' Hall.

Skirting the house to the south, east and the rear, were the formal gardens of Tudor inception, their original designs virtually unchanged through generations of gardeners. Flower beds of symmetrical shape were defined by minute box hedges, whilst taller hedges wrapped their arms lovingly round the rose garden with its marbled seats, as if to contain the sweet heavy perfume. Here too was the orangery and, bordering the kitchen gardens, a mosaic of herbs, fragrant and prolific.

For much of the year the Manor stood, its feet deep in flowers, its magnificent chimneys reaching towards the sky, mullioned windows blinking their patterns of russet and gold, changing chameleon-like with the coming of the Spring, to a delicate Kendal green.

Helen loved everything about the Manor and its environs. Whenever afternoons permitted she would go to her own special place in a corner of the orangery. Here in her day-dreams she saw ladies in rich Tudor finery gossiping in clusters, couples deep in conversation, planning their secret trysts. Always the men were carbon copies of James, whom she adored. Whether dealing with Annie Dennison, Prinny or little Rosa his charm and courtesy were unvarying and she loved him for it. Thirteen years her senior he may be but, as she often told Walter,

"Perhaps James will wait until I'm quite grown-up and then marry me."

If Walter appeared disconcerted and silent on this subject she assumed it was because boys in their adolescent years did not like to discuss such matters.

Her own views on men were very confused. James was her hero with Mr. Dennison a close second, then came Walter who, after Rosa, was her very best friend. Always she thought of her father and Bert Hinton as threatening. Apart from fleeting glimpses of the latter, both were now removed from her life. Just five years old when her father left home, the memory of his nightly home-comings remained with her for many years. The smell of ale and tobacco which permeated everything. His clumsy movements and slurred speech all adding to the picture Mam had unwittingly drawn for her of men being both unpredictable and unreliable. Whenever Mary saw him coming up the path in that state Helen was told to take Rosa upstairs and shut the door. But in their small cottage a closed door was insufficient to drown the sound of angry voices.

Usually they argued about money or, as Helen now realised, the lack of it. But there were other sources of contention. If Dad sat down at the table in his shirt sleeves Mam would refuse to serve him. There was something else. Something unspeakable. Sometimes Dad wouldn't go as far as the privy at the bottom of the garden, relieving himself near the back door. Never had Helen seen her quiet well-spoken mother so angry as on these occasions.

"You're like something out of the Bible," Dad complained to Mam, "you're forever pestering me with your eternal 'Thou shalt nots'."

"And you, you're like nothing remotely connected with the Bible unless it's the Prodigal Son. You do nothing but squander the funds it takes me hours to earn. When did you last bring home any money, instead of taking it out of the house?"

"That's not fair. There's no work to be had and you know it."

"Not within a two mile radius, but I notice that you're quite capable of walking a good deal further than that if you want to join your friends drinking and gambling."

Later Helen, plucking up courage to ask Mary what 'gambling' was, shuddered to learn that in the barns and middens her father frequented at night-time, dogs and cockerels were encouraged to fight each other, to the death. On good days, Jim Calloway, darkly handsome, would ruffle his daughters' shining tresses and refer to them as his 'little copperknobs'. But looking back it seemed to Helen that there had been few good days and too many when they were sorry to see him arrive home.

She remembered well the night Mam locked him out. At first he had shouted abuse and threatened to break down the door, but eventually the effects of the alcohol took over and he slumped comatose on the garden path. Roused by the early morning chill he found at his side a bag containing what clothes he possessed and a few guineas. Helen heard Mam talking to him through the locked door, telling him she was giving him the opportunity to do what he had always wanted

- go away to sea. At first he protested loudly, but at last all was quiet and peering out they saw that he and the bag were gone. Twenty-four hours elapsed before the door was unlocked and Mam started to relax. They had never seen him since.

There was no feeling of regret at his departure, rather an easy adjustment to their new lifestyle. Three places instead of four at the table, quieter evenings and an absence of those incessant arguments.

Occasionally the older Helen wondered about him, stared at the globe with interest and asked questions.

"Where's the nearest big port, Prinny?"

"Liverpool, on the West Coast, the other side of the Pennine range", and ever anxious to capitalise on a learning experience, "let's find it in the atlas."

"It's a long way. How would someone get to Liverpool from here?"

"Let's work it out shall we?..." Prinny knew the reasons underlying Helen's curiosity and decided that factual knowledge was preferable to speculation.

"Are there lots of big ships there?"

"Of course, and there are special ships which carry people who want to emigrate."

"What's 'emigrate', Prinny?", Rosa was also showing an interest.

"It's when people leave the country they live in, to go to another country and start a new life."

So, Helen pondered, their father could now be on a completely different continent. Slowly she traced her finger across the globe westwards from Liverpool. He could be in North or South America, the West Indies even...

"Why don't we ask Lord Craybourne about this? In the Manor library there are sure to be books about ships and about the lives and cultures of people in the Americas."

Exploring this new avenue of study Helen, whilst never regretting her father's departure, yet felt a sense of awe that he could now be separated from them by a vast ocean.

For her part, Elizabeth Craybourne was hopeful that this indeed was the case. Jim Calloway's advent into their lives had caused nothing but trouble. Noted for her charm and elegance, those closest to Elizabeth knew of the vein of steel which underlay the serene exterior. This it was which enabled her to keep going following her husband's sudden death and the ensuing disclosure in his personal letter that Mary was his daughter. That in such circumstances he should have asked her to safeguard his grandchildren's futures was in many ways more devastating than the facts themselves. Young men of his class often had liaisons with female servants. Providing everyone was discreet it did not present a problem. But when a child was involved...

The cruellest blow was that he had not seen fit to confide in her earlier. Nevertheless, she had tried to carry out his wishes. Had intended warning Mary about Jim Calloway, who no doubt wanted to get his hands on the small capital Mary had inherited. But, too late! Returning from her vacation, Elizabeth found them already married. Within a few years there were two little ones and Jim was spending and drinking freely. Thank heavens Mary had sent him packing whilst there was still some money left.

Following Jim's departure Elizabeth had been able to assist Mary much more, knowing that other tenants would see nothing wrong in the support she was giving to the young mother and her children. Only when Mary came to her with the heart-rending news that she was terminally ill, did Elizabeth tell Mary that Oliver, Lord Craybourne was her natural father. Retrospectively, Elizabeth realised that the knowledge had left Mary more relieved than shocked. No longer did she have to worry about what would become of her children. Mary knew Lady Craybourne as a woman of her word and her reassurance that the girls would be cared and provided for with financial assistance in their adult lives had brought a glimmer of colour into Mary's ashen face.

At last Elizabeth sensed that Mary felt she could face whatever the coming weeks would bring, secure in the knowledge that her darling girls would be able to stay together and their welfare watched over by someone she trusted implicitly.

And so it was. With Prinny she discussed frequently the children's welfare. Rosa's bubbly extrovert personality was already evident and presented no problems but Helen's questions, her uncertainties showed an obvious need to keep alive her mother's memory. They encouraged her to talk about the past.

"You know, Helen, your mother's prowess with her needle and in particular her lace-making, were legendary in this area."

"Legendary ... ?"

Elizabeth smiled, "Well-known, famous."

"Famous?"

"Friends of mine from miles away regularly placed orders with her."

"I didn't realise. I mean I knew her work was beautiful but . . ."

"It was quite exquisite. I've put on one side some of the pieces she made so that you can pass them on to your children. I'm quite sure that they will become family heirlooms -treasures that is."

Following Mary's death the children were not taken to the cemetery until the spring flowers were in bloom. They were no strangers to the place, previously the focal point of Sunday afternoon walks, bearing flowers for the graves of Mary's parents.

In Craybourne as elsewhere the tradition of taking flowers to family graves on Sundays was firmly entrenched and an occasion for meeting friends and exchanging news. Prinny did not approve! After consultation with Elizabeth she agreed that the girls be taken every few weeks, if only to ensure that they maintained as large a group of social contacts as possible.

As Prinny had anticipated Annie had wasted no time in completing her interrupted saga of Mary's supposed origins and her marriage to Jim Calloway. Prinny subdued her usual reluctance to listen to such gossip, on the premise that any information she could glean regarding the children's background might well prove useful in caring for them.

Physically they were most attractive children. Helen's red-gold hair was more biddable than Rosa's tumble of auburn curls, but both had the pale magnolia skin common to redheads, although Rosa already bemoaned her own liberal sprinkling of freckles. Helen's eyes were green, startlingly so when she wore shades of blue or the paler colours, whilst Rosa's were flecked with grey. Both children were small-boned and slightly built. The influence of their lady's maid grandmother Sarah was, Prinny thought, very evident. Clearly Mary had been schooled well in speech and good manners and had passed these on to her own children. Their speech whilst Northern was never 'broad' and Prinny was thankful that she had seen no evidence whatsoever of the reportedly uncouth behaviour of their father, Jim Calloway.

That they were very different in temperament she had already established. Helen, a quiet thoughtful child, weighed up the pros and cons of any situation before coming to a decision. Scrupulously tidy, her school books were immaculate. Rosa was the reverse! Gregarious and untidy, she rushed into things, often without thinking, and her written work was peppered with blots and alterations. Obviously, Helen bore the imprint of her conscientious mother and Rosa that of her out-going, but unreliable father. Letty reprimanded herself. She should not even be thinking in such terms. Assumptions of that nature about children were unforgivable. After all her task was to ensure good qualities were enhanced and problems eradicated. In spite of the blots, Rosa was an intelligent child who soaked up information like a sponge and, more importantly, retained it. It was Helen who needed constant reminders of her mother's existence and perversely had the greater need of a father figure. In John Dennison's company she happily learned about his beef and milk herds, Hislop's pure-bred pigs and the multitude of farm creatures in which he took such a pride.

"These little hens are bantams, Helen. Right little beauties aren't they? And this chap is the cockerel - he's a real smarty-pants."

Helen chuckled. "It's funny you should call him that. I was just thinking that those ruffles round his legs are like trousers."

"I've often thought the same. Now luv, you take this basket and gather up the bantams' eggs, then we'll go and see what we can find in the hen coop."

In the kitchen the garrulous Annie found it difficult to interrupt Rosa's incessant chatter for long enough to answer her questions.

"Why did you put flour on the board and on the rolling pin? Why did you put grease on that tin? Why are you brushing the top of the pastry with that slippery stuff? Could I try one of the buns? Please..."

Helen learned that Craybourne boasted another farm,Featherstone, and that it was situated some two miles along the valley. Too far for the girls to walk, their first visit was in the July following Mary's death. After several days of high temperatures, Prinny abandoned lessons for a holiday period and there was animated discussion as to how the free time should be spent.

"We could have a picnic Prinny. Go out in the fields somewhere. Take our tea." As always, Rosa's excitement bubbled over.

"The trouble is..." Helen hesitated, not wanting to dampen Rosa's enthusiasm, "we know everywhere round here so well. Perhaps we could go to the other side of the village."

"I've got an even better idea". Prinny had warmed to the subject. "We'll go out to Featherstone... that is if Mr. Dennison will spare Walter to take us in the small cart. Then we can picnic on the lower part of the mountain". Squeals of delight from the girls and the decision was made.

Two days later at 9.30 a.m., one of Mrs.Waring's hampers was brought across from the big house and stowed in the cart. Next, the girls were wedged in with blankets and cushions. Then Prinny joined Walter on the front bench seat and with a quick 'Walk on' to Bella, they were on their way.

Nestling at the foot of the Pennine Range, the reaches of the farm extended upwards until green gave way to rocks and scree, ribboned with waterfalls. It was from Featherstone that lambs had been brought the day prior to Mary's funeral and this journey made Prinny even more aware of the time and effort which had gone into that thoughtful gesture.

If Featherstone and its surroundings were delightful, the same could not be said of its occupants. With the exception of Ned who was both shepherd and odd-job man, they were a strange group. Bea Featherstone, mother of the farmer, was almost blind and shuffled around with her stick of knotted elm, continuously muttering and cursing everything around her. The farmer himself was a surly uncommunicative man and his small son seemed to be at great pains to avoid any contact with the party from Craybourne, disappearing around corners whenever they caught sight of him.

"It's a right shame about t'little lad," Ned said in answer to Prinny's questions. "Whatever sort of a life is it for him here? Can't do anything right as far as his father's concerned and has to do things for t'old lady no grandson should have to do and especially at his age!"

Embarrassed, Prinny attempted to change the subject, but Ned was now in full spate.

"Good thing t'farmer's got his own dogs because I wouldn't let him anywhere near my two. He's as harsh on them as on t' boy. Half mad with temper sometimes. You never get t'best out of anything that way - human or animal. I'm only staying 'til we bring t'sheep down to winter in t'valley, then I'm away. Mr. James understands. T'flocks are well down in size so I b'aint really needed now."

He grinned at the two girls waiting patiently by the cart.

"What about some nice cold milk? Set you up a treat it will for your walk. It'll be 'ot climbing yon hills."

Milk had never tasted so good, Helen thought. The small dairy was cool and inviting with its stone slab and covered pitchers of milk. The pearly streams frothing and bubbling their way into tall beakers were deliciously cold, slaking their already considerable thirst. Bella was unhitched, watered and moved into the shade then, armed with hamper and blanket they set out.

"Prinny, I'm hot and my legs are tired". This from Rosa after fifteen minutes of steady walking.

"Don't worry Rosa, I know it's hot and we're not going to go much further. You see the stream over there? That's come right from the top of the mountain. We're going to walk as far as that so that you'll be able to put your feet in the water .

With such an attractive target in view, Rosa now forged ahead. Destination reached, the blanket was spread on the ground, their hamper carefully placed in the shade of a cluster of gorse and then the youngsters rushed to dip their toes in the stream. An early lunch and the hamper revealed a veritable feast. Pieces of cold chicken, hard boiled eggs and slices of ham, Yorkshire tea-cakes, thickly buttered, pots of jelly and a clutch of nectarines from the Manor hot-houses. All were greeted and consumed with a succession of pleasurable 'Oohs' and 'Aahs' washed down with lemonade and ginger beer until, replete, they each found a shady spot and stretched out.

It was an afternoon of shimmering, almost tangible heat. Skylarks sang and hovered in the soaring blue and the gorse and tussocky grass gave off their own musty scent. Helen saw the boy first.

"There's someone over there Prinny, someone watching us."

"Surely not...?"

"Yes, she's right Miss Pringle. Looks like the lad from the farm. Wonder what he's playing at? Shall I go and send him packing?" In this all-female company, the young Walter was eager to demonstrate his masculinity.

"No! No don't do that...He's probably just curious." After Ned's comments, Prinny felt sorry for the boy.

"You don't think he's hungry, do you ,Prinny?" As usual Helen's sensitive nature considered less obvious reasons for the boy's behaviour.

"I doubt it. Living on a farm, there's usually plenty of food. No, I expect he doesn't see many young people, so he's just enjoying watching you girls and Walter."

Aware that he had been seen they saw the boy pick his way across a rocky patch, slide down one of the scree gullies and continue to the valley floor.

"I don't think he liked us!" Rosa said.

For the first time in his adult life and certainly as the butler of Craybourne Manor, Haig was undecided what to do. Prinny's valley picnic with the girls had left him distinctly ill at ease. Contact with Featherstone farm and Craybourne had previously remained tenuous, but now,... He had seen Michael Featherstone only once when the boy was barely out of long clothes and still bearing the rounded features of the very young. Impossible then to tell just who he was like.

With a thump Haig put down the silver coffee pot he was carrying, causing Mrs. Waring to look up in surprise.

"Haig, are you alright? You'd be the first to say 'Ha'penny off the silver' if anyone else had done that". Then, seeing his expression, "For heaven's sake man, what is it? Are you ill?"

"No, at least... Flo, I need to talk to you, but not here, privately."

"Why don't you go into your pantry and sit yourself down. I'll join you in a moment and we'll treat ourselves to a nice drop of sherry. His Lordship won't mind, you look fair mithered." Accustomed to giving rather than receiving orders, he made no demur and went into the Butler's Pantry.

There was no-one else in whom he was prepared to confide, Mrs. Waring's loyalty to the Family equalling his own. She had joined the household when Oliver was first married and they had together watched with sadness the deterioration of that unhappy union. Flo Waring had always considered Oliver a man great integrity and for Elizabeth, the second Lady Craybourne she would, as she frequently said "Give my right arm."

"I couldn't possibly tell his Lordship and I don't want Lady Elizabeth to know - ever! But at the same time, someone ought to know. You see, I don't know if he's ever been told. And now there's the boy to consider..."

"You're not making any sense, man. What boy are you talking about?"

"Oliver Craybourne's grandson."

"Oh my Lord, you're not saying there's more wrong side of t' blanket bairns?"

"Not more...just one, Michael Featherstone."

"The boy over at t' farm. Don't be daft!"

"It's true, I'm sure of it. Don't forget I was here when his Lordship was seventeen. Only a few years older and I knew what he was going through."

"How d'you mean? Going through...?".

"I can't go into details, it's too embarrassing. He was a young man, still being treated like a boy and full of tension. He was ready for, well..."

"You mean he was ready for a woman?"

"Yes, just so." Haig's relief that she'd understood without further explanation was obvious. "He went out that morning saying he was going for a ride along the valley. When he came back I knew straight away something had happened. There were his clothes for a start. Grass stains on his lovely trousers, shirt wrongly buttoned up - you know. His manner was different too. He was flushed and a bit flustered, wanting to be on his own. Yet in a funny way I could tell he was pleased with himself. When he said he'd stopped at Featherstone's for a drink I knew what had happened."

"Sounds to me as if you're putting two and two together and making six."

"Oh no. You didn't know Bea Featherstone then but I did. She was if you'll excuse me, what men would call 'easy'. All flashing eyes and showing too much flesh. Whenever she came into the village the men were round her like bees round honey. She was newly married then but as the time went by and no babies appeared on the scene they started to poke fun at her husband Si, saying he wasn't man enough for her. You know the sort of thing."

"You still haven't said why you're so sure..."

"Well to begin with there's not another soul lives within miles of the valley. I made a note of the date and afterwards made it my business to talk to the folk at Hislop's, very discreetly of course, about what was happening at Featherstone's. Sure enough in a few short months I hear she's pregnant and Si's like a pouter pigeon at having put paid to all the rumours."

"All the same..."

"Mrs. Waring, I'm as sure as I'm sitting here that young Michael's Oliver's grandson. What I don't know is whether Sam Featherstone was ever told. Bea's gone to pieces now, almost blind and from all accounts very confused. But supposing she has told someone, left any proof around? There might come a time when the family tries to make something of it. After all Sam Featherstone would be the eldest son and heir to the Craybourne title."

"I never heard the like! That nasty bad-tempered man."

"But what should I do?"

"Absolutely nothing. You've got it all off your chest now. You know me, I can be as silent as the grave if needs be and especially when it comes to protecting that dear man and our young Lordship. That Bea woman might never have been sure herself who the father of her child was."

Haig began to relax. "You're right. But at least someone else knows now. I just want to do the right thing by the family. But they've just had one nasty surprise dropped in their laps and enough's enough."

"It'll be our secret. I still think your imagination's got the better of you...", Haig started to protest, "but just put it out of your mind and enjoy your sherry. Now, I must get on, there's a leg of pork needs putting in the oven." And with that she bustled away.

Why does she hate me? Helen puzzled over the question for the umpteenth time. There was no doubt that the Honourable Daphne, just three years her senior, displayed towards her real signs of animosity. Just the other day on their weekly visit Haig was escorting them across the hall when hearing a movement she looked up and saw Daphne glaring at them from the head of the stairs. She had silently watched their progress to the Dining Room and then flounced away out of sight. Being shown to the Dining Room was a departure from the usual, but Lady Elizabeth was there all smiles, explaining that she thought they might like to see the table fully laid.

"Ooh..." Rosa drew in her breath sharply, "it's lovely. Are visitors coming to have tea with you?"

"Well not quite. We have tea in the drawing room, but in here we have dinner and we would usually say 'Guests are dining with us'".

Through such barely susceptible corrections and the feeding in of new information, Elizabeth hoped that together she and Prinny were preparing the girls for whatever their lives might bring.

"Such a lot of knives and forks..." Helen looked puzzled.

"Cutlery, and tablecloths and napkins are napery."

"But how do you know which piece of cutlery to use?"

"It's quite simple really Helen, this is how it works..."

In her bedroom Daphne was fuming. Mama was at it again, coaching these grandchildren of her father in good manners. What next? Lessons in deportment? Tuition in Latin and Greek?

All my life I've heard nothing but good about my father. Always cracked up to be some sort of saint and now this! Seems their idol had feet of clay. How can Mama take it so calmly? Another one with saint-like tendencies. Hope it's not catching. Most women would have ranted and raved and got rid of every reminder of Mary and her brood. Not Mama. Instead we're having the full Lady Bountiful routine.

The worst thing of all is that I'm related to those girls. Heavens, I think I must be their aunt! If I'm to be perfectly honest I'll also admit to being jealous of their gorgeous hair. They didn't get that from the Craybournes, we're the insipid pale blonde variety. I guess their good-for-nothing father was responsible, which makes him good for something after all. One thing's for sure, in a few years' time they'll both be turning heads - other people's that is!

Chapter Six

Autumn, and Prinny decided to make a second picnic visit to the Featherstone area. Already the mornings and evenings hinted at Winter but the days were still warm and oozed golden light. The sheep had been brought down into their winter pastures and Ned had left. With this exception nothing had changed. Only the dogs yapped and snarled on their arrival and Walter went off in search of a human presence.

He found Bea in the farmhouse kitchen. A kitchen which was so far removed from his experience at Hislop's that he stopped aghast on the threshold. In her rocking chair the old lady mumbled and cursed. The unsavoury smells of stale food, dirt and urine made him gag and he stepped quickly back into the clean mountain air. Since Ned's departure it was obvious that things had deteriorated rapidly. Ned would never have tolerated these living conditions, would have insisted on some sort of order being established. No sign of the farmer. Only the merest glimpse of Michael who quickly disappeared into the depths of the barn. Rosa ran to the door and called inside.

"Come out Michael. Come out and come with us."

No answer. They went to the dairy and Prinny took coins from her purse as Walter poured milk for each of them. At least here it seemed clean enough. At Helen's insistence they took from the hamper a large piece of chocolate cake and wrapped it in oiled paper. This they left with the coins on the stone slab. Rosa ran back to the barn.

"We've left you cake Michael. It's in the dairy."

On their return Helen was pleased to see the cake had gone.

"I expect the rats enjoyed it", Walter joked.

"Don't be silly Walter", Rosa reprimanded him, "what would they have done with the paper?"

The mountains' long shadows cloaked the valley on their return and Prinny shivered. Winter was almost on them. Soon these hills would be covered in snow and the valley impassable and soon, very soon, she would have to face her next hurdle, Christmas.

In fact, Christmas presented no problems at all.

"You'll be with us for Christmas Day." It was a statement of fact from Annie and brooked no arguments. An early visit to church was followed by a gargantuan meal in the farmhouse kitchen. If Helen relived the events of last Christmas in Piggott's Lane she made no sign. Afternoon tea in Annie's parlour and Rosa's carefully pronounced "Would you care for some cake?" reducing them all to laughter. Blind Man's Buff, dominoes and Snap. Gifts for everyone. The girls rosy with excitement and on their return to Orchard Cottage, the three of them quite exhausted.

A crisply cold Boxing Day morning, and Prinny and the girls walked along the lanes around the estate. Back at the cottage for soup, ham and pickles and then at 3.30 to the Manor for tea. On this occasion the presence of her own children had been insisted upon by Lady Elizabeth. Daphne, sulky in lemon taffeta, eyed the girls moodily. They were very pretty in Elizabeth's presents to them, matching dresses of jade green. Robert handed round plates and food with his customary sardonic smile. Of Elizabeth's children, only James was genuinely pleased to see the girls and anxious to put them at ease.

Helen sat near the window. Occasionally she would put out a small hand and stroke the thick pile of the velvet curtain. I hope to God her hands are not greasy, Daphne thought. Her mother was more charitable, noting the child weigh in her hand the large tassel, running her fingers through its silken fronds. She's so quiet and so tactile. Loves the smell of things too, leather, books, whatever... Handles them reverently and smells them. Very sensitive...

Elizabeth eyed her own children. James is a darling, but these other two...I sometimes find it hard to believe they're flesh of my flesh.

"What about some carols?" In an attempt to submerge her own disquiet, Elizabeth was uncharacteristically hearty. At a signal Daphne moved towards the piano and they started singing. All that is, except Helen. Her eyes moved from the singers to the room and its contents. The walls with their silken sheen of cream and gold, the sweet-smelling Christmas tree with its red taffeta bows, the rich patina of the polished surfaces. Around the room, light sconces of delicate Dresden. Oh to run her fingers over those exquisitely formed porcelain flowers, to feel the ridges of the ribboned plates of Sèvres which adorned the mantelpiece. It was all too beautiful...

Daphne saw her leave the room. What was she up to? Having a little snoop perhaps. Wonder if Mama has ever even considered that these girls might be light-fingered? Accompanying "The Holly and the Ivy" to its conclusion, she then excused herself. Sounds eventually led her to her Mother's boudoir. Unmistakable sounds of sobbing. The door was wide open and seeing her, Helen got up quickly, "I shouldn't be in here. I'm so sorry..."

"Stay where you are and sit down." Daphne closed the door. "Whatever's wrong? Are you ill or something?"

"No, it's just, well last Christmas we were with Mam, Mother that is. Although she was very sick we did sing some carols and I was just..."

"Remembering... of course. Only natural. Would you rather be on your own?"

"No! Thank you. It's nice to talk..." Helen hesitated," to you. There was something else made me cry. Mam loved pretty things. And well, the Drawing Room, it's so beautiful. I was just thinking how she would have loved it all, the tree and everything."

I've been imagining her to be some awful monster and she's just a little girl grieving for her mother. God forbid it should happen, but how would I feel? Especially when I've been such a pig to Mama lately.

"It's always the same you can never find a hanky when you need one. Have mine Helen, it's quite clean, though not very big." Daphne produced a dainty piece of cambric, "There, dry your eyes. We're going to go up to my room now so that you can wash your face and tidy up before we join the others."

Relief washed over Elizabeth as Daphne re-entered the room holding the small Helen's hand. I was wrong! Daphne has inherited some of our better family traits after all. Thank you Lord.

Michael Featherstone was just eight years old when he received his first lesson in working the sheep. Unloved, uncared for, he was as yet unaware of his origins. It was true that Gran had once shown him her treasures and where they were hidden, but he was not good at letters and any significance the objects bore had bypassed him.

He had thought it a strange collection. The wedding ring, too small now for her swollen arthritic fingers, a brooch of cheap paste bought for her marriage and, torn from the fly-leaf of the family Bible, a crude representation of a tree, each apple denoting a member of the family. It was the ten-year old Sam who had pencilled in the Featherstone family names. Folded in the piece of paper was a small corner of cambric, obviously cut from a handkerchief; it bore the initials O.M.C. Through the name of her son's father had been drawn a line, obliterating the S.F. so that the apple now bore instead the painstakingly copied initials O.M.C.

Of a certain day in the September of 1860 Bea now had no recall, but Haig's suppositions regarding the coupling of the Lord of the Manor's son and the farmer's wife had been accurate in almost every detail.

Autumn had been a mere suspicion on the breath of early morning when the young Oliver rode out in an attempt to ease the restlessness in his body. The past weeks had seen his manhood wasted in a series of vivid dreams, the embarrassing results of which had led to a variety of subterfuges. Hidden pyjamas, a sheet hastily dried behind locked doors. There was no-one in whom he could confide, certainly not his austere parents, nor Nanny to whom he was still 'my little boy'.

Lazily folding clothes in the shade of a sycamore tree, Bea Fatherstone watched his approach, noting the litheness of the young body, the breadth of his shoulders, the animal energy now bathed in perspiration after the long, hot ride.

"A drink maister? It'll cool thee down."

In a flurry of apron and blue cotton skirt she entered the dairy, emerging with a tall mug and pitcher of ice-cold milk. Oliver, thirst slaked and his horse stabled, announced his intention of spending the day walking on the lower ranges of the mountains and, without further ado, set out. At twenty-eight Bea Featherstone was sexually frustrated, her overworked husband's greatest need at the end of the day being a desire for sleep. Now, abandoning her task with alacrity, she followed Oliver, maintaining a discreet distance, whilst keeping him always in her sights.

When he stopped by a foaming water cascade and removed his riding boots she was, to his astonishment, suddenly at his side, hair black as ebony, cotton skirt lifted to show flashes of bare legs. The swell of brown breasts above the square cut bodice, the hint of whiter flesh below and the dark dampness of her armpits all evidence of a femininity foreign to Oliver's experience.

"Going for a paddle, maister? But your lovely trousers, you mustn't get them wet, 'ere, let me 'elp you."

Suddenly, as her slightly coarsened finger-tips started to unbutton his clothes, stroking and caressing, his skin began to burn and he knew that his engorged manhood must explode before he could touch her. And so it proved, to his frustration and humiliation! Now, consolingly, reassuringly, she helped his uncertain fingers to unbutton her own straining bodice, directing his inexpert hands to her nipples erect with anticipation and finally, to the silky darkness between her thighs. Black hair tumbled over white shoulders, she lay amongst the heather, legs splayed invitingly, awaiting his readiness until at last the seed flowed again and he was able to penetrate the territory he had dreamed for so long of possessing. As he lay, deep inside her, her own orgasm was such exquisite ecstasy that her deep-throated exclamations of satisfaction eventually gave way to gurgles of amusement at her pupil's quickly learned lesson.

"Are you all right, lady?"

His polite enquiry and the term 'lady' produced further giggles.

"I'm fine, maister, and I wouldn't mind betting your 're feeling a mite better for having got all that dirty water off your chest. Now you know how it's done you could come and see me again. 'E's always away Thursdays - goes to market..."

The youth, drowning in his embarrassment, muttered something about going away and that he was sorry for what had happened. As he rode away her coarse laughter and scornful voice echoed around him."Sorry... like 'ell thou art. Thee's 'ad a reet good time and so 'ave I. Come again..."

The delights of her flesh and the success of his own performance suffused his being on the long ride home. It had been an idyllic day, but one too dangerous to repeat. Had the object of his passion been a young single girl on the estate a blind eye would have been turned to the liaison, but a relationship with an older, and more importantly, a married woman, would be considered reprehensible. Great though the temptation was, better to avoid visiting Featherstone again before his departure next month. At least now he would join the Guards feeling that he had been 'blooded', that he was not without sexual experience. Of the child born from the seed sown that day Oliver Craybourne was never to know.

For Si Featherstone the birth of Sam, the boy he believed to be his son proved a watershed. Confident now in his marital bed, his manner out of it became one of burly aggression. Nervous of evoking his violent temper, he was treated with respect by the other hill farmers. The boy Sam inherited with ease the aggressive characteristics of the man he called 'father'. And into this atmosphere his own son

Michael was born to a mother who saw early death as a happy release from a life at the beck and call of two cruel , insensitive men.

At first unnerved by the presence of strangers on or near the farm, Michael began to enjoy the visits from the Craybourne party, observing its members closely, whilst maintaining his distance. Came the day when his father, away at the market, left instructions to hand over some lambs to 'the lad from Hislop's' and Michael was at last forced to speak to Walter. The lambs safely stowed in the cart, Walter asked for a drink and suggested they sat down together whilst he drank.

The boy was quiet, too quiet he thought. Several more visits were to take place before Walter felt Michael trusted him, did not flinch when he raised his hand in the most casual of gestures. If the relationship became important to the boy, it proved of value also to Walter. There was no-one else in whom he felt he could confide. Here was a willing, uncritical audience.

To him Walter spoke of his hopes and dreams. The Dennisons were so kind, how could he tell them that as soon as he was old enough he would leave them. And Helen. However remote his dream, he could not upset Helen by telling her one day he would go away. To Michael he could speak of a life outside that of the farmyard. Bustling towns, other means of earning a living. Armies of men trained to fight, sailing overseas to hot countries, seeing the world and all its wonders...

Michael too, began to indulge in such dreams. Dreams which took him away from the stink of the farmyard ordure, away from the misery of Featherstone. Dreams which were shattered only by the whine of his father's cane across his legs.

A rare visit to Harrogate and Prinny noted with amusement that the girls were behaving absolutely true to form. Helen, at fourteen almost a young lady, was quietly taking in everything around her, whilst Rosa gregarious as ever, chatted to anyone who would listen. They were now she said, a la Lady Elizabeth, "taking tea at Betty's restaurant". Toasted currant teacakes, custard tarts, Indian tea and the most exotic of cakes.

"I must have one of those". Rosa's forefinger extended towards a flower of lime-green marzipan petals, its heart a swirl of cream.

"Manners Rosa!" Prinny's eyebrows lifted in mock horror at both gesture and utterance,

"Sorry Prinny," Rosa laughed, "but they look so delicious and pretty too."

Helen's eyes were not so much on the cakes as the other occupants of the restaurant. One would think a flight of exotic birds had settled here, she thought. Such hats! Feather trimmed and chiffon swathed, as their owners moved and spoke they fluttered and dipped, creating a spectrum of fluctuating colour. And the dresses! Ladies came here of course not only to consume tea and cakes, but to meet friends and to be seen. Inevitably the visit to Beti's would be followed by a gentle stroll around the gardens of the Spa town. On such a stroll who knows whom one might encounter? Only the smartest of ensembles were suitable for such occasions.

They had travelled by carriage with James, who today had business in the town and was to meet them at five o'clock for the return journey. It was by no means the first time they had accompanied him on business trips. Whilst other properties were sited further afield, the family factories were in Halifax and its environs and he had on occasion taken them there and to Huddersfield and Leeds.

On one such visit he had shown Helen inside one of his woollen mills. Her overpowering recollection had been one of noise. As far as the eye could see the looms clattered about their business, with voices shouting instructions above the din.

"The material has a weft and a warp, Helen, see the threads running in different directions. The shuttle carries the weft, or the woof as it's sometimes known, and it weaves in and out creating texture and strength. Yes, the noise is a problem. People do have to shout to make themselves heard. They do say this is why North country people are developing louder voices than the rest of the country!"

Always Helen's hero, his treatment of her now as a young lady rather than child, endeared him to her even further. Often she pondered on his kindness and their circumstances. Yes, her mother had been a faithful servant to the Craybournes, but she was comparatively young, not a retainer like Haig and Mrs Waring, years and years her senior. Yes, Lady Elizabeth had obviously valued Mary's work very highly and her Ladyship was noted for her kindness, but... always, as Annie Dennison had done some years earlier, she wondered why Elizabeth had done so much. Helen had now been told that there was some money for Rosa and herself, money left by Mary, the proceeds from the sale of her grandparents' stores. Perhaps Lady Elizabeth was taking care of the money for them and at the same time was using some of it for their needs.

Various approaches to Prinny on the subject had drawn a blank. If she knew more, she certainly wasn't saying. The most Helen could get her to say was,

"When you're twenty-one you'll be able to take over your own affairs. I'm afraid you'll just have to wait until then."

Seven years... It seemed a lifetime. Although, the seven years since her mother died seemed surprisingly to have passed quickly.

There had been some changes of course. Robert was now at Oxford University and they were seeing less and less of Walter. I must ask Annie why he doesn't visit us any more. Probably finds us boring little girls now that he's so grown up, Helen thought.

At least Daphne is reasonably friendly when she's at home. 'Doesn't exactly seek me out but at least doesn't go to great lengths to avoid me. What curious remarks she made on that last visit.

"If I can possibly avoid the coming out business, I shall do so. I know I'll have a battle royal on my hands with Mama, but so be it."

"Coming out?..."

"Yes, when I'm eighteen. All that dressing up and going off to Court, being a debutante, doing the Season, you know."

Helen, reluctant to admit ignorance, nodded, privately thinking it all sounded delightful.

"I have other plans. Been keeping my eyes and ears open and reading...Do you know what a Suffragette is?"

"Not really... something to do with voting?"

"Quite right! Suffrage is voting and a Suffragette is a woman who wants the right to vote. We haven't got that now you know."

"We?"

"Women, you goose. You and me. This is a man's world created by men, for men and it's about time it changed. A lot of women are determined to see that happen and I want to be part of the struggle. Because I don't think there's any doubt that's what it will be. But not a word to anyone... it's our secret."

A shared secret for Helen and for Daphne the kernel of an idea which was to grow and grow. Perhaps Helen could be of real assistance to her in the future. Doing well academically, according to Prinny, Helen was an absolute greenhorn when it came to knowledge about life and in particular, about life in society.

I've got two years to work on it. Two years before that awful dressing up charade in London. By then Helen will be almost sixteen. If I can persuade Mama to let me take her with me as some sort of maid or companion, that lack of knowledge could well enable me to escape Mama's ever-watchful eye. Rotten of me to use Helen in such a way, but if there is to be a battle royal between myself and Mama then "all's fair in love and war." I shall have to be extremely well-behaved for the foreseeable future if I'm to pull it off... Daphne started to make plans.

Chapter Seven

March 1907

Lying between the cool sheets, and listening to the sounds, muffled by heavy curtains, of awakening London, Helen contemplated the past few days. Their journey by rail from Halifax to King's Cross had been an adventure in itself. Never had she seen such grime as existed in the northern town. The busy cobbled streets, the endless rows of houses, smoking mill chimneys; all came as a shock after her quiet rural existence. Then the train itself, frightening and yet exhilarating, like some monster spewing out on its breath towns and countryside in a never-ending stream. In the further shock wave of her first impressions of London, Halifax shrank to normality. Here the stream of traffic, the variety of its nature, left her literally speechless.

Helen regretted that Lady Craybourne had been unable to accompany them. Momentous decisions had to be made about Robert's future and until these were taken her Ladyship must stay at the Manor. He had been 'sent down' from Oxford a year ago, which Prinny had told her, meant he was expelled and could never go back. That he had done something terrible was obvious from Lady Craybourne's shocked pale face and James's fierce expression. Just what it was Helen couldn't imagine, but, judging from Prinny's tightly pursed lips there was a strong possibility that she knew and an even stronger one that she would never be prevailed upon to say. Prinny had explained that several important men from London had visited Craybourne a few days before requesting that James take a post in the Government. There was little doubt that the idea appealed both to him and his mother. So far as Helen could determine, Robert was the main problem.

Robert himself seemed singularly unperturbed by the fuss, spending much of his time reading poetry, often aloud and, as far as Helen could gather, travelling to Leeds and Bradford and sometimes London to meet his friends and visit art galleries and theatres. If James did become a Government official, and the idea obviously appealed to both him and Lady Craybourne, he would have to spend a great deal of time in London. In that event it was obvious that Robert would be of little help in managing the estate.

In the pale light, which now crept around the sides of the curtains, Helen surveyed the room with pleasure. She had never slept anywhere so grand and this room she knew was as nothing compared to the one Daphne occupied. For some reason there had been long discussions between Lady Craybourne and Prinny before it was decided that she should travel as Daphne's lady's maid. Perhaps they were worried that she wasn't yet ready for such duties, but Miss Pringle had told her that young girls of her age often started their training by looking after the daughters of the nobility. It was all very puzzling. The evening dresses with their matching accessories, the sets of delicately embroidered underwear, or lingerie as she must remember to call it, the fans, the hats ... oh, the hats!

Perhaps they were trying to protect her from Daphne's moods but strangely, throughout the journey, Daphne had been almost friendly. Of course, in the face of her own amazement at the wonders of the city Daphne had appeared somewhat blasé, bored even, but then that was to be expected, she had after all seen it all, done it all, on numerous occasions. When Nanny Glossop slept, which she had done for most of the journey, Daphne had seemed at her most relaxed, talking of things which to Helen were rather puzzling. Why should Daphne think women hadn't sufficient rights? What more did they want to do? Surely someone like Lady Craybourne was happy; she seemed to organise, to control things, and enjoy herself at the same time.

Close by the tinny-sounding church bell struck the hour of seven and with a quick movement Helen got out of bed and drew back the curtain. The sun which had filtered through the leaves of the trees defining the square, now speared its way into the room. It was going to be a lovely day!

Daphne too, was awake. How to bring her plans to fruition? How was the Honourable Miss Craybourne to escape from the mass of expectations and social conventions which entangled her? Retrospectively she realised that her early years at school had been a vacuum, a time when she had felt herself to be a misfit both at home and at school.

On vacations from her Kentish boarding school she had watched the Calloway girls with curiosity mixed with contempt. So, Mama and La Pringle had it in mind to turn these little ducklings into swans, hence the weekly visits to take tea in the Manor drawing room, she supposed. No doubt the little darlings were being initiated into the awesome rites of balancing cake-plate and tea-cup in one elegant gesture. If that was the limit of their ambitions, good luck to them. They were both pretty enough to break a few men's hearts, if that was what they wanted. Strange, really - Mary had been pleasant enough to look at, but ordinary, whilst no-one could ever call her Titian-haired daughters that. They were, to be honest, rather beautiful. No doubt Jim Calloway was responsible. By all accounts, that thickly curling black hair, the dark eyes and quicksilver, disarming smile had all added up to a very handsome man.

But, she was digressing; she must think things through. There was no doubt that the summer of 1903 had changed her life. When news reached Craybourne that a Mrs. Pankhurst had formed a union to fight for women's suffrage, Daphne had felt excitement welling up inside her. This was what was wrong with her life, she was leading an entirely futile existence and therein lay the root of her dissatisfaction with everything and everybody and clearly, she was not alone in that. If women in their hundreds, thousands even, felt as she did, perhaps changes could and would be made. She refused to contemplate the awfulness of marriage to some nitwit, devoid of brains, because he happened to be the 'catch' of the season. No, as soon as possible she would join the W.S.P.A. and convention could go hang!

Easing herself higher on the snow-white pillows with their deep edging of crochet, she smiled, recalling the look on La Pringle's face when the Suffrage movement was mentioned, a look she had at first thought spelled disapproval. Their mutual amazement at finding they had at last established a point of reference in their relationship, even, dare it be said, a measure of rapport, seemed now, looking back, quite comical.

Returning for her last two years at Kent, to the astonishment of her tutors all was changed. Gone was the apathetic, uninterested approach to her work, now there was so little time in which to find out all she needed to know about history, politics, the Constitution. All would be grist to her mill.

Robert had been a bloody fool. Mama must surely have always been aware that he was different. Even as a child she herself had sensed it, though only now understanding the full implications. Her unladylike habit of listening outside doors whenever serious discussions seemed to be afoot, had resulted in the information that Robert had been found in bed naked with someone; that the someone should have been male rather than female had exacerbated the crime in the eyes of the Rector of his College. That worthy gentleman had informed Mama that the Honourable Robert Craybourne had been found behaving in a way considered dishonourable in the extreme and that he had brought grave disrepute to his College. No wonder Mama had barely spoken for days and James by comparison had, uncharacteristically, snapped and snarled at everyone. There had been no scandal, or none that she was aware of, either at school or on her visits to London. No doubt they had the Rector to thank for that.

I shall go on loving Robert all the same. In spite of, no, even perhaps because of what he is. She smiled again, remembering. A few years ago we used to fight like cat and dog. I thought he was arrogant and patronising and I know he regarded me as a bad-tempered, spoiled little brat. Now I know him to be sensitive, intelligent and appreciative of all the best things in life - art, music, poetry. He's witty, charming and has a sense of colour any woman would give her eye-teeth for. I'm digressing again! If I deviate from what Mama believes to be the straight and narrow, she'll have only James and if he isn't there ....No, I can't afford to dwell on that, I've got my own life to live.

Daphne's sharp little face was serious. The silver-blonde hair of the Craybournes was her best feature, the granite-grey eyes beneath it being too closely set for beauty, whilst her mouth hinted at a sensuality her somewhat angular body denied. Without the necessity of being outright deceitful, things had worked out much as she had hoped, Nanny Glossop and young Helen being hardly likely to prove a hindrance to her plans. Her Aunt would be a different matter. Louisa, Lady Eynsford, her mother's sister, with whom they were to stay for several months, was quite a shrewd lady. However, a widow of forty-two who frankly admitted to hating her widowed state might be too concerned with the search for a second husband to worry about her niece. On the other hand she was currently acting in locoparentis for her sister's child...? There was little point, Daphne told herself, in meeting trouble half way. One thing was certain, Uncle Cecil was far too preoccupied with his gout and the onerous task of escorting his sister to the many social activities necessary in her continuing search for a mate, to worry about Daphne.

Strange the differences that pertained between siblings. Mama was invariably composed, cool, unflappable, whereas Aunt Louisa was sharp, volatile and completely unpredictable. As for Uncle Cecil, well, he was a lamb, doing pretty much what he was told. No, he wouldn't be a problem; in fact he might well prove to be quite useful.

There had been one difficult day when her mother had done a great deal of heart-searching as to whether it was right for Helen to accompany her. After all it wasn't every day that an aunt set out accompanied by her niece, or half-niece, the latter in a comparatively menial capacity. The nub of the problem was that Helen had obviously not yet been told the whole story. That, and her age. Here a few chosen seeds sown in the direction of La Pringle had borne fruit, Daphne having pointed out that many of her contemporaries at school were already 'looked after' by girls of Helen's age learning their trade as ladies' maids.

Possibly that had tipped the scales, but whatever it was, here they were in London and she could now start putting her own plans into action. A tap at the door and a little maid appeared. Her face shy beneath the gofferred cap, she bore a shining brass ewer of hot water. In her wake was a second maid who with a polite 'Good morning' set down a tray of tea and biscuits at the bedside and then with a swish the curtains were drawn back from the huge windows, revealing a morning awash with green and gold. Daphne smiled to herself. It was going to be a lovely day!

The sun was not shining over Featherstone. For several days a thick mist had shrouded the upper reaches of the mountains, twisting wraith-like into the lower gullies and ravines. On two occasions Michael had been forced to abandon the idea of taking lambs for the Manor kitchens to Hislop's. Today a break in the mist saw his departure, thankful to be away from the farm and his father for a few hours.

At what hour of the day the control of Sam's two alsatians snapped during another of his irrational and savage bouts of cruelty would never be known. From the moment their fangs sank deep into his throat, he had lain and died in his own blood. Gran, receiving no answer to her urgent calls for assistance and her need to be taken to the privy becoming increasingly imperative, struggled from her rocker to the yard, almost falling over her son's prone body. Her claw-like hands, trying to identify the object, were soon covered in the sticky cloying substance she knew to be blood. With a sudden awareness, her sharp intake of breath gave way to uncontrollable gales of laughter at the knowledge that she had outlived the son who had brought such misery to her old age.

Staggering from side to side in her blindness, she sank at last exhausted under the same sycamore tree from the shade of which the young and beautiful Beatrice had first seen Oliver. Her back against the bole of the tree, head slumped forward, the spreading darkness on her skirts indicating that the visit to the privy was no longer a necessity.

Thus, on his return, Michael found her and, a few seconds later, the body of his father. Armed with Sam's shotgun, he made a brief search for the dogs, eventually deciding that they had gone to ground fearing retribution. With the mist creeping further down the valley he speedily fed the livestock and then transferred the humans, both living and dead to the cart. Moving like an automaton his one objective being to return to Hislop's and the human contact which Gran could no longer provide. With difficulty, the ungainly bundle that was now Sam Featherstone was dragged and lifted into the cart's well and concealed with sacking. Next Gran, cocooned in blankets, was wedged in the corner. His grisly task completed, Michael turned his back on Featherstone and set out for Craybourne.

Chapter Eight

Three days after their arrival in London, Lady Eynsford announced her intention of, that morning, escorting Daphne to the House of Aston, the fashion house on which she graciously bestowed her patronage. Helen was to accompany them. Met at the entrance by a footman in the grey and pink livery of the House, they were escorted to the main viewing room.

It was another world. Curtains in the palest pink cascaded down the walls, interrupted only by mirrors whose gilt frames were encrusted with cherubs. The mirrors reflected lamps shaded with pleated pink silk and low circular tables bearing vases foaming with pink blooms. The very air breathed perfume. For years afterwards Helen was never to reach for a perfume bottle without recalling the impact of that first moment when the perfume was almost as tangible as the essences and flowers from which it was culled. Moving forward to greet them, Aston's senior vendeuse, all pale blonde sophistication, directed them to the elegant gilt chairs upholstered in velvet of silver grey, then stood, notebook and pencil at the ready.

"Lady Eynsford," the vendeuse bobbed a curtsey, "How may I assist your Ladyship?"

"Nothing for me personally today, Miss Wilmott. This is my niece, the Honourable Miss Craybourne."

"Miss Craybourne." Another stately bob and inclination of the head.

"She is coming out this season and will need a number of day and evening dresses and, of course, her Court presentation dress. If we might see what is left of your Spring collection, together with any further designs you have to offer."

Leaving her client briefly, Miss Wilmott speedily relayed this information to disembodied voices in an adjoining room and, within moments of her return, the House of Aston started to display its wares.

Never had Helen seen such an array. Exquisite gown followed exquisite gown in such a rainbow of colours and such a myriad of fabrics and design that Helen began to feel pallid to the point of invisibility. Daphne's usual forthright manner seemed to have waned in this ultra-feminine atmosphere. Under pressure from Lady Eynsford she admitted to "quite liking the aquamarine" and agreed the lime evening dress to be "quite eye-catching." Eventually, at Lady Eynsford's insistence, four evening dresses were selected, with little enthusiasm on Daphne's part. Other purchases, she informed her aunt she would prefer to leave in abeyance pending her mother's arrival.

Now Daphne and Helen were taken to a smaller room lined with mirrors and here Helen assisted Daphne in removing her outergarments. Another assistant appeared who took the necessary measurements and once Daphne was re-attired they were ready to leave. Emerging from the dressing room they found her Ladyship deep in conversation with a lean and handsome gentleman, Mr. Aston himself. Lady Eynsford now exhibited a fluttering coyness which Helen had not previously witnessed, a coyness which continued throughout the introduction of her niece.

"Ah, there you are, Daphne. May I present Mr. Neville Aston, who owns this charming establishment - my niece, the Honourable Miss Craybourne."

"Delighted, Miss Craybourne."

Neville Aston bowed low over Daphne's hand, but whilst murmuring the appropriate phrases to Daphne, Neville Aston's practised eyes took in the second girl. Obviously the lady's maid, or rather a trainee.

Sixteen, possibly seventeen and a stunner! He'd never seen such poise in so young a girl. The budding figure with its slender innocence was provocation itself. Her neat little head was supported by a slim elegant neck and surmounting all, that brilliant halo of hair which looked as if it was longing to break forth from the restraint of her hat. Her clothes were - well, not bad for a menial, she obviously had some idea of colour and style, but whatever she wore, nothing could detract from that pure oval face, the alabaster-like skin and those astonishing sea green eyes.

Lady Eynsford and Daphne and indeed Helen herself would have been amazed to know that Mr. Aston was even conscious of her presence. In fact he could have given quite an accurate assessment of her height, weight and measurements.

As they were escorted from the premises it was arranged that Miss Craybourne would attend for a fitting in three days time and that her maid should call the following afternoon to receive materials for the shoemaker so that he could proceed with evening pumps to match the soirée dresses selected.

Neville Aston had no compunction about what he planned to do. Had Helen been Lady Eynsford's own maid he would, with reluctance, have abandoned the idea, but any one of a dozen girls could fulfil the tasks the girl would currently be carrying out for Miss Craybourne. Given a few moments alone with Louisa Eynsford he was sure he would be able to persuade her that to accept his offer would be in the girl's own best interests.

Mr. Neville's' smooth charm belied the fact that he was an astute businessman. There were many pretty girls around, but this girl had the charismatic quality he sought. More importantly, she was exactly what he had been looking for. In Helen he would create something quite new. To date, modelling for a House such as Aston's was regarded as prestigious, but only within the trade itself. Music hall stars achieved fame, notoriety even, but his mannequins remained lady-like, unobtrusive and anonymous. This he proposed to change. He had been searching for a face and figure such as Helen possessed. Qualities which could, with the right training and publicity, bring untold wealth into the Aston coffers. Neville Aston had always prided himself on moving with the times, on sensing the mood of a society ready for change and adapting accordingly. When he had inherited Astons it was a House of Mourning, catering specifically for wardrobes for the bereaved, its fittings rooms awash with acres of material in funereal black and deepest purple. Whatever one's shape or size, here bereaved families would find the clothes convention demanded and, as circumstances required, quickly.

But Neville had soon realised that even the most grief-stricken of ladies wished to look their best and that any stock slightly outmoded was not in his own best interests. Soon his meticulous attention to current styles and detail ensured a growing reputation and clientele. What more natural now to suggest to Madam that once her period of mourning was over and she was "feeling more herself" she might care to visit Aston's again to see its 'other' range of garments and to ensure that glimpses of the very best of these were available on her pre-funeral visits. Within months those 'other' clothes were to become the main attraction and the sombre mourning garments, whilst retained, were relegated to smaller, less conspicuous display areas.

Within five years the House of Aston was acknowledged as one of the leading London Fashion Houses, having, to Neville's delight, 'creamed off' from other houses a number of very important customers. True, he had had occasionally to turn a blind eye to certain incidents in order not to lose the patronage of those members of the aristocracy who were not so scrupulous as they might be. He smiled wryly recalling the large quantities of mourning clothes sent 'on approval' to a widowed Duchess. The majority of the garments had been returned to him after the funeral, their necklines and shoulders dusty with powder. Quite obviously they had been worn. He smiled again, it must have been a very smart funeral - a pity he couldn't take the credit for that...! But, his lips were sealed. The Duchess was now a regular customer and in her wake had brought a number of important ladies, their accounts, and their figures, substantial!

But, times were changing. Class barriers were breaking down and women were, he felt sure, about to take a more active role in society. Eventually, more and more women from all walks of life would demand clothes of better design and quality but would have neither the time, the inclination, nor the money to visit establishments such as Aston's. The next five years would see many changes and that was where Helen's youth was such an asset. He would train her as a mannequin, mould her in his techniques ensuring that, unlike his other mannequins, she became well known in London and its environs, nationally even. She would be seen at the best places and with the right people. She must visit Ascot and Henley, the theatres of course, ride on Rotton Row and walk in the Strand. When the time was ripe he would use her as an important factor in his plans to bring about the massive changes on which he had been brooding for some time. A bell, announcing the imminent arrival of more customers, broke his reverie. Today he was convinced that he had seen the girl who could help make some of his plans materialise. It was inconceivable that she should turn down his offer, but if she did, then his search would be resumed ...

A smile of welcome lighting his face, he turned to greet his next client.

Chapter Nine

Michael and Rosa first met in the graveyard of Craybourne Church eight days after the deaths of Sam Featherstone and his mother, Bea, for, as Michael had anticipated, Gran had not survived the evening's events and died at Hislop's in the silent hours before dawn.

Rosa had brought flowers on the anniversary of her mother's death and Michael had come to see that headstones were in place on the family graves and to ease his own guilt. His feelings were confused. His father he could not forgive, even in death. The suffering he had inflicted on Gran and Michael and on the animals around him would not lightly be erased. There was, Michael felt, a bitter irony in the fact that it was a part of that animal community which had put an end to his father's life but, and his guilt surfaced again, he himself could have been more supportive to the old lady. He could perhaps have more frequently diverted some of his father's ill-temper onto his own shoulders. He felt another pang of remorse, recalling that he had not had her treasures buried with her as he'd promised. The fact was that he could not face going back to Featherstone for a long, long time, perhaps never. Walter had collected Michael's clothes and the only other items he had requested, a clock which had belonged to his mother and a pearl-handled knife, Si Featherstone' s pride and joy. Other personal items, documents etc., Walter had bundled into a box ready for Michael to examine as and when he felt so inclined. Doubtless he would find Gran's treasures there and perhaps the Vicar would allow these to be put into the ground near her at a later date.

Oliver Craybourne's two grandchildren, their views of each other obscured by a huge Victorian gravestone depicting a large angel of indeterminate sex, its wings outspread, almost collided at the intersection of the paths separating the lines of graves. Both now in their teens, the tall flaxen-haired boy, grown past his strength, and the vivacious girl, glowing with health, surveyed each other. Rosa's hair was darker than Helen 's, a deep glossy auburn, her eyes hazel flecked with grey. Always more volatile than her sister, she had retained that effervescent sense of humour which delighted everyone with whom she came in contact. Now, in spite of the sweet sadness of earlier reminiscences and their sombre surroundings, she laughed as they recoiled from the near-impact and started to apologise, her North Country accent almost totally obliterated by the veneer of gentility imparted by Prinny, whilst Michael's speech was as broad and as roughly hewn as the environment in which it had been fostered.

Rosa had known of course of his father's death. The village had been agog with stories about the circumstances. The boy's tortuous journey through the fog back to Hislop's, his father Sam's cruelty to humans and animals, a cruelty which had reaped a harvest no-one could have ever envisaged. Now she was surprised to find the boy who'd shown such courage was morose and introverted to the point of rudeness. He did not volunteer information and made conversation difficult. On that first morning however, Rosa had sufficient chatter for them both. She had caught sight of him on many occasions at the farm, she told him, but he'd always seemed to be going somewhere, doing something, it wasn't until today that their paths had crossed. This elicited no response from the boy, nor did her explanation that the remark was meant to be funny. It was obvious that, to date, Michael had found very little amusement in his young life. He must come back with her and meet Prinny, she said, after all he was living practically on their doorstep. She brushed aside his reluctance and soon he was installed in the living room of the neat little cottage with a beaker of milk and a slice of fruit cake before him, Miss Pringle's own version of the North Country 'stay-bit'.

Michael seemed to find that good lady's quiet calm manner reassuring and gradually she learned his plans. He wanted to try something quite different from farming and Walter, on his behalf, had spoken to Lord Craybourne, before he left for London. His Lordship had said there was plenty of work to be had at the Longroyd Mill in Halifax and Walter had arranged lodgings for him in that area. He was to start work on Monday week, but would go to Halifax on the previous Saturday so as to get 'settled'. When he left, promising to visit them again before his departure, Miss Pringle expressed her concern.

"I fail to see how the boy can possibly settle to that sort of existence after the open air life he's been used to."

"Mark my words Prinny, there's more to Michael Featherstone than meets the eye. He looks so skinny, frail even, as though he's never had enough to eat poor lad, but he must be stronger than he looks or he'd never have been able to do what he did and then make that awful journey. Somehow I don't think you need worry about him."

But worry about him she did, as indeed did a number of people, the Dennisons, Mrs. Waring, Walter and Haig. All were part of a good-natured conspiracy to compensate the boy for those years of misery. Annie Dennison speedily altered clothes Walter had outgrown and on the day of his departure for Halifax she and Mrs. Waring vied with each other to produce enough goodies to keep him going for a considerable number of days.

It had been arranged that Michael would return to Hislop's at weekends and Miss Pringle suggested a weekly lunch date each Saturday with Rosa and herself. Prinny, aware of her own limitations, had, with Lady Craybourne 's approval, arranged for Rosa to receive tuition from the newly appointed Curate of Craybourne, who was now pressing his opinion that in due course Rosa should make application for university entrance. Rosa's lessons were on Saturday mornings, so Michael could arrive when he wished and they would all eat together at one o'clock. Rosa had hoped that Michael might be encouraged to walk across and meet her from the Vicarage, so that they might return to the cottage together, but finding him week after week deep in conversation with Prinny, she decided he preferred that lady's company to her own! Several months were to elapse before she realised what was happening.

The realisation that she was no longer having to ask Michael to repeat himself or explain an idiom was gradually borne in on her. This was Prinny's contribution to the conspiracy. The roughest edges of Michael's speech had now been honed away. Working in a city, meeting people of different types, had already played its part in removing that awkward introverted manner and to this Prinny had been adding other knowledge. Whilst Rosa had been working at her Latin, Greek and French, Michael's oracy skills had improved beyond all recognition.

Throughout his life Michael was to associate Rosa with colour and laughter. It was almost, he thought, as though an artist had taken his palette and, selecting the most vivid glowing colours, painted and shaded her face and hair. Her ready laughter was a tonic which he drew with pleasure into his humourless existence and, with the resilience of the young, he found the memory of those awful years starting to recede. Michael had a distant relative of Walter to thank for his living quarters in Halifax, a terraced house in Albert Street, home of the Sykes family. Pillars of the Methodist Church, Arthur and Lydia Sykes regarded even the consumption of a fruit wine as bordering on mortal sin. Sunday dinner's vegetables were prepared on Saturday so that, the weekly joint sizzling in the oven, the whole family could set out for chapel leaving their little maid-of-all-work, Jennie, to cope with the remainder of the household chores. On arrival, the two children were ushered into the Sunday School, Arthur took up his stance at the rear of the church to issue hymn books to the congregation as they arrived, whilst Lydia exuding self-righteousness and overtly conscious of her Sunday finery, particularly her hat with its lavish adornment of cherries, took her seat in the family pew six rows from the front. With the opening chords of the first hymn, Arthur would slip quietly into his place beside her and soon her somewhat strident soprano and his gruff baritone would swell the volume of the rumbustious hymns.

When, during the service, the Sunday school children filed into their places in the front pews, Lydia's eyes would glitter with pride at the manner in which the Sykes offspring conducted themselves Other children might fidget or slouch, whisper even, but Lionel and Frank, never. Their lusty participation in the singing was enough to stiffen Lydia's already upright spine. After dinner the children went to Sunday school again and afterwards, weather permitting, were met by their parents for a sedate walk through the park or a visit to the churchyard to put flowers on the graves of Grandma and Grandad Sykes. In the evening parents and children attended Chapel together.

Michael usually returned from Craybourne just as the Sykes family returned home from evening service. Now came a general atmosphere of relaxation. With the removal of Mrs. Sykes' hat, Mr. Sykes' neck collar-stud and the boys' collars, the tension of being on one's best behaviour eased and, together, they sat down to a cold collation of meat, pickles and potatoes, followed by toasted Yorkshire teacakes, liberally spread with butter and jam. In spite of their inhibitions and pretensions, they were well-meaning, kind-hearted people. Aware of Michael's background, Lydia was anxious that, although only a lodger, Michael should see and experience family life at its best. It was several years before Michael realised just how much he had to thank that relative of Walter for. Other lodgings which he was to see and of which he heard were neither comfortable nor homely, whilst in the well-regulated Sykes home, food was plentiful and meals appeared at regular intervals, so that within a few weeks Michael's spare frame had started to lose its gauntness.

Here too, at Michael's disposal, were books and newspapers and, as his mind at last shrugged off the stultifying cloud of unhappiness in which it had been for so long shrouded, he began to find more and more pleasure in finding out what was happening in the world outside Craybourne.

Flora Hinton was never to recover from the weight of guilt she felt on watching Mary's coffin lowered into the cold earth. Hadn't she wished for months that the woman would go out of their lives so that Bert might once again show some real interest in 'his little Flora'? Hadn't she often prayed that God would remove this blight from her life so that all would return to normal, or what had previously passed for normality?

Impossible now to penetrate the separate world into which Bert seemed to have retreated and she had little enough energy or inclination left to try to do so. Within a few hours of returning from the church Flora turned to what was to become her main source of comfort, food. Never eating to excess in the presence of her family, her burgeoning size was a source of wonder to them and they readily accepted her explanation that the problem was glandular. Gluttony became the dominating factor of her life. When the house was empty she would lock the doors, draw the curtains, bring out food from its many hiding places and start to eat, the sadness evoked by the departure of her elder son Tom, to work on a farm over the Pennine ridge, being assuaged by vast quantities of suet pudding topped with rivers of syrup. The more unhappy she was the more she ate, until the once rounded young woman disappeared inside the undulating layers of flesh.

Annie Hinton was, at ten, a miniature version of the plump and pretty Flora Hinton on her wedding day, with darkly curling hair, laughing eyes and an overtly feminine manner developed as a protective veneer in the presence of her boisterous brothers. As a member of a rural community, she was not unaware of animal sexual activity, but its implications with regard to human beings were to her, as yet, somewhat obscure. Certainly Flora had imparted no helpful knowledge other than the fact that she must not be afraid when her 'monthlies' started, as these were a sign that she was growing up and could soon have babies.

The first time her father touched her, Annie, thinking about it afterwards, decided it was a mistake. She was washing up in the scullery and he reached out and across her for a towel, then as if steadying himself, his hand slid down over her budding, hard little breasts. She had drawn back quickly and without a word he had gathered up the towel and left the room. A few months elapsed before something much more alarming happened. Flora, peering with her tiny eyes through the smudge of face obliterated by layers of fat, was busy at her interminable crochet and Bert was sitting staring into the fire when Annie, already in her nightdress, passed him on her way to bed.

"Got a good-night kiss for your old dad, then?" he asked, pulling her onto his knees. Annie, surprised at this unexpected show of affection, relaxed, lying across his knees, staring into the fire, her back towards Flora. She was aware that his hand was stroking her thigh and that it was pleasantly soothing. Suddenly that awareness gave way to alarm. His hand had slipped under her nightie and, the fingers still moving and stroking, were working their way steadily upwards. When he touched the part of her she had understood to be private, she felt her cheeks flame. Should she tell him to stop? Hadn't her mother seen? Why didn't she stop him? Surely it was wrong for any one to touch her there, even her father... or was it? She stole a glance at him. He still looked the same, except that his cheeks too, were flushed and there was a peculiar hardness under her buttocks, a hardness she'd never felt before on his lap. With a jerk she sat up, jumped off his knee and blurting out the word, "Night", she scuttled up the stairs.

Any doubts she might have had disappeared the night he came to her room. Flora was visiting a neighbour and Annie and Sidney had been in their beds for an hour or more. Waking with a start to the feel of large hands moving over her body, she let out such a piercing scream that a bleary-eyed Sidney rushed in to see what was wrong. In the half darkness her father's form moved forward to assure Sid that it was alright, he could go back to bed, Annie had only had a bad dream. Annie now shocked and frightened and sensing a threat she could not have verbalised, asked that the lamp be lit and that Sidney stay and talk to her until she felt better.

From that day forward she watched every move her father made, ensuring that she was never left alone with him again. If Flora had to go out then Annie said she had to go out too, to give old Mrs. Harrison a hand, or that she was needed to run errands at Hislop's. At night-time, the wooden stool in her room was pushed behind the door, on the pretext that the door banged in the draught and disturbed her.

When Flora died as a result of the heart-strain caused by her obesity, Annie was just twelve years old. With premature maturity, she knew she could no longer remain in Piggotts Lane and quickly dismissed suggestions that she would work either at the Manor or Hislop's, knowing that these would both entail living at home. Her announcement that she had decided to go and get work in one of the Craybourne mills brought forth a storm of abuse from Bert. Why couldn't she take a local job and stay at home and look after him and her brother? Her quiet "You know why", silenced him. Gloomily he watched her preparations for departure.

On the day Sam Featherstone's life was terminated by his own dogs, Annie Hinton said a tearful goodbye to her brother, bade a cool farewell to Bert Hinton and set out for Halifax.

Chapter Ten

In the privacy of her room Daphne read again the letter from Mrs. Pankhurst, briefly welcoming her to the ranks of the Suffragette movement and informing her that meetings were held daily in a number of houses and apartments. Addresses and dates were appended so that Daphne could select the area and date on which she wished to attend . The list showed that Christabel Pankhurst was to hold a meeting on the following day, in an apartment just off the Embankment. Ideal, Daphne decided, but how to evade Aunt Louisa's protective vigilance?

In the event, there was no problem. Louisa announced that she and Cecil would be taking tea with some Australian friends the next afternoon. Cecil was anxious to check on his property interests in Perth and Sydney and she was looking forward immensely to seeing again her old friends Hugh and Dorothy Quilley. She regretted that the invitation did not include Daphne, but assured her that she would probably have found it incredibly dull listening to their gossip. With Helen's visit to Aston's already arranged, Daphne knew she would only have to wait for Nanny Glossop to collapse into her postprandial nap before leaving the house. It was perfect.

The first person she saw on entering the room at the appointed meeting place, was Wiggie. To be precise, Miss Muriel Wigmore, mistress in charge of languages at Daphne's former school, Fairoaks. Wiggie was kneeling on the floor beside a long, low table, opening a number of large brown paper packages.. Daphne saw that these contained leaflets which Wiggie was stacking into neat piles on the table. Smiling broadly at Daphne's astonished expression, Wiggie rose to greet her, hand outstretched.

"Miss Wigmore…." The articulate Daphne was lost for words.

"Muriel please, or Wiggie. . it's first names only here and we're not in school any longer."

In an attempt to subdue her embarrassment, Daphne turned to the other occupants of the room. Assembled were a dozen or more ladies, all deep in animated conversation As Wiggie introduced her to the different groups, Daphne experienced a growing feeling of disappointment, noting that there was only one woman here who could be identified as working class. Here she had hoped to meet women from all walks of life. The reason for the omission was quickly explained by Wiggie.

"You've touched on something of which we are all deeply aware. Yes, the fight is currently being fought by upper and middle class women for the simple reason that working women, however supportive to the cause, do not have the time. Working all day and attending to the needs of their families in the evenings allows them little freedom. They also feel, rightly or wrongly, that they would not be sufficiently articulate to speak on the Movement's behalf." Nevertheless, Wiggie was convinced that there was a vast amount of support for what they were doing, support which was as yet relatively untapped.

Annoyed that she had not reasoned this out for herself, Daphne now agreed that there was quite a good representative cross-section, even, as Wiggie pointed out with glee, a chorus girl from one of the Music Halls, surely the bastion of male chauvinism!

Much of what they did, she explained, was dull, tiring, but very necessary work. Handing out leaflets, standing for hours outside the Houses of Parliament, talking to women in shops, public houses, or the streets and yes, that included the prostitutes, but, and now her eyes lit up, when they went into the Commons or a political meeting with the deliberate intention of creating a disturbance, then it could be rough, but exciting!

Daphne had first met Muriel Wigmore three years ago when, fresh from Oxford, Wiggie had joined the staff of Wells. Their relationship had survived the usual 'crush' of a younger girl for a woman a few years older. Wiggie, in spite of her inexperience, being fully aware of the official school attitude which frowned not only on particular friendships between staff and pupil, but between the girls themselves, had managed to tread the fine line between encouraging Daphne in her work and showing her kindness, without displaying the overt friendship which would have attracted suspicion. A young woman of great integrity, Muriel Wigmore had realised during Daphne's final burst of academic interest the direction in which her interests were being channelled, but had at no point admitted her own allegiance to the cause of women's suffrage. Now, meeting as young women on equal terms, with an objective they found mutually challenging, they could at last relax in each other's company and friendship.

Small and neat with brown hair and a rather freckled complexion which was the bane of her life, Mu Wigmore's grey eyes now twinkled with anticipation as an impressive lady in an expensively cut dark-green ensemble advanced towards them.

"Here comes Christabel," she said and, smiling, moved forward to make the introductions.

Daphne had much to think about on the way home. The reaction of her fellow suffragettes, on learning the reasons for her stay in London, varied from covert disapproval to amused disbelief.

"My dear, you can't possibly be an activist for women's rights and 'do the season', I mean... you'd be something of a laughing stock. Can't you just hear the jibes. 'wanting the best of both worlds!' Muriel had tentatively suggested that if and when she felt she could make the break from her family commitments, then there would be room for her in the apartment Muriel shared with Amy Reece. Amy worked in a book-shop in the mornings and Muriel had obtained a part-time teaching post in London so that they were both provided with the minimum amount of money necessary for survival, plus the free time needed to devote to the cause. Daphne herself could probably get a part-time post, assisting at a local school, or perhaps she had sufficient funds to manage without this?

To the latter Daphne had made no response, feeling instinctively that to underline further differences between herself and other campaigners was inadvisable. The truth was that she had plenty of money. Craybourne's wealth came not from the estate itself, but from the vast areas of land owned in Halifax, Leeds and Bradford, land that now burgeoned with flourishing woollen mills. In two short months she would be eighteen with access, albeit limited, to the fortune left her by her grandfather and in the interim period there was little doubt that her dress allowance would suffice - it was probably more than Muriel and Amy earned in a year.

As her cab turned into St. James's Square, she was startled to see James's car outside No.8. A flustered butler opened the door to her and Daphne was ushered into the drawing room where a far from cool Lady Craybourne awaited her. It was infuriating enough that the telegraphed wire announcing their impending arrival should have gone astray, that her sister and brother were not at home, but it was particularly infuriating and extremely curious that no-one seemed to know the whereabouts of Daphne.

"I understand that Helen is at the House of Aston. Perhaps you would be good enough to explain your own movements."

Gone now were Daphne's hopes of talking to her mother quietly and dispassionately about the changes she wished to make in her life-style, changes she now acknowledged as inevitable. The afternoon's visit, her enrolment as a member of the Women's Social and Political Union, her desire to do something for women, all women, which had started as a mere idea, was now in full spate.

Seeing that his mother was momentarily incapable of speech, James started to point out at length the drawbacks, which were considerable. Daphne had never done a day's work in her life, had always lived in comfortable, pleasant surroundings, meeting nice people. Wincing at the word 'nice', Daphne parried these arguments with her own, concluding by embracing the still rigid Lady Craybourne, saying how sorry she was for the unhappiness this would cause her, knowing what pleasure Elizabeth would have derived from her daughter's season in London. The sincerity of her words, the uncharacteristically warm embrace and the tears which followed, seemed at last to rouse Elizabeth from her state of shock and they sat silently for a time, arms locked around each other.

At last Elizabeth spoke. "So, it is decision time for the Craybournes, all of us." And, in answer to Daphne's unspoken question, "Yes, James will be staying in London. The Prime Minister wants him in the Lords as a spokesman for the Government on a regular basis and James has decided to accept. The Home Secretary is under pressure and James is to assist him where possible. The new Labour faction in the Commons has so many young men, that Campbell-Bannerman is determined to strengthen his own party with young men of the same calibre. It's a great honour for James, you know. You should be very proud of your brother, obviously the excellence of his law degree and his stalwart work in Yorkshire has gone before him."

Anticipating Daphne's next question, James explained, "I've appointed an Estate Manager at Craybourne, well qualified chap called Leslie Bateman. Walter will be acting as his assistant on the practical side. He's twenty now you know and a tower of strength."

"As for Robert, your uncle is even now discussing with his Australian friends, the possibility of Robert going out there."

"Mother, you can't banish him as if he was some sort of leper. We did away with prison ships and all that years ago."

"My dear, hear me out, please. Robert is not going to be forced to do anything against his wishes. He has at last realised that he can't spend the rest of his life without any worthwhile goal and has expressed a great deal of interest in going to Australia. There are one or two artistic ventures afoot there which he feels might appeal to him. If...and it is still a large 'if' he decides to investigate any one of them more thoroughly, then he will return to Australia with your uncle's friends next week."

Daphne, almost speechless at the rapidity with which all their lives appeared to be changing, was only too aware that she was in no position to criticise, as a major part of the Craybourne family changes must be laid at her own door. If events in their own household could in any way be said to mirror events in society, then the Pankhursts and Wiggie were right and this was going to prove an era of vast social change.

"It will no longer be necessary for me to stay for the season,"Elizabeth continued, "but I do intend staying until your eighteenth. Even campaigners for women's rights are allowed to celebrate birthdays, I suppose? You won't deny me that pleasure my darling? I do so want to give you a lovely, lovely party."

But now Daphne was in no state to reply. Her mother's sudden and unexpected capitulation and Elizabeth's loving smile had created in her such a wave of relief that Daphne could only embrace her mother as her own tears started to flow.

Helen, too, had decisions to make, but arriving at No. 8 St. James's Square and finding that usually well-regulated household in something of a state of shock, she decided that her own problems must be temporarily shelved.

Lady Craybourne's explanations about Daphne's plans created further turmoil in Helen's mind. Following Daphne's departure she would no longer be needed. It seemed as if fate was giving her a massive push in the direction of Aston' s. Surely she was meant to seize this opportunity with both hands? A few short weeks ago, days even, the thought of spending several months in London, caring for Daphne's clothes, helping her dress, accompanying her on walks, had seemed all she could wish for. But now she had seen Aston's, talked to Mr. Neville, Helen felt there was much, much more. She hadn't understood some of his plans, but even if what he'd said was a pipe dream, she knew in her heart of hearts that working in those lovely surroundings, wearing elegant clothes all day and yes, in spite of her shyness, even parading up and down displaying those garments, would be much more fun, more satisfying than gathering up someone else's discarded clothes. Tomorrow she would talk to her Ladyship, ask her advice.

Elizabeth's first reaction was one of scepticism. Helen was a beautiful girl; perhaps this Aston fellow's intentions were less than honourable. A word with her sister reassured her on that score. The only rumours ever connected with Neville Aston, and those unproven, were those involving men and whilst this might be unsavoury, at least it should ensure that his reputation with regard to the many females in his establishment would remain unsullied. Recalling Robert and the Oxford scandal, Louisa pressed on hastily, pointing out that Aston was a most astute businessman and his fashion house set fair to becoming the most prestigious in London.

The obvious excitement of the usually retiring Helen was proof enough that she desperately wanted to join Aston's. That she would not do so unless Lady Craybourne' s approval was given, was equally obvious. Elizabeth decided that during the next forty-eight hours she would make her own investigations. Her first appointment the following day was with her bank manager, who ensured her that Aston's was not only solvent, but flourishing. Next, accompanied by Louisa, she descended on the fashion house itself where Neville, slightly nonplussed at her Ladyship's searching questions and interest in such a junior member of her staff, attempted to allay her fears. He agreed that during training Helen would be working long hours for little pay but, and this with a deprecatory smile, Aston' s was an important House and one in which many girls would be only to delighted to work. Young men occasionally visited Aston's escorting their mothers or sisters, but in such circumstances, indeed at all times, there would be an abundance of chaperones. Not until Helen was eighteen would he embark on the second stage of his plan to make her a well-known figure and he would certainly ensure that on any visits in this connection she would be provided with suitable escorts. Smilingly he added that he felt these would never be in short supply.

All agreed that the most critical factor was where Helen should live and to this Neville Aston had already given some thought. One of his senior assistants, a Miss Tindall, whom Lady Eynsford no doubt remembered, was now retired and living in the Kennington area. In order to supplement her income she now had two Aston girls staying there and could accommodate a third. This would serve the dual purpose of Miss Tindall being able to keep an eye on the girl and enabling Helen to enjoy younger female company. Elizabeth's own assessment of Neville Aston as being first and foremost a businessman with no ulterior motives and Lady Eynsford's obvious approval of the selection of Miss Tindall decided the matter. The visit was not concluded however before Neville was informed that Lady Craybourne was always concerned for the wellbeing of her staff and tenants and particularly so in the case of such a young and innocent girl adding with a rather steely glint that she and Lady Eynsford would be watching Helen's progress at all times. Helen was to remain at St James's Square for a week, during which time she would be taken to visit Miss Tindall and all necessary arrangements made. With that good lady's address firmly tucked into Lady Craybourne's handbag, the two ladies departed, leaving a bemused Neville Aston thinking that the behaviour of ladies of high society never ceased to astonish him!

Informed of the meeting's discussion and its outcome, Helen and Daphne retired to their respective rooms, the former overjoyed and not a little nervous, Daphne amazed at this further unexpected turn of events. Unseeing, she stared from her window at the scene below. Quiet little Helen, who would have thought it? Well, they say "Still waters run deep!" The idea hadn't originated with her of course, but that she should have even considered accepting, been interested enough to talk to Mama about it. And now Mama's approval - wonders would never cease.

There truly must be a wind of change in the country if Mama was prepared to countenance not only the Suffragettes, but women working in something akin to 'trade'. One could see that the movement with its middle and upper class overtones might just be acceptable in Mama's circles, if only as a harmless diversion, an escape from 'ennui' and of course going into service had always been acceptable for those who didn't have to do it! But trade had always carried its own taboo and this girl is, well 'sort of' family. Not that Helen knows. Mama's decision not to tell her on the grounds that if the girl was starting a new venture the last thing she needed to be told was of her illegitimacy might be questionable, not least on the grounds of individual liberties, but I suppose it is understandable. It will be fascinating to see how she copes.

I thought my challenge was big enough, but she's still a baby and a 'country cousin' to boot, correction, for cousin read niece, step-niece, or whatever relation she is.

I shall make my own gesture to progress by inviting her to this birthday party Mama insists on giving. Helen and Wiggie and some of my new friends should add quite a fillip to that little gathering and at the same time remove some of the starch.

Now - no more procrastinating, I really must sort out what to take to Wiggie's. Practical garments only, and plenty of warm ones. I have a feeling that some of next winter's vigils at Westminster could be rather chilly....

To Helen's delight, some of the contents of Daphne's wardrobe later found their way in her direction. Although two inches taller than Daphne and still growing, the now popular non-trailing and slightly shorter skirt lengths meant that Daphne's dresses could be adapted and Helen's skill with her needle made light work of the darting and tucking necessary to accommodate her slimmer figure.

Whilst the girls proceeded with their packing, Elizabeth Craybourne visited and approved Miss Tindall. Her bank manager received a second visit during which certain financial arrangements were discussed. Once again Helen was summoned to the drawing room. Here she was informed that a bank account had been opened for her for the sum of two hundred pounds. Helen's eyes widened in amazement. The money would not be available to her until she was eighteen unless, and her Ladship now spoke slowly and emphatically, she was in difficulties, in which case, it was hoped that she would in the first instance contact Lady Eynsford. Should she not be in residence, then Helen was to go to the bank, where the manager would advise her. Pre-empting the next question, Elizabeth explained that this money had been her mother's and that an equivalent amount would be available for Rosa at a later date.

After the girl had left her, Elizabeth wondered if she had done everything that Oliver would have wished. Over the years the girls had lived comfortably with Prinny, all their expenses having been borne by the money he had left for Mary. Rosa's education was continuing with extra lessons locally. A bright scholar, Prinny was already suggesting that, if finances were available, university should be considered for Rosa. It would be good for the girl to mix with her contemporaries. Her social life to date had, of necessity, been very limited, although amazingly, this seemed in no way to have affected her natural outgoing nature. At all times she seemed so vibrant, so full of enthusiasm, that half an hour in her company could prove exhausting. No, there was no need to worry about Rosa....

It would be possible to make more money available for Helen, but would that be wise? Helen, as Mary before her, might find herself being used by some unscrupulous character, anxious to acquire an easy living. No..hopefully, Neville Aston's plans and her own built-in safeguards would ensure that Helen was happy and her future secure.

Daphne posed yet another problem. Whilst she seemed so confident and worldly-wise she would very soon have access to the trust fund set aside by her grandfather, if she became involved with anyone peculiar, and organisations such as the W.S.P.U. invariably attracted a few cranks, then who knows what might happen?

Elizabeth Craybourne sighed deeply. A few years ago she had thought that three children were quite enough to cope with, now her small family had expanded to five and, with the exception of James who seemed at last to have found his niche in the House of Lords, she felt very responsible for each one of them. Reaching for her eau de cologne, she delicately dabbed her temples and wrists, then lying back on the satin cushions of the chaise longue, closed her eyes, determined for a few precious minutes to shut out the world and its attendant problems.

Eynsford House

Dear Rosa and Prinny,

I can hardly believe the events of the past few days. The most amazing news is that I am to remain in London and work here at the House of Aston's. This is the fashion salon of which both Lady Craybourne and her sister are customers. (The correct word is probably 'patrons') At first I shall be assisting in the workrooms and, I hope, gradually progress to something more important. I know that you will be sad that I am not to return home of the end of the summer, but I think you'll both agree it is a wonderful opportunity for me.

As you know I love everything to do with clothes and fashion. The variety of material textures, the patterns and styles here are unbelievable. You, Rosa, are obviously developing into quite an academic, but I feel I have inherited this love of textures from Mama. Remember her beautiful lace and crochet work? One thing I've learned here at Eynsford is that whenever 'Madam' has a new outfit, any lady's maid worth her salt retains a spare piece of matching material so that in the event of a scarf, hat decoration or even an evening purse being required it will be made up and result in a totally matching ensemble.

Daphne is going to help fight the cause of the Suffragettes and tells me that you, Prinny, will not be surprised to hear this After her birthday she is moving in with friends, although Lady C. has made it clear she is only permitting this because of three factors. One, Daphne is to live with a Miss Wigmore who used to teach her in Kent, two, her aunt Lady Eynsford will always be on hand and three (and this is the other wonderful news!) James himself is to be in London for much of the time. I know we had heard rumours that he might join the Government - now it is confirmed. I could not be more thrilled. I am to live at the house of a Miss Tindall, where other young ladies who work at Aston's also have rooms and I am well aware that this is going to seem very, very strange. But to know that James will be here in London for much of the year will be for me, most reassuring.

Lady Elizabeth has been so very kind, constantly trying to ensure my safety and comfort. She has given me permission to write this letter and asks me to assure you Prinny that she will be in touch very soon.

My final piece of, for me, lovely, lovely news, is that I am to attend Daphne's party. I have my own personal invitation, handsomely engraved, which I shall always treasure. Be assured that after the event I shall be writing to you with the minutest details recorded!

I cannot be sure what the next few months will bring, obviously many new experiences. Sad as I am that this will mean being deprived of your company for some time, I know dearest Rosa that you will be quite safe in our beloved Craybourne and that you and dear Prinny will be mutually supportive.

Please give my love to the Dennisons and to Walter (it's so long since he and I spent any time together), and my regards of course to Mrs. Waring and Haig - in fact to everyone you can think of.

Say a little prayer for me that I don't make an absolute fool of myself on the very first day.

My love always to you both,
Helen

Chapter Eleven

As was to be expected, Eynsford House was a hive of activity on the morning of May 25th, Daphne's coming of age party. Presents had been handed over the previous evening and Lady Eynsford had requested that the girls occupy themselves in their rooms until late morning. Helen spent some time with Daphne ensuring that every item of her evening ensemble was in immaculate order.

The dress of ivory satin, severe by Helen's standards, was relieved only by the apron-like sculpture of the skirt, which lifted to the waist at the rear and from there cascaded into a fall of satin ruffles. Tucked into the folds of these were rosebuds of the palest lavender and ribbons of green. An unusual choice, but one about which Daphne had been adamant. A corsage of miniature orchids of the palest mauve had been ordered, the choker of pearls and the tear-drop pearl earrings were from the Craybourne collection and her silver-blonde hair was to be dressed in a chignon into which pearls and lavender rosebuds would be threaded.

"It's lovely, Daphne, absolutely lovely."

Helen carefully laid the white kid gloves in their folds of tissue paper.

Daphne grinned, remembering her own reluctance to have any part in 'these dressing- up charades."

"Yes, I'm pleased with the result."

At first she had grudgingly thought she must accept the party with as good a grace as possible, but now realised how much she was looking forward to having her family and friends brought together for this special occasion. After all, it wasn't such a bad idea to have one last good fling, before seeing how the other half lived, and, realistically, facing goodness knows what privations.

Sadly, Robert wouldn't be with them. There had been no acrimony at his departure. He himself had seemed full of excitement and his gift to Daphne of a fur-lined travel rug was accompanied by an entirely typical note.

"Sweetie, this I feel sure will prove far more useful than any of the silver knick-knacks I've looked at. It will make an excellent bedspread. A little extra comfort should never be decried. Starving in a garret might sound romantic but it's probably the quickest way to lose one's ideals. Be happy and fulfilled. My love always, R."

Sensitive as always, how she would miss him! Daphne swallowed, then spoke positively,

"I'm going to join mother for coffee".

As Daphne bustled purposefully along the corridor to her mother's room, Helen returning to her own sanctuary, now experienced the second pleasure of culling together the ensemble she herself would be wearing.

Never had she possessed anything so beautiful! The primrose chiffon had been a gift from Lady Craybourne and Trenchard, Lady Eynsford's maid, had sketched the design and undertaken the major task of cutting out the precious material, leaving only the stitching for Helen to do. When the garment was ready for fitting, it was Trenchard who, with a sure eye for colour and style, had trimmed the neckline and bustle. She would allow the introduction of no other colour, insisting that Helen's gorgeous red-gold hair was a sufficient accessory on its own. From her superior age of twenty years, Trenchard's further admonishment -

"No jewellery please, Helen. With your looks there'll be no need to create any other diversions," produced from Helen one of her rare flashes of humour.

"Oh, Trenchard, you mean I can't wear the tiara? And it's so beautiful."

Trenchard's head jerked round in amazement, then, as she caught the sparkle in Helen's eyes, both girls collapsed in giggles.

The silvery chimes of the clock on the landing, alerted Helen to the fact that it was mid-day and, having fulfilled Lady Eynsford's requirements, she could now vacate her room. She was totally unprepared for the sight with which she was confronted. The staircase and entrance hall had been transformed. The magnificent curve of the balustrade with its imposing newel post was covered with hooped swags of greenery, interspersed with white and purple ribbons and clusters of white roses. The perimeter of the hall was lined with green tubs containing half standard bushes of white roses. In front of these, creating the effect of a solid bank of flowers were bushes of white camelias, their glossy dark leaves the perfect foil for the pure white blooms they bore. The heavy perfume of flowers filled the air. Moving next to the dining room, Helen stood enthralled. The huge dining table had been re-positioned to stand in front of the three long windows which overlooked the Square. It was covered, as were the small gilt tables brought in by the caterers, with napery of the palest lavender. Greenery cascaded in loops and trails, each frond enhanced by the paleness of its background. In the centre of each table was a sunken well containing bowls of white rosebuds and small purple orchids. The trailing green fronds from these centrepieces fanned out, star-like, across the tables.

Ready to receive all the culinary delights planned for the supper buffet, the large table had, at regular intervals, silver épergnes bearing roses and orchids, culminating in the centrepiece, a silver tree standing some three feet in height, its branches open-ended to contain orchids of the deepest purple which cascaded down on to the lavender damask, like some exotic weeping willow.

Stunned, Helen tried to take in all the exquisite details.

"It all sounded rather funereal, but I have to admit the finished effect is quite charming, don't you agree, Helen?"

"Oh yes, your Ladyship," Helen hesitated, "I too thought the choice of colours .... well, rather unusual, but it's quite beautiful."

"I don't think you've yet worked out what that rascally daughter of mine is up to, Helen." Lady Craybourne smiled at Helen's puzzled expression and continued. "These are the colours under whose banner Daphne will soon be operating - the colours of the W.S.P.U., that is the Women's Social and Political Union. She thought to surprise me, but I have, in fact, in store for her a little surprise of my own."

And surprise Daphne she did, for that evening Lady Craybourne's own ensemble, details of which she had not revealed, consisted of a sumptuous dress of lavender tulle lace over taffeta, flounced at the hemline and bustle with lace of a deeper shade. The Craybourne emeralds and her fan of ivory and lavender feathers cleverly incorporated the colour scheme which Daphne had insisted upon.

"Just because I was reluctant to let my fledgling leave the nest for the unknown doesn't mean 1'm not in total support of the Suffragettes' aims". Lady Craybourne informed a somewhat rueful Daphne, who was once again reflecting on her good fortune in having a parent, who was not only shrewd and kind, attributes which didn't always co-exist, but was also stunningly elegant.

From her discreet vantage point in the corner of the balcony overlooking the hall, Trenchard watched the guests arrive and listened to the mellifluous voice of Crimp, the Butler, as he formally announced them. The receiving line was just inside the double doors leading to the ballroom and consisted of Elizabeth, Lady Craybourne, James, Lord Craybourne, Daphne and her aunt, Lady Eynsford.

The slim, primrose clad figure of Helen could be seen just beyond, the aureole of red-gold hair striking even at this distance, her tension obvious from the way she constantly fidgeted with the buttons of her long evening gloves.

Trenchard, whilst admiring her own handiwork, thought, "Poor kid, she's scared out of her wits and no wonder. I've never known anything like it... First, she arrives as some sort of lady's maid, although heaven only knows, she's as green as they come. Never had the handling of decent clothes before, that's for sure. Then, before you can say knife, she's landed herself a job at Aston's of all places and what girl wouldn't give her eye teeth for a good job there? And now to cap everything, she gets an invite to this party. I can just imagine Lady E. inviting me to one of her do's. Pigs might fly! It's more than weird, it's downright peculiar. Even if Cookie's right and she's some sort of poor relation, I can't see they'd think it necessary to invite her to tonight's posh do.

"Mind you, the girl's got style, real style. That dress is terrific, and I did a great job there but come on Trench, admit it, with her looks and figure she could probably wear a sack and make it look elegant!

"Another thing, the girl's sort of aloof, not chilly aloof, but detached, finds it difficult to let her hair down. Seems as if she doesn't quite know where she fits in - not surprising really, as that's just what the rest of us feel - and let's face it, nobody seems about to enlighten us!

"I think Cookie's right and 'it's a touch of the elligitimates', but couldn't be Lord Craybourne who's responsible surely, he's too young but if it's someone else in the family, how come Lady C. is going to such lengths to be kind to her?... I don't know, it beats me..."

In retrospect, it seemed to Helen that she had passed the whole evening in a dreamlike trance. That this would be the mere forerunner of many others much more lavish and spectacular she had no way of knowing.

In the early hours of the morning, as sleep still eluded her, she could only reflect on the evening's many wonders... the kindness of James, Lord Craybourne, her first taste of champagne and the delicious tickling sensation it produced in her nose, the buffet's delicacies and the cake! An amazing frosted icing concoction, four tiers high. The fruit ...grapes, pineapples. nectarines.... And, most delightful of all, Muriel Wigmore. This small, vivacious young woman with her glossy brown hair, twinkling hazel eyes and retroussé nose was a source of wonder to Helen. Her conversation was witty and informed. She seemed to recognise so many of the guests and a non-stop stream of comments were relayed to Helen sotto voce.

"He's from the Foreign Office" ... "Amazed to see her here, she sings with the Metropolitan Opera Company" ... "That one's a rake, he pinches bottoms, so look out!" ... "He's tipped to be the next Archbishop of York" ... "She's having an affair with the Duke of...." So it went on until Helen was totally bemused by the kaleidoscope of colour, faces and information she was trying to assimilate.

Throughout the whole evening there had been only one small sour note when James had introduced Muriel and Helen to Diana Smith-Weever, a school friend of Daphne, whose father was also in the House of Lords.

It was quite obvious from the proprietorial manner in which Diana clung to his arm that she was hopeful of becoming more than just a friend. It was also painfully obvious that James had forgotten that Muriel had taught at Diana's school and Diana's shocked expression at being expected to socialize with someone who worked for her living and a further young person who, whilst introduced vaguely as 'another branch of the family', was clearly rather insecure, not quite top-drawer, was immediately apparent. Her brilliant blue eyes passed icily over them, assessing the home-made gowns, the lack of jewellery, then she purposefully drew James away, saying in her languid drawl,

"I really must have a word with dear old General Minter, he's my godfather you know". Her words hung in the air like sharp pointed icicles.

Wiggie grinned ruefully at Helen. "She was always a vain, arrogant child. Pity someone didn't teach her some manners when she was small, it's too late now. Come along, I'm starving!"

And allowing no time for any brooding about the snub Helen was led towards the dining-room.

The first pale primrose streaks of dawn banded the curtains before Helen finally fell into an uneasy sleep. On awakening, the collage of dreams had faded, with one exception. She was standing on the dais at Aston's wearing her primrose dress and a tiara of diamonds. Before her stood Diana Smith-Weever, blue eye blazing with anger as she screamed, "I hate it! I hate it! With hair like that she should never wear diamonds. Off with her head!"

'I blame Prinny for that', Helen thought, 'too much Lewis Carroll in my formative years!'

Then as the knock on the door heralded the arrival of her morning tea, she began to ponder on the changes the next few days would bring.

Chapter Twelve

Life at Miss Tindall's was a far cry from the luxury of Lady Eynsford's town house. Darkened by years of London fogs, 17 Acacia Terrace, Kennington, was fronted by a small patch of lawn. Defining its perimeter a few shrubs struggled half-heartedly for survival.

A typical London terrace house, Helen's new home consisted of two floors with attic rooms and a basement. The attics had been converted into comfortable bedrooms, each paying guest having her own room and the use of the large sitting room. In the corner of this was the dining table. Here, Miss Tindall joined them for meals, retiring immediately afterwards to relax in her own small cosy retreat on the second floor.

In the basement, one room had been adapted to serve the dual purpose of washing and bathing. Here was housed the boiler or 'copper' so that as the water heated so the chill was removed from the room. It was a simple matter to take the zinc bath down from its hooks on the wall and fill it from the copper. This removed all necessity for carrying bath and jugs of water up flights of stairs and worked well.

The austere appearance of Miss T. as the girls called her, grey hair drawn severely back into a bun, tiny gold rimmed spectacles, belied her kind heart. As Neville Aston was well aware she kept a watchful and kindly eye over 'her girls'.

Sonia had been with her for two years. At twenty two she was a professional freelance model who worked for Neville Aston and other haute couture houses. When a fashion house presented its Spring and Summer or Autumn and Winter collection, she was much in demand. At other times she would await specific requests to model privately the court ensemble, honeymoon lingerie, etc.

Sensing in Helen a potential rival, Sonia's attitude was at first polite, but distant. However, Helen's diffident manner, her delight in each new experience, genuine admiration and requests for advice soon resulted in the beginnings of real friendship.

Betty worked in the finishing room at Aston's. Here were added the delicate seed pearls, bugle beads, jet trimming, fringes and embroidery, which could transform a well cut but simple garment into something really exclusive. Betty's creativity of design and the quality of her embroidery had been brought to Aston's attention and although now only eighteen years of age, she was an established member of his workforce and one whom other fashion houses would have very much liked to acquire.

They were a mixed bunch. Sonia, the sophisticated, wordly-wise older girl; the Cockney sparrow Betty, always with an ear to the ground for what was happening 'on the street'; and Helen, the country girl, well educated by their standards, with a rather quaint out-moded way of speaking, well mannered and extremely well spoken, but according to Betty, a complete innocent, with no knowledge of city life, no idea of what it was like to earn one's living and, more importantly, no idea of what it was like to live and work with others, regardless of compatability.

Nevertheless, the different personalities within the Tindall house-hold did much to prepare Helen for the latter. During those first twelve months she acted as assistant, first to the cutters, then the seamstresses, finally moving into Betty's finishing department. She went out with the buyer to see where and how the materials were selected and sat in the office of Mrs. Groves, the chief vendeuse, noting the names and requirements of the clientele and absorbing the code of behaviour expected of Mrs Groves' role. Occasionally the client required total anonymity, with the account being settled by someone else's husband. On other occasions the client seemed to want the world to know that her little darling had acquired the catch of the season and was shortly to be married.

Helen's first fitting attendance, ostensibly to assist Mrs. Groves, proved a revelation.

"I couldn't believe my eyes, Sonia, she had a monkey with her, a real monkey in a cage!"

"Helen, my lamb, you have obviously met our American friend, the redoubtable Mrs. Monaham and her marmoset, Bibi. Quite an experience!"

"That amazing cage, all gilt and red velvet ... The fitters were none too happy I can tell you when she opened the cage door and let Bibi scurry about all over her, and them, whilst they were trying to do their work."

"They may not have liked it my sweet, but 'caveat emptor' and all that".

"Caveat what? What are you talking about Sonia?".

"Caveat emptor - Latin. Means the customer's always right and we can't win."

"There's something else I wanted to ask you. Is Nancy in some sort of trouble? Mr. Aston seemed to be talking to her very seriously just before lunch."

"Oh, that would be just the usual warning. Nan's going away next week, abroad would you believe, and Mr. A. always spells out his pre-holiday instructions. No sitting in the sun, no exposing your face and body to any extreme weather elements, and if you should come back with the suspicion of a sun-tanned skin, you can expect your marching orders straight away."

"Why is he so funny about that? Does it really matter so much?"

"My poor innocent .... tanning is for peasants, farm labourers and people of that ilk, according to Aston. Never seen Lady C. with a tan have you?"

"Well, no .... she has the most beautiful skin."

"There, you've answered your own question, my child. If your face is to be your fortune, look after your skin and it will look after you. Like it or not, Neville Aston does know what he's talking about and he's a lot kinder than some of the employers I work for. Take Lina, we always know when it's her time of the month... puffy eyes, blotchy skin and ready to faint after five minutes on the fitting dais under those cruel lights. Mr. N. can't say anything, of course, would never do, but he always manages to discreetly swop her fitting commitment as soon as he knows and sees to it that she goes to the rest room for a cup of tea 'until she's feeling more herself'' as he so delicately puts it."

Once or twice a week Mr. Aston would tell one of the dressers to prepare Helen in a particular ensemble and she was then permitted to enter the viewing room. Always this happened at the end of the day when the room was empty and the House of Aston officially closed. There, Aston would drill her in the art of displaying a garment to its full advantage, until her diffident manner at last gave way to one of total confidence, his often quoted aphorism of Oscar Wilde, 'Chins are being worn rather high this year', resulting in an elegant, proud bearing which he knew would ensure respect in any surroundings.

The fact that Helen was able to adapt to the casual, sporty image required for country tweeds and walking dresses, radiate a somewhat racy look for the more flamboyant of his designs and, when necessary, appear as demure as a debutante at her first ball, were part of the chameleon-like quality which Aston saw as a most valuable asset.

Helen's first modelling assignment, two months before her eighteenth birthday, was a low-key affair. Although married to an American, Mrs. Howard Culpepper spent much of her time in England to ensure her two sons' admission to the Guards. On this occasion the purpose of her visit was to provide her god-daughter, about to 'come out', with the requisite court dress and accessories. Within the parameters of the guidelines for the ensemble, materials had been selected at an earlier visit and the dress was in the final stages of completion. As Miss Nugent's measurements and those of Helen were almost identical it was agreed that Helen should model the complete outfit in order that the young debutante might note how best to negotiate the train and head feathers whilst curtseying.

The muscles of Helen's stomach knotted with nervousness as she was assisted into the draped white chiffon. The silver tissue train was then added, its sheen shot with blue and trailing the regulation eighteen inches. Next came the three foot tulle veil floating like swansdown over the glossy red-gold chignon, and into its retaining band the three white traditional Prince of Wales feathers were fitted. Helen's feet were slipped into the silver shoes, the elbow-length white gloves smoothed over her slender arms and she was ready. Or, almost .... As she left the dressing room, one of the girls pressed into her hands a small cluster of white flowers.

"The girl's a knockout."

Her speech laced with the Americanisms acquired from her husband, at the end of the viewing Mrs. Culpepper bore down on Neville Aston.

"'Fraid my little mouse will be a poor advertisement for your wares, but c'est la vie. Where did you find this little charmer?"

"Some sort of ward of Lady Craybourne and her sister, not sure what the connection is exactly." Neville Aston chose his words carefully, realising that Mrs. Culpepper would have relayed this information into some of the more important drawing rooms of London by the end of the week.

"So, she's not one of your usual working gels, fascinating …. but, of course, that would account for the poise, breeding always tells."

Neville Aston murmured something unintelligible, noting with pleasure that Mrs. Culpepper's sons, the elder resplendent in his Guards uniform, had arrived to escort the ladies home. Neither did it escape his notice that the eyes of both young men were fixed unswervingly on Helen, until, excusing herself from Miss Nugent, she discreetly withdrew. For a first testing of the water it had all gone exactly according to plan. He would have a small celebration all on his own. A very large glass of champagne!

Chapter Thirteen

17 Acacia Avenue

My Dearest Rosa,

How are you, little sister? I feel so guilty that we are far apart and meet so infrequently. Not being with you for my eighteenth birthday was a particularly bitter pill. My love and thanks for all your good wishes and for the lingerie cases, which are so very pretty. How did you find the time with all your studying? Lady Craybourne has assured me on several occasions that I must not worry about you, as you are well and working hard. I cannot imagine my little Rosa at Oxford, but, knowing it to be your dearest wish, I pray that your dream will be realised. One day, perhaps, women will be permitted to work for a degree - what a step forward for our sex that would be!

By comparison, my own life seems decidedly frivolous! Can you imagine how amazed I was to be invited to the races at Ascot by one of our customers, a Mrs. Culpepper? When the invitation arrived for me at the Salon, Mr. Aston looked rather smug and muttered something about 'Stage 1'. He then explained that for this and any similar occasions, I would wear ensembles provided by the House of Aston. (This was quite a relief, as I certainly didn't possess anything grand enough for Ascot!) He spent some considerable time in showing me how to pose for photographers, without, as far as I could gather, appearing to do so! Should I be approached by journalists from 'The London Illustrated Evening News' or 'The Tatler', I was to give my Christian name (to which he has added an 'a') and say that my clothes and I both come from the House of Aston. I enclose a photograph of me from the L.I.N. with Mrs. Culpepper's two sons and Victoria Nugent, her god-daughter.

It seemed strange at first to be referred to as just 'Helena' (no surname) of Aston's and, even stranger, that the photographers have appeared at several other events to which I was invited. We seem to be getting just the publicity N.A. wanted. I can't help feeling that he knows someone, somewhere, who is pulling a few strings on his behalf.

I thought at first my escorts might have objected to this intrusion of privacy, but not so! So many of these young people seem to progress from one lovely event to the next, without a care in the world. It is impossible to equate this with the hard lives of the people we know in and around Craybourne. Can you believe for instance that anyone would change their clothes five times a day? Victoria tells me that on a typical day she would change from her boudoir robe to a riding outfit, followed by an ensemble for luncheon, then relax in a loose and flowing tea robe, finally dressing for dinner. If she were playing golf, or walking in the afternoon, it might necessitate another change. I estimate that at least four hours of her day must be spent in changing and titivating. Amazing. However, on the credit side, with a few exceptions, such as Diana Weever-Smith, (remind me to tell you about her sometime), the young men and women I have met do not seem nearly so fussed about status as we were only a few short years ago and they often laugh at themselves and the stupidity of the 'rules' with which they were indoctrinated as children.

I must not appear too critical, as clothes now form a large part of my own life. Neville Aston is anxious to develop ranges of clothes for women who would never dream of setting foot in his Salon, but who shop at departmental stores such as Dickins and Jones. Whilst I am currently meeting a great many 'social butterflies', I am aware that there are many, like me, who work for their living and do not have the time or always the inclination to make their own garments. I'm sure N.A. is right in thinking there is a large untapped market there.

Once his collection of ready-made clothes is complete he plans to launch it at Dickins and Jones, with viewing in the evenings and on a Saturday to ensure all the working girls have the opportunity to attend. He has already arranged several outlets in London and photographs of some of the garments will be released to the principal newspapers, so that people will know exactly where a garment can be purchased. Of course there is always the danger (perish the thought!) that one might meet someone wearing an identical garment and I suppose people who can't bear the idea of that will continue making their own.

But enough of me and my affairs. I cannot begin to tell you how homesick I sometimes get for Yorkshire. Passing Covent Garden or catching a glimpse of a street vendor's barrow with its profusion of flowers is enough to transport me to the gardens of Craybourne. Spring time is probably the most difficult of all. After a London winter of interminable fogs, I long for the clear bracing air of the Dales and the drifts of daffodils and bluebells in the parkland.

I am realistic enough, however, to count my blessings, often! One of those for which, in retrospect, I am now very grateful, is the unobtrusive tuition we received from Lady C. when she invited us to take tea with her. Do you remember? That and Prinny's careful attention to detail at the dining table, has ensured that I rarely feel at a loss, even when the circumstances are very 'posh' (e.g. dinner at the Savoy!) and the company quite exalted.

Do give my love and best wishes to Prinny, I will write to her soon but I know that you will convey all my news.

My regards to friends on the estate and to you, little sister, and Prinny of course,
All love, always,
Helen
P.S. Write to me soon.

Orchard Cottage,Craybourne

Ma Chére Hèlene,

As you can see my acquisition of the French language moves on apace. I must confess that this is largely due to the fact that, for a time, I thought myself in love with Charles Tremayne, (the young curate who tutors me) and my state of mind produced an obsessive addiction to my studies. However, fear not, I have now decided that this was a foolish schoolgirl passion and have decided to save myself for an Oxford Don - one of the younger ones!

In comparison with your own activities, our lives here are spent very quietly. However, with Christmas only three weeks away there is now a quickening of pace and preparations are gathering momentum. I am very hopeful you will be able to join us. Lady C. is currently in residence and says it has been provisionally arranged that you should join James who is escorting Daphne and her friend (a Miss Wigmore?) by rail. We, that is Prinny and you and I, are all invited to the Manor for Christmas luncheon, so if any other invitations are forthcoming for Christmas, however, tempting, please, please, make sure you turn them down!

It has been exceptionally cold here, with ponds and ditches frozen over. This morning the sun was actually shining and we woke up to a world of crystal. Everything was transformed. The sun shone on trees, bushes and fences with their fragile coatings of ice, making them gleam and sparkle - it was like fairyland.

Prinny and I had tea with Lady C. last week. I thought she looked rather tired and was disturbed to note a distinct tremor in her left hand, which she was at some pains to conceal. Surprisingly, her hair is quite silver now - she's surely only in her early fifties? In any event, her hair colour is quite stunning with those pale blue eyes. As always, she was the picture of elegance in a corded silk dress of deep cinnamon - a product of Aston's no doubt and I imagine that the lace and tassel trimmings were probably your Betty's handiwork?

Michael Featherstone still visits us regularly on Saturdays. He is vastly different now. Reserved by nature, he has acquired a quiet confidence and is quite articulate on the subjects close to his heart - divisions between the rich and poor, the woollen industry and animal welfare. The latter was certainly to be expected. Having seen his father consistently abuse their own farm animals, particularly the dogs and horses he says it is time some society was formed to offer protection to all animals. It sounds rather far-fetched and he agrees that until there are much better conditions for humans it is unlikely people will devote much time to worrying about animals.

The Methodist influence of the family with whom he lives is strong and he is now reading a great deal about the Quakers and the revolutionary way in which they have provided their workforce with both excellent accommodation and pastoral care.

Prinny is delighted, she has always said that in Michael Featherstone there was a caring, strong minded individual waiting to emerge. Of course he has changed physically too; at just sixteen years, he is almost six feet tall and his hair which was blonde to the point of whiteness has darkened so much it will soon be the same colour as mine - I tell him it's the coal-laden atmosphere of Halifax that is to blame.

A few months ago dear Walter who was so successfully assisting Leslie Bateman in running the Estate, suddenly developed itchy feet and felt the need to seek 'pastures new' before he got too old! He joined the army, has already had one promotion and, according to the Dennisons, his regiment is now on its way to India.

Prinny sends you her love. As always she is a tower of strength and when I get despondent about my studies, which does happen on occasions, is always there to encourage and make suggestions. These could be anything from practical comments about research to more frivolous ones such as 'Go and sit in the sun and make daisy-chains for the rest of the afternoon.' She is still one of the youngest people I know and will be so if she lives to be one hundred.

We are counting the days to your visit and I am praying for snow, so that you may be forced to remain here for some considerable time!

Fondest love,

  Rosa

Acacia Terrace

Dear Prinny,

What a wonderful Christmas! I am of course writing to Lady Cranbourne and enclose my letter to Rosa, but I am all too aware that, as always, you were the master mind behind our own Christmas arrangements, ensuring everything ran smoothly and everyone's needs were considered. It was a delight to be back at Craybourne with you and Rosa and to see everyone at the Manor and our friends on the Estate, particularly at the farm.

London is amazing and my life continues to be very exciting - I am so very lucky! Nevertheless there are times when I long for the tranquility of the Manor gardens and the peace of our little sitting room at Orchard Cottage.

My love and thanks always,

  Helen.

27 St. James's Ave., Kensington, January 1911

My Dear Lady Craybourne,

My sincere thanks to you for your hospitality and many kindnesses during the Christmas season.

Having for so many years been forced to spend the festive season alone, I cannot begin to tell you what a delight it was to celebrate within a family group.

Craybourne Manor is, I have no doubt, a lovely place to be at any time, but what an extra joy to wake up on Christmas morning to a white world 'deep and crisp and even'. To an outsider like myself, it is very apparent that there is a deep sense of belonging amongst your tenants and I now fully understand why both Daphne and James speak of Craybourne in such loving terms.

I am aware of your concerns about Daphne. She is a strong-willed girl, but not, as might have been the case a few years ago, head-strong. Now her actions are tempered by her innate intelligence and she has learned to delay any action until the matter in hand has been thought through.

She and I co-habit very happily, albeit our living standards fall very short of the comfort provided at Craybourne! I do assure you that she associates with no-one you would feel unable to meet - although that is not to say you would necessarily always approve of their views. But to approve the views of all one's acquaintances would, I am sure you will agree, be very rare indeed.

Although deeply committed to the cause of Women's Suffrage, I fear that neither Daphne nor I are the stuff of which martyrs are made. On occasions we have questioned the motives of those who constantly thrust themselves into the public's eye. Before participating in any of the movement's actions, we discuss privately the implications of those actions and exactly what benefits may or may not accrue from them.

It was a joy to have confirmation from James that within the two Houses are a great many closet supporters of the W.S.P.U. One day they will have the courage to show their true colours and then, (oh happy day!) women will win the right to vote and relinquish this somewhat burdensome torch we now carry.

Meanwhile Daphne and I will continue to heckle speakers in the Commons, conduct meetings, hand out leaflets, and lobby M.P.'s and almost anyone whom we think will be of use to our cause.

If I have digressed from my courtesies, it is because I sensed you still needed some reassurance about Daphne's welfare. Should I have ever have any cause for concern on her behalf and feel it is something with which I cannot deal personally, be certain that I will make contact with James immediately.

For making me so welcome in your lovely home, all my thanks.

Kindest regards,

Muriel Wigmore.

In later years Helen was to look back upon the period at Miss Tindall's with a wave of nostalgia. Away from the Salon, Sonia took the two younger girls under her wing. Saturdays and Sundays became special times for them. On occasion they would rise early to see the riders in Rotton Row. Often they strolled in the parks and picnicked at the riverside. Listening to the band in Hyde Park was a 'must' on Sunday afternoons as was tea at Lyons Corner House. Seasonal changes became associated in Helen's memory with the different foods. In the summer they enjoyed ice creams from the Italian vendors, delicately licking their fingers free of raspberry vinegar. Feeling daring, they sampled sarsaparilla wine and declared it not so thirst quenching as ginger beer.

Betty's Cockney accent would broaden considerably when they stopped to buy apples from one of the costermongers. When she and the barrow boy had shared a joke together the girls would find that not only had they received the best fruit on the stall but a few extra apples for good measure. In the Autumn and Winter they regularly attended Thés Dansants. Sonia had painstakingly taught them both the rudiments of ballroom dancing, somewhat difficult in a cluttered room, twelve yards square. Nevertheless, their knowledge was sufficient to enable them to accept those early invitations onto the dance floor. Helen recalled only too well the very first tea dance when, with Sonia already dancing, she and Betty sat quaking in their shoes. Afterwards they could never quite decide whether they were more nervous of not being asked, or of accepting and tripping over their partner's feet.

The very best treat of all was a visit to the Music Hall. Helen had loved every moment of those evenings. They always made sure of an early start so that they could stay in the foyer and see everyone arriving, the girls being particularly interested in those in evening dresses, recognising instantly Aston garments and those from rival fashion houses. Stage costumes were also a source of fascination. Clearly these garments were very structured so whether the wearer was sitting or dancing, her outfit draped beautifully.

With hindsight Helen was able to see in later years that as she became better known in the fashion world, these private occasions dwindled and her new role in society, crafted by Neville Aston, started to absorb all her free time. Whilst the new life proved full of wonderful occasions and challenges, the mature Helen realised it had lacked the innocent spontaneity of that golden time when they were three young women in London, footloose and fancy free.

Acacia Terrace, Kennington
July 1911

Dearest Rosa,

I have met an amazing young man - an Indian. When I first saw him my first reaction was that he had the sort of suntan Neville Aston would never permit! Then we were introduced and I found him quite delightful. He is studying at Oxford with Richard Culpepper and as his name is fairly long and unpronounceable, everyone refers to him as Jai, (as in I).

 This is my first real encounter with a foreigner, other than Americans who hardly count. Jai is different from anyone I've ever met. His manners are impeccable (much more so than the English boys) and he has a quiet charm and a rather dry sense of humour.

The day after we met he invited me out to tea and suggested The Promenade at the Dorchester, which is just about my favourite place in the whole of London. Neville Aston tells me Jai is rich. Certainly he doesn't seem to have money worries as do the other students and even some of the debutantes and their escorts. He doesn't of course, mention anything of that nature and seems fairly reluctant to discuss India, other than to tell me "It's a land of contradictions". When I asked him to explain, he said, ambiguously, "One day you'll find out for yourself".

Thursday

 My apologies, Rosa. Three days have passed since I started my letter and all my good intentions about completing it, seem to have gone by the wayside.

The university is now 'down' for the summer vacation, so Jai is in London permanently and seems to want me to spend every available non-working moment with him. Neville Aston has been very generous in this respect but (can it really be a coincidence?) Jai and I have been rather plagued by the press. We've been photographed at Wimbledon (he's a keen tennis player), at Henley Regatta, and when dining and dancing at the Savoy. On that particular occasion Jai was annoyed. From the press I learned that Jai's father is ruler of a province of India, but Jai insists that there are dozens of them - provinces and rulers! He did say his family are Rajputs, that is descendants of the original Hindu military and ruling caste of India, but my knowledge of Indian history is insufficient to understand the significance of that.

Neville's Spring launch of his ready-made range has sold beyond his wildest dreams. Now, in addition to photos in The Tatler of "Helena of the House of Aston seen at the Cliveden Hunt Ball", we have The London Evening News with "House of Aston's Helena boards a motor-bus wearing a clerical grey braided two-piece and coral silk tailored blouse. Note the convenience of the slightly shorter skirt length". I still have to pinch myself to make sure it's real, when I see my own likeness staring up at me from the newspaper!

Work on the Aston Autumn/Winter collection is now completed and will be shown next week. Some of Neville's long-standing customers see these new collections of ready-made garments as a threat to their designer clothes. Personally, I think those will always be available to the very rich. Neville is right though in thinking that changes are taking place. Even a country-bred girl like me is aware of it. A great levelling out seems to be taking place in London, with no-one too interested in class barriers any more, (except for a few old die-hards at the Salon). Perhaps it's because class has little relevance here where so many people are out at work.

You remember that Prinny used to talk about the nouveau riche? Well, London is awash with them, spending their money and enjoying life. Good luck to them I say. And yes you would be right in thinking I feel somewhat strongly about it. After all my own fortunes have changed dramatically during the past few years and now meeting Jai - I feel I have been so lucky. I have nightmares about going into a room where everyone stands up and points a finger at me, shouting "She's a sham, an impostor, she shouldn't be here". Jai laughs at me. He knows all about my origins of course and says the British are far too concerned with background. I find that very strange coming from someone whose countrymen are so divided by caste, but when I try to discuss it, he changes the subject!

An enormous bouquet arrived for me yesterday, with a card from Jai saying it was the anniversary of our meeting six months ago. I felt quite overwhelmed and Miss Tindall and the girls were very impressed. We filled eight vases. There were long-stemmed roses, carnations, scabious and scented stocks and clouds and clouds of frothy white gypsophila. Our sitting room is like a bower and smells gorgeous.

Much love to you and all at Craybourne.

Helen.

Acacia Terrace,

Rosa Darling,

I think, no I know Jai's going to ask me to marry him! Before you say we've only just met , it must seem like that to you but we have been seeing each other almost every day for several weeks now and, well, he has become very dear to me.

The trouble is I'm not sure if I'm ready to make that sort of decision. What I do know is that since Mama died, although I care about many people, particularly Prinny, you, little sister, are the only person I really love. I feel that Jai has filled a void in my life - one I wasn't even aware of until recently. I so much enjoy being with him, but love... well, I've only read about that in books and all this silly nonsense about wealthy Indian princes which even my friends whisper about, is guaranteed to put anyone off! Jai looks after me and is concerned for my welfare. You know Lady C. , James and Daphne are all very kind, but often I don't see them for months at a time and with no Prinny to cluck around after me like a mother hen, I confess to enjoying being cosseted by Jai.

The most important news I have kept until last. We are coming to see you! Yes, I did say we. It is Jai's idea and he has attended to all the arrangements. We are to travel north by rail on Friday, August 10th, accompanied by someone called Karim - he is a sort of manservant to Jai whom I didn't even know existed. Jai has hired a car and Karim will drive us from Leeds to Craybourne. Tell Prinny I will be writing, but I don't want her worrying about accommodation for Jai and his servant. Rooms have already been reserved for them at the Craybourne Arms.

Jai is so considerate, he feels it is time he met you and Prinny and as Lady C. has been so kind to me/us, I am to write to ask if she will receive us during the weekend. I am hopeful that, as the House will be in its summer recess, James might also be present. He has met Jai, although very briefly. On two occasions when Jai and I were dining out, we've bumped into James and to my surprise and delight, each time he was accompanied by Muriel Wigmore. It seems the languid Diana (Weever-Smith) had better look to her laurels!

You can't imagine how much I'm longing to show Jai our beautiful Yorkshire Dales. August should be just right for us to enjoy picnics so start thinking about all the places we must visit and you can give us a conducted tour.

Selfishly, this letter is all about me, but I am very mindful of the fact that you are waiting to hear from Oxford about your entrance examination and besides that everything must pale into insignificance. I do so hope all will be resolved by the time we travel North and we can sit up late into the night discussing your plans - and perhaps mine too!

My love always,

Helen

Chapter Fourteen

By the time he travelled North, James knew a great deal about Jai. The Culpepper lad had been a mine of information. Unlike the other Oxford students, Jai was not housed in rooms in college. He had rented a house in the city and in residence with him were Karim, who seemed a very superior sort of manservant, a male cook, and a young woman, Aliya, who served at table and helped generally about the house. The question of Aliya's 'general duties' had resulted in a great deal of ribaldry amongst Jai's fellow students, but Richard Culpepper was adamant that on his visits to the household everything was very correct, with the girl subservient and her presence unobtrusive.

From the Foreign Office, James learned that Jai's father was indeed the ruler of Jaishalpar and one of the Raj, the Indian princes with whom the British Government had, albeit superficially, cordial relations. 'Wealthy' was considered an understatement for the sort of riches the family enjoyed. The Maharajah was in poor health, attributed on the grape-vine to his former racy lifestyle. His 'Western' education amounted to three years' tuition from a young English teacher, the only apparent result of this being the acquisition of several expensive motor cars.

A stroke some eighteen months ago had left him partially paralysed and Jaishalpar was currently being governed by Jai's mother, a good woman with a social conscience. In spite of this, James was also informed that there were rumours, unproven, of inexplicable savagery in the area. Traditionally, the Raj was a close-knit unit, reluctant to discuss its members, but British personnel had noted an unwillingness amongst the Indian princes for close association with the Jaishalpar family.

It was difficult to make much sense out of this. India was a country where in certain areas 'the survival of the fittest' obtained. It was known too, that factions within the Raj were constantly at loggerheads, so that stories could be based on mere speculation or malice.

Certainly it was insufficient evidence on which to mount any reasonable objections to Helen marrying Jai, if that was indeed her intention. Although since Mary's death, his mother had kept a watchful eye on Helen and Rosa, neither she nor Prinny was their legal guardian. Other than offer advice, or in dire circumstances attempt to make her a ward of court, there was little they could do.

Slipping his watch from his pocket, he saw there was at least an hour's travelling time before they reached Leeds, time for forty winks.....James closed his eyes and succumbed to the soothing rhythm of the train.

Their departure from King's Cross had all the hallmarks of a Royal Progress. The small elegant procession moving like an oasis of calm amongst the smoke-filled station, its vaulted ceilings reverberating to the cacophony of hissing steam, powerful machines and bustling crowds.

Soon the group was the cynosure of all eyes. Leading the way, a self-important porter ensured that no obstacle impeded their passage. Then came Jai, whose aura was one of authority hinting at arrogance. Darkly handsome in his Western clothes, he was the perfect foil for Helen. She was well-known now to Londoners. Working girls and fashionable ladies alike sighed with admiration, noting each detail of her midnight blue suit with its ruffles of silver grey lace at the neck and wrists. Today the red-gold of her hair was almost concealed beneath the large brimmed hat, its crown covered with tiny silver osprey feathers. One gloved hand on Jai's arm, the other holding her rolled silk parasol at just the right angle, the epitome of elegance.

Behind them walked Karim, carrying their two dressing cases and checking from time to time to ensure that their luggage porters remained close at hand.

Once ensconced in their carriage, Helen sank back with pleasure against the freshly laundered covers which protected the wealthy from any undue contact with smoke-impregnated furnishings. She removed the glove of her left hand to study again the magnificent ring. How heavy it felt. She turned her hand in the sunlight to catch the shafts of emerald green beauty.

"The nearest colour I could get to your eyes,"Jai had said. And there was another ring, still in its small velvet box. This would be placed on her finger when the English wedding ceremony had been performed. The rings, Jai had explained, were designed to complement each other... the betrothal ring, a huge square-cut emerald and its 'keeper' eternity ring with emeralds and diamonds alternating in a gold setting. Together, Jai had added, they would attempt to complement their beautiful wearer.

"I long to show you India, my India," Jai had said. "Indian women are noted for their beauty and grace, but you my darling will outshine them all. I know that I am asking you to leave your own country and loved ones, but I will ensure that you never regret it. I will surround you with lovely things worthy of your beauty and together we will find true happiness."

She had accepted his proposal of course, that had always been inevitable. In retrospect she could wish he had spoken more explicitly of love, rather than her beauty and grace, how much he admired her and wished to take care of her. But then she recalled his boyish charm as he had talked, at last, of India and how he would enjoy sharing with her its wonders.

His suggestions that there should be two wedding ceremonies, one in England at the church of her choice and a Hindu ceremony in India seemed entirely reasonable. During the sea crossing Helen would be chaperoned Jai added, as he could not regard her as his wife until after the Indian wedding. Again this was thoughtful and entirely acceptable. Neither was she unduly alarmed at his statement that any children should be brought up as Hindus. Helen did not regard herself as other than a good Christian who attended church irregularly. She was vaguely of the opinion that all religions believed in an all-powerful force for good, so must have many bases of commonality.

Her biggest concern had been leaving England and Rosa for an indeterminate period but, as Jai pointed out, Rosa was about to commence a new life herself. His further assurances that there would be no problems about she and Rosa exchanging visits removed any misgivings Helen might have had.

Today his charm had given way to a morose mood and once seated, his disappearance behind a copy of The Times indicative of his unwillingness to converse. Helen pondered on the inconsistencies of his behaviour. Always in public the perfect escort, gracious and charming, there had been occasions when they were alone when he had seemed slightly off-hand, almost ill at ease. The only conclusion she could draw was that, like herself, he had built up a public facade of confidence, but was in fact inherently shy. After all, it was quite an ordeal for a young man to leave his country and the culture in which he had been brought up, and then have to associate with peers with whom he had little in common. Smiling at her own reflection in the carriage window, she resolved that together they would help each other in overcoming this trait.

Jai's first sight of Yorkshire was not salubrious. Within minutes of crossing the border, the rain began to slice against the windows, coursing like huge tears down the grimy surfaces. From Leeds any view was obscured by driving rain, with Karim concentrating on following signs and Helen desperately trying to give him some assistance. By the time they reached Prinny's cottage, they were feeling chilly and despondent. Helen, the more so, because Jai seemed so aloof, annoyed almost, as if she should have in some way ensured that the weather behaved itself whilst they were travelling. Arriving at Prinny's cottage, all was forgotten in the warmth of their welcome. Tea in the sitting room, glowing with flowers and a cheerful fire ("August or not, it's raining and miserable and that's when you need a fire most" Prinny had said), had been a happy occasion.

Rosa, the extrovert, vibrant with good health and elated by her sister's presence, dominated the conversation. There were exclamations at the sight of Helen's ring, kisses and congratulations and more hugs and congratulation when the letter was produced offering Rosa a place at Lady Margaret Hall College in September. Then there were the gifts from Jai, Rosa's parcel, "I think you'll find this useful at Oxford", containing a dark green leather dressing case with brass fittings and her initials in gold. As Rosa delightedly examined its contents, Prinny opened her own small package to find an exquisite cameo brooch. The gentle way in which she lifted the brooch from its surrounds and fingered the delicate relief, expressing more than any words, her pleasure at the gift.

At 5 o'clock precisely Jai made his excuses, firmly refusing all invitations to stay and dine with them. He reiterated his earlier words to Helen, "You ladies have much news to discuss and many plans to make," and, confirming that he would call at 11. a.m. the next day, he departed for the Craybourne Arms.

When Prinny finally retired, leaving the girls to gossip late into the night, she was hard pressed to crystallise her reservations about Jai. Charming certainly, perhaps too charming. Helen clearly hung on his words and yet he never to her expressed any term of endearment or, for that matter, looked at her lovingly; even allowing for the culture differences this was odd. Revelling in Rosa's admiration, he had given all her questions serious consideration. Could this be because his lengthy answers made him once again the focus of attention?

With the experience of maturity, Prinny culled together the various signals which 'en masse' were indicative of a somewhat arrogant, self-centred nature. She well knew, however, that any such suggestions to the girls whilst in their present state of euphoria, would be dismissed as totally groundless.

Perhaps James and Lady Craybourne would be able to help. Thrusting the problem from her, she attempted to sleep.

The previous day's rain had given way to brilliant sunshine and Helen, enjoying her walk through the Manor grounds, drank in the sights and sounds she had so loved as a child. She stopped to chat with Len, the old gardener, congratulating him on the grounds' immaculate perfection. Huge stone urns spilling over with deep blue hydrangeas flanked the drive; clustered conifers, varying in shape and colour, threw pools of shadow onto the lawns and, long before their kaleidoscope of colour came into view, the air was redolent with the heavy perfume of roses.

Lady Craybourne had asked to see Helen at three o'clock, suggesting that Jai join them for tea at four o'clock. With her in the cool green drawing room was James and, the courtesies having been exchanged, Lady Craybourne came straight to the point at issue, their concern for Helen's welfare. Did Jai intend marriage? Was he returning to Oxford, etc., etc. Helen smilingly removed her glove, revealing the superb emerald and told them of Jai's plans for their future together, his need to return to India earlier than planned because of his father's deteriorating health.

James and Elizabeth were somewhat nonplussed. Everything Jai was suggesting sounded entirely reasonable and acceptable - with one exception. Elizabeth Craybourne was adamant that Helen should not travel to India without an English speaking companion. Helen's comment that she would have Jai, was dismissed. Jai might have to absent himself for lengthy periods to visit different areas of the province, Elizabeth pointed out. Supposing Helen was ill, to whom could she turn for sympathy, or ensure she was getting the correct treatment? When she was with child, Elizabeth forged on regardless of Helen's blushes, with whom would she converse on the difficult days? There was absolutely no question about it, an English speaking female companion must accompany her to India. Could Helen think of anyone - without family ties - who might fulfil this role, perhaps someone from Aston's?

"I think perhaps...." Helen hesitated, "I think Betty might come with me. Neville would hate to see her go but ...."

"Betty? The girl who does the wonderful embroidery?"

Helen nodded. "She's one of a very large family, but there's no-one for whom she is directly responsible. She's often said she would love to travel."

"A splendid idea. The girl's got a good head on her shoulders. Let's hope she agrees." Lady Craybourne was more than pleased with this suggestion. She had met Betty and knew her to be a most competent, level-headed young woman. Her family background and London upbringing had obviously made her very worldly-wise. She was not the type to panic and had just the vein of steel which Helen might on occasions need.

James excused himself, leaving the two ladies so that his mother could explain to Helen her own mother's origins and the reasons why the Craybourne family were keeping such a watchful eye over Rosa and herself.

For Helen it solved the enigma which had puzzled her subconsciously as a child and more overtly as an adult. So many things had not seemed to fit. The contrast between her father, the coarse Jim Calloway and her fastidious mother, whose manners and speech were so correct, had made their union inexplicable. With the exception of the Vicar, none of the villagers she met had Mary's refinement. Of her grandparents she had known only that they kept the village stores. Now, with the full story, the mystery was unravelled. She knew from personal experience that senior servants in large households acquired a great deal of knowledge both directly and indirectly through their employers; that ladies' maids, butlers, senior footmen and parlourmaids learned how to move and speak decorously and gained a great deal of information about politics and world problems, merely by keeping their eyes and ears open. This was how her grandparents had learned, ultimately transmitting that knowledge to their daughter. How fortunate she and Rosa had been that Prinny had taken up this torch on Mary's death. From her they had gained a real insight into, and love of, literature and history. They had pored over maps, discussed politics, visited art galleries in Leeds and Bradford and had, in fact, received a very rounded education from which she, Helen, was now reaping the benefit.

At Aston's she had always felt that her mode of speech and many of the topics she found of interest had set her apart. She now realised how and why this had occurred.

Having allowed the girl some minutes to collect her thoughts, Lady C. gently brought her back to reality.

"You can now understand, Helen, why I have a very special interest in your safety and well-being. My husband, your grandfather, was a gentle man in every sense of the word. He wanted the best for his family, his workforce, his tenants. You and Rosa are a part of our family and James and I want you to know that we are always here ready to support you in any way that we can."

The tremor in Elizabeth's voice suggested she was not feeling quite so calm and composed as she appeared and Helen saw that the movement of her left hand on which Rosa had commented, was suddenly more marked. With a spontaneous, uncharacteristic gesture she crossed to Elizabeth, lightly kissed her cheek and said, "I do understand and I am very appreciative of all you have done and are doing for Rosa and for me. We'll try not to let you down."

"My dear, we are all so proud of you and what you have accomplished." Clearly moved by Helen's unexpected show of affection, Elizabeth now steered the conversation into calmer waters.

"It's almost four o'clock, perhaps you would ring the bell for tea. James will meet your fiancé and bring him through to join us.

As Helen crossed to the bell pull, Elizabeth thought what a lovely young woman she had become. Her movements were relaxed and graceful. The magnificent eyes which, chameleon-like, seemed to change with the colour of her apparel or surroundings were today rendered almost turquoise by the blue of her tea-gown. Possibly because of her youth, the girl was still a curious mixture, a mélange of sensitivity and innocence, yet capable of a directness which was unnerving.

Curiously, Helen had not mentioned Jai's wealth and status. With the exception of her magnificent ring, clearly of great value, he seemed to have lived fairly modestly in England. Yet, according to James, his background was one of opulence. Because of this, one might have expected Helen to exhibit some sign of nervousness or excitement. Had Jai deliberately withheld information from her regarding her new life-style? Certainly wherever she went she would be both a credit to herself and a prize indeed for the man she had agreed to marry. Admirable enough, providing the acquisition of that prize was not his sole reason for the marriage.

Only Helen was aware of Jai's displeasure at the one major decision he had not instigated. Within the last few days she had learned to recognise the tightening of the small muscle at the left corner of his mouth. He explained to Lady Craybourne that he had anticipated that Aliya would fulfil the role of Helen's dresser and chaperone. On a less serious occasion Helen would have been amused at the quizzical way in which that good lady's eyebrows shot heavenwards. Pre-empting her next question, Jai added that Aliya was a female servant in his household and yes, she did speak English quite fluently. Now it was Helen's turn to register surprise, albeit covertly. A young woman in Jai's Oxford household, speaking fluent English. Why hadn't he mentioned her before? Every day she seemed to discover something new about Jai. New, and occasionally disturbing.

Elizabeth was speaking, courteous as always.

"I can see Jai, if you will permit us to address you so familiarly, that you have given a great deal of thought to Helen's comfort and well-being. However, I am sure you will agree that what is required is not so much a servant as a contemporary, someone with whom she can be completely relaxed. I have already pointed out to Helen that there could well be occasions when you have to leave her for lengthy periods and for a young girl living in a new country, accustoming herself to a different climate and culture, many problems could arise. I feel sure you will understand and grant me this small favour."

In the face of such polite opposition, how could Jai refuse?

With the approval of Rosa and Prinny, Helen had decided to be married in London where lived the majority of her friends and contemporaries. It was now agreed that the venue should be St.Margaret's, Westminster and Helen happily accepted James's offer to give her away. Rosa, Prinny and Elizabeth would travel south for the occasion and at this point Jai announced his intention of providing both the wedding breakfast and whatever was necessary to ensure that the Manor staff and tenants were able to enjoy a small celebration. The wedding date was fixed for Friday, 22nd September, Jai having already ascertained that the ship Eastern Star would depart for the Far East on the following day.

Elizabeth stood at the open window, the sunlight casting her shadow on the faded green silk taffeta which covered the walls. As she watched the young couple walk away from the Manor, the warm summer breeze gently stirred her gown's lace-edged sleeves.

There was another matter which troubled her deeply, one which she could not bring herself to discuss with James and which she had felt inadequate to discuss with Helen. Whilst in her early years the girl had been closely associated with farm life, it was very unlikely that she had any knowledge of what marital relations involved. Prinny, entrenched in her spinsterhood, would certainly not have conveyed such information. The girl seemed so vulnerable, she could only pray for her happiness.

If Helen had any doubts at all, they were dispelled during those few days in Yorkshire. Jai was once more the most delightful of companions, always anxious to please and unselfish in his acceptance of the fact that Rosa should accompany them on all occasions.

Each day, long before the last fingers of mist which defined the valleys, had been burned off by the sun, they were already in the car, a picnic hamper stowed in the boot. With Jai at the wheel, they visited the beauty spots Rosa had selected, climbed the great rocks which stood guard over Ilkley, wandered through the ruins of Fountains Abbey and balanced precariously as they crossed on stepping stones the river at Bolton Abbey.

Sometimes they picnicked in lush green fields where Jai made chains of buttercups and daisies and ceremoniously presented them to 'his ladies'. At others, they ate amidst the heather, high on the moors, looking out across ridge upon ridge of undulating beauty.

If Helen occasionally wished that Jai would be more loving, more passionate even, she would reprimand herself severely. It was foolish of her to blame Jai for behaving so correctly. It may well be that such contact was not permitted under the Hindi religion. When they were married all would be resolved.

Chapter Fifteen

From the Maharajah Elect, Jaishalpar,
Craybourne Arms, Yorkshire

Ashok,

The girl is mine! She is such a beauty, such a prize. When I tell you that her face is a perfect oval with a skin that is the colour of pearls, pale but with a translucid quality; her eyes at times as green as emeralds and her hair almost defies description, sometimes gold sometimes red, you will perhaps begin to realise why I coveted her from the start. About my height, she has the tiniest of waists, yet her curves undoubtedly suggest the hidden delights in store.

I have had, to coin an English phrase, to 'play my cards carefully'. Her rapid rise to fame has already made it necessary for her to make many adjustments, coming as she did from a quiet rural background. Had she known too much about me or how we will live, I feared she would have shied away from further massive changes. As it is, such knowledge as she now has about our status in India has largely been gleaned from the English press and, dear cousin, I know you will agree that we are only too well aware of their inaccuracy!

It was always obvious that many other suitors were interested. The English were even prepared to forget their rules about class and accept her because of her newfound celebrity status. In much the same way as they accept me of course, "Ignore his skin colour, he is after all one of the Raj!" The competition was fierce, but as you well know, I am at my most determined when under pressure.

Ashok, she will be such a jewel in my collection and our progeny cannot fail but be magnificent. Her name by the way is Helena.

No mention is to be made of Metta. This information she will glean in due course. Once under my control, I can determine the how and when of this.

Unfortunately, the aristocratic lady who keeps a watchful eye on my betrothed (more of this when we meet), and who lives in a faded ancestral home in the North of this cold country, was implacable on one point and we are now to have an addition to our party, a Miss Betty Carter (such an ugly name!). She is a London-bred girl, whose accent I fear you will have great difficulty understanding. As Helena's friend, she is to be treated as a guest, rather than a servant. I leave you to make all necessary arrangements.

Please check the arrival date and time of the Eastern Star departing from Tilbury on Sept. 23rd and arrange hotel accommodation in Bombay.

I trust my dear Mutti has not been interfering too much with our agreed handling of matters in the province. It will be good to be home and take up the reins once more.

Salutations,

Romesh

Dearest Rob,

The most amazing news! Our little wrong side of the blanket step-niece, whose face is guaranteed to 'launch a thousand ships' is associating with one of the Raj - and by that I mean closely associating. Wedding bells, rumour has it, are imminent.Can you believe this girl? Her rise from naive country girl to top mannequin has been nothing short of meteoric and now this! I've met the erstwhile husband and he's very smooth! Entirely westernised - I think. Can one ever be quite sure? By all accounts he had an English tutor from the age of five and is just completing his second year at Oxford. Well travelled, naturellement! He has a sort of feral grace which makes me feel that behind that urbane facade there is a tiger waiting to spring. Darkly handsome, of course. You can imagine that together they form a most impressive duo. James insists that Jai (derivation of the name of their province) is fiendishly rich but if Helen has registered the fact she's not saying anything about it. I can never decide whether the girl is very naive or somewhat stupid.

My own affairs plod on from meeting to meeting. Thank heavens for Wiggie who keeps me sane, particularly when Emmy (Pankhurst) is doing her Royalty act, which seems to happen more and more frequently. There are times when Wiggie and I feel we just cannot agree to her demands.

Wiggie is incidentally seeing quite a lot of James and I have to say she is just what big brother needs to prevent him from becoming a complete sobersides.. I defy anyone to remain serious for too long in Wiggie's company. Wouldn't it be quaint if my former teacher became my sister-in-law?

So, you are now helping to take the wonders of cinematography to the outback of Australia - fascinating! I shall expect detailed reports at regular intervals. Until my next bulletin with news of the beautiful Helen and her Indian prince and the belted earl and the lowly schoolteacher...

Adieu, dearest Rob, my love and prayers always for success in all you do.

Daphne

Eastern Star October 2nd

Rosa Darling,

Heaven knows when this will reach you, but, as promised, I will try to keep you au fait with events. Looking back, the wedding still seems like a dream filled with beautiful people.

Neville was wonderful in producing our dresses so quickly. (Judging by the bevy of photographers he still managed to get max. publicity for Aston's). I am glad we insisted on ivory, as I feel for both of us, white is too stark.

Didn't Jai look incredibly handsome? I can't wait to see him in his full Indian dress. Not much longer now before I see his home and I have a serious case of 'butterflies in the tummy' at the thought of it.

Jai was so right in booking us into a hotel for the night of the wedding. We were reasonably well rested by the time we joined the ship. (Claridges was, as you would expect, absolutely sumptuous. Betty was quite speechless at its grandeur).

A quite wonderful surprise was awaiting me on board. In my cabin were four huge teak wardrobe trunks which Betty and I opened with great excitement. Each one was velvet-lined and they contained fabulous outfits for a variety of occasions. There are day and tea gowns, ball gowns, satin and velvet cloaks, fabulous hats and accessories and even lingerie! Obviously Neville had been given carte blanche and having all my measurements, plus the knowledge of my preferences in wearing apparel, had happily complied with Jai's instructions to assemble this wonderful collection.

Jai brushed aside my thanks. He says there will be occasions when we will entertain or be entertained by the British, both the diplomatic corps and the regiments based out there. Apparently an Indian wardrobe awaits me in Jaishalpar as I shall be expected to wear a sari on formal Indian occasions. However, as he pointed out, I would probably prefer this style of dress for much of the time as it will be so much cooler and more comfortable than our own garments. I needed no convincing! I love the thought of wearing a sari, the few I have seen have been so beautiful. I think Betty is going to find the different ornamentation of great interest.

To date, there has been only one occasion when I felt decidedly unwell and had to decline both dinner and breakfast the following day. Betty has had several bouts of sea-sickness, but seems to recover very quickly I suspect she is so excited at the events of the last few weeks, that she is absolutely determined not to miss anything whilst confined to quarters. She is, incidentally, starting to make good use of the journal - her leaving present from Aston's. She is determined to keep a comprehensive record of our life in India so that her family can enjoy reading it at their leisure at a later date.

We were rather surprised when Jai suggested that it would be correct for Betty to address him as 'Sir', but she has quite cheerfully complied with his request. Everyone on board is most deferential to Jai and on the subject of modes of address, the other day I heard him referred to as 'Highness'. Isn't that amazing? Hitherto, I've tried very hard to dismiss all this nonsense about Indian princes and mannequins as Ethel M. Dell rubbish but there is little doubt that, the closer we get to India, people are becoming almost more ingratiating by the hour.

Are you now happily settled in Oxford? I do hope so and that you are meeting lots of soul-mates with whom to discuss your many interests. Prinny must be missing you terribly.

It already seems ages since we were at Craybourne and seeing my lovely Dales. The sea in its many moods is very beautiful, but I would exchange it readily for the sun on the heather-covered glories of the Yorkshire moors.

Only to you can I say this little sister - the nearer we get to Jai's homeland, I become not only excited, but apprehensive. Is that strange? I love Jai dearly, but even here I feel he is not relaxed with me as I would wish. However, I must put these thoughts from me, no doubt when our Indian wedding ceremony has taken place and I am truly his wife all will be well.

I pray always for your happiness and success dearest Rosa,
Fondest love
Helen

Betty's Journal

Hotel Maidan, Bombay
India at last! Sighted Bombay at 1.30 p.m.

Earlier Helen received a message from 'Sir' that he would appreciate it if she wore the dress of cream, braided with peach satin. Strange request, we both thought - until we saw him! For the first time Jai was in full Indian garb and he was a sensation. Immaculate cream trousers and tunic braided with peach, a cream turban with heavy gold pin which held a chevron of peach coloured feathers. Together he and Helen formed a beautiful colour coordinated picture and, perhaps, as Helen suggested, a symbolic one of a union between East and West.

When we assembled on deck, the Captain and senior officers were lined up to bid us farewell. Karim and Aliyah left first to supervise the luggage, then Sir followed by Helen, with Yours Truly bringing up the rear.

At the foot of the gangway we were met by another very gorgeous young Indian, who made deep salaams to Jai and to Helen. He was introduced as Ashok, Jai's cousin and escorted us to two huge cars which were waiting for us As you know, I'm somewhat vague about cars, but I asked Karim and he identified them as a Rolls Royce and a Dion Bouton laundelette. Both were of the palest yellow with interiors of ivory and gold. Helen, Jai and Ashok travelled in the first car, with Karim, Aliyah and myself in the second. My glimpses of what was happening beyond our entourage was of hustle and bustle, with what appeared to be hundreds of white-clad Indians milling about and shouting at each other.

It took us about ten minutes to reach the Hotel, but what horrific sights en route. People lying by the roadside, children half naked and obviously starving - quite awful.

By complete contrast, inside the Maidan all is calm, cool and orderly. Things happen upon request. The floor seems, like the ship, to be still moving, but no doubt that sensation will persist for a time. Even the bed seems to be floating.

Friday
10.0 a.m. left for Jaishalpar this time in three cars. Jai and his cousin, who had business to discuss, Helen and I, Karim and Aliyah.

Today, I was able to absorb more of our surroundings. Clustered around each village is a huge patchwork circle of fields. The bullocks, their horns painted vermilion, seem to plod sleepily on no matter what occurs. By contrast, clouds of birds, startled by the approach of our cars, rush screaming into the blue arc of the sky. Everywhere the scent of sandalwood.

One stop, late morning, at a private home, where we were welcomed with much bowing of heads and elaborate salaams. Tea was served with tiny biscuits decorated with orange peel and pistachio nuts, dusted with white sugar - they looked much too pretty to eat!

About 1.p.m. our driver indicated that we should look ahead and we saw a palace! Jai's home looks just like one of those huge fluffy cream cakes sold by the best London shops. The whole effect is one of the palest pink with touches of gold, which send shafts of light everywhere as they are struck by the brilliant sunshine. It was quite breathtaking. Helen and I just looked at it, then at each other, and gulped.

Once inside the high perimeter wall, we passed through an avenue of lime and mango trees then under a huge golden arch which brought us into a fairyland of gardens with, unbelievably, English type herbaceous borders with strutting peacocks which scuttled shrieking for cover as the cars approached. Lotus-shaped marble fountains cascaded water into lily covered pools and the air was heavy with the perfume of roses and jasmine.

In front of us was a huge courtyard, its perimeter defined on each flank by some fifty elephants. They were so splendid! Their backs covered with brocade, faces and trunks painted with the most brilliant colours. Each had a plaque on its forehead and, can you believe it, anklets and necklaces of silver and gold. Standing by each was an attendant - his mahout.

Flanking the marble pillars and stairs to the front entrance was the palace guard, one hundred men in scarlet jackets and white trousers. As the cars came to a standstill we could hear music playing (I couldn't see a band anywhere) and the guard and elephant attendants all came to attention. What we were hearing was apparently the national anthem of Jaishalpar and it's played every time a member of the royal family passes through the golden arch. I have visions of the musicians perched in trees, hiding behind shrubs etc., all waiting for the signal to start playing!

Watching Jai, sorry - Sir, standing to attention and acknowledging the salute, it was some moments before I realised that another figure had appeared on the scene. At the top of the marble stairs stood a tiny figure in a vivid green and gold sari. Suddenly all eyes were focused upon her. Jai went up the stairs, bowed deeply, made his salaams and then stood at her side as Ashok escorted Helen to meet her future mother-in-law, Her Highness, the Maharani of Jaishalpar.

Chapter Sixteen

Repeatedly, the irony of her situation struck Helen in the pleasantest possible way. She who had made light of the stories of wealthy Indian princes as being over-glamorised nonsense was now in the most fairy-tale of palaces and about to marry a very rich and influential man. The tiny charismatic figure at her side was royal. Guards came to attention as she approached, female attendants froze in their tracks. Yet there was about her a warmth with which Helen could feel an instant rapport. As the Rani escorted her around the suite of rooms which were to be her own, Helen's delight and amazement became more and more apparent. A cool verandah opened onto a cloistered garden, vibrant with exotic blooms. Three small pools were linked by streams, with here and there small shaded arbours. A bathing pool of pink marble was screened for privacy, but its colour glowed faintly from behind the trellised marble surround, as intricate as filigree lace.

Totally overwhelmed, the girl turned to the Rani clasping the small brown hands tightly within her own. Accustomed to the cool politeness of the English, the Rani smiled broadly. This girl she could like! But she was so vulnerable. Stifling a wave of pity, she explained that Helen would always have a female attendant within call on the veranda. The girl, Ila, had a limited knowledge of basic English, but was skilled in the arts of massage, make up and arranging hair. Another girl would be responsible for Helen's wardrobe.At this point she opened one of the sliding mirror-faced doors in the dressing rooms to reveal saris in every hue and texture imaginable. Indicating that she would have time later to examine these more closely, the Rani continued. A guard would be on duty outside Helen's rooms at all times and should a problem arise with which she needed assistance then he was to be sent with a note to the Sirdar in the same corridor. Pre-empting Helen's question she explained.

"We have six Sirdar's here, each responsible for some aspect of the Palace management. These are not servants but men of superior families - what you would call the aristocracy."

"1t's all so …. impressive, so big....I'd no idea...." For the first time Helen's voice faltered as the enormity of her changed circumstances hit her.

"You are tired, my dear. There is much more you need to know, but it can wait until another day. Now I suggest you either ask your friend to join you in the pool, or let Ila prepare you a bath, then you and - Miss Carter isn't it? should rest for a while so that you are refreshed before we dine this evening. There will be occasions when your friend will be invited to join us for dinner, but this evening we dine en famille and Miss Carter will join the Sirdars.".

In spite of her delight at the Rani's command of the English language and the rapport she felt they had immediately established, Helen was soon to bless Elizabeth Craybourne's foresight in her insistence that a friend should accompany her. It was obvious that the geography of the palace was not going to be mastered within a few days or even a few weeks, but together the girls explored, giggling discreetly at the incongruities and gasping at the luxury of it all.

They found a cluster of dining rooms of varying size and styles. The walls of one, overtly British and capable of seating one hundred guests, were covered in Landseer paintings, its marble floor concealed under Axminster carpet, the mahogany sideboards laden with Wedgwood and crystal. The walls of a smaller room were draped in blue silk, its table covered in exquisite Flemish lace, with in each corner huge vases of Sèvres porcelain, bearing great clouds of mimosa and jasmine. The Rani had told them that the great durbar room was large enough to host four hundred guests and would be used for this purpose on the occasion of Helen's wedding.

Dinner on the evening of their arrival had proved something of an ordeal. The delicious meal prepared by a French chef, one of the three in residence Helen learned, was served Western style in deference to Helen. Conversation proved desultory, for the first time Helen becoming aware of an undercurrent between the Rani and the two young men, Jai and his cousin Ashok. Whilst outwardly polite and deferential Helen was quick to note on a number of occasions, the veiled insolence in their replies.

Ashok's wife, Hamida completed the family party, but as her English vocabulary was monosyllabic, there was no help from that quarter.

Jai had escorted Helen back to her rooms, kissed her perfunctorily and, on the point of departure, announced that the wedding would take place on the following Thursday. Helen's role in the ceremony would be explained by the Rani.

It was a sombre Helen who, assisted by Ila, prepared for bed. More and more Jai seemed like a stranger. He made no attempt to bridge the divide which seemed to be widening between them and any attempts of her own to do so were brusquely brushed aside. Ensconsed at last in the ivory bed at the room's centre, she looked out at a full moon through the softly stirring clouds of mosquito nets, slipping at last into a troubled sleep.

The sound which woke her sent her pulses racing and the perspiration oozing from her pores. There it was again! The roar of a large animal and so close at hand. Drawing back the nets around her she caught up her robe and called loudly for Ila. Slowly the girl appeared from the verandah, drenched with sleep and uncomprehending.

"Ila, what is it? What is that sound?" The great roar once again filled the room and now the girl understood. "Highness's tiger, Memsahib," she smiled broadly, "No be afraid. Him in cage. No get out."

Helen sank back on the edge of the bed, her terror receding. A tiger and obviously close by. Something else to see tomorrow.

The next day saw Helen and Betty, escorted by the Rani herself, visiting the zenana. These were, the Rani explained, the quarters for women who kept complete or partial purdah and the Rani's own suite was within this section of the palace. The girls were shown the magnificent tiger, Zizi, presented as a cub to Jai on his first tiger hunt.

Helen noted thankfully that the animal had a huge area in which to exercise and, even more thankfully that armed guards were always in attendance.

"But who are the women who live here in the zenana?" Helen asked

"The wives of our Sirdars, Ashok's wives...." At the lifting of Helen's eyebrows, the Rani continued, "Yes, my dear, I did say wives. You met Hamida the other evening, she is in partial purdah and may be seen by her husband and other male members of his and her family. Ashok has two other wives who keep total purdah. Ours is a polygamous society."

"Then that means that Jai, that is Sir, I mean His Royal Highness could ....?" Betty hesitated.

"Yes my dear, that is exactly what it means. My son, like his cousin, is entitled to take several wives."

The words dropped into Helen's mind like stones into a deep well, falling for a long time, before making contact within the depths of her consciousness and then reverberating until she was almost deafened by the roaring in her ears. Noting her distress, the Rani suggested they sit in the gardens for a while, indicating to Betty that she wished to speak to Helen alone.

"My dear, there are many, many aspects of our culture which it will be difficult for you to accept. Romesh, Jai, as you call him is my son and whilst there will always be the bond which exists between mother and child, I am not blind to his faults. He has been brought up to rule this province. My husband is not a good man and my son at an early age indoctrinated with beliefs and codes of behaviour which I cannot condone. He was encouraged to discover his manhood here in the zenana at the age of fourteen and has never since felt the need to restrain those desires for any reason whatsoever."

Observing Helen's stricken expression the Rani steeled herself to continue.

"Forgive me, child, there are certain things I dare not disclose on pain of death and that is an expression I do not use lightly, but at least you should know that my son, like his tiger, is a predatory animal, used to getting exactly what he wants. Clearly and for obvious reasons, he has desired you greatly and is prepared to give you anything you wish just to have you here with him. Beyond that, I do not know what he plans."

"Highness - there are so many things I don't understand....If he desires me and has gone to such lengths to bring me here, why does he never speak of love?"

The Rani's smile showed her relief at knowing that here was a question to which she did have an answer.

"Sadly, my own opportunities to teach Romesh how to show and accept affection were denied me whilst he was still small. There is another factor however. Our culture does not readily encompass such declarations. We speak with admiration and respect of beauty and other qualities. We describe the wonder of love's fulfilment as it relates to nature and the elements, but of that which is closest to our hearts we do not easily speak."

112

As a downcast Helen left the zenana, the Rani brushed aside the attention of her serving girls and retired to her small boudoir. She was overwhelmed with misgivings. Had she said too much? Had she said enough? She was under no illusions that should Romesh be in any way suspicious of her conduct he could make life for her very difficult indeed.

How long before Helen found out about the Princess Mumtaz who still lived in purdah at her father's palace in the foothills of the Himalayas? She and Romesh had been married since he was sixteen. As Hindi tradition demanded Mumtaz had been married before the onset of menstruation. Just twelve years old and, as she herself had been, of small physique, consummation of her marriage and the first pregnancy had occurred before her bones had set and strengthened. The resultant miscarriages had been of little surprise to the women of both families.   Only their menfolk seemed oblivious to the fact that these disappointments were the direct outcome of their own lusting after younger and younger females. Jai now spent one month at his wife's home each year hunting and fishing with her father and brothers and enjoying his marital rights. Perhaps 'enjoying' was not quite the right word, she thought wryly. Of that marriage, to his annoyance, there had been as yet no progeny. A succession of miscarriages had ensured that the Princess had speedily lost favour and the likelihood of the union producing a successor was becoming increasingly remote.

How long too, before Helen found out about Metta and the small boy who lived right here in the zenana? Her own instructions had been to keep them out of sight until after the wedding. Metta was already sullen at the restrictions placed upon her. Soon, very soon, Helen would know of their existence.

What were her son's intentions for this naive young girl? In Helen's own eyes and in British law they were man and wife. If she should learn of the Princess Mumtaz prior to her wedding would she head for home as quickly as possible and, more importantly, would Romesh allow her to do so? His loss of face amongst the Rajput and the British Raj if such news became public would be considerable. It was incredible that none of the former had seen fit to inform the British Foreign Office that he already had a wife, with such information the wedding in England would never have take place. Clearly the Rajput's resentment at being questioned about one of their peers had resulted in a closing of ranks on this issue.

That Romesh indulged in deviant sexual behaviour the Rani was in no doubt. On his father's instructions, women of all ages, men and boys had been brought to him since puberty. Just what demands he would make on the inexperienced Helen, she shuddered to think. Her own experiences at the hands of her cruel, depraved husband were buried deep in the recesses of her mind.

Other questions were taxing her sorely. The girl had not mentioned conversion at any time. How did Romesh propose getting her through the wedding ceremony? And, a further hurdle. It was accepted that Romesh was a law unto himself, that he would soon be ruler of Jaishalpar and rulers were above caste. Nevertheless, some of his contemporaries would still believe that Helen, a foreigner, was 'untouchable'. Yet to keep her in purdah would deny him the opportunity of displaying his prize....If only she could read the mind of her devious and unpredictable son, then, forewarned, she could attempt to assist Helen in some way. Only her gods could help her now. Wearily she left the boudoir and entered her prayer room.

After a troubled night Helen had made a number of decisions. Using Betty as a sounding board, she had decided that it was indeed the fault of both Jai's upbringing and his culture which had left him unable to express his love and offer her terms of endearment. Hopefully, as she told him of her own feelings, he would learn to respond in the same vein. What she felt for him must surely be love? In his absence she longed to be with him. In his presence she longed that he should hold her closely; longed for the physical contact about which she had read, yet never experienced. Always she clung to the thought reiterated by the Rani, that he must have desired her a great deal to have married her and brought her several thousand miles to his homeland.

That Jai was already sexually experienced did not disturb her as much as the Rani had feared. Men were after all always expected to 'sow their wild oats' and one inexperienced partner in the marital bed was probably sufficient! That he could, if he so wished, take other wives was something she could never have anticipated. But, in their naivety, she and Betty decided that once married to Helen this would never be a consideration. Helen would ensure that Jai was kept blissfully happy. Together, in this fabulous palace, they would produce a succession of princes and princesses to ensure the continuation of the Jaishalpar dynasty.

In the small hours of the morning she dreamed of standing before Prinny who was pointing to a blackboard on which were the words 'Cause' and 'Effect'. Over and over again came Prinny's voice saying "But Helen, have you really thought the problem through? Have you considered it from every angle?"

The next morning, having decided that all the problems presented on the previous day could be resolved, the girls set out on a further exploration of their surroundings.

Entering one corridor they came across a niche in which was seated, cross-legged, a negro. The lower half of his body was wrapped in a white dhoti, whilst his naked torso was draped with row upon row of magnificent pearls. The girls stopped, awestruck, at this bizarre sight. Chuckling, the negro touched the pearls, inclined his head and "You.. Highness". Moving away down the vaulted marble corridor, chattering animatedly about this latest discovery, they were brought to a standstill again, by the sound of raised voices.

One piece of knowledge Helen had acquired during her brief stay in India was that here voices were never raised. Everyone wore an air of langour and signals of approval or displeasure were noted without comment.

Displeasure was however, now being expressed volubly by two people speaking in rapid Hindustani. Helen and Betty had recognised the voices as those of Jai and the Rani before the couple came into sight. Immediately Jai turned and walked away from them, whilst the Rani clearly distressed, waited for them to join her. In an attempt to cover their embarrassment at stumbling on a family quarrel, the girls started to ask about the negro wearing the pearls.

Gradually the Rani's hands, which had been fluttering like two small brown birds, settled against the deep blue of her sari.

"Ah, the pearls... .They are my wedding gift to you, dear Helen." Betty gasped loudly, then coughed to cover her confusion. "All Hindi brides," here the Rani hesitated looking distressed, "all Hindi brides wear pearls. The man from your London jewellers, Aspreys, is already here. Tomorrow we will arrange a fitting, so that the collar is adjusted to the correct size for you."

Helen stammered her thanks and asked the question which had plagued the girls since they first saw the negro. "Why is the black man wearing them? There must be a reason..."

"The best reason in the world Helen. His skin is like velvet, its texture adds lustre to the pearls and they improve with being worn. When they are yours, see that Sharma wears them several times a week and they will retain their beauty."

The Rani, now sufficiently recovered from her altercation with her son noted that Helen showed no signs of strain this morning. Clearly she had decided to accept her situation and go ahead with Jai's plans.

"This afternoon you are to be presented to the Maharajah. Please be ready at three. Tomorrow at ten the pearls will be fitted and then may I suggest that you - and Miss Carter - Betty, stay with me to discuss the order of Thursday's ceremony."

The great bed of the Maharajah resembled too closely a catafalque, Helen decided. On its raised platform, with a guard at each corner, it was an awe-inspiring sight. behind the ruler stood his chattri-bearer, holding over his sovereign's head the royal canopy, as he would bear his ruler's standard in times of war. And at the far end of the room below an oriel window, the throne of the Rajput rulers, its cushion covered in crimson brocade. Incense burned in smoking silver urns, mingling with the perfume of flowers and spices. But no fragrance however pungent could mask the over-riding odour of approaching death. It was obvious that this was to be a token visit. Any communication with the Head of State, clearly under total sedation, being out of the question.

Leaving his father's cheerless quarters, Jai was all charm. With enthusiasm he showed Helen the pilkhanna, the huge stables where the elephants were housed. He laughed and shared Helen's delight when at his suggestion she gave an elephant the command 'Beht' and watched him lumberingly sit down. Her spirits lightened even more when they next visited the tennis courts and Jai suggested she and Betty might like to have lessons from the resident professional coach.

"A tennis coach, here in an Indian palace?"

"My dear Helen, you must rid yourself of the British notion that we are all savages out here! We have been playing tennis for many years and do not forget that in addition to our family members we have a very large staff here, the Sirdar's, their families, our administration staff, senior military personnel - I do assure you the coach is kept well occupied. I thought perhaps you and Miss Carter might enjoy the experience."

"Oh Jai, we'd love it. In England it might be considered quite daring, but here, it will be so private and such fun. There is one thing I don't understand..."

"Yes?"

"You often mention other people who seem to be in the palace for long periods of time. If that is so, why do I never see them?"

"My dear Helen, of necessity their quarters are far removed from your own, besides which it would not be considered seemly for you to meet, except for specific meetings such as we have discussed. Your status here demands that you remain aloof at all times."

Later in her room, Helen pondered over his comments. Was he really saying that her world was to be limited to contact with himself, Betty, the Rani, Ashok, the ladies of the zenana and her personal attendants?   No, that couldn't be what he had meant. Hadn't she been told previously that there would be a considerable amount of entertaining and being entertained? That entire wardrobe of English clothes he had bought her. What would have been the point if she was never to meet anyone, go anywhere? It was all puzzling. Something else she needed to discuss at length with Betty.

Betty's Journal.

Tuesday

I never ever dreamed that people could live like this anywhere in the world. I've just discovered that there are twenty gardeners here, that the tennis coach has an assistant and twelve ball boys, two men are employed just to look after guns and no fewer than ten men spend all their days sweeping the drives and pathways. Each of the sixty elephants has his own mahout who lives with his wife (or wives if he can afford it!) in a compound close to the pilkhanna.

Living in this palace is almost like being on another planet. There is no news of the outside world and why do I have the feeling when I'm dining with the Sirdars that even if something important was happening in England or anywhere else they would be reluctant to tell me?

Three days ago Helen donned a sari for the first time and has been wearing one ever since! Ila showed us how to wrap the length of lime-green chiffon (about eight yards long) around Helen's waist to form a skirt with a pleat at the front. It was then crossed over the bodice. The final effect was stunning. Helen insisted that I try one too and I chose a fine cotton in terra-cotta bordered with cream. It looked and felt delightful. They are so much cooler and more comfortable than our English garments. The Rani has promised me a dozen saris and Helen says I must keep the one I first tried.

N.B. Have just realised that this will mean I own thirteen - a good thing I'm not superstitious!

Helen has now received her instructions for Thursday.

At ten she goes to the zenana where she will be bathed with perfumed oils, make-up applied, hair dressed in a smooth chignon and robed in her wedding garments. First a blouse of gold and a half-slip of red chiffon. Then the wedding sari of red (for good fortune) Benares silk shot with gold. Her collar of fabulous pearls goes on next. It consists of ten strands, the longest reaching to waist level. The clasp itself is worth a fortune. Two rose-shaped clusters of diamonds, each about one and a half inches in diameter are clipped together so that, as the man from Asprey's explained, they are very secure and the weight of the collar is evenly spread. Even so, they are in total quite heavy. I tried them on yesterday. Sensational!

After the robing, ivory bangles will be added - (all Rajputana brides must wear these) then Ashok's gift of diamond and pearl earrings. The final touch is a garland of flowers so that on meeting Sir they can exchange these as a symbol of their devotion.

Her gift from the Maharajah has already arrived, obviously selected by the Rani. It is a parure of emeralds with matching bracelet and huge drop earrings. This, with her engagement and wedding rings complete the set. They are quite breath-taking! The Rani suggested that she should never wear these with shades of green, but, from experience, rose pink was a good background for displaying the real beauty of the stones. One problem I rarely encounter is which jewels to wear with which outfit! At this rate Helen will soon have sets of precious stones for every day of the week.

She seems completely bemused by what is happening to her. Jai's changeable attitude is so confusing, but she seems resigned to being already married to him and making the best of things.

Back to the wedding arrangements - once she is dressed and the signal is received to proceed, Helen will be carried in a silver palanquin by male relatives of Sir to one of the small durbar rooms. Here will be assembled only the priests, male members of the family, the Rani of course and the Rani's senior female attendant. The couple will sit under a silver wedding pavilion and the ceremony performed. The Rani has said Helen must only move as directed and should incline her head when the Rani indicates, keeping her eyes, above the face veil, downcast at all times. (I couldn't help wondering how on earth she would see the signal with her eyes glued to the floor, but no doubt someone could always give her a nudge!) Following the service a silver thal (tray) of food will be brought for the couple to share. Helen's first task is to take food with her fingers and offer the first mouthful to her husband. He then offers food to her.

From there the couple will be carried, this time in gold palanquins, to the large durbar room where Princes from other states and several hundred guests, including Yours Truly, will be assembled. They'll all bring gifts of course, as if there were not enough amazing objects here already.

117

N.B. Why does the Rani seem so ill at ease? It's obvious that she is already fond of Helen, so that's not the problem. Perhaps, as hostess, she will just be relieved when Thursday is over?

St. Hilda's College, Oxford

Helen Darling,

I do so hope this reaches you before your wedding day - Indian style. I shall be thinking of you and I know Prinny and everyone at Craybourne will be doing so.

I am loving it here. Everyone seems so enthusiastic about their subjects (and has plenty to say about other people's!) and the city is quite beautiful.

James is so very kind. He wrote to me the other day, enclosing two five pound notes for 'running costs'. I gather he now sees Wiggie very often. She and Daphne chained themselves to some railings outside No. 10 a few weeks ago and were jailed for several hours. More recently Daphne cut her leg badly in a scuffle with the police at Westminster. In spite of all this, James implies that they both become more disenchanted with the Pankhurst regime as time progresses. Daphne is fortunate to have two such level-headed people around to ensure she does nothing foolish.

Since leaving Craybourne, I have become more aware of how easy it would be to unwittingly make some dreadful mistake. Don't be alarmed I'm not planning anarchy or anything of that nature, just growing up sufficiently to be aware that there are very devious people around and life is full of pitfalls.

My regards to Jai and to Betty. Our letters obviously constantly cross. Jai's 'stately home' sounds absolutely fantastic and I can't believe you had to go to India to get tennis lessons! I long for pictures of you in your beautiful saris - is that going to be possible?.

Love always dearest Helen,

Be happy,

Rosa

***

Helen stirred and opened her eyes. So much had happened in her short life. Grievous things and latterly, wickedness she had not dreamed existed. If Rosa's last letter from Oxford was anything to go by, even there she too had become aware that life was not all sweetness and light. A far cry from their rarefied existence at Orchard Cottage.

On the credit side they had good friends. Yet, the prospect of meeting those friends again, now that they were aware of her own humiliation, was overwhelming. What a stupid romantic fool they must think her and they were so right. But this was not the time to falter. With Betty's help and Walter's strong right arm she would get through the next few hours. As the huge funnel blasted its warning of their approach, Helen rose from her deckchair and moved towards the ship's rails.

Chapter Seventeen

As the 'Pride of the Orient' docked at Tilbury, the small welcoming party scanned the faces of the passengers, eagerly searching for Helen and Betty. When Helen, escorted by Walter, at last came down the gangway, James, Rosa, Daphne and Wiggie each reacted in their own way to her changed appearance. James embraced her awkwardly, as if fearful that her fragility would break under pressure. Rosa and Daphne, both usually so vociferous, were too overcome for words and it was left to Wiggie to bridge the silence by enquiring about the journey, Helen's health etc.

Daphne, shocked beyond belief, could hardly conceal her feelings. What had happened to the happy, glowing girl who had left England a few short months ago? The sea voyage's duration had done little to remove the unnatural pallor. Her figure was alarmingly slim and, worst of all, her beautiful eyes seemed slightly unfocussed, as if still so clouded by pain and horror that everyday images were no longer sharply defined. By contrast, the little Cockney had blossomed and was now amazingly handsome! Overweight before, she was now quite svelte, glowed with good health and had developed an air of authority which clearly was effective. Certainly those around her were most attentive as she gave rapid instructions regarding the disposition of the luggage.

Hovering at Helen's elbow was Walter. A Walter who, whilst registering a blend of embarrassment and delight at the warmth of Rosa's greeting was totally at ease meeting James and Daphne again and greeting Muriel Wigmore for the first time.

Inexplicably Daphne felt a wave of pride. Walter's relaxed demeanour underlined for her all that the Suffragist movement was attempting to achieve. A few short years ago Walter had been a farm boy with little or no prospects, but rebelling against such stagnation, he had joined the Army, learned from his experiences and was now a man of the world, well-travelled and able to hold his head high in any company If only the Suffragettes could show the women they represented that only when they had the vote and could be seen to be thinking individuals with minds of their own would they earn the respect of men which they so richly deserved.

Behind Walter was another man in uniform, a Sergeant Wilson. A large thick-set man with smiling eyes, he clutched Helen and Betty's dressing cases as if they contained the crown jewels and he'd fight to the death anyone who attempted to take them from him! It did not escape Daphne's notice that his eyes followed Betty's movements appreciatively, nor the fact that before she was completely swamped by her own family, they had made some arrangement to meet again.

Speedily, James's party were settled in waiting cars and as they left the docks the figures of Walter and his Sergeant quickly disappeared from view amidst thronging crowds and waiting vehicles.

Prinny, thought Daphne, would see that as symbolic, the conclusion of something-or-other, but I wonder...?

For a week Helen was cared for and cossetted at Eynsford House. The instructions left by Lady Eynsford, currently visiting Sydney with her brother, had been that everything must be done to ensure Helen's comfort. In fact, no such instruction was necessary. Always popular with the staff, they had followed Helen's elevation in the world of haute couture with enthusiasm and gasped with delight at the press reports of her wedding to an Indian prince. This was the stuff fairy-tales were made of! Now her frail appearance and the obvious signs of stress resulted in a closing of their protective ranks in an endeavour to make her well again.

James's physician advised a week of total rest, a diet which included plenty of fish and red meat and at least two glasses of port daily. All business commitments were to be delayed until Helen was looking and feeling much better. Once he was satisfied with her progress a sojourn in the country was recommended and here he added, smilingly, that the air in Yorkshire was very bracing at this time of the year!

Helen's jewellery and Betty's precious stones had been lodged with Asprey's for valuation, together with the 30 tiny gold ingots stitched into their funeral cloaks. It was agreed that a representative from Asprey's be asked to call on the girls one week hence. James was to investigate Helen's legal position with regard to the marriage contract and to make the strongest possible representations to the Foreign Office with regard to the behaviour of Prince Romesh. From now on all his activities would be closely monitored and such information known to the Army in his locality would also be studied.

Having carried out the Doctor's instructions to the letter, to the delight of Cook and the rest of the staff, Helen was once more greeting them with the ready smile they remembered and had lost her look of total exhaustion. Throughout the week Rosa, undeterred by her sister's long silences, attempted to entertain Helen with anecdotes about her tutors and fellow students at Oxford. The first occasion when Helen's chuckles bubbled into unrestrained laughter marked for Rosa the turning point in her road to recovery.

Now Helen was able to reciprocate with stories of the opulence which surrounded the Jaishalpar Palace and its occupants. Rosa had seen the jewels which had been taken to Asprey's. They were amazing! That huge diamond and those magnificent pearls - at least Helen wouldn't be walking away from all this heart-break empty-handed. That Helen shied away from more personal details about what had happened did not disturb Rosa. She herself felt guilty that she should have been so easily taken in by Jai, had so readily succumbed to his charm. Rosa had been told that the marriage had broken down irrevocably, that a sham 'marriage' had taken place abroad and that Helen had had a miscarriage. The scale of Helen's betrayal was so enormous that her reluctance to talk about it was understandable. Rosa had little doubt that her sister would provide other details as and when she felt ready to do so.

By the time Rosa returned to Oxford they were able to exchange light-hearted admonishments.

"Take care of yourself. Plenty of fresh air when you get to Craybourne and it will be very, very fresh. Remember you haven't been used to that for a long time."

"Study hard, but not too hard - I don't want you to return to Craybourne looking like a wraith."

"Look who's talking!"

"Rosa, be serious. We're no longer short of money. Make sure you get plenty of good food and oh, just enjoy yourself!"

Before Helen had time to miss Rosa's exuberant presence, Betty arrived. Removing her beige duster coat to reveal a smart amber-coloured day dress, she laughingly explained that these were part of Aston's ready-to-wear collection.

"But I have been to the Salon and told Mr. Aston that we'll both be needing clothes having left our wardrobes in India. He wanted to give me a job on the spot but I declined. Naturally I didn't go into details, just told him you hadn't been too well and we were going to Yorkshire to get the roses back in your cheeks."

"I wondered who had told Neville I was here. Look!" Taking Betty's arm, Helen led her into a small sitting room filled with flowers. Pointing to a huge vase filled with a striking combination of red and pink carnations she said, "Those arrived from him this morning - aren't they beautiful? And typically eye-catching!"

Laughingly Betty agreed, then, uncharacteristically serious, said "There is one thing Helen... about Neville. I felt there was something not quite right."

"What on earth do you mean?"

"Well, it wasn't what he said, so much as his appearance. You know as well as I do that Neville is absolutely fastidious about that... suit, cravat, hair, always have to be just so."

"And?"

"All I can say is, he didn't look his usual immaculate self. I did wonder if this going into the ready-to-wear industry hadn't worked out quite as he'd hoped."

"He probably just had a bad night and had to rush this morning. I'ms ure he'll be coming to see me as as he can manage it and I hope we can arrange for you to be here too, so we can make a dual assessment. You know the saying 'two heads are better than one.'"

"I'll go along with that, and still on the subject of appearances it's good to see you looking so much better. Perhaps now we can get down to making plans. The thought of all these precious stones is beginning to keep me awake at nights." Without more ado they made a number of decisions.

When the man from Asprey's called the following day he was to be given instructions for altering the pearl necklace. Two strands of a good length were to be retained and a new clasp fitted. The two longest strands were to be used to form a choker necklace and matching bracelet, splitting the rose-diamond clasps to form fastenings for the two items. One rope of pearls was to be made up as a necklace for Betty. The suite of emeralds was to remain intact and stored at the Bank. Asprey's were to be asked to find buyers for the huge diamond and for the bulk of Betty's stones. One sapphire from the latter was to be cut to form a pendant and matching ring.

There were no problems pertaining to the alterations. Mr. Collins' suggestion that the five remaining pearl ropes be sold was met with a polite but firm refusal. This precious gift from the Rani was on no account to be sold. Conversely, nothing given to her by Jai was to be retained. Together with the ingots, Asprey's estimated that Helen's items were worth approximately three hundred thousand pounds. Betty's stones and her ingots were valued at between fifty and sixty thousand pounds. By the time Mr. Collins left them, the girls were reeling under the impact of the wealth now theirs.

James escorted them to the Bank the next day and, at the girls' request, remained present during discussions with the Manager. A pink man with a prominently displayed gold hunter, he became progressively pinker as more details of the jewels held by Asprey's were placed before him. From the sale of the ingots each girl had ten thousand pounds, placed immediately in her account. The set of emeralds was duly placed in the Bank's vaults, together with the remaining ropes of pearls. On the departure of Lord Craybourne and the two young ladies, the Manager, quite overcome by the morning's excitement, sent for his Deputy and eschewing the decanter of sherry at his elbow, requested a large glass of whisky.

Another week elapsed before Helen and Betty were ready to leave for Yorkshire - a week in which they both commissioned clothes from Aston's and bought from his other range. Amongst the purchases Mrs.Endicott had made for Helen was an unusual bolt of rose coloured silk, shot here and there with threads of silver grey and emerald. Neville, asked to create an evening dress from this, enthused endlessly over the material's unusual design. "With materials such as this at my disposal, I could win back some of the business which seems to be slipping away."

"All that's needed is a trip to the market in Bombay," Helen joked, then seeing his serious expression, asked if business was really so bad as he implied.

"I probably cut my own throat, by moving into the 'off-the-peg' business. The haute couture trade seems to be drying up and people with bigger organisations than mine have now moved in and can handle the big stores' everyday trade more efficiently. But I mustn't bore you with my petty worries. Compared to the problems building up in Europe they pale into insignificance."

Helen, cocooned in Jaishalpar, within a regime which had been deliberately non-communicative about world affairs, expressed rather shame-facedly her ignorance of recent events.

"An attempt was made here in London earlier this year to resolve the problems in the Balkans. Sadly, it looks as if it was to no avail. There's still tremendous unrest out there and I'm afraid all the signs are that war is inevitable."

This conversation, more than any other, at last galvanised Helen into action to remedy her lack of knowledge. She started to read avidly the daily newspapers and to ask questions of all and sundry.

From Daphne and Wiggie she learned that the promise made by the Liberals to complete the passing of a Conciliation Bill aimed at giving the vote to a number of wealthy women was still unfulfilled. Daphne and Wiggie declared themselves totally against legislation of this sort, believing it to be against the aims of their association. Whilst accepting their campaign must be kept at the forefront of public attention, they deplored the latest arson campaign, in which letters in pillar boxes were set alight, empty buildings burned and monuments attacked. Clearly disenchanted with the W.S.P.U. leadership they too were more concerned with the problems building up in Europe than home-grown affairs.

There was one brief visit from Walter, who explained that he was unable to leave for Yorkshire as planned. All officers returning from duties overseas were being given crash courses in modern warfare. Many, like Walter, had been operating in different climatic conditions and it was now essential that they be prepared for fighting in a variety of different terrains and temperatures. Additionally, they were being taught to drive and service vehicles, it being recognised that horses would play only a minimal role in any ensuing warfare.

Walter's air of strain they attributed to the fact that his holiday had been delayed and he had much to think about. The latter was certainly true! He was torn by a welter of conflicting emotions and doubts. Some years ago, as a lovesick youth, he had deliberately removed himself from Helen's company, knowing that her education was rapidly creating between them an unassailable barrier. To have found her again at a time when experience and travel had broadened his own horizons and education, was an unbelievable stroke of good fortune. Once again she had needed his strength, had turned to him for advice. Now two other barriers had surfaced. The knowledge of Helen's wealth had been the first body-blow, the second that he might be sent overseas again, this time into the thick of battle, each in itself sufficient reason for him to abandon any notion of ever telling her how much he cared. As he returned to the Barracks, the fat black clouds looming overhead seemed to symbolise a future which was gloomy and unpredictable.

For the fifteenth time in half an hour, Prinny stirred the fire. As it sputtered and burst into flames, she moved to the window, straightening one curtain, then moving another to see if the car was in sight. Nervously she touched the brooch at her throat. Was wearing it a mistake? With fingers stiffened by arthritis, she traced the cameo's relief, a sensation which always afforded her pleasure. It was nonsense to think in those terms. They couldn't after all, remove all traces of Jai's existence from their lives.

Still holding the curtain, she sat on the window seat. Seven short months ago she and Rosa had waited for another car, a car bringing the man who was to wreak such havoc in their lives. If only she had had the courage to speak out then. To tell the girls that she suspected their hero to be both insensitive and self-centred. Elizabeth Craybourne had also admitted to a feeling of unease in Jai's presence, but neither she nor James had experienced her own sense of revulsion. She smiled wryly. Perhaps even surrogate mothers have instincts when their young are threatened! In any event, she had said nothing and Helen had been brutally damaged by the association.

How would Helen now look and behave? Would the loss of her naivety have changed her personality? Hitherto Helen's greatest charm had been the air of innocence which seemed at odds with her elegant sophistication. But now.... Prinny's eyelids drooped as she succumbed to the soothing murmur from the glowing grate and the warmth of the cosy room.

The westering sun was setting as Simmonds, the Craybourne chauffeur, brought the car to a standstill. On the instant that Helen stepped from the car a sword of sunlight sliced between the hills enclosing the valley, the Manor and its environs in a golden caul. Temporarily blinded, Helen paused and instantly the remembered scent of the aromatic herb garden enveloped her. She was home. Helen rushed forward and as Prinny's angular figure wrapped its loving arms around her, together they wept.

The ensuing days were of total relaxation. Prinny had never made demands on her relationships with Helen and Rosa and made none now. The girls breakfasted late, gathered bluebells from Walter's secret copse and strolled in the Manor House gardens. They took tea with Elizabeth, James and Muriel Wigmore, who had accompanied them from London. Helen was saddened to note the further deterioration in Elizabeth's condition. The trembling had now spread to the other arm and on occasions she seemed slightly confused as if some part of the conversation had escaped her. By contrast, the rapport which now existed between James and Muriel was a pleasure to witness. Quiet and diffident by nature, James blossomed daily in the warmth of Muriel's gentle teasing.

"I want to show you Yorkshire, my Yorkshire," Helen announced one morning.

"Obviously, we are feeling much improved." Betty smiled at Prinny.

"Yes I am," Helen answered.

"The weather seems settled and I'm going to show you Ilkley and the moors and York Minster - and we must have tea at Betty's in Harrogate".

"Now that sounds like several places, not necessarily too close together. How do we get there?"

"Goodness, you're right, it could be quite complicated. We'd better get out the time-tables."

Betty giggled and Helen looked at her suspiciously, "What have I said? What is so funny?"

"It isn't you particularly, it's us. We've got all this money and could probably buy half a dozen motor cars and we're talking about buses and trains."

"You're right again. We'll buy a car and learn to drive."

"What, just like that?" Betty had stopped laughing.

"Yes, just like that".

There had been a car at Craybourne for some two years, James having found it more convenient to keep one vehicle in London and one in Yorkshire, travelling between the two by rail. Simmonds was on hand to drive Elizabeth as necessary but it was agreed from the start that as such outings would be infrequent he should carry out other duties in and around the Manor.

James made several suggestions when Helen first broached the subject of cars to him. First, that Simmonds would be available for much of the time to take Helen and Betty on their sight-seeing outings, secondly, that he and Simmonds would undertake to teach the young ladies to drive, in this Muriel insisted on being included, and last of all that he and Simmonds would be happy to advise them on their choice of car. In this way, as James pointed out, once he and Muriel had returned to London, Helen and Betty would be able to continue their lessons and gain confidence in the quieter environs of Craybourne. Without more ado the first outing to Ilkley and the moors was arranged together with another visit to Leeds, accompanied by James and Muriel, with the express intention of looking at cars.

There were moments when Betty, her perceptions heightened to a high degree of sensitivity during the events of the past months, would sense a need on the part of Helen or Prinny to talk. At such times Betty would be seized by a sudden urge to 'stroll to the village' or 'walk over to the farm', leaving them in private. On one such occasion Prinny embarked on a subject she felt could no longer wait.

"James and I have often discussed Elizabeth's health. We are both realistic and know that there has been and will continue to be a steady deterioration. We have agreed that when it becomes necessary I shall move into the Manor. Elizabeth still has her personal maid, Johnson, but there is a limit to what her duties encompass or indeed to what she or Elizabeth would wish included. I already assist Elizabeth with correspondence and, sadly, she will soon need her food cutting at mealtimes and assistance with her bath. These are the services I shall be happy to give to an old friend but to do this properly I must be under the same roof. What I am trying to say, dear Helen, is that I feel the time has now come for me to make such a move. I hope you will not feel I am abandoning you so soon after your return in such unhappy circumstances. Had your friend not been here I should have felt even more guilty, but at least I know now that you will not be alone. It goes without saying that you and Betty are to stay here just as long as you wish. This is your home. And Rosa's home too of course. If, for any reason, you should not be here during her vacations, then she is to stay at the Manor with Elizabeth and me."

"You've thought of everything Prinny, as if I would ever feel you'd abandoned me. Of course I - we - must help Elizabeth in any way we can. She and James have done so much for me - for all of us. Just so long as you feel up to this, after all you're not a spring chicken any more!"

"My dear, I shall be living in the lap of luxury with a staff in attendance and friends around me, which is a great deal more than the majority of single ladies in their declining years could ever hope for."

"Single you may be but you do have a family of your own, Rosa and me, and I'm sure James and Daphne regard themselves as some sort of nephew and niece, not to mention your other young friends Walter and Michael Featherstone. You are not and never will be alone and don't forget please that I now have money, lots of money.

"If there's anything and I do mean anything you need at any time, you're to let me know. Promise you'll do that."

"Thank you my dear. Of course I would let you know, I promise. Now let's be practical. Would you like me to arrange for someone to come in each day to clean the cottage and prepare a meal? Neither you nor Betty seem very expert in the kitchen - I'd hate you to starve!"

And so it was settled. Two weeks after Helen and Betty arrived at Orchard Cottage, Simmonds, assisted by a boy from the farm, carried Prinny's clothes and her most cherished personal possessions over to the Manor and the girls were once again on their own.

All traces of apathy vanished, Helen now eagerly joined Betty in discussing over and over again plans for the future and how to utilize their 'fortunes'. They would build a hotel in Leeds and turn it into the equivalent of London's Dorchester. They would build a factory with a model village for its work-force as the Quakers had done in the Midlands. They would buy cinemas and show only Mary Pickford films! As the suggestions became more and more ridiculous they invariably collapsed into giggles. Always, they came back to the same fact, that it was useless to tackle something of which they had no knowledge whatsoever and always they were forced to recognise that the one field in which they were most conversant was that of clothing and fabrics, their decoration and accessories. Perhaps they should go back to London and talk to Neville Aston, he might have some ideas. But they were in holiday mood and the thought of leaving the pleasures of Craybourne for the heat and grime of the city was not a tempting one. After all, as they repeatedly reassured each other, Helen needed to convalesce. Happily they drifted from day to day, the hours punctuated only by driving lessons.

Eddy Wilson's letter brought them down to earth. Walter's Sergeant friend had written in a manner totally at variance with his downright character. Having enjoyed Betty's company on the journey home, he said he would welcome meeting her again, but realised she probably had many calls upon her time, etc.,etc., and would understand if this should not be possible. Betty was nonplussed by the diffident tone of the letter.

"I don't understand him, Helen. We really got on well on the boat, but that meeting in London was not a success. He seemed ill-at-ease all the time, as if he was choosing his words carefully and sometimes wondering what on earth to say next."

"Perhaps..." Helen hesitated.

"Well, go on, perhaps what?"

"It might be the money..."

"The money..what money?"

"Yours, you idiot - THE MONEY! He's bound to know by now that you have a sizeable fortune. Perhaps he feels you'll be looking for a partner in a different set."

"I never heard such rubbish. I'm surprised you should even think of it. As if money makes any difference to feelings. Well, if that is the trouble and I'm certainly not convinced that it is, what should I do?"

"I'm the last person in the world you should be asking for advice! It all depends on how you feel about him. Do you want to get to know him better?"

"Yes I do. He's extraordinarily sensitive which is amazing for an army man. I like that. And don't forget that with four brothers I have some ready-made samples to measure him against. If I don't get to know him better, I'll always wonder if he was Mr. Right, the one with whom I should have been happy to trip up the 'apples and pears.'"

"Finding Mr. Right seems to be fraught with all sorts of hidden hazards," Helen interjected caustically.

"Well naturally, you would feel that and who could blame you? But for every Jai in the world there must be several hundreds of decent fellows prepared to be eternally loyal and to love his wife 'until death do them part.'"

"You're right, which is getting be an annoying habit of yours. Invite him up here for a weekend by all means, but I think it would be better if he stayed at the Craybourne Arms don't you?"

"Of course. Wouldn't have considered anything else. After all I'd hate to offend Lady Elizabeth and Prinny's sensibilities and have him staying here unchaperoned!"

"What does he do in the Army, Betty? I don't think you ever told me."

"I probably did, but if you were still in the glooms, you didn't register. First and foremost he's a soldier, a cavalryman. But, like Walter, he was brought up on a farm, in the Newbury area, where there are quite a few racing stables. Apparently he was always hanging around these as a young lad and picked up a great deal of helpful knowledge about horses. He's now recognised as a good judge of horseflesh and makes a lot of purchases for the Army. He obviously was involved in some scouting for Walter and I think on one occasion, actually with him in the field, which is how they come to be such firm friends. When shall I ask him to come?"

"Suggest the weekend after next. Oh, and ask if he's any news of Walter. It's about time he was allowed to start his holiday."

Eddy's acceptance was duly received and a room booked for him at the village inn. He sent no news of Walter and before they were able to welcome Eddy to Craybourne, Helen received another male visitor.

She recognised him immediately. Fifteen years rolled away as she watched him walking up the path to the front door of the cottage. The set of his shoulders, the slightly rolling gait were unchanged and when she opened the door and their eyes met, his were of that remembered periwinkle blue. As he raised his hat she saw there were changes - the goatee beard, the neatly shaped sideburns and the sheen of silver on the crisply curling black hair.

"Will you not ask me in, so that we can talk?" The Irish lilt was there still, but the voice deeper, the speech sharper, more defined than she remembered. Without speaking, she showed her father into the small sitting room.

"Perhaps I should have written first, but I thought you might not see me. Heard you'd had trouble of some sort - thought I might be able to see you right."

"If you've come about money .... there is none."

"I suppose in a way I have come about money." She turned away abruptly. "But certainly not for a hand-out from you or anyone else. May I sit down?" Without waiting for a reply, he moved to the window seat from whence she had seen his arrival.

"Let me put the record as straight as I can Helen. I was rotten to your mother and I'm ashamed of that. She was right to turn me out. Life's strange, but because of that, things started to come good for me. I did what she suggested, worked my passage to Canada. Out there, you know, they're not so concerned with who you are, if a chap's prepared to work hard he can do anything, go anywhere, make it right to the top. I worked and saved until I could afford a fishing boat of my own and then another, and another, until I had a whole fleet of them. Sold them lock stock and barrel for a tidy sum last Autumn and arrived in Liverpool in the Spring to go into partnership with a man I'd met in Canada. Reed his name is, owns a shipping line. Whilst I was waiting in one of the offices, I saw a small piece in one of the papers about your return home."

"How did you know it was me? It's been so long...."

"I know Canada's a long way away, but I did see English newspapers from time to time - the chaps bring them over on the boats and resell them. Everyone's glad to have news from home. I'd watched your progress and I knew that you were the Helena they were talking about. What happened out there? Did he knock you about..? You never know with coloureds."

"I'd rather not talk about it."

"I know you'll think it's easy for me to say this now Helen, but I was very sad to hear about Mary. If I'd known earlier, much earlier, I like to think it might have changed my attitude. At the time I was just a stupid youngster with no thought for anything but my own pleasures."

"Yes, it is easy to say that now. How did you find out about her death and why on earth didn't you come back to see if we were all right, Rosa and me? We were two small children on our own. They could have sent us to a workhouse..."

"Not quite on your own Helen. One of the lads from the village sent me a note, said his wife stood over him while he wrote it! The shipping company traced me. I knew the Craybournes would look after you. After all," a sharper note had crept into his voice, "it's traditional, isn't it, for the gentry to look after their workers and tenants, the widows and orphans, the frail and infirm? Her Ladyship never approved of me, so what happened couldn't have come as much of a surprise. Don't forget I was on the other side of the Atlantic and at that time didn't have two pennies to rub together, let alone the wherewithal to look after a family. I was told Miss Pringle was looking after you and Rosa here in this cottage. She seems," he grinned wryly, " to have done a first-rate job."

"Yes, she's been wonderful to us, like a mother..., ".she hesitated..."You probably know then that Rosa is at Oxford and you've obviously read about my problems."

"Sort of... no details. I know you became quite a star in the fashion world. I can't tell you how proud I felt when I saw pictures of you in the papers. Don't worry about this Indian marriage Helen, you're young enough to start again and, well this is why I said that in a way I had come about money, I want you to know that if there's a problem about finance, I'm really quite well-heeled now so I could always help out with that."

For the first time Helen smiled, "I don't know what to call you..."

He grinned back at her. "Let's not make it difficult. I answer to both Jim and Captain."

"Well..Captain, thank you for the offer, but Rosa and I really do have enough money for our needs. The Craybournes have been very kind to us. Some time I'll tell you about my marriage - but not today. Now, Prinny would never forgive me, I'm forgetting all those lovely manners she taught us. Shall we go into the kitchen and make a cup of tea?"

There Betty found them an hour later, laughing over Jim's anecdotes about his early fishing-boat days and his lack of expertise. He left them with invitations to visit him at the Liverpool offices of the newly established Reed and Calloway line, promising to keep in touch by letter. "Although my skill in that department doesn't quite measure up to my head for business ..."

Elizabeth and Prinny pursed their lips and were certainly not convinced that Jim Calloway really had made good and was now a responsible business man. Indeed, Helen herself still felt she would need some reassurance on that score. But, against all the odds, she had warmed to him. Yes, there was still 'a touch of the Blarney' about him, but she had believed him sincere and after those singularly humourless months in India had welcomed his masculine humour. Now, she could see where Rosa's bubbling vivacity had sprung from and why, all those years ago, her serious minded mother had fallen for Jim Calloway's youthful rakishness. As they watched his departure, Betty summed up both their feelings, "What a charmer!"

Chapter Eighteen

Helen was only mildly surprised to see that Eddy Wilson was accompanied by Walter. Whilst a rather edgy Betty offered Eddy her hand, Helen embraced Walter warmly, dark memories of what an earlier equally innocent gesture had evoked, pushed firmly to the recesses of her mind. Betty relinquished the heavy tea-tray with its large fruit cake, donated by the Manor kitchen, into Eddy's more capable hands and, once settled, they talked.

The young men were told of Prinny's move, but not of Jim Calloway's visit. Helen read extracts from the latest of Rosa's letters, extolling the virtues of a young man called Alex and expressing joy at being in such a beautiful city in the Spring and Summer and concluding that she was looking forward tremendously to being at Craybourne for the summer recess. It all oozed with Rosa's zest for life and echoed so vividly her exuberant mode of speech that from the superiority of their advanced years, the four of them laughed together.

The girls related their driving experiences and Walter and Eddy reciprocated, the two men expressing their admiration that the girls should be taking such an avant-garde step.

"We've decided not to go ahead and buy a motor car, as we'd planned." Helen was immediately aware that the remark was a mistake, reminding the men of the value of money and its purchasing power, something they were trying to forget.

"Why is that?" Walter attempted to sound casual.

"We haven't yet decided what we want to do, that is, what we're capable of doing. This will almost certainly affect where we live, so it seems silly to rush into anything. All we are sure of is that we're certainly not going to sit around doing nothing for the rest of our days."

"Seems sensible enough," Walter commented. Then, quite deliberately, and equally obviously, changed the subject.

He said he would be staying at Hislop's farm with the Dennisons and announced his intention of asking Simmonds if he could borrow the Manor carriage, now little used, so that the four of them might drive around the country lanes together.

"After so long in India, these English views seem like heaven to me and I've no intention of looking at them through clouds of petrol fumes."

They made plans for the following day, then Betty announced her intention of showing Eddy the short cut to the village and they left together.

Helen now gave Walter an account of her father's visit. Like Lady Craybourne and Prinny, Walter was reluctant to believe that this particular leopard had changed his spots, privately wondering if Helen had once again been sweet-talked by a man who just wanted something from her. He could not but agree though, that as her own finances had not been discussed, no harm could come from further meetings, but was adamant that should the Captain at any time try to borrow or beg money from her, she was to contact her solicitors at once and ensure that Jim Calloway could at no time get his hands on her fortune. On this somewhat sour note they parted. He, all too conscious of her financial vulnerability and how he too, would be seen as just another fortune hunter. She, wondering why the afternoon which had started so happily, should have ended so coolly.

"It's quite ridiculous that we haven't met before,"Helen said smilingly, "Betty and I have been here almost four weeks."

"For the first two of those weeks I was in Scotland and since then," Iain McNeal shrugged, "well, let's say, there's been plenty to occupy my time."

Elizabeth had invited the girls and Walter and Eddy to join Prinny and herself for dinner and at the same time, officially meet her new Estate Manager. He was a typical Scot, Helen decided, or rather her idea of a Scot. A slim six footer with dark brown hair and eyes almost as dark, his face in repose was very serious - the original 'dour Scot', she mused. She had to admit though that his slow smile was worth waiting for. His was not a token movement of the lips but a suffusion which encompassed the whole face.   "Even if only his eyes were visible, I would know when he smiled" Helen thought, "it's as if someone had switched on a light inside his head. Amazing!"

They were, Prinny decided, a small but elegant gathering. Elizabeth in her now favourite silver-grey, Helen stunning in rose-pink silk, delicately etched with silver leaves and Betty wearing a jewel-bright amber taffeta, ideal for her complexion. Walter and Eddy, not to be outdone, were resplendent in their dress uniforms and Iain wore with some panache the tartan kilt of his clan. Neither was she displeased with her own appearance. Her dress of deepest green had ruffles of cream lace at the wrists and neck, the latter reflecting light onto her face, now somewhat flushed from the responsibility of ensuring that everyone was being properly looked after.

More and more of Elizabeth's duties now devolved upon her and she realised somewhat guiltily that she was enjoying it! Whoever would have thought that she, a spinster with no prospects whatsoever would one day be running an establishment such as this? Now she started to relax, noting that Vickers was dispensing drinks with his usual expertise and the parlourmaid was diligent in presenting canapés at regular intervals. Vickers had been at Craybourne for some five years, replacing Haig who had first come to the house as a young man when Oliver was a youth.

Prinny had always admired Haig. Like so many in his position he had known everything that was happening at the Manor and she had often thought that if anyone was capable of writing the Craybourne family history, he would be the ideal person. But in all the years she had known him, she had never heard him repeat gossip or say anything detrimental to the family, and now, his lips still sealed, he was living in the village with his niece, enjoying his well-earned retirement.

She crossed the room to speak to Eddy. Only he still appeared slightly ill-at-ease although everyone present seemed to be aware of this and doing their utmost to make him feel welcome. Eddy would have been the first to admit to his own discomfort. It was all very well for Walter, he knew these people, but Eddy couldn't rid himself of the feeling that he had more in common with Vickers and the parlourmaid than withhis fellow guests. And yet, by all accounts, Iain McNeal was a gamekeeper's son, Helen was the daughter of a seamstress and a ne'er do well father, Prinny was a clergyman's daughter and his lovely Betty was an ordinary London girl with no pretensions whatsoever. Walter, he knew, was from a similar background to himself. Put like that, it did seem that out of the lot of them only Lady C. herself was really top drawer. And what a lovely lady she was, chatting happily to Walter as if he was a duke or something, instead of a lad who'd once been a farmhand on her estate.

What a couple of innocents they'd been when, he a private and Walter a sergeant, they first went out to India. Farm life had taught them both certain tracking skills and quickly they had acquired more. Soon they were in the same scouting party, one of a number which kept a discreet but watchful eye on possible sources of trouble in the Jaishalpar area and beyond, sometimes travelling as far as the foothills of the Himalayas. It had been on one such mission, when Prince Romesh himself was under surveillance, that they had learned of his marriage to the Princes Mumtaz.

Away from the Barracks for days at a time, they learned to work as a close-knit unit, knowing that their very lives were dependent upon each other's skills and watchfulness. The day which was fixed forever in Eddy's mind had started well. The pink flush of dawn was streaking the mountains when they emerged from the copse which had provided their shelter for the night. The early morning air with its freshening breeze was cool and they and their horses felt refreshed. They were first alerted by the steady beating of drums accompanied by a low rhythmic chanting. Quickly they returned to the shelter of the copse, each man dismounting and holding his horse's head to allay any signs of nervousness.

The funeral procession at last came into view, emerging segment by segment from its pall of dust. First, a makeshift pallette of string and straw bearing the body, wrapped in its red funeral cloth. Then came priests and musicians, closely followed by a roughly made palanquin. Behind this was a cluster of women and bringing up the rear were two bullock carts piled high with fuel - cow-dung cakes, dried and ready for burning. Surging around the whole were some seventy or eighty chanting, gesticulating men, all in a state of unnatural feverish excitement.

The procession moved parallel with the copse. Not until it was within fifty yards of the hidden watchers, were they able to discern the occupant of the palanquin. What had been hitherto a smudge of brilliance amidst the grey, was now defined as a small girl, bedecked in gold and silver tinsel, with cascades of brilliantly coloured necklaces and bracelets. She sat upright, her eyes wide and unseeing.

"Suttee!" Walter's smothered exclamation was followed by a string of expletives. "Looks as if they're all drugged to the hilt and they've filled that poor kid full of bhang as well."

Relentlessly the procession continued forward, skirting the copse and moving towards the forest's bulk.

"We'll attack now and get the girl away to a place of safety", the young subaltern floundered, "Or, perhaps..."

"With respect, Sir", Walter spoke rapidly but firmly, "at the moment there are too many of them milling around the girl and we don't yet know if any of them are armed. Once they reach their funeral point, they will be forced to split up to attend to their different tasks. The pyres will have to be built and the girl will have all her finery removed and be dressed in funeral clothes. She will not be placed on the second pyre until the first has been ignited and is well ablaze. With this strong breeze, we might just get some smoke cover, if she is prepared down-wind of the fire. If you're agreeable Sir, I suggest you take the other three and create a diversion by circling round and round the palanquin and the attendants. Wilson and I will go inside your circle and attempt to get the girl onto one of the horses. We should all wait at least ten seconds after the lighting of the first pyre to allow the smoke to drift."

And so it was done. Luck was with them and the palanquin was set down at the edge of the forest clearing. As the flames roared upwards, smoke oozed and billowed from the perimeter of the pyre, drifting steadily towards the area where the girl and her attendants now waited. Unheard by those closest to the pyre the sound of the horses was drowned by the roaring and crackling of the hungry flames and the frenzied chanting of the watchers. But at the rear, the crowd heard and started to fragment, moving towards the alien sounds. As Walter had surmised, the constant circling of the four riders had created its own swirl of dust, into the heart of which he and Eddy carved a swathe through bewildered handmaidens and dragged the girl to Eddy's horse.

Once re-mounted, Walter fired two shots over the heads of the men now struggling to unseat them, their hands clawing and tugging at the girl's bare legs. The press of men fell back for a precious moment, sufficient time for them to spur their horses forward and away in pursuit of the others.

It was then that their luck ran out. The subaltern's horse, well-trained to deal with all types of noise was struck on its hind quarters by a stone, and startled skittered to a standstill. A knife thrown with force and accuracy winged towards its now stationery target and struck the young man between the shoulder blades. He slumped forward onto his horse's neck, but in the seconds before he could slide to the ground, Walter had left his own mount and leapt onto the saddle behind the young officer.

Swiftly the horses galloped away from the melee of angry shouts, waving arms and wickedly glinting knives. The confusion and smoke and dust, the acrid smell of the fire in their nostrils, speeding their flight. They did not stop until several miles had been put between themselves and the angry mob. A mob deprived of its sacrifice to the gods, deprived of the stimulation of seeing the look in the eyes of a small girl change from passive acceptance to wide-awake terror as the first of the cruel flames reached her.

The knife had not touched Philip Jordan's heart, but the wound was deep and he had lost a great deal of blood. Quickly his condition and that of the girl was assessed. The wound was roughly packed with bandages in a crude attempt to staunch the flow of blood and then they turned to the girl. Still stupefied, she seemed completely unaware of her surroundings and, wrapped in her mashru, the ceremonial cloth of silk and cotton, was like a limp rag doll.

"They were obviously determined she wouldn't wake up too early and try to change her mind about suttee - that is if she ever agreed to it in the first place", Walter commented savagely, "at least it will make transporting her easier."

Walter's frightened riderless horse had followed them. He now instructed that with the exception of Eddy, who would continue to hold the girl, each horse would in turn carry the double load of one man and Philip Jordan, allowing one horse in rotation a period of rest.

It took them twenty four hours to reach the nearest medical assistance at Fort Lokhari, sixty miles from their own Barracks. Once recovered from her large dosage of bhang, the girl appeared well, but frightened. She told them that her name was Lakshmi and she was ten years old. She was the widow of Kumar Manjiah, a zemindar who had just died at the age of fifty three. It was exactly five months since her wedding day. Shock and revulsion reverberated around the fort as this information was passed from mouth to mouth and a home was quickly found for her with a family of Hindus, committed to the cause of removing all unsavoury practices from their religion.

The condition of Philip Jordan, for several days giving serious cause for concern, slowly started to improve. When debriefing finally took place, it was his deposition outlining the events which advised that Walter should receive a commendation for bravery in the field, he having been most at risk, both when placing the girl on Eddy's horse and again when dismounting to save his senior officer from falling from his mount, a fall which would have meant certain death at the hands of the enraged mob.

And so, "For enforcing British law in India, regarding the abolition of the practice of suttee and in so doing saving a life and for disregarding his own safety, thereby saving the life of a British officer, etc., etc...." Walter was awarded both a commendation for bravery and promotion to the rank of Second Lieutenant.

The chink of glasses aroused Eddy from his reverie and returned him to the reality of the Craybourne drawing room. No-one could have deserved promotion more than Walter. Funny though how these awards never seemed to mention the really clever part. Not panicking - deciding what should be done quickly and then putting it into action, there was the skill and that's where Walter always had the edge. I just hope if I'm ever in a nasty situation again that he's the bloke alongside me. Mind you, you'd never think to look at him now just what a cool customer he is. Glass in hand, smart as paint, he looks quite the socialite!

Oh Lord, I should be talking to someone! Here comes Prinny to read me the riot act. Now what would be a suitable topic of conversation?

At the other side of the room Helen had now learned that Iain's home was in the Kinross area, where his father was game-keeper on a large estate. He told her, somewhat reluctantly, that his parents had been disappointed when, after a year at Edinburgh reading Physics, he had left to learn how to run an estate, as Assistant Factor for the Earl of Cleish. Pre-empting her next question, he pointed out that whilst the Craybourne Manor estate in itself was not extensive, he was also responsible for the oversight of large tracts of land in and around Halifax and had embarked on a programme of building artisans' houses.

"There are large work-forces in the city Miss Calloway, and everyone needs somewhere to live. Initially, the Estate will let the houses, but if all this becomes too much to handle, then we'll sell to landlords who are happy to buy land and houses complete".

"You don't feel this may invite exploitation by unscrupulous landlords?"

"Of course that is always a possibility. The Estate itself could do just that - charge too much, allow houses to fall into disrepair. Only when there is legislation to protect tenants will they be safe from such malpractice."

Oh dear, Helen thought, whilst I agree entirely with what he's saying, I do wish he didn't have to sound quite so pompous about it all. Saved from further comment by Vickers' announcement that dinner was served, she took Walter's proffered arm and followed Elizabeth and Iain into the dining room.

The girls enjoyed the company of Walter and Eddy for the ensuing few days before Eddy returned to Newbury to spend time with his family. Immediately, Walter's visits became less and less frequent

"It's the money again," she told Betty, "I've got to talk to him".

The next time Walter made a courtesy call, Betty hastily made her excuses and Helen faced Walter across the kitchen table.

"There are things we need to say to each other," she started.

"Oh yes... there are hundreds of things I'd like to say, if I were in a position to do so." This from Walter, bitterly.

"Such as...? No, I'm being unfair. Let me say it. You care about me ... and have perhaps done so for a long time?"

"Yes , but . . .

"Listen Walter, I know only too well that you felt you couldn't say those things because my circumstances have now changed so dramatically. But there is something you must know. It's an age-old cliché, but I really do regard you as a brother. You are an old, very dear friend and I'm sorry, but I can't visualize you in any other role. If I loved you the money would make no difference at all - I wouldn't let it.

"Perhaps it's too early after...?" He looked at her hopefully.

"No, please don't find excuses for the way I feel. I'm sorry my dear, but I can't see any possibility of changing." His head sunk onto his arms. "What I would hate now more than anything is that this should affect our friendship. Already you've started to call less and less - avoiding me in fact. I need you, Walter. I needed you in India and I need you now. There's a cruel man out in India to whom I may or may not be still married and there's a charming man in Liverpool who may or may not be after my money. I need your strength, your experience of men and the world and your continuing love and advice. Please, please don't deprive me of those."

When she looked at him pleadingly with those beautiful eyes, he knew he could not refuse anything she asked of him.

Letters were always received with pleasure at the cottage, but never had one been pounced upon with such delight as their first communication from the Rani. Both girls had written expressing their gratitude for her many kindnesses and, on James's advice, had carefully avoided putting into words details of their escape, or her part in it. This reply, so evocative of her persona, reduced them both to tears. Whilst her spoken English was very good indeed, she had clearly laboured over this epistle, not being prepared to entrust even her father's scribes with the information enclosed.

She and her retinue of faithful attendants had reached Damrishar without mishap and had been warmly received into the bosom of her family.

"They refuse to shun me because I am now a widow, believing this tenet of our Hindi creed, to be both cruel and outmoded."

From her informants at Jaishalpar she had learned that Jai had indeed nominated his son, Niaz, as his heir and that he had now announced his intention of marrying Metta and making her his Second Highness.

"I had not thought he would ever marry a daughter of a Sirdar, but for Metta I am happy. This will mean that she will still retain some contact, however small, with her son. I also suspect that Romesh is once again following the pathway of expediency. The British have been very reluctant of late to accept adopted heirs as succeeding rulers to the Raj princedoms. By marrying Metta he ensures there can be no query that Niaz is his rightful heir and as such must succeed him. Always he is watchful and attempting to thwart everything they say and do.

"I am wondering dear Helen, if your Lord James has yet found out about your marital status. I know the British Government wishes now to prevent British girls from marrying Indians. I have been reading a book by Pandita Ramabar. She is speaking often for the cause of high-caste Hindu women, particularly widows. Although some suttee still takes place secretly, since the British made it illegal many thousands of young lives have been saved.

"I wish to do something to stop the practice of young girls, still children, being married as I was. Also to remove the stigma which is applied to all widows. Married before puberty to men many years older than themselves, they are often widowed at a very early age so merely exchange the misery of their marital status for that of despised widowhood.

"Please tell your friend to convey to the British Government that I wish to play a part in the righting of these wrongs. I am feeling very strongly that I must not spend the rest of my life cloistered here. I realise now that there are many women, and men, who are determined to make these changes. If this does not happen, then logically without regeneration, our culture will not survive.

"Before leaving Jaishalpar I asked Almeera to bring me something from your room that I might keep as a memory. (I fear this is not the right word). She returned with the beautiful shawl with its patina of pearls and embroidery, created by your friend. Perhaps I am wrong to keep this? Please say if in doing so I am causing you offence. The shawl is now with other treasured possessions in my puja chamber. It is a part of you and your friend to keep with me in my heart and prayers.

May your god be with you always, Brijial, Princess of Damrishar, Junior Maharani of Jaishalpar"

Helen swallowed a sudden large obstruction in her throat and waited until Betty had finished reading.

"I suppose....." she hesitated.

"Yes, you suppose...?"

"Betty, I know if we asked her, she would send me the shawl but... well, it was your gift to me and I really need to know how you feel about this."

"We couldn't possibly ask it of her, having read this. It's really the most charming, moving compliment. In any event, the shawl was a part, however small, of your life in India, something you obviously want to forget. I've often wondered if I wasn't tempting fate using all those seed pearls. Didn't someone once say that pearls are for tears?"

"You're now being very wise - after the event! If one listened to every old adage and superstition we'd never do anything - we'd have to live like nuns! So, we're agreed then that the Rani keeps the shawl. After all you can always make me another one - minus the pearls, if they worry you!"

Laughing, Betty left the room and Helen picked up the letter again. Her respect for the Rani grew with every new revelation about her early years and this letter was another indication of the strength of her character, a character which could have been soured by her experiences, yet still was able to show compassion for Metta and happiness that her small son would not yet be taken from her and lost to her forever. Had Jai been ill, Helen knew the Rani would have wished to nurse him, all her maternal instincts resurfacing to meet his needs. The only person whom the Rani had never forgiven was her husband, the man who had deflowered and abused her, a wicked man, intent only on satisfying his evil appetites. That such a young girl had managed to retain her self-esteem, ultimately acquiring a dignity and sense of justice which commanded the respect and admiration of those around her, was quite amazing. Rarely did the Rani allow herself the luxury of tears and if she ever indulged in doubts or self-pity these were reserved for the privacy of her puja room.

'I wish I had half her resilience, 'Helen brooded. 'There aren't many, if any, men around willing to chip away at this carapace of resentment I've built around myself. Even Betty unaware of it, thinks, bless her, that I'm quite cured. Yet any man touches me, even James or my father, I want to break that contact as quickly as possible. I only just stopped myself from doing that the other day. I'm sure Muriel noticed. She's just too polite to ask me about it.'

She returned to the letter. The Rani had reminded her that the wheels of the law were certainly grinding slowly on the question of her marriage, in fact nothing seemed to have happened for weeks. She would write to James.

Chapter Nineteen

The first hints of Autumn were fingering the hills and dales when Helen and Betty travelled South again. Walter had apparently resigned himself to Helen's dictum and enjoyed the girls' company whenever this was proffered, even managing to adopt a teasing attitude towards Betty regarding her association with Eddy.

Helen having expressed a wish to see where her sister lived and worked for much of the year, the two girls escorted Rosa back to Oxford. Finding 'the dreaming spires' much to their liking, they spent a happy week exploring and, on occasions, when Rosa's Alex happened to be on hand, punting on the river.

From there to London, where Muriel and Daphne had not only found them furnished rooms close to the Embankment, but had organised a Mrs. Beeton to come in daily. She was, as Betty frequently remarked 'a character' . A true Cockney, her speech was littered with rhyming slang and Helen was grateful that Betty was around to interpret. Small and stout with ankles which cascaded over her shoes she bustled about, singing tunelessly as she worked. Unlike her namesake, this good lady's efforts in the kitchen proved incapable of producing a meal worth eating. Her standards of cleanliness, however, left nothing to be desired. Funds they might have a-plenty but employing a cook the girls decided, was out of the question.

"Too bossy!" Betty surmised.

Helen nodded agreement. "We wouldn't have any privacy at all. At least Mrs. B. disappears when her cleaning's finished."

And that was that. Neither of the girls had ever been required to do any serious cooking and found their previous experience limited to such peripheral items as fairy cakes and rock buns. However, they experimented until they were able to produce meals which were tolerably appetizing and, more importantly, edible!

Helen reflected on the fact that coincidentally they were now all in the South again. 'All' being Rosa in Oxford, James at the House of Lords, Walter and Eddy at their Knightsbridge Barracks and Muriel and Daphne in their Kensington flat. The latter had now declared their allegiance to Sylvia Pankhurst and her breakaway organisation, the East London Federation of Suffragettes. Helen was moved by their stories about conditions there, stories which Betty, having lived on the fringes of such hopelessness, was able to confirm. They told her of women with drunken husbands, women who whilst beaten regularly, struggled against all the odds to bring up their children. These stories touched a still-raw nerve in Helen. She asked if money itself could do anything to alleviate conditions and their ready acquiescence resulted in a cheque for one thousand pounds. A similar amount donated by Daphne had provided a lifeline in the form of meeting rooms where women could bring their children, meet others and receive advice and assistance. This further gift would mean the opening of more such centres.

Writing the cheque gave Helen a frisson of satisfaction. How ironical it was that some of Jai's money would now be used to counteract the sort of situations Jai himself was all too capable of creating.

A few days after their arrival in London a meeting was arranged with Neville Aston. Both girls were shocked by his appearance. Usually so debonair and pin-neat, his cravat was slightly awry and his suit rumpled. What was even more alarming was his slightly distrait manner. Nevertheless when, the pleasantries over, they settled down to the reason for their meeting, whether he saw any future for them independently in the world of fashion, they found he had not only given the matter considerable thought, but was extremely lucid on the subject.

"I think evening wear is your field. You, Betty, already have amazing skills with beadwork and fabric decoration. I believe the war will see the end of haute couture, it's in its death throes now, but I suspect that ladies, or perhaps I should say women, will always be prepared to buy something special for evening wear.

"Nor should you stop at just dresses. That shawl you mentioned, Betty, with its silver threads and overlay of seed pearls - well, evening cloaks and shawls could be another big seller, perhaps to match a chosen dress. Satin shoes and bags could be similarly decorated. Hats, gloves - fans might even make a come-back - then there's jewellery ..."

"Stop! Stop!" Betty and Helen were both laughing, but already flushed with excitement.

"Neville. . .you re wonderful. That sounds exactly right for us."

Helen laughed again. "It's so clever of you to come up with such a brilliant idea, Neville. We could start small here in London, then perhaps try Leeds and then well, the potential is enormous."

"I think it is enormous, to my knowledge no-one has specialised in that field before and if a lady can find under one roof everything she requires to complete an evening ensemble , then this will save her a tremendous amount of searching. The sort of intricate work you can do, Betty, will always be in demand. If you can coach others in those skills then you have the makings of a first-rate business. Another thing I wanted to talk to you about - that material you brought back, Helen. Get some more or similar, in fact get as much as you can, as soon as you can. War could mean a cessation of trade imports, so do a little stock-piling now!"

"Neville, this is all very generous of you but.." Helen hesitated, "are you quite sure we won't be encroaching on your territory? That's the last thing we'd want to do."

"Absolutely not, darlings. No-one and I mean no-one seems to be ordering complete seasonal ensembles any more. Everyone is in a state of limbo just waiting to see what the next few months will bring. I'm afraid..."

"Yes, you're afraid...?"

"I was merely going to add that if there is any market left out there, I'm afraid that the Maison Céleste has cornered it. But that's quite enough shop talk. Now my dears tell me, in spite of the obvious unpleasantness you encountered, about which we will definitely not speak, India still must have been a truly fascinating experience surely...? Do tell..."

Leaving Aston's they discussed Neville's appearance and manner.

"You were absolutely right Betty, but without being downright rude, I don't know how we can find out what is the problem. Clearly he's given a lot of thought to the effect war will have on business generally and the Marie Céleste salon seems to have taken much of his haute couture trade, but he's a shrewd business man for heaven's sake and used to bouncing back whatever the difficulty. It might be a purely personal problem and we certainly can't go down that road. He's given us some wonderful ideas and I think we'd better start putting some of them in practice right away."

Within a few hours of leaving Aston's they had put certain suggestions into action. A wire was sent to the Rani asking if she had any trade contacts, particularly in Bombay, and outlining their interest in materials of unusual design. A further wire was sent to Jim Calloway asking if the Reed, Calloway Line had any ships currently in the Far East or any due there in the near future. Advertisements were placed in two London newspapers, stating that young ladies of sixteen years or over, with expertise in embroidery and decorative work were invited to apply for positions of interest.

"Are we rushing things?" Helen asked doubtfully.

"Definitely not! The next step is to find a workshop and salon. Tomorrow we'll start looking at property."

It was not to be. The news of Neville Aston's suicide by hanging reached them early the next morning. The policeman who brought the information said that Neville had been found by one of his staff, the doorman. "There was a letter addressed to you Miss Calloway," the policeman coughed his embarrassment, "it's now with the Coroner, Ma'am."

The next few days were an unpleasant haze of interviews, Post Mortem details, the Inquest and, finally, the funeral. With the assistance of Aston's Chief Vendeuse, the girls had assembled friends and clients, members of the trade, staff and former employees. Sonia, Miss Tindall and the seamstresses rubbed shoulders with members of the aristocracy, all humbled in the presence of sudden, unexpected death. The results of their efforts afforded Helen and Betty as much satisfaction as was possible in the circumstances. The packed church, redolent with the fragrance of expensive perfume, the banks of lilies flanked by huge clusters of purple and black ostrich plumes, all seemed a fittingly exotic 'final curtain' for such a flamboyant creative artist.

Helen's sadness at the loss of the man who had always regarded her as his protegée, was exacerbated by the letter left for her.

Helen Darling,

I fear I've come to the end of the road - that is, of my own particular road. Since my sister Margaret's untimely death and with the business sinking fast there's little here to encourage me to stay. Nothing else appeals and the possibility of having to go away to fight is anathema to me. So, my dear, I'm bowing out. Don't be distressed. I've done much of what I set out to do, and, more importantly, I've enjoyed doing it.

There's no money to speak of, but I do want you to have the Salon. The property itself is in a good situation so is therefore of some value. I can think of no-one else in whose hands I would rather see it. There is sufficient stock to dispose of and clear existing debts and then, my dear, you and Betty will be able to start on your own venture.

My gratitude for your affection and consideration in the past.

I wish you well, always,

Neville

P.S. Remember! Life goes on.

They had not realised that he was so alone and this caused Helen great distress. No relatives had appeared at the funeral, in fact no-one outside his working life seemed to know or care about his demise.

That he should have made their start so much easier, by deliberately setting their feet on the pathway he'd suggested, was typical of his generous nature and together the girls mourned the fact that they had not earlier sensed his loneliness. But, as he had admonished, 'Life goes on' and their plans, albeit now considerably revised, began to take shape.

The Aston premises were large, comprising the Salon and numerous fitting rooms, extensive work-rooms, two offices and Neville's flat. Too large, they decided for the small exclusive business they had in mind. However, their immediate need was a permanent base in London, so plans were drawn up to extend the living area to include three bedrooms, two sitting rooms and the latest in bathroom and toilet fittings. Existing stock was sold. Then came the unpleasant task of dismissing the Chief Vendeuse and ten members of staff. The cutter, two seamstresses and two trimmers were retained, together with the book-keeper and Alf, the doorman, who was to assist where needed. The main salon with its beautiful pink and gold furnishings and a second large viewing room were dust-covered and closed.

Work commenced immediately with Helen overseeing the alterations and Betty submitting several designs to the workroom in order to establish her own working guidelines. This was a different Betty from the girl who had travelled out to India a year ago. The experience of travelling, meeting people from all walks of life, the sojourn in a royal palace with its multitude of servants, the good times and the subsequent heart-ache had all played their part. This Betty was no longer a

142

subordinate, a Cockney girl with a brilliant flair for design and needlework. She now spoke with authority, knew what she wanted and expected to get it. As Alfred told his wife one evening,

"You remember that little mousey gal, Sal, you know the one wot used to do the beads and fings in the workroom and then went off to India with Miss 'Elen? You should see 'er now! My Gawd 'ow she's changed. I tell yer she's got them women sorted an' no mistake and those two new gals we've got - well, I reckon she's got them scared out o' their wits!".

That wasn't in fact true. The two new girls, Flora and Maud, both selected from the advertisement applicants, had already worked out that Miss Betty's bark was a great deal worse than her bite and that, in any case, anyone who could turn out the sort of beautiful work she did, was worth listening to.

From the Rani came a reply to their wire and hard on the heels of that, a second from the contact she had arranged. Iswar Ram was a fabric merchant, who would be most happy to supply materials, several samples of which were already on their way. Jim Calloway wrote to say he would be in London at the beginning of November and that a ship was leaving Bombay at the end of that month, calling at Tilbury. There would be sufficient space in the hold for up to one hundred bales of material. A wire from him would ensure that this space was reserved for them.

"One hundred!" Betty was aghast. "That's ridiculous, we can't handle that many. Besides each dress must be different, we'll have far too much of each design."

"Just a minute Betty, let's think it through. Remember we're no longer dealing with haute couture. Surely the same base material could be used for several dresses and shawls. Each will still be completely individual, because each of your surface designs will be different."

"You're right, the final product will always be unique, that's obviously what everyone wants. I suppose if Neville was right about the war and goods not being able to get here, it does make sense to buy in a stock of material."

"If the samples are what we want Betty, we'll not only fill the space the Captain has on this trip, we'll order a further and larger consignment for the next one!"

The Rani's offer of assistance to the British in India produced a very positive response from James. He was authorised to assure her that the Government would be delighted to accept. As he told Helen, people of the Maharani's standing and with a reputation for possessing a sound social conscience were exactly the type required for the new Commissions being set up to examine various cultural practices not acceptable to the British, nor to many Indians. That such practices were inextricably linked to different religions made it imperative that each religious discipline was represented in any discussion forum. Ruefully he added that he wished he could be as forthcoming with news of her application for annulment, but as yet there was nothing to report.

Helen had little time to brood about the lack of news as the next few weeks saw the girls busily occupied with a variety of tasks. The first samples arrived from India and were approved. Their apartment was completed and, on Betty's insistence, the name 'Helena' was now inscribed in white and gold over their street entrance. She brushed aside Helen's protestations that they select a new, more impersonal name for their venture. "Your name already means fashion and style to an awful lot of people, we'd be stupid not to make the most of it." Their launch into the fashion world was to take place the following April, so as to allow ample time for material deliveries and the making up of some twenty dresses and a variety of accessories.

There had been no window showcase at the House of Aston, so an innovatory move was to enlarge one of the windows at street level in order to display their wares. Whilst dresses could be made to order, the purchaser selecting her own material, style and the design to be appliqued, there would always be a range of dresses in standard sizes ready for immediate purchase, each differently trimmed and finished. Contracts had been set up with shoe and bag manufacturers and a milliner. As these people were supplying only basic shapes each stockist agreed that the items would be sold under the Helena label.

Jim Calloway's visit in November was brief, but he was full of admiration for their progress and assured the girls of the continuing co-operation of the Reed Calloway Line. In the early part of December Helen received two communications of significance, the first confirming that her marriage to Prince Romesh, now Maharajah of Jaishalpur had been annulled. Whilst the Prince's religion permitted the taking of several wives, the fact that he had not informed Helen before their London marriage of an existing wife in India was not acceptable in British law. The antagonism of a number of the Rajput to the British Government, as James had suggested, was now resulting in a hardening of attitude towards those Indians who stepped out of line.

Helen had expected to feel elated at the news of her annulment, but the earlier remembered feelings of guilt and shame came flooding back as she read the impersonal legal language. As a small girl she had felt guilty after her mother's death. Had she done something wrong and was being punished for it? Could she have kept her mother alive by acting differently? Now she was engulfed by the whole gamut of her uncertainties. She must have been at fault in some way or Jai would never have done this to her. Should she have stayed on in India, tried to establish a better understanding, to recreate the love she had at first thought to be theirs? But always at the back of her mind she heard the quiet measured tones of the Rani.

"My son removes from his orbit all those who question or refuse to agree to his wishes."

And then Prinny's voice, steely and firm, "Anyone who knowingly deceives another person as Jai did you, is not deserving of your love or loyalty."

Let it lie, she told herself. This is the end of that particular unpleasant episode. I have now started afresh and must look forward, never back.

The second envelope contained an invitation to attend a small dinner party celebrating the engagement of James and Muriel. Also, the surprising information that Robert had returned from Australia and was already with his mother at Craybourne. Guests at the dinner would be Helen, Daphne of course, Walter and Richard Culpepper. Clearly Richard had been chosen as someone whom she knew, although had not met for some time, but Helen was surprised at the inclusion of Walter. Her surprise would have been even greater had she known that his invitation was at Daphne's request.

Having long tired of the hedonistic young men brought up in the rarefied atmosphere of upper-class society, living in London had made Daphne aware that there were many types of men about whom she could not be dismissive. Her sorties into the East End on suffragette matters had revealed many ill-natured coarse bullies, but there were others who, in spite of the rigours of their environment, in spite of childhood conditioning, had yet retained a sense of purpose and, amazingly, a respect for womanhood. There were some too, who did not fit readily into any catalogue of stereotypes.

Such a man was Peter Fairburn, a printer of Kentish origin, whose overtures she had to date refused. Having served his apprenticeship as a typesetter for a local newspaper, he had on impulse at the end of one hop-picking season, joined the throng of East Enders returning to London, in order to see if life in the big city suited him. Ten years later he was still there. Now, at thirty, a well established member of a printing firm in Acton and a staunch supporter of women's suffrage, he assisted by doing their printing in his off-duty periods.

'Just my luck,' Daphne had thought on numerous occasions, 'I'm sick and tired of those spineless creatures I've been seeing for the last few years, but now I'm faced with the other extreme. Peter is a real man, hard-working, kind, steady and yes, let's be honest - dull! The only subjects he gets steamed up about are Christabel Pankhurst's dictatorial ways and cricket!'

Suddenly out of the blue had come the suggestion that she join the welcoming party at Tilbury and there was Walter with his glamorous aura of service in India. She was impressed by his easy manners but sensed that they concealed the rough edge of his manhood lying very close to the surface. He was, she decided, more masculine than either of her brothers! And, his hair bleached by the Indian sun, his skin bronzed by it, very handsome indeed. She had wanted to see him again.

She listened now with pleasure to the interchange between Walter and Richard. Not for Walter embarrassment or prevarication when asked which school he had attended, just an easy, "Locally - the village school and after that my education was on the farm, then the army and India." The young guardsman having not yet notched up any foreign service was impressed. Without a public school background, Walter's current rank was a clear indication of some outstanding talent or promotion in the field.

Whilst Walter's behaviour was pleasing to Daphne he was very confused by hers. He remembered her as an obnoxious arrogant child, who seemed to upset everyone with whom she into contact. Tonight her manner was deferential, almost demure. His opinion was sought on a variety of topics, the threat of war, women's suffrage, Indian independence, whether women should drive automobiles. He had an uneasy feeling that it was all an act, but was at a loss to understand why. Helen was also puzzled by Daphne's uncharacteristic and somewhat cloying attitude towards Walter. Where was her rapier-like conversation, the sharp and often cruel wit? It was almost a relief when this surfaced.

A sudden lull in the conversation left Richard's cultured voice supporting the idea that thirty was the correct age for women to be given the vote and only then to women of substance, property owners, etc. Daphne's icy retort cut through the somewhat stunned silence which followed.

"It's sad to know how many there are so conditioned by our male-dominated society that they cannot approach this subject with an open mind. If the vote is only given to women of substance, we'll be merely propping up a class system which is both unfair and vastly outmoded."

"Oh heavens, I'd quite forgotten how much you and Muriel are involved with all this - sorry Daphne. But just for the record, my father's an American so I haven't suffered so much from 'conditioning' as you call it, there's not much of a class system over there."

"You have got to be joking! You haven't long since abolished slavery. Are you seriously trying to tell me that your parents number amongst their friends people from the wrong side of the tracks or even, dare I say it, coloured people?"

"Now, now. No more talking shop this evening. In case you'd forgotten we're here to celebrate. Who's ready for more champagne?"

Muriel's easy manner quickly diffused the situation and left Walter to cover his amusement. We all operate double standards, he decided. They're talking about removing class taboos and washing it down with a champagne which would have cost a working man half a year's wages. I suppose I'm a sort of middle-man, one foot in either camp. Perhaps that's why I was invited. No, I'm being unfair. There has to be some interim stage, changes of this sort don't occur overnight. At least they're making an effort, unlike some with their backgrounds. They do go out into the East End and they are trying to help the women and children there. Why Daphne had to give me that 'butter wouldn't melt in my mouth' routine I can't imagine. That outburst was more typical of the little monster I remember. Intrigued by her enigmatic behaviour he invited her to go to the theatre with him the following week.

Helen, overhearing the invitation and Daphne's acceptance, left James's rooms feeling confused. She had thought by now that she knew Daphne well, that they were good friends, but this 'little woman' act was a side of Daphne she had never seen before. It seemed that repeatedly her judgement of character was called into question. She must be very, very careful in the future. One error in that direction had already resulted in heartache and tears.

Chapter Twenty

Rosa stopped on the staircase, savouring the moment. It was Christmas Eve and in the hall the pine tree's distinctive aroma mingled with that of spruce. From the kitchen came teasing odours of all that was delicious, succulent hams baking, sweet-centred mincepies, crisp and golden, emerging from over-worked ovens and, overlaying all, the scent of spices and aromatic herbs.

For the first time Rosa was actually staying in the Manor and enjoying every minute of it. With the influx of young visitors and adorned in its Christmas finery the house had shed its faded elegance and glowed with warmth and colour. Tonight it breathes Christmas, she thought, and, moving on into the drawing room, was quickly absorbed into the convivial atmosphere of pre-dinner drinks.

"You didn't go home for Christmas, Iain?" Helen asked

"Obviously not! No, my sister and her brood were descending on my parents, so I knew I wouldn't be missed. I also knew that here the company would be delightful."

A compliment no less! Either he's already partaken of too much Christmas cheer, or once again my judgement of character is proving badly flawed. Politely she responded.

"It's certainly wonderful for Elizabeth to have all her family around her again and pleasant that we are such a young group. I believe Daphne and Robert have some very foolish games organised for later."

"In that case I should warn you that charades is my speciality. As a frustrated thespian I inflict my underused skills on as many audiences as I can find - especially captive ones!"

Helen still stunned by the transformation of dour Scot into this witty amiable companion was relieved when they were joined by Robert, a vastly different Robert from the hedonistic young man of whom Prinny used to speak so disapprovingly. Tall and lean, his brown hair layered with gold by the Australian sun, he exuded good health. Gone was the rather cunning, wary expression. Now Helen warmed to his ready smile and thoughtful eyes. Clearly he had overheard Iain's last remark.

"And I think it only fair to warn you, Iain, that I'm no mean slouch myself when it comes to charades. You should also be prepared for the fact that since living 'down under' my vocabulary has been considerably extended. Some of those new words might prove rather taxing for the uninitiated!"

Helen left them laughing together and moved across to speak to Daphne. The antipathy Daphne had sometimes shown earlier in their relationship had now given way to a good-natured bantering and from this had emerged a comfortable friendship. Clearly Daphne had assumed that Helen was some sort of empty-headed clothes-horse and an ill-informed country cousin to boot, whilst she had still thought of Daphne as a spoilt little rich girl, prey to various whims and fancies. Both now knew differently. Helen admired Daphne for sticking to her principles, giving up her cushioned society role and immersing herself in the cause of the

Suffragettes, whilst Daphne had learned that inside Helen's elegant head was a shrewd well-informed brain.

Nevertheless, Helen was still puzzled by Daphne's behaviour at Muriel's dinner party. It smacked of just the sort of empty-headed nonsense which Daphne normally decried. Putting on an act for the sake of a man, any man, wasn't really Daphne's style at all. Helen was intrigued to know how the evening with Walter had gone and found Daphne just as anxious to tell her.

"Unmitigated disaster, Helen, from start to finish! I still think he's rather gorgeous, but when it came down to rock bottom, our conversation didn't have too many meeting points -if any! His experiences are all outside mine, and mine at the moment are far removed from his. Let's face it, Walter has since childhood really only been at close quarters with women on farms. They work hard, very hard, but there's usually plenty of food around and their husbands are less likely to go out and spend all the money on drink as they would in a city - probably much too tired! The women he saw whilst in the army would be either bird-brained social butterflies (sorry to mix the metaphors) or camp followers - neither of them exactly typical. Because of this he's never really given much thought to women's place in society or whether they should have a voice in how that society develops."

"But Daphne there are other topics of conversation. You didn't have to discuss the Suffragette movement all evening!"

"I tried. We both tried. To be honest we were both ill-at-ease most of the time. Neither of us seemed to be able to rid ourselves of our origins, you know Lady of the Manor, farmhand etc., all that stuff. Ironical isn't it, I thought I'd shed that skin, but obviously it still shows. I think he felt exactly the same, either that or he's still carrying a torch for you and, don't look all surprised, everyone's well aware of how he feels. What really annoys me, if I'm honest, is that I was all prepared to show the Pankhursts just how avant garde I was by not only supporting the Cause, particularly of those of the lower echelons but actually marrying one of them. Now I've shocked you! But you must surely know by now, I'm all talk - not really wicked at heart."

"There are times when you give a very good impression of being so. I certainly never expected a maiden aunt of mine to behave in such an unseemly fashion". Helen's reply was straight-faced.

"Niece you forget yourself. Mind your manners child." Unable to control their laughter any more and with wine-glasses waving dangerously, they collapsed onto the nearest sofa. Muriel, hearing their laughter, looked fondly across at the silver-haired lady who had made all this possible. It was her generosity of spirit which had drawn Helen and Rosa into this family group. Oliver Craybourne must have been a wonderful man to have warranted such love. Most other women would have felt no sense of commitment to these grandchildren of his, born of an extra-marital relationship. But Elizabeth by example had somehow overcome the feelings of resentment at least two of her children had exhibited. Of course, the children in question were now adults. They had had time to reflect on what was important in life and what their own priorities would be. Realistically, Muriel acknowledged that Helen's money would have also played a part in changing attitudes, removing any residual traces of bitterness. The Calloway girls could never now be accused of self-seeking. No longer had they need of other people's money.

"Darling, that is much too serious a face for Christmas Eve. Is everything all right?" James looked anxious.

"Of course. I was just reflecting on my good fortune in having such a wonderful mother-in-law."

"Well, if such thoughts are the order of the day, I'll certainly drink to the two special ladies in my life." Taking her hand, he drew her to the nearest window-seat and until dinner was announced, indulged himself in being close to her, breathing in her perfume and enjoying her animated and incisive conversation.

The dining-room was a picture and Prinny felt an overwhelming sense of pride that she had played a part in achieving this. Silver and crystal, crisply starched napery, all were reflected in the gleaming surfaces bearing the patina of years of loving care. Huge copper bowls held a tapestry of yellow, bronze and gold chrysanthemums and from the glowing pyramids of fruit, grapes cascaded.

Three village girls had been employed to supplement the Manor staff for the period prior to and during the Christmas houseparty. Even so the preparations had seemed endless. Lavender-scented linen had been brought out from chests, washed and aired. Bedrooms long unused were prepared and in the kitchens preserves and cooking ingredients were checked and rechecked. Elizabeth had determined the menus and their accompanying wines. And at last the final touches were made. The pine-tree with its scarlet candles and pretty baubles was placed in the hall and, throughout the ground floor, reception rooms were made gay with holly, spruce and mistletoe and a multitude of scarlet ribbons. Prinny had no worries about the quality of the food, Mrs. Waring was a very able captain of her ship and judging by the entrée dishes was already steering an excellent course.

Elizabeth was coping well this evening, buoyed up by the joy of having all her children together once more. Prinny had to admit they had turned out well, far exceeding anything she might have expected from them. Not that she included James in any of this, he had always been a tower of strength, but Daphne, who would have thought she'd have the courage to do the things she'd done for the W.S.P.U.? As for Robert, whatever his sexual proclivities (and her forays into English literature had implied it was unlikely that these would have changed), he was still a lovely young man. She astonished herself that she was able to think like this. There was a time when she would have shunned him, felt that any association would in some way soil her. How wrong she had been.

On the days before Christmas when Elizabeth had felt unwell she and Robert had of necessity spent a considerable amount of time together. His assistance with all manner of matters concerned with the preparation of the house had been invaluable, but most of all Prinny had enjoyed his company at dinner, appreciated his dry humour and the anecdotes of his travels and work in Australia. The two had developed a rapport, the roots of which for some time, she was unable to analyse. Gradually she recognised in him an empathy with those whom he felt like himself to be 'outside' society's norms. It took her slightly longer to realise that it was because she herself came into this category that the young man was drawn to her. Rarely had she thought of herself in those terms. However, there was no denying that a spinster with little money to speak of was not the most favoured of society's creatures. She glanced down the table at Robert and his sister. Their characters were now so far removed from the spiteful schoolgirl and arrogant playboy she remembered that it was difficult to equate them with the same people. She motioned to Vickers to pour her another glass of wine, smiling at Rosa's astonished expression.

As planned, dinner was concluded by the time the village carol singers arrived. Speedily they were ushered into the hall and lights other than the tree candles and their own lanterns were extinguished. It was an informal occasion with Elizabeth and Prinny seated on the oaksettle and the younger members of the Manor party on the stairs. Soon they were all joining in the familiar tunes and Helen, impressed by the quality of Iain's baritone, wondered what other surprises this enigmatic character had in store.

Neither had he understated his talent at charades. When he and Rob joined forces the results were hilarious and Helen found herself laughing as she had not done for many months. After Elizabeth and Prinny had retired the youngsters turned back the carpet in the morning room, put on the phonograph and danced until midnight. Then, suddenly serious, they toasted Christmas and each other. War was not mentioned, but each thought of it, wondering whether Christmas would be so light-hearted another year hence and whether all or any of them would be celebrating the festival together.

To church the next day on rime-covered paths which crunched under their feet. Christmas lunch and the exchange of gifts was followed by a further walk to greet those at Hislop's and tenants living close by. Then in the evening it was time for songs round the piano; Daphne proved an excellent accompanist with the ability to play by ear anything they requested.

Daphne first started to feel unwell on Boxing Day. She recalled feeling very cold when the carol singers brought the chill of a winter's night with them into the hall. And she had had a persistent cough for several days. Typically, she refrained from mentioning any of this until others remarked on her flushed cheeks and the cough which had become increasingly noticeable.

The doctor's diagnosis of bronchial pneumonia shocked the household, his frequent calls leaving them in no doubt as to the seriousness of Daphne's condition. Five days passed during which the house itself seemed to hold its breath and walk on cushioned feet. Five silent days before the Doctor at last declared 'an improvement' and started to discuss convalescence. Meanwhile Helen had wired

150

Betty that she would not be returning to London until the middle of January. James and Muriel had also delayed their return and when at last Daphne's temperature dropped considerably everyone relaxed and settled down to a restful few days.

At least that was the idea. In fact Daphne was a demanding patient who required a constant stream of visitors to alleviate the boredom of staying in bed. On one such spell of duty, Helen found her anxious to continue their Christmas Eve discussion about the men in her life.

"I wanted to tell you about Peter. He's a printer, a good one and a real help to our East End group, does all our work at minimal cost. He's a lovely kind-hearted man. I just wish he had a bit more dash - he's so staid, so predictable."

"Daphne, I have to say this, you really are the limit! You seem to want your bread buttered on both sides. First you complain, constantly, that the dashing ones are empty-headed and now you've found someone who's not empty-headed you want him to be full of dash and sparkle!"

"Touché. You're quite right. I suppose if you're in love you see everything through rose-coloured spectacles and believe the object of your love is everything you want him to be, regardless of what's he's really like. You know, like Titania falling in love with the ass."

Silence - and Daphne suddenly aware of her gaffe, rushed on.

"Sorry Helen, what crass stupidity on my part. I was always good at opening my mouth and putting my foot in it."

Helen laughed. "Don't apologise. I can talk about it now - or at least I'm making myself do so. Yes, love's rose-coloured spectacles can have a blinding effect and even when you do notice faults, you're naive enough to think you'll be capable of changing them. My mother made that mistake and so did I, so be warned... I've thought about this quite a lot, Daphne. Real love must be when you accept someone with all their faults, knowing that they feel the same about you. Who knows you might in time get to love even their quirks or idiosyncracies."

It was Daphne's turn to laugh. "Like Peter's hands always stained with messy printer's ink you mean? No, I shouldn't joke about him, he's a good friend and I'm fond of him. You must meet him Helen. So far we've never met socially, but perhaps I should be thankful for what I've got, or what seems to be on offer and stop baying for the moon".

"I don't know about baying for the moon, but I think Prinny will be baying for my blood, if you talk any more. Turn over, Aunt, and go to sleep."

Helen made her way to the study and curled up in the large leather chair by the glowing fire. This had been her grandfather's domain. On many occasions he must have sat in this chair, handled with love and care the books all around her and in here he had died. Strangely this did not make her feel sad or alarmed, on the contrary, it gave her a comfortable feeling of stability.

Christmas had brought gifts from Jim Calloway for Rosa and herself, matching sets of silver and crystal trinket boxes. He expressed his intention of being in London at the end of January and the hope that he could call on her again. Perhaps his change was the most remarkable of all. Are we like snakes, she thought, shedding our skins, and with each new growth acquiring a different persona? Or is the chameleon a closer comparison, with the Captain and the rest of us hiding our real selves behind neatly constructed different facades? Why was she so conscious at this time of people changing - Daphne, Robert, her father? Perhaps the changes were not all on the part of the observed, perhaps she, the observer, had changed too. This obsession with change was probably symptomatic of coming to terms with her disillusionment about Jai. She really must attempt to identify people's finer qualities, rather than adopting the more negative view of looking for faults.

Muriel entered the room and Helen abandoned her self-analysis.

"Sorry to interrupt Helen, but I really do need to talk to you. Do you mind?"

"Of course not", Helen jumped up and pulled another chair to the fire. "Is anything wrong?"

"Au contraire - it's just that I have a favour to ask of you, well of you and Betty really. As you know James and I are planning an Easter wedding and I wondered if you would be prepared to design and make my dress and those of the attendants?" Helen attempted to speak.

"No dear, hear me out first, please. I know that you plan to specialise in evening wear, but this wouldn't be so very different an exercise would it? You see I would dearly love a dress decorated with pearl and crystal, which is after all Betty's forte. Elizabeth is giving me the dress as a wedding gift so this is not only going to be the most expensive dress I have ever owned, but far and away the most beautiful. I hope you and Daphne will be my attendants, together with some small nephews and nieces.

"Before you decide, there's something else I think you should consider. The wedding will be before your launch, I don't wish to sound immodest but with James an M.P. and me the new Lady Craybourne the press are bound to be interested. This would mean you would have advance publicity in The Tatler, the London Illustrated, plus any number of newspapers. Surely that would be good for business?"

"And I thought Neville Aston was the astute one when it came to publicity! I must talk to Betty first of course, as she'll be doing all the spadework, but it sounds a wonderful idea and it does occur to me that this might be a natural extension of our business if the market for evening wear should dry up. Our generation hasn't experienced a war before, but if people should stop giving dances and parties then our business might grind to a halt. On the other hand even in wartime, people will continue to get married and a girl will always want something special for that. I'll talk to Betty and yes, I'll be absolutely thrilled to be one of your attendants."

"There's more, I'm afraid. Something which occurred to me when I met a friend who was going to Neville Aston's funeral. She complained bitterly that she had been scouring her wardrobe desperately trying to find something that was both black, and suitable, to wear on that occasion. Surely there's a market there?"

"Obviously there is, but Neville Aston actually scaled down that side of his business, so it clearly wasn't paying."

"I can understand why Helen. It's the haute couture which is just too expensive. Funeral clothes need to be ready so quickly. Surely that must mean a natural market for ready-to-wear garments. People need to know they can select something smart which won't cost the earth, something that can be quickly adapted to their fitting and most important of all, can be ready in 48 hours."

"I suppose you wouldn't like to join our Board of Directors, Muriel? You're probably right in thinking that haute couture has priced itself out of the funeral wear trade, after all we're talking about clothes with limited usage. Ready-to-wear sounds much more sensible. You are aware, I suppose, that you have probably trebled our business venture in the space of about five minutes! Any other ideas?"

"Yes, there is, but it's nothing to do with business.. that is, it certainly isn't something which will produce any revenue."

"Intriguing....do go on."

"I wonder if you would be prepared to help Daphne and me set up some sort of dressmaking school in the East End? You see, so many of the young women become mothers before they've learned how to keep house. There's no money to buy clothes and they haven't the skill to make them. I thought we might look for a couple of rooms, one for machining and one for cutting out. Then, if a couple of senior experienced women worked with them the girls could learn to put together a simple dress and how to make clothes for their offspring. There'd be no shortage of takers if we make the lessons free."

"And we could beg off-cuts and unwanted materials from people in the trade, Muriel, it's a splendid idea. There are several seamstresses we had to get rid of when we made new plans for the business. I doubt if they've all found work. I'll happily get in touch with them and find three or four prepared to do this and I'll be glad to meet their wages. You can count on us for maximum help."

"Helen, you can't imagine what a relief it is to find someone who'll actually do something to help, instead of just talking about it! I'm sure it's through this sort of basic assistance and education that we can improve the lot of some of these poor women. Incidentally, going back to wedding talk, we've made it clear to Elizabeth that we plan no changes here at the moment. In London I'll be moving into James's rooms, which, thank goodness, are big enough to house two. It does mean though that Daphne will be on her own, unless of course she decides to ask anyone else to join her.

"But now I really have said everything I came to say and I've interrupted your quiet hour for much too long, so I'll leave you in peace. The snow doesn't seem to be settling, so James and I are going to take the dogs for a walk, or they're taking us, I'm never quite sure which! Don't forget you're having a driving lesson this afternoon - weather permitting."

Helen settled back in the armchair. The conversation with Muriel had reminded her of the formidable amount of money in her bank. For-mi-dable! The drawn out

French pronunciation was precisely the way she thought about it. Frightening, and for that reason its existence was pushed to the recesses of her mind and rarely given an airing. Being able to help with Muriel's project would be very satisfying and her ideas for the business seemed sound enough but, Helen reflected, I am so lucky, even if the whole venture falls apart it would not be the end of the world. There will still be my cushion, that fortune for-mi-dable! A comforting thought. She was lucky, very lucky. She smiled at the leaping flames. It was a long time since she had thought of herself in exactly those terms.

On the evening of December 31st a somewhat petulant Daphne was allowed downstairs to 'see in' the New Year. Disgruntled, because the concession had not also included dinner downstairs, her mood was ignored by the others and in the face of their gaiety quickly dispelled.

At one minute before twelve Iain left the house. Then, as the carillon from Craybourne Church joyfully welcomed 1914, he pounded the heavy brass knocker of the Manor's front entrance and asked to be admitted. Bearing a piece of coal, some bread and milk he wished them all the luck they wished themselves and handed over the gifts, with the assurance that the house would always offer a warm hearth, food and drink to all who needed them in the coming year. When Daphne suggested that the boy from Hislop's could have saved him the necessity of going out in the cold by 'first-footing' in his place, Iain threw up his hands in mock horror and lapsed into broad Scottish dialect.

"Wheesht lassie, have ye no sense? D'ye nay ken only a dark-haired mon can bring in the luck? What mair coud ye wish the noo' than mysel' a raven-haired Scot, crossing your threshold at midnight, bearing gifts?"

The outburst of laughter brought colour at last to Daphne's wan face and Helen noticed that her eyes now followed Iain's movements with interest. A combination of dash and intelligence? Helen mused. No doubt about the latter, if a high forehead really does denote brain capacity. He's not as handsome as Walter, or Rob for that matter, his face is too angular. In repose that dark hair and the deep-set dark eyes give him a dour, even glowering expression, but now when he's clowning around they're most striking.

Vickers' appearance with the champagne was the signal to salute the New Year with an additional toast from Elizabeth that the newly engaged couple's wedding year should be especially happy. Tonight her skin seems almost translucent, Helen thought. Her frailty makes Prinny's angular figure look almost robust by comparison.

When the young people were finally alone the mood was sombre. Heralding the New Year had made it impossible to avoid contemplation of what it might bring. This time there was no attempt to cloak their feelings on the matter.

A serious James, speaking from his informed position, felt any war in Europe would involve a very different type of fighting than that previously experienced. It was well known that the Germans had experimented with and probably produced many new weapons. He trusted that our own Mills bombs and the newly developed Vickers machine gun would prove a match for these. If this was the case then he believed that any war would prove to be one of attrition - a question of who could hold out the longest. Certainly there would be much less hand-to-hand fighting, little use of horses in the battles themselves and, with the more powerful weapons, greater loss of life. It was after all, he pointed out, some years since Britain had been involved in any major conflict. The Boer War had been of comparatively short duration and policing India and Northern Ireland could in no way have prepared our armies for what might lie ahead. The Territorials, it was true were trying to make good this deficiency but.... his voice trailed away, then once again gathered momentum. If the agreed Balance of Power in Europe was upset by any country big or small, the inevitable consequence would be that all countries in the agreement would go to battle stations.

Robert was inclined to optimism. "There's always been trouble in the Balkans, James, as you well know. Probably always will be. No country wants war after all, too damned expensive for one thing. No, more than likely this will all blow over and this time next year we'll be laughing at what Jeremiahs we were!"

"I'd be most happy to be proved wrong, but however limited, I'm still glad of my training." Whilst reading Law at Oxford, James had been part of an army cadet force and now expressed his intention of enlisting immediately war was declared. Iain had already joined a local territorial group, and both felt they had fragmented knowledge of what might be required. Robert's only experience was of hard living on journeys through the outback, "Though I doubt anything can be more demanding than that!"

The girls too, considered what their role might be in a country at war. "We must certainly keep the driving lessons going," Muriel declared, "if the men are away, women will be needed to do all sorts of jobs. It's a selfish thought, but we might at last have the opportunity of showing what we're capable of."

The church clock was striking two as they bade Iain and each other goodnight, wishing each other pleasant dreams. Yet they were somehow all aware that the gaiety they had enjoyed at Christmas and earlier on this New Year's Eve had slipped through their grasp. Had this articulate, intelligent group of young people begun even to suspect the accuracy of James's prognosis their dreams would have been far from pleasant.

James received the message from Haig on January 3rd. A typically formal note requested that his Lordship be kind enough to call at 2 Oak Tree Cottages before returning to London. James was shocked by Haig's appearance. Now seventy nine years of age he had lost the sleek well-fed look of a man in good health and enjoying a compatible occupation. His whole body seemed to have shrunk, to such an extent that James realised he would have passed him in the street unrecognised.

Haig's reasons for relating his version of Oliver's coupling with Bea Fatherstone all those years ago were soon apparent. He believed that Oliver's grandson, Michael, might have amongst his grandmother's possessions, evidence which would lead him to the truth regarding his forebears. If that was the case, wasn't there a possibility that he might make some claim against the estate? The old man shook with anxiety when stressing that he didn't wish Lady Craybourne to be troubled with this matter. Of the incident itself he made light, leaving no doubt as to where he apportioned the blame.

"She was the one at fault, Sir. He was just a young innocent who happened to be in the wrong place at the wrong time and fell right into her trap.

"She'd been watching him for some time, knew the young gentleman was all mixed up, with his feelings.... you know what it's like Sir, when you first come to manhood." He coughed. "I wouldn't want her Ladyship to know, Sir, even though it happened all those years ago. She's not well and this would upset her. To be honest, Sir, it's all this talk of war that's made my mind up about telling you. You see, just suppose you and Master Robert go away to fight and anything unpleasant was to happen and you didn't... Well, don't you see Sir, if this lad has any proof he might just feel as a male descendant that he could put in a claim for the title and everything else. That's what I was afraid of, Sir, I'd hate to think of Craybourne being in the hands of someone who wasn't proper family. Your father was a good, kind man and I feel I must do what I think he would want. I might not be around much longer myself and I just thought someone else ought to know the whole story."

As James strode back to the Manor he pondered his best course of action. The old man had made two very valid points regarding succession to the Estate and the likelihood of a war having an effect on that succession. Clearly everyone, except his mother, and there he agreed with Haig, must be informed. 'Everyone' would encompass Robert, Daphne, Muriel of course and Helen. Perhaps Rosa was too young? He dismissed this idea almost immediately. Rosa was an intelligent young woman living her own life at Oxford. She too, must be included. Helen and Rosa were blood relatives who had a right to this knowledge.

It was 10.30 p.m. before James had his opportunity. As soon as Prinny and Elizabeth had left them, he related all the information given to him by Haig.

"My word, the old man certainly did know how to sow his wild oats!" Robert exclaimed. "Sorry ladies, but it's difficult for me to equate all this roistering around with the gentle man we knew as our father."

"Rob, will you be serious for a moment?" Muriel spoke sharply sensing James's irritation with his brother's lighthearted reaction. "Haig is right in thinking there might just be long-term repercussions which could affect us all. Obviously the first thing we should do is locate Michael Featherstone. He could be anywhere."

As Rosa's laughter rang out they turned as one in her direction. "He could be, but in fact he's right on your doorstep, living in Halifax and, brace yourself James, helping to run one of your, that is the family's mills."

"Good Lord, there is a Featherstone at Lea Bank. Never connected the two but then, there was no reason why I should, it's a common enough name in these parts. So the M. Featherstone I see on the mill reports refers to Michael. a good worker, if what I see there is anything to go by."

"Now we know where he is, what next?" Daphne asked. "Do we make the first move or leave well alone?"

"I'm for the latter."Rob was serious now. "He might never need to know. After all Haig might be wrong in surmising that the old lady left Michael some sort of evidence of his father's parentage."

Helen was the next to speak up. "He might be wrong about that, but we can't be certain that Bea Fatherstone didn't at any time tell her grandson who his grandfather really was."

"If that's the case he hasn't done anything about it yet, so the likelihood of his ever doing so is remote. Besides which a verbal comment wouldn't cut any ice in a court of law. His lordship would have to have tangible proof to substantiate any inheritance claim and I feel like Daphne that we should leave well alone."

"Right Robert, what about the rest of you? Are you all agreed that we do nothing?". Four heads nodded simultaneously in response to James's question. "It goes without saying I hope, that Mama is not to hear a whisper of this and as she and Prinny are so close now, that means excluding Prinny as well".

"There is one thing, James..."

"Yes, Rosa?"

"Prinny did for a long time correspond with Michael. She hasn't mentioned him recently, but I don't know if they're still in touch."

Daphne couldn't conceal her astonishment. "Prinny corresponded with Michael Featherstone? I'm amazed that a boy from the back of the beyond is literate enough to hold her interest!"

"Sister dear, that's a most patronising remark from someone who is supposedly a champion of the working classes."

"You're quite right Rob. I didn't mean it quite as it sounded. I just can't imagine what the two of them would have had in common."

Rosa laughed again and the frisson of tension that had been building steadily since James had started speaking, was quickly dispersed.

"I think that if and when you ever meet Michael Featherstone you will be in for quite a shock. He's not quite the country hick you might imagine and remember it's a few years since I've talked to him, so even more changes are likely."

"Well judging by the accounts I've received from Lea Bank you're right Rosa, he's doing well, very well. He can only be about twenty and he's already moved up from tenter to overseer. Floor manager will be his next step and that can't be far away."

"Helen", Rosa turned to her sister, "you remember the Hintons? Annie left home just after her mother died and went to Halifax to look for work. Just before I went to Oxford, Prinny had a letter from Michael saying that he and Annie were seeing quite a lot of each other. Goodness, I've just realised that this makes me some sort of cousin to Michael. Now that we share the same grandfather. How weird!"

Each now returned to the privacy of her own bedroom and mulled over this new revelation about Oliver Craybourne. Helen pondered on men's sexual needs, needs which so often placed them in unpredictable situations. Oliver had been much loved and admired, but even such a man had fallen prey to bodily urges, the results, of which some fifty years later might well prove troublesome for his family.

Had Jai been so very different from this man and all others? Perhaps Bea Featherstone had deliberately seduced Oliver but it was she who had borne the child, something which could easily have complicated her life. There should be some way in which women could be protected from men who enjoyed themselves and then left, uncaring that their seed could become flesh and blood.

And a woman also had needs, sexual needs. On the few, the precious few blissful nights that she and Jai had shared he had aroused in her feelings she had not known existed. Feelings which had taken over her whole being. These, in spite of the later horrors, she recalled more and more frequently. Only now was she beginning to realise that a woman's sexuality might also be a potential force in its own right. And, smoothing the sleek satin of her nightgown she was becoming aware that once sexuality had been awakened it would not readily be subdued. Soon, it would start to make its own demands.

Chapter Twenty One

Helen fingered the edge of her frilled jabot. The telegram was typical of Jim Calloway. Usually his communications arrived a mere two hours before he himself descended on them. The request that he might see her alone was surprising and a little disturbing. Hitherto his visits had consisted of informal chats over tea or coffee with Betty and herself. If his and their business permitted, a walk along the Embankment or in Hyde Park was arranged, or a quiet dinner. Always Betty was included in the invitation. Helen preferred this, not yet feeling sufficiently at ease to be alone with him for very long. Now, she decided that her office offered the best opportunity for privacy and asked Betty to make sure they were not disturbed.

His presence filled the small room. Unsure as always of her role in his presence, Helen accepted his quick kiss on each cheek, thinking as she went through the motions of taking his coat, offering a seat, etc., that the alternative of shaking hands with her father would be too ridiculous for words!

He came quickly to the point.

"I'm here to ask you to invest in my business Helen."

Her eyes slid away from his face. 'Oh God, not the money again.' she thought, 'just as I feared. What now?'

"It's not quite what you think," he smiled, "hear me out. Archie Reed has had enough - he's seventy four, hasn't been too well of late. His Doctor has warned him it's time to put his feet up. He'd hoped to have a son or a grandson to take over, but that wasn't to be. He's got two daughters, one's a spinster, very much into good works, the other's a widow, husband died of typhoid fever about ten years ago. No children. Neither of the daughters is the least interested in the business, but human nature being what it is, they could always use more money. Clearly, they're putting pressure on Archie to get it all cut and dried before - well, before he gets any worse. So, he wants to sell his share - about forty thousands' worth, all up. I said I'd try and find a buyer...". He hesitated. "Helen, I know in your eyes I've got a bad track record with regard to money, very bad, but that was years ago when I was just a silly kid. Since then I've worked hard and saved hard to get where I am today. Ours is a good business - a sound investment."

"I'm sure you're right, but as you well know I'm about to start a big venture of my own, something which will take, is taking now, all my time and energy. I know nothing whatever about shipping lines and trading - and I'm afraid like Mr. Reed's daughters I've very little interest in finding out."

"I know that if I tell you it's not necessary for you to know anything about it, you'll be even more suspicious of my motives, but to be frank that is exactly the situation. I know where I'm going. I have the knowledge and the expertise to run the line. If Archie is bowing out I certainly don't want anyone else coming in and trying to change things or telling me how to run the business. The bottom line is

159

that I desperately need your money either as an investment or as a loan. Of course I wouldn't expect you to even consider this without taking advice, so I've brought the Company books with me and if you say the word I'll hand them over to your Bank or anyone else for examination."

"You've obviously thought of everything!" Helen smiled, and at last Jim relaxed.

"I know I've got a nerve coming here, but I would like to direct the way Reed and Calloway develops. I know I can do it, if only I'm given a free hand."

"If... 'if wishes were horses', as Prinny used to say. Listen J.C., sorry I really can't call you either Captain or Jim....if my Bank Manager approves then I'll give the matter some thought, I'll need three weeks, say. Is that all right?"

"Helen you're a trump. If you do decide in my favour, I'll see you never regret it."

"Don't worry, if I decide in your favour, I'll see I never regret it."

Jim heard the warning behind the smile and was glad to hear it. This lovely girl of his was now getting herself back on course. Hitherto the quieter of the two children, she was now showing more spark and determination. It would be some time, he thought, before anyone deceived her again and when that happened, he didn't particularly want to be around.

As Helen had anticipated, James was pessimistic about J.C.'s request.

"Asking you to buy a few shares would be one thing, but a half share in the Line is a huge undertaking. Think how much of your money would be tied up in it and more importantly, how much would be at risk."

"But I'm not using the money, in fact it's something of an embarrassment. Perhaps this would be a solution."

"Well, if it's worrying you that much, a good many worthy causes would be only too willing to relieve you of the problem!"

"I know that James and I fully intend helping where and whenever I can, I just don't want...well, I don't want to be rushed into anything before I'm absolutely sure that I'm making the best possible use of the money."

"That's sensible enough. Why don't we leave further discussion until we've got a detailed report from the accountants and then have another chat?"

Jim's other business in London proving more protracted than at first expected, he called again on Helen three days later, to see if the girls had time to take chocolate with him at Charbonnel's. Helen and Betty were not alone. They had asked Sonia to call to discuss arrangements for the launch, at which she and three of her mannequin colleagues would be modelling. Sonia was in the throes of bemoaning the decline of the haute couture trade and the effect it was having on work available for models, when Jim Calloway was ushered in, his arms full of flowers. Chameleon-like she changed immediately. The wilting lily of a few moments ago suddenly glowed with animation. Hearing Jim's invitation and its courteous inclusion of herself she quickly accepted saying that if the girls were too busy she would be most happy to accompany him. And so it transpired. Jim and Sonia departed for Charbonnel's leaving

Helen and Betty to resume some of the tasks which had built up during Helen's longer than expected Christmas absence.

Sonia was delighted with Helen's father. He was after all only fortyish she assured herself and hadn't she always preferred older men? Clearly he was well-heeled. The immaculate suit and hat, the neatly trimmed beard and hair, the silver case in which he kept his cheroots, all spoke eloquently of money. That was a bonus because what really appealed was his matter-of-factness and the roguish twinkle never far from those blue eyes. This was no bland effeminate dandy however, evidenced by the down-to-earth expressions which from time to time crept into his conversation; expressions which Sonia knew would have been taboo in the majority of drawing rooms.

Jim in his turn was captivated. This handsome willowy blonde veered between coquette, woman-about-town and comedienne! He liked these quicksilver changes and found her graceful movements a feast for his eyes. For years he had lived a bachelor existence. There had been women of course and plenty of them, he was too virile for the celibate existence, but never since Craybourne had he co-habited with a woman. All those years ago he had found Mary's fastidiousness irksome. Now, amazingly, it was this very aspect of femininity which he found a source of fascination and attraction. It was as if the raw maleness of those years at sea had created an imbalance leaving him starved of the delicate female touches which he now absorbed like a sponge. He drank in Sonia's graceful movements as she gently eased her skirt before sitting, the way she unbuttoned and removed her gloves and her habit of smoothing a tendril of hair over her ear. Sonia nibbling delicately at a petit four was an art form in herself! She saw and revelled in his absorption, carefully expanding the time taken on each of these movements, very aware that together they made a most handsome couple.

His suggestion that they see each other that evening Sonia accepted with alacrity. She would, she roundly informed him, take him to the best pub in London where they could eat 'bangers and mash' and sing songs round the piano. Inwardly he marvelled at the fact that she could behave like a duchess in Charbonnel's, but was not above visiting more homely establishments and, he felt sure, letting her hair down. What a woman!

By the time Jim Calloway left for London he had two major causes for concern. One, whether his daughter would accede to his request and his course of action if she refused and the second, how soon he could correctly make a bid for Sonia before some much younger beau beat him to it.

The first question was quickly resolved. Within two weeks he received a wire from Helen. Her accountants had approved the accounts, (she did not add how fulsome their approval had been) and she had decided to invest the sum requested. Would he visit London as soon as possible to iron out the legal practicalities of her becoming a partner? Grinning at the sombre photographs of himself and Archie surmounting the office fireplace he spoke aloud in the empty room. "Sorry Archie old chap you're going to have to move over, to make room for my girl. She's a real stunner and no mistake. Can't wait until some of our clients see her picture up there! Can I go to London she says? I can and I will. Perhaps I can deal with that other matter at the same time. And kill, if you'll forgive the expression, two birds with one stone."

Daphne did not return to London until mid-February, Elizabeth being concerned that she should be really fit before being once again exposed to the rigours of London fogs. Muriel and Peter Fairburn were both delighted to see her, the former grateful for Daphne's advice and support as the preparation for her Easter wedding gathered momentum. Peter's delight was at first tempered by Daphne's frail appearance. Having grown accustomed to the strength and forcefulness of her character, he discovered in himself a new vein of protectiveness on seeing her now subdued and apparently vulnerable. His offers to escort her were more readily accepted and he began to wonder if she might at last be receptive should he attempt to put their relationship on a more intimate basis.

Two weeks after her return to London they went together to a meeting of the East London Federation of Suffragettes. Oblivious to the speaker, Peter's attention was focussed on the small ungloved hand lying so close to his own. On an impulse he covered it with his work-stained fingers, waiting for a reaction. Daphne continued to look straight ahead, but the gentle curling of her fingers into his own delighted him. So often in her company, his instinct had been to dampen her impetuosity, to bemoan the fact, as Prinny had done so many years ago, that she had not been disciplined more as a child. He realised now just how much he had enjoyed the parry and thrust of her conversation, the quick riposte, the touches of asperity. He smiled wryly resolving to make the most of this newly compliant Daphne as it was unlikely that this blissful state would endure very long. When at the end of the evening there was no protest as he gently tucked her arm through his, he decided that things were definitely looking up.

The workroom of Helena Modes was bristling with activity as the Easter wedding and the opening of their salon started to loom on the horizon. In her office Helen, having dealt with the paperwork awaiting her, was just starting on a letter to the Rani, when Betty burst into the room.

"I've had the most brilliant idea, at least I think it's brilliant."

Helen pushed back her chair and put down her pen. She was used, well almost used, to this new Betty, who since announcing after Christmas that she and Eddie had reached an 'understanding', seemed full of enthusiasm for whatever job was at hand.

"I'm working on the beadwork design for the bodice of Muriel's dress and as James's seat is in Yorkshire, I decided to include the white rose of Yorkshire. Then I thought why shouldn't we include this on all of our garments - a tiny white rose. After all you're from Yorkshire too. It would be our symbol, trademark if you like and it would signify that only garments bearing that sign were genuine 'Helena Modes'. What do you think?"

162

"The idea is great. But Betty, you're doing it again! Why not something representative of your part in all this?"

"I knew you'd say that, so I did give it some thought. There's London Pride and Bow Bells of course, but both too complicated to reproduce. I'd rather stick to the rose idea, if you agree."

Helen capitulated, "I suppose we could have small silk labels made up with the rose and our name."

"We could, but to begin with let's do it by hand. Once we've agreed the exact shape and size it won't take one of my girls more than say, fifteen minutes to add the rose either incorporating it into the design if the dress colour allows, or stitching it into the lining or facing."

"How's the wedding dress coming along?"

"The foundation's finished and I'm trying to decide between two ideas for the decorative work. I need another opinion, come down and tell me what you think."

Acknowledging that her letter to the Rani would have to wait until the evening, Helen followed Betty down the stairs.

By the time Jim arrived in London, Helen's solicitors had the necessary documents ready for signature. These ensured that Helen's investment bought her an equal partnership in her father's business, with all the rights that entailed. Jim's good humour was so infectious and her Bank Manager so full of encouragement regarding the viability of the shipping line that Helen felt it would be churlish not to echo their enthusiasm in some way. With this in mind she arranged a small celebratory dinner party at their flat. They were six in number, Betty and Eddy, Walter, Sonia, Jim and herself.

Helen and Betty, having finally succumbed to the necessity for employing a cook/housekeper, were slightly apprehensive about this, their first serious entertainment. Amy Colston was a Scot, whose train-driver husband had died some two years earlier. Since that time she had worked in a hospital kitchen and was now clearly delighted to have good china and glassware on which to display her considerable culinary skills. If the girls were apprehensive, she was not, her confident demeanour underlining the fact that tonight she was determined to show her mettle.

Eddy was his usual quiet self, Helen noted. These days Betty had such an abundance of aplomb and enthusiasm that it was easy for him to remain in the background. I wonder if he'll always be happy with that situation, she mused. Betty, like me, has changed so much in these last months. Will Eddy be able to keep pace with her if she continues to change? Is this what the men in Government and elsewhere have against the suffragettes? We've never held the reins before. Are they afraid that if and when we do, there's the danger that they'll be pushed into the background? Only when women have money do they seem to have any power, any authority. It shouldn't affect men's attitudes, but it certainly does! For me the

163

best thing about having that 'formidable fortune' is that it's given me a freedom of choice, the opportunity to attempt all sorts of things which would have been out of the question. I can never be grateful enough to the Rani for making that possible for me. Now she covertly watched as Eddy quietly complimented Amy on the excellence of the food. He couldn't be more different from Jai she thought, his kindnesses, unlike Jai's showy gestures, are totally unobtrusive.

During the meal it occurred to Helen that she had rarely seen Sonia in male company. Hitherto with Betty and herself Sonia had been very much the leader, the experienced older girl, always good company and fun to be with. Now Helen saw that, seated between Jim and Walter, two very personable males, she was enjoying herself to the full. Sonia had in fact, accepted Helen's invitation with glee and was now somewhat nonplussed. She had wanted very much to see Jim Calloway again, to reassure herself that his interest was not transitory.

Tonight she was confronted by not one but two, apparently unattached, delectable males. Jim was handsome, mature and doing very nicely if the implications of this dinner were anything to go by. Walter on the other hand was handsome, probably penniless -but young! Not quite so sparky as Jim of course, but after a few hours in her company, who knows? It was possible they both had other fish to fry elsewhere and Jim did have some of the hallmarks of a philanderer, but 'nothing venture nothing have! ' Walter already enchanted by his delightful dinner partner suddenly found himself the sole recipient of her most brilliant smile.

Only to herself would Helen admit her pleasure at J.C.'s suggestion that the shipping line now be renamed. Rejecting 'Calloway and Calloway' as more appropriate for a firm of solicitors and dismissing out of hand Sonia's facetious proposal that 'Calloway and Daughter' might set a precedent, they all agreed that the simplest and most apt title was 'The Calloway Line'.

Jim declared his intention of informing all mercantile offices and national newspapers of the new partnership. As they together raised their glasses to toast its success, Helen wondered if she had misconstrued the look of speculation which Sonia had turned upon her father. Pondering why this should trouble her, her mind leapt back to an afternoon in Hyde Park, when Sonia svelte and skittish in tailored coral had announced emphatically that she intended marrying a rich man. The others had laughingly questioned how she would ensure this and her answer had been razor-sharp, "Simple - I shall consider no others!" Now, as Sonia dazzled Walter, Helen saw the cloud which crossed Jim's face. Doesn't he realise it's probably for his benefit? It looks as if Sonia has got her rich man well and truly hooked!

Amy's comment as they retired did nothing to quell Helen's misgivings. "Your father seems right taken with yon friend of yours, Sonia. An' if ye'll excuse me saying so Miss Helen, I canna help thinking she could be a right handful!"

Chapter Twenty Two

Easter Saturday, April 11th, 1914

Craybourne Church was packed for the wedding of its Lord of the Manor. Those who couldn't squeeze into the back, lined the walk from church door to lych gate. The day was bright but the breeze cool, and Prinny fussed between Elizabeth and Daphne to ensure that neither was unduly exposed to its chill.

Inside, the church was fragrant and bright with orange blossom and spring flowers, and Muriel radiant in her white fairy-tale dress. Encrustatians of pearls and crystal covered the bodice and spilled into panels which narrowed, frond-like, at the hemline. Her cloud of veil was secured by a simple circlet of pearls entwined with orange blossom and she carried a posy of white and lemon rosebuds. Helen and Daphne's dresses were of the palest lemon velvet with sashes of green and the small bridesmaids and pages wore variants of these colours. The over-all effect was springlike and charming. Robert was an elegant best man and Muriel, in the absence of any male relatives of her own, was given away by Lady Eynsford's brother who had, since Daphne's party, declared himself completely captivated by Muriel's charms.

In addition to family and mutual friends the reception was attended by James's colleagues from both Houses of Parliament and members of the local nobility. Whilst all were scrupulously polite, Helen nevertheless knew that she was under scrutiny and started to wilt under the impact of so much open and covert interest. At the very moment when she felt herself to be at screaming point, Robert appeared at her elbow and, with profuse apologies to those around her, insisted that she was urgently needed elsewhere. 'Elsewhere' proved to be his mother's boudoir, a small haven of tranquillity in which she gratefully drank the tea he brought her and for a few minutes let his nonsense wash over her, until she felt her flagging spirits lift and knew she was ready once again to wear her 'sociable' face.

"How did you know?" she asked him.

"My dear Helen, you had taken on the look of a fox at bay. And, I might add, those around you looked increasingly like a pack of hounds, particularly the female of the species!"

The next morning Helen travelled to Liverpool, having promised her father that she would spare him three days to visit his offices and staff, meet the owners of other mercantile businesses and those of the Calloway Line's Captains in port. Their first stop was her hotel, both to deposit her luggage and to take luncheon. When, coffee finished, they were ready to leave, Jim handed her a small package.

"I thought you should have a memento of the founding of our partnership...it's just a trinket."

The trinket proved to be a gold brooch. Five small enamelled flags were strung along the gold pin and when Helen looked up questioningly, Jim explained, "They spell out your name in seaman's code. Five letters - I haven't added that extra 'a' because to me you're still Helen, the name your mother wanted, indeed insisted you should have. I thought something to do with the sea would be appropriate...."

"It's lovely J.C. and such a wonderful idea. Thank you. I'd like to put it on now, if you'll help me."

So, to the amusement and curiosity of other diners, Jim carefully pinned the colourful little brooch to the collar of her smart grey travelling suit. Then, whispering in her ear, "Let's give them something to think about!", he kissed her cheek and, tucking her arm through his escorted her from the room.

Helen found her father an excellent host, anticipating what would afford her most interest. At the sight and sounds of the docks, memories of her journeys to and from India came flooding back. And as the creaking and sawing of timbers, the rattling of masts mingled with the constant activity of loading and unloading, she wondered how it was possible to establish order out of seeming chaos.

The Reed Calloway offices were housed amidst the conglomeration of buildings used for storage and victualling. The building was on two levels, its ground floor housing the clerical staff who seemed to Helen's inexperienced eye to be in danger of drowning under the creeping tide of burgeoning files and stacks of paper. Upstairs were the partners' offices, a secretary's room and a small waiting area. It was immediately obvious on entering Jim's office what had determined the layout of the building. The unbroken view across the Mersey with its fringes of activity was panoramic. Below and around them everything moved, but at the heart of it all was the river which by comparison appeared almost static.

Jim had often admired the fact that his daughter never felt the necessity to fill silences, waiting always until she had something worthwhile to say. What she said now was "It's impressive" and he knew she referred not to his business, but to that which fired his own imagination, the power of the river itself. Always he had felt a child of the sea, appreciating its changes of mood; now he felt a new affinity with his daughter. He sensed that she too acknowledged the power of the sea and its tributaries, the force which had generated the very cities into which they continued to pump life-blood.

Helen was now staring at the portraits over the mantelpiece of an unusually stern Jim and the moustachioed Archie. Smilingly, she asked him to unwrap the slim package he was carrying for her. Her own face stared up at him, its colourful beauty shining forth despite the sepia tones. The wide-set eyes stared back at the viewer, her mouth even in repose, sweetly sensuous. A sharp expulsion of breath pre-empted his delighted exclamation.

"Tomorrow - when you come again tomorrow, this will be in its rightful place and now there's something else you should see."

He ushered her downstairs and into an adjoining workshop, where two men were painting a sign some 15ft. long spelling out for all to see, 'The Calloway Line'.

"That too, will be in place tomorrow, couldn't quite manage it for today."

His delight was catching and she started to enjoy more and more the novelty of her situation and the ambience of this male-orientated environment.

The following day she was introduced over glasses of sherry to the other Directors. Without exception, they seemed to have reached their three score years and ten but, she decided, it was perhaps just the abundance of white hair and moustaches which gave that impression. They blinked at this bird of paradise set down in their midst, rubbed their ear lobes and clicked their teeth, before being won over by the gentle creature who, they decided, was far too decorative to prove in any way threatening.

"That's the difficult lot, the old brigade. You'll enjoy the company of the captains rather more I think," Jim grinned at his daughter.

On the afternoon of the next day three of them presented themselves for inspection by the new partner of the Calloway Line. Perhaps it would be more correct to say that it was she who was under inspection, Helen mused, as the first bearded gentleman took her gloved hand in his own. Jim had laughingly introduced them as "Tom, Dick and Harry" and this they enlarged upon. "Thomas Sibbick ma'am at your service", "Richard Thornton, delighted to meet you ma' am", "Henry Gurney ma ' am. My compliments, Jim, the decor has certainly improved since my last visit!"

The ice broken, they all sat down. A nervous looking youth produced a tray of tea, which was speedily augmented by whisky and the anecdotes started to flow. Helen saw her father in his own world, at home with these men and they with him. He deferred to their knowledge as master mariners, whilst they in turn were equally deferential when matters of commerce were discussed. Four other captains she learned were on the high seas and one newly appointed master was visiting the dry dock where his new ship was nearing completion. Jim had another surprise for her, "I know how busy you are but I'm afraid I'm going to ask you to make this journey again in four weeks' time. Your launch will be over by then and I'm sure Betty will be happy to hold the fort for a few days. I need you for a christening on May 9th."

Helen registered surprise and he laughed, "Our new ship, that is yours and mine, will be hitting the water on that day. I want you to be here to christen her Helena and yes, this time I've added the extra 'a', somehow it seemed to flow better. Tell your sister the next one will be Rosa and she can do the honours!"

It was a weary Helen who boarded the London train and bade farewell to her father. In a few short days there had been the excitement of the wedding, her own ensuing 'Spanish Inquisition' by Yorkshire's high society, the pleasure of seeing Rosa and catching up with her news and, finally, the different experiences and personalities encountered during the Liverpool visit. Tom, Dick and Harry, once relaxed, had been like a comedy turn, each determined to outdo the others with his reminiscences. Tom, she decided, was like his bristly carrot-coloured hair, all fire and brimstone, immediately on the defensive if he suspected that anyone was laughing at, rather than with him. Harry probably did have a girl in every port, compliments flew too readily to his lips. Of the three she certainly preferred Richard Thornton. He was polite without being deferential, pleasant without Harry's suavity and quietly amusing.

Now, she really must give some thought to the Helena launch and sort out a list of priorities for the next few days. That is, after she had closed her eyes for a moment or two. The two elderly ladies sharing her compartment, smiled and whispered to each other in a proprietorial manner as Helen slept soundly and the train steamed steadily southwards.

Two days after her return, Helen was once more in dockland, this time in Tilbury to examine a warehouse available for rental. The store-room at the Bond Street premises was now crammed to capacity with material from India and mindful of Neville Aston's recommendation regarding some stock-piling, a further large consignment was on its way from Bombay, this time with the emphasis on all-purpose materials. The warehouse certainly met their major criteria that it should be clean and dry. It was also about four times as large as they had anticipated. On two levels, each main area had been sub-divided and she noted there was loading access to both levels. A section had been added to the facade to provide two offices and two utility rooms. Impressed with the state of the building and its proximity to the heart of the docks, Helen asked the agent to grant her a twenty four hour reserve on the contract.

Back in her office she used the newly installed telephone to ring Jim Calloway. Would there be any occasion when he might require storage at Tilbury she enquired and explained the reason behind her question. "Yes", was his unequivocal reply. "When the war starts," he added, (always now she noted, it was 'when' and not 'if') "it could prove very useful for us to have several of our ships based at Tilbury. Storage areas will be in demand - in fact they might well be requisitioned by the Government, but we'll meet that if we come to it. Grab it now while you and can and we'll share it and the cost. All right? If things snowball for us at Tilbury, we'll also be glad of some office space. In the meantime organise a couple of camp beds for one of those front rooms would you?" "Beds?"

"Yes, when the warehouse is full we'll have to employ a watchman to make regular visits; meanwhile I'll get a couple of the lads off each of our ships docking there to use the building as a base during their stay. It'll be cheap digs for them and someone policing the premises for us."

Buying into the Calloway line hadn't been such a bad idea after all, Helen thought as she replaced the receiver, it was proving quite an educative experience! In Liverpool her father's undoubted business acumen had given her a number of ideas and his advice about the warehouse was short and to the point. Smiling, she picked up her pen and added 'Beds' to the list of items requiring attention.

The next morning having signed the contract confirming a five year lease on the building, Helen set off for the East End to look for a suitable building for Muriel's dressmaking school. Neither of the first two properties she was shown had a single room large enough for what Muriel had had in mind. The third was a solid corner property, some fifty years old, with two good sized rooms, one on each level. Each of these had huge windows allowing maximum light, ideal for sewing rooms. There were other smaller rooms, a kitchen and a lavatory. One room would be a children's playroom and another at ground level was needed to house babies in prams, when it proved too wet or cold for them to be left in the garden. The garden was a bonus. Most of the children would have come from terraced, artisans' houses, fronted by a yard or, if lucky, a tiny patch of grass. Helen felt quite elated at the prospect of children playing hide and seek in and around this well-established garden.

Muriel and Daphne had agreed to organise the purchase of long tables for cutting and sewing, together with a long sideboard, extra shelving and storage cupboards. Helen had spoken to a trade contact about sewing machines and Fred Bloomfield had promised her six for the price of five, providing she bought from him all other ancillary items. He it was who put her in touch with a supplier whose stock of material had recently been damaged by burst water pipes. In some cases only a fraction of the bolt had been damaged and about twenty of these were now in Helen's possession. Three seamstresses were ready and waiting for the 'off' and although Muriel was not due back from her Paris honeymoon for some ten days, Helen felt that with the assistance of Daphne and Peter Fairburn everything would be in place for her return. Whitechapel had been selected as an ideal area for the school to be sited because of its proximity to the church hall where most of the meetings of the East London Federation of Suffragettes were held. It was also where Peter worked. He assured them that there were already at least two dozen 'takers' for the scheme with quite a few ditherers, clearly waiting until they received feed-back from the others, before committing themselves. All had young children and the mothers themselves were to take turns in looking after them helped by Annie, the fourteen year old daughter of the senior seamstress. Daphne and Peter were full of enthusiasm when they saw the property and immediately set about making arrangements for the furnishings to be moved in.

At the Salon Helen found a letter from the Rani awaiting her. After the preliminary felicitations she wrote that there was 'disconcerting news from Jaishalpar'. The British authorities had prevented two acts of suttee but in a third case the information had reached them too late and a sixteen-year-old girl had died.

"I can hardly believe that this should happen in a province where for so many years I tried to educate our people against such practices. As this was not an isolated case I suspect there has been a deliberate plan on the part of Romesh to flout the British and incite trouble. He knows also my view on this subject and that I have now joined the conference to debate the issues of child marriages and suttee. I fear that because of his disapproval a young girl had to die. I have at last had contact with many like-minded people; first of all at an Indian women's meeting in Bombay and then in February at a five day conference in Delhi where women and men, Indian and British were represented. Our first task was to determine our aims and objectives and it was most reassuring to find our hearts and minds so much in unison.

"Metta keeps in touch with me, secretly. She tells me my grandson grows tall and strong and is a very loving boy. I pray daily that she may be spared the heartache I suffered.

"I was pleased to learn of your annulment. Your life is now full of many pleasant things I feel. I pray it will continue so and that you will find true happiness.

"My felicitations to Lord Crayboune and your friend on their marriage. To you and Miss Carter all good wishes on your business venture. Please ask if you think I can assist you further.

"Remembering you always with affection"

Yes, Helen decided it would be quite in Jai's character to attempt to make his mother's new position untenable by ensuring that British law was flouted in the province where she had lived for many years. Shuddering at the thought of what suttee entailed, she joined Betty in the main Salon.

Here, men had been working under Betty's direction to prepare for the launch. The six foot square dais had been doubled in size and the wall behind it was now a shimmering waterfall of vivid Indian materials cascading from ceiling to floor. Around the perimeter of the room white pillars had been placed, each one now entwined with greenery. In one corner a cluster of shrubs of varying heights were interspersed with miniature lemon and orange trees. The effect was exotic and charming. Betty however did not seem pleased.

"Thank goodness - I wanted to see you."

"Is something wrong?"

"It certainly is! It's Sonia - again. This is the third time she's let me down this week. I really don't know what to make of it. I called a run through for ten o'clock. - it's now mid-day and not a word! I've sent the other girls off to have some lunch. The question is what should I do next?"

"Could she be ill?"

"She wasn't ill on the previous occasions. On the first she said she'd misunderstood, had got the dates mixed up. The second time she arrived - very late, said something about having over-slept. Now Flo says she's sure she saw her in Oxford Street this morning with a young officer. Walter, would you think?"

"Quite likely, but who she was with is beside the point. She obviously wasn't where she was supposed to be. She has a responsibility to be here to rehearse with all of you and ensure everything goes like clockwork. That's what we pay her for. I think we should give Alf a message to take to her home now, saying that we expect her tomorrow and if she doesn't turn up we'll find a substitute."

"That's a bit steep, isn't it?"

"It's what is necessary. We have a business to run and we can't let her presume on our friendship by playing fast and loose with us. After all, she's the one who's always complaining that there isn't much work around. We've got a hundred people coming on Friday expecting to see a slick presentation of what we have to offer. We can't afford to take any chances. I'll write that note now."

Within minutes Alf had left the building and in less than an hour a somewhat irate Sonia appeared asking what all the fuss was about. For the first time Helen was aware how their roles had changed. No longer was she the younger inexperienced girl looking to Sonia for advice and guidance. She was now the employer, an owner of property, a woman of substance as they said in Yorkshire, with the experience of marriage and travel behind her. This new persona of hers saw Sonia as a rather flighty young woman who had abused both her friendship and hospitality. Keeping a rein on her anger, she spelled out the necessity for Sonia's presence at ensuing rehearsals, a fact of which Sonia was well aware.

"No problem darling. Of course I'll be here, it's just that - well something cropped up this morning and it was too late to get a message to you."

Helen did not press the matter. Working under a cloud of animosity was unlikely to produce happy results and the results were all-important.

Early on the Friday morning flowers arrived from Covent Garden. Hard on their heels came the caterers, setting up their champagne buffet with speed and efficiency. One corner of the main salon contained a display of artwork showing designs for decorative work and samples of the different ornamentation available. Helen had taken heed of Muriel's comments and the smaller salon, draped in purple, grey and black, invited clients to inspect ready-to-wear mourning clothes from Helena Modes. The range was smart and unfussy. Extra trimming it was pointed out, could be added as desired.

At eleven o'clock. the noisy salon thronging with women of all ages and a sprinkling of male buyers was suddenly silenced and the parade began. At its conclusion the plaudits were considerable and there were requests from a number of established stores that contracts might be discussed regarding regular supplies of selections of evening dresses. Buyers also showed a great deal of interest in the mourning clothes. Here too it seemed some regular contracts could be agreed. This contracted work was exactly what they had hoped for, knowing it would form the backbone of their business. Before the buffet was completely dismantled, Helen and Betty hastily seized glasses of champagne and laughingly toasted each other and 'Helena Modes'.

"That's the first of the Helenas launched, the second could be a slightly damper experience!" With that, Betty left to ensure all her precious dresses were carefully rehung.

At the morning's end as Helen supervised the disposal of various hired items, a uniformed figure appeared. Walter first of all congratulated Helen on what he gathered had been a huge success then, looking slightly sheepish, asked if Sonia's duties were concluded.

"Good heavens yes, she's still in one of the changing rooms though. Shall I get her?"

"No no. I'll wait, if I may. We're just going to have some lunch..." Walter hesitated, "Would you care to join us ?"

"Thank you.... but I'm afraid it's out of the question. As you can see there's enough here to keep me occupied for quite some time."

"I'm glad all's going well for you now." Walter had started diffidently, but now gained confidence. "You know, sometimes I can hardly believe it, little Helen in her white pinafore smock in Piggott's Lane, now a partner in a shipping line, partner of a dress emporium, a very wealthy lady and a doer of good works in the city."

"Oh yes, the formidable fortune - let's not forget that!" He looked puzzled and she smiled.

"It's a private joke. And I don't know about the doer of good works bit, that really hasn't quite got off the ground yet."

"But it will, Sonia was only telling me.... " He stopped.

"Yes, Sonia was telling you..?".

"Oh - just that you'd found a house in Whitechapel for the dressmaking school and that you'd also found a warehouse in Tilbury. You're quite amazing!"

Helen could only guess at Sonia's knowledge of the warehouse. Either she had spoken to Jim on the telephone or he had written to her. Certainly neither she nor Betty had discussed this with any member of the staff. Interesting!

"I don't know about that. It's not until you attempt something that you know what you're capable of. When Mother was ill I had to grow up very quickly and probably built up a resilience to dealing with unhappy situations. In the last few months I've built up even more. By now I've grown a very hard shell..." Before she could finish Sonia came swanning into the room in one of her 'Look at me, I'm a mannequin' moods."

"Darling - I'm sorry, have you been waiting ages?" Clearly she was hopeful that this was the case."

Walter was obviously discomfited, both by the mode of address and the question. "No - haven't been here long. Helen's been keeping me company."

"Of course." The grey eyes raked the two of them, looking for signs of intimacy. Clearly nothing untoward had been said and Sonia, airily bidding Helen farewell, made a flamboyant exit, suggesting that Walter should hurry as she was 'starving'.

Helen spoke quickly, determined to spare Walter further embarrassment. "Isn't she incredible? Just how she keeps that figure of hers I'll never know, she's always eating!"

With that they were gone and she could relax. Clearly Sonia was having regular contact with Jim. She had already told Helen that after the launching of the S.S.Helena, he was coming to London for at least a week. That Jim should have conveyed this news to Sonia rather than herself implied a close relationship or one that he hoped would be so. Helen admitted to a slight apprehension that this liaison might in some way affect both her business and personal relations with Jim

Calloway. What puzzled her was why, suddenly, Sonia was seeing so much of Walter? They were all free agents of course, but knowing Sonia's marital aspirations, Helen hoped fervently that Walter was not going to be hurt again.

Walking down the Strand with Sonia on his arm, Walter had no reservations whatsoever. Spring was in the air and the admiring glances taking in Sonia in her chic flame-coloured suit and the handsome young officer, fuelled his sense of wellbeing. At Simpsons he was entertained during lunch by stories of what it was like to be behind the scenes at such times as this morning's presentation. There was no time for modesty, Sonia declared, two or three dressers helped to thrust or pour models into one outfit after another. "And," she announced coyly, "the really slim fitting light-weight dresses mean a minimum of undergarments. So you're wriggling out of a dress and suddenly find you're standing there, as naked as nature intended."

He was alternately delighted and shocked by her chatter. None of the girls he had known, whatever their station, had talked in this racy fashion. It set his pulses racing and he started to wonder what this gorgeous creature looked like 'as nature intended'. Covertly she watched him from under long lashes. Hooked, line and sinker he was! They'd have a rare old time during the coming weeks. But she'd be careful of course. A few kisses and caresses, enough to keep him anxious for more, but nothing to jeopardise her big chance. She'd now ascertained there was nothing here for her except a good-looking beau who could escort her around town and be happy to pick up the bills en route. Jim, on the other hand, would be just right for her. They had the same lack of respect for convention, the same somewhat bawdy sense of humour, but were both capable of putting on the style when necessary. And, most important of all, Jim knew how to make money and did not seem averse to enjoying spending it. Soon, very soon, if she played her cards right, people would be referring to her as 'the rich Mrs Calloway'. Smiling into Walter's adoring eyes, she squeezed his hand affectionately.

Chapter Twenty Three

Helen felt a mounting wave of nervousness and excitement. She had lunched with Jim and the Captains, Henry and Richard, and now saw from the office windows that the earlier clusters of people had grown to a crowd of several hundreds.

Jim rubbed his hands with satisfaction.

"It's because they know who you are lass. The men want to see if you're as bonny as they've heard and the women,well, they want to see that too but they also want to see what you're wearing. I reckon you'll satisfy the lot of them on all counts, you're a right knockout!" Grins and grunts of acquiescence were directed at Helen and she felt her qualms subside a little. She had chosen her outfit carefully to ensure that she was clearly visible against the darkness of the ship's underbelly. Her two piece was of a brilliant jade-green with copper-coloured frogging down the bodice and matching braiding at hem and cuffs. So that all could see her face and hear her voice she had selected a hat with the brim lifted on one side and fastened with an aigrette of copper. The effect was striking and elegant.

Waiting for her cue on the small platform, she was fascinated by the pinkness of the sea of faces gazing up at her. The clothes of the crowd merged into a dull grey, but the faces shone forth, bright and pink. Grinning or earnest, they seemed to her strangely vulnerable. As the bottle struck the great ship and she started her ponderous slide, the roar from six hundred throats was deafening. Then, as she came to rest in the waters of the Liver, a cheer shook the platform causing it to shiver and vibrate. At Helen's slight stumble, Jim took her hand and raised it with his own. Again the crowd roared its approval and when they left the podium to retrace their steps to the Calloway offices, Helen felt in danger of being engulfed by so much good-humoured back-slapping and the flood of hands which pressed approval on them from all sides.

It was Richard Thornton, Helen noted, who was the first to see her to a chair, take her bag and gloves and offer her some form of refortification. Not the inevitable sherry, but a small glass of whisky. "Medicinal!" His eyes twinkled at her and she felt grateful for the thought and better for the stimulant. Whilst Jim and Henry enthused over the smooth launching of the Helena, Richard informed her that he would be docking at Tilbury in the second week in July and hoped that he might then take her out for dinner. Her ready acceptance delighted him and when he excused himself, pleading a ship to be readied for departure the next day, he took a long look at the slim elegant figure, whose brilliance lit up the sombre office, hoping that he would be able to retain the image for eight long weeks.

On her return Helen found that work in the sewing rooms at Bond Street was brisk as Betty and her team fulfilled the new contracts. Four firms had each ordered twelve evening dresses and there were some two dozen additional private commissions. Whilst thirty dresses could be drawn from those displayed at the opening, there was still a considerable shortfall to be worked on. To cope with this two more skilled seamstresses and another cutter had been engaged.

At the Whitechapel house a routine had been established on a rotation system. Ten young mothers were being given lessons for two days weekly, with a further ten alternating. Friday of each week was retained as a day when the seamstresses tidied the workrooms and prepared work for the following week. The scheme had now run for two weeks and Muriel and Daphne were enthusiastic about its potential. They were grateful for Helen's assistance, both practical and financial. With regard to the latter, they believed the house to have been taken on a long term rental basis. In fact Helen had bought the property. A survey had shown it to be of sound construction and at the back of her mind was the feeling that should the school eventually outlive its usefulness, then the building might prove useful in another capacity. In any event, it could always be sold.

Muriel and James had visited Yorkshire once since their return from Paris and reported that Elizabeth's illness seemed to be in remission and she was reasonably well. Rob was spending more and more time with the Yorkshire territorials and Prinny - well Prinny was the same as ever, unfussy, unflappable, meticulous.

"Can't imagine what we ever did without her," James remarked often. Two days before their arrival at Craybourne, Haig had died.

"I never saw that man put a foot wrong." James had said. "He was an exemplary butler and now even in dying he's made it conveniently possible for me to attend his funeral. I'm grateful for that".

The tenants and villagers were also grateful. To see the Lord of the Manor and his Lady paying their last respects to a man who had served the family faithfully for many years was right and proper. Trouble might be looming in Europe but there were some things which should remain constant. With gusto they raised their voices in the Doxology, satisfied that almost everyone had managed to find something in a 'good black' and that the old man had been given a 'send-off' worthy of him.

Helen had seen little of Sonia or Walter since the salon opening, but Eddy was a regular visitor, taking Betty out several times a week when his duties permitted. It had been arranged that the three of them should drive to Oxford on the Whitsuntide weekend and spend a couple of days there with Rosa and Alex. On the Wednesday prior to this, Helen received a call from a distressed Rosa. At first almost incoherent, it was a few moments before Helen understood what she was saying and its implications. Alex had been unwell for several weeks nothing specific, just listless and plagued by a persistent irritating cough. Succumbing finally to Rosa's plea that he see a doctor, he was told immediately that he had tuberculosis. One lung only was shadowed and the doctor had advised that rest, fresh air and good food would all assist towards a full recovery. It did mean though that he must leave the University at once and would not be permitted to return until he received a clean bill of health. There was more.

"The doctor asked to see me too, Helen. He examined me and asked the most embarrassing questions - he wanted to know whether Alex and I .... It was awful. He said even kissing can pass on the disease and although he says I'm all right at the moment, he wants to see my health monitored for several months." At this the tears started again.

"I can't believe it. Everything was going so well. I've been getting good grades and my tutors seemed really pleased with me. Now this. Poor Alex and poor me. What about all our plans?"

"Stop crying, Rosa, and listen. We've got to be practical. Yes, it's rotten luck, but the doctor obviously believes Alex will be all right if he follows medical advice. That's the first problem dealt with. With regard to you and your studies - it's June next week, so you would soon be down for the summer anyway Only a few weeks will be lost. If you agree, this is what I think we should do. We'll drive down as planned and bring you back to London with us. I can help you pack and we'll send your trunk by rail. Make arrangements at the College about returning in the autumn. Stay with me for a couple of days, I'll make sure you rest and it will give us chance to talk. Much as I'd love to have you stay longer, I think London is the last place for you to be at the moment. What you need is Yorkshire's bracing air. I know there won't be young people around, but when Rob's at home, I'm sure he'll be happy to take you out and about. Normally I'd say please yourself whether you stay in the cottage or at the Manor, but in the circumstances I think it has to be the latter if Elizabeth agrees and I'm sure she will. Prinny can then sure you get plenty of rest, have regular meals and eat your greens."

Rosa had stopped crying.

"You're right, Helen I'll only miss two or three weeks' lectures. I could have regular check-ups from the Craybourne doctor and do lots and lots of reading ready for the Autumn."

"In the fresh air." interjected Helen.

"Yes ma'am! In the fresh air. Perhaps it won't be so bad after all".

Further details having been agreed Helen replaced the receiver and pondered again at the new traits which had surfaced in her own character. She had surprised herself at the authority with which she had spoken to Rosa, the speed with which the plans had crystallised. After all Rosa was the quick-witted one, the extrovert, never at a loss in any situation. It would be nice to think this new confidence had burgeoned out of unhappiness. Nice, but would it be honest? Resilience perhaps, but confidence? If it were true then she would have had something to thank Jai for after all. But having now met some of the 'scholars' at the dressmaking school, she knew the former rarely applied. More often rejection and ill-treatment resulted in a lowering of self-esteem and a resultant lack of confidence. At least this applied where financial circumstances were such that the recipient was unable to walk away from the problem. But when she could walk away.... Here was the nub of the matter. However embarrassing and frightening its possession had been at first, realistically it was the 'formidable fortune' which had given her a new voice and a growing sense of purpose.

Eventually, a somewhat subdued Rosa was seen onto the Yorkshire train, promising faithfully to keep Helen informed of her activities. Her lengthy letter a few days later showed the old Rosa to be in control again. The Craybourne doctor had confirmed that currently she showed no signs whatever of T.B. and had smilingly informed her that her decision to come to the 'most healthy place in the country' could not be bettered. The bracing air of the Yorkshire moors was just the ticket for blowing away cobwebs. He had no qualms about the quality of the food she would be eating, or the regularity of her intake, knowing of old Prinny' s watchful eye. As a regular visitor to the Manor, he knew of the daily calls to the kitchen by the boy from Hislop's bearing huge cans of creamy milk, baskets of brown eggs and the yellowest butter in Yorkshire. Another caller was the gardener with his trugs of fresh vegetables and each day at four o'clock precisely, the squeak of the window in the butler's pantry told the household that a second gardener had left his offering, a basket of dessert fruit from the hothouses and gardens. Throughout the year there flowed into those baskets a steady stream of golden pears, nectarines and peaches, green figs, succulent grapes. No, the young Miss Calloway would have no problem in that department.

Rather pertly Rosa added that the doctor had no objection to her reading and continuing her studies - provided she did so in the fresh air! As Helen had predicted, Rob was being very kind and supportive. He had met her in Leeds and driven her to the Manor. Already they had plans for a visit to the county fair and another to Harrogate to take tea at Betty's restaurant.

lain McDonald sent Helen his regards. On their way from abroad were several tropical trees destined for the new Craybourne arboretum and he was planning a visit to London docks to oversee their transfer from thence to Yorkshire. This would be about the second week in July and he would like to telephone Helen then and, if she were free, arrange a meeting.

Helen put down the letter. It's more than likely that Iain's trees are on Richard's ship, she thought ruefully. They are very personable young men and I'll probably enjoy getting to know both of them better. More than that I am definitely not ready for. My life's full enough as it is and there's so much more I feel I could do, given the time and opportunity.

Her work at the Salon was, unlike Betty's, not onerous and she found herself spending more and more time with Muriel and Daphne. The former had found that when the House was sitting, there were long periods when James was occupied and since her marriage had picked up the threads of her campaign with a new sense of urgency.

"I'm even more conscious now of the fact that we, you, Daphne, Rosa and I are all privileged people! We three might have had some struggles, only Daphne was born with a silver spoon in her mouth, but let's face it we've experienced nothing such as these East End women have to contend with. Sorry, Helen, you perhaps have, I keep forgetting what a rotten time you had last year. It's just that sometimes I think of the rarefied atmosphere of Fairoaks School and in spite of all the staff's efforts, the shallowness of some of the girls there. Girls like that awful Diana Weever-Smith. Girls for whom capturing a man seemed to be life's ultimate goal. You know I think I could have lived my life quite happily without a man - I'm pretty independent and I think I'm a survivor. Meeting and loving James was for me, a bonus, and a family would be another wonderful addition. I never forget how fortunate I am."

Together the three young women organised the opening of a second dressmaking school, the aim always being to turn out young women capable of making a simple dress for themselves and garments for their children. After ten weeks if they had accomplished this they left, taking with them the garments they had made. Often the rudiments of basic cooking were taught covertly, with deliberate discussions being started at lunchtime as to how certain dishes had been prepared, their cooking times, costings, etc.

From this arose the decision that a second building should be found to serve the dual purpose of a sewing and cookery school. Mile End was selected as a suitable area and eventually a house was found there, twice the size of the Whitechapel site. From beginning to end, with the building furnished complete with cookers, its quota of sewing machines, and so on, the whole exercise took four weeks. Once again the girls were unaware that Helen had purchased rather than rented the building.

By the time the second week in July came round, Helen felt she was ready for a break. London was basking in a minor heatwave. Everything seemed to bear a coating of dust and people were increasingly irritable in the sticky heat. On this particular morning Helen sank gratefully into an armchair. The room was relatively cool due to Amy's foresight in drawing the curtains to prevent the sun's rays fading the carpet. Not a breath of air stirred them. Amy brought her coffee and handed Helen a small parcel.

"Came an hour ago...I ken it's from your friend across the sea"

Helen turned the package over. It was, as Mrs. Colston said from India, but the writing was certainly not that of the Rani. She broke the seal and pushed the string over the corners releasing the folds of paper. Inside was a piece of soft white material and.... Helen recoiled so violently that the small table at her elbow rocked, slopping coffee in all directions.

Her hand shook as she gingerly lifted from their wrapping several pieces of blood-stained satin. She recognised the material. With it the memories came flooding back. She was seeing Jai for the first time in full Indian dress, just as they were about to disembark at Bombay. It was the same. cream satin edged with apricot, now bloodied and scored. Underneath the material was a piece of the official notepaper of Jaishalpar Palace.

"The Beast is dead, killed by his own kind. We are free at last."

Jai was dead, but by whose hand? There had been no communication from the Rani, yet this package would have taken several weeks to reach England. Unseeing, she stared at the windows as a flurry of air quickened the curtains. Automatically, she crossed the room, closed the windows and drew back the curtains and, as the first silver spears of rain struck the panes, the tears slipped down her cheeks. She remembered the strong handsome lines of Jai's face, his charming smile, the lithe body, taut with pent-up energy. In this moment, she focused only on the good things which had first drawn her to him.

She looked again at the message. Only Metta could have sent it and Helen imagined her feelings of release and relief that her son could not now be marred by the perversions of his father. But what would Metta's position be now with Niaz still tiny and the cunning Ashok waiting in the wings? Helen decided to do nothing for twenty-four hours. If no other news had reached her by then, she would contact Walter and ask if the Army could glean some further information.

Zizi was fretful. Dinner was late and something was lodged in the soft pad of his front left paw. When Jai at last arrived, accompanied by Niaz, the child's squeals of delight startled and irritated the animal further. Jai loved an audience, even that consisting of a three year old and the menial guards. Spearing the first joint of meat he stepped into the cage, cooing and crooning to the huge beast as to a small child. "Here it is, Your Magnificence, what you've been waiting for, but you're going to have to catch it first." Several times he teasingly waved the food towards Zizi, drawing back swiftly as the animal lunged forward to take the joint.

Zizi snarled. He was tired of this game. The smell of the raw meat had whetted his appetite. Already he drooled in anticipation. Again Jai waved the speared meat but as Zizi lunged he missed his footing, stumbling slightly backwards, throwing up his left arm to steady himself. In that gauche movement Zizi's paw flashed out to take the meat and unwittingly raked Jai's upheld arm with her searing claws. Jai did not cry out, but suddenly he was engulfed by fear and instantly Zizi was aware of it. Enraged that food was still being denied her, as the blood poured from his arm she smelled newer, fresher blood and the smell of his fear spurred her on. With a spring her velvet body was upon him. For a few seconds time stood still as the guards watched petrified. At last they sprang into action and pushing the child back, leapt into the cage throwing food into the far corner and with their goads urging Zizi away from his victim. The noise had alerted others. Niaz was quickly removed from a scene which he did not comprehend and horrified attendants removed the body of their ruler, whilst keeping a wary eye on the sullen tiger.

Metta and Ashok were duly informed and within an hour Metta's father, a Sirdar, had called together senior officers of the Palace to make a decision regarding the succession. Ashok presided over the Council. He proposed that he should act as Regent until Niaz was considered competent enough to rule. Ashok was not popular. His cruelty was on a par with that of Jai. Since boyhood they had been agents of evil and the recent act of suttee and other aborted attempts had been carried out by Ashok on Jai's orders. Now there were undercurrents of discontent that the regime was in danger of continuing as before, substituting one malevolent ruler for another. Metta's father, fearful for his daughter's position in all this, suggested it was fitting that the Junior Maharani (the Rani), be asked to return to the Palace as Regent, stressing her popularity with the people. It was not to be. Ashok's subversive threats ensured that the status quo was maintained with himself in power. And so the people of Jaishalpar prepared to bury their potentate.

Walter arrived early to see Helen, before the postman delivered the Rani's letter. He saw that the news of Jai's death had already reached her and asked if she wished, indeed could bear, to hear the more detailed information he had received. When he had finished she sat pale and composed, then opened the letter from India. She exclaimed at seeing the notepaper heading, "But this is from the Palace - at Jaishalpar...?".

Walter hesitated. "There is more, Helen, and it's all horrific. Are you sure you can cope with this?"

She nodded mutely and lowered her head as his words flowed over her. Ashok and Jai had made a pact that should anything happen to Jai, a final insult to the British authorities would be that his wife committed suttee. That Metta would never voluntarily agree to this, they were well aware. That night Metta's father had 'died in his sleep' and without his protection, Metta herself had been an easy target. Drugged by Ashok's guards, she had been placed on one of several flower-banked conveyances beside the funeral pyre and only when the latter was alight had the flowers been swiftly brushed from her face and her own pyre ignited. That British dignitaries had speedily left the scene, leaving soldiers to arrest those responsible, had in no way diminished the success of Ashok's macabre scheme.

Now Helen's tears flowed freely and it was some time before she could see clearly what the Rani had written.

"A great evil has occurred here Helen. Whilst mourning the loss of my own blood and bone and what might have been, I cannot help but feel relief that his barbaric rule has been brought to a halt. Even after death his wickedness reached out to ensure Metta died as a 'gesture' to the British. My followers alerted me and I was brought here swiftly. Ashok has been arrested and banished from this province. Following a term in prison, his movements will be observed at all times.

"I am appointed Regent to my grandson and will ensure that he becomes a caring, just ruler. This may at first limit the amount of work I can now do for other causes, but my first duty must be here in Jaishalpar. I know you will understand that.

"You are in my thoughts and prayers."

Helen folded the letter.

"Now it is really finished. I suppose I always felt that whilst he was alive he would perhaps somehow at some time have an effect on my life... and now he no longer can. It does seem...."

"Yes, Helen...?"

"I can't help feeling that however horrible, there's a sort of poetic justice in all this. To the world Jai showed a veneer of politesse in the same way that he thought Zizi was tamed, civilized if you like and could be relied upon never to harm him. But beneath the surface both were feral beasts and if crossed in any way, they reverted to type."

"You could argue, of course, that Jai's upbringing prevented him from being anything other than he was."

"Walter, it seems that for as long as I can remember I've been making excuses for Jai's behaviour. It's because of that unnatural upbringing that, whilst I weep for the child who has lost his mother, I can only be eternally grateful that someone with the Rani's wisdom and strength is now going to be responsible for him."

Well aware that something disastrous had occurred, and more than a little curious, Amy's entrance was right on cue. Glowering at Walter who seemed to have made whatever was wrong worse, she suggested he should bring the tray of tea in from the kitchen whilst she ushered Helen into the bathroom to repair the damage to her tear-stained face.

Chapter Twenty Four

Helen felt disappointed and frustrated. She had looked forward to Iain McNeal's visit and to his company. He would have all the news from Yorkshire and her mind would be diverted from the harrowing events in India. In the event he proved a poor companion. Gone was the lively personality she had warmed to at Christmas. Once again he was the dour Scot, who at their first meeting she had thought him to be.

There was news from Yorkshire of course. The most startling being that Rob had enlisted and was now with the Yorkshire Green Howards, under canvas at Ripon. "What a strange paradox, that Robert, who at Christmas was the most sceptical about the possibility of war, should be the first of us to be directly involved."

"Just bowing to the inevitable I suppose." Iain answered gloomily. "At least now he'll have a reasonable time to be trained. The majority will just be thrown in at the deep end."

But when Helen asked, "Then why don't you do the same, enlist and get some real training now while there's still time?" he seemed rather taken aback.

"It'll be over long before they get to my age group. Robert's right, those in their twenties will be the first to go."He paused, "I am in the Territorials you know."

Yes, Helen reflected, but undergoing some sedate exercise on the moors, once or twice a month, is not quite the same as the hard training for war which the enlisted men will be receiving. On any other occasion, recalling James's comments at Christmas regarding the duration of the war, she would have challenged Iain's assumption of its brevity, but the dullness of the evening was having a soporific effect on her and she wanted to see it to its conclusion as speedily as possible.

Unaware of the reason for Rosa's prolonged stay in Yorkshire, he reported that she was looking 'bonny' , that Lady Craybourne was much the same and if Prinny was feeling her age, she certainly wasn't complaining about it. The hydrangeas were out in their masses throughout the park and the rose garden was a picture. And that was it! During dinner Helen introduced various topics but all seemed to die from Iain's lack of enthusiasm. She had enjoyed her pre-dinner sherry and wine with her meal, but Iain had declined both. Perhaps he was ill and the soda-water he ordered was to calm his stomach. If so, he was too embarrassed to offer any explanation and she too polite to ask for one.

When the evening finally creaked to its conclusion she felt only relief that he had gone. However puzzling his ambivalent behaviour might be, it need be no concern of hers. The next time he wanted to see her, the answer would most definitely be no!

By contrast Richard Thornton's visit was a delight. Jim Calloway had telephoned to say he was coming to London for a few days to tie up the details of making Tilbury a permanent base for some of the Calloway ships. He proposed appointing Richard captain of the Line's flagship and that this and five other vessels would in future berth at Tilbury. Due to meet Richard on his arrival, he suggested Helen might like to go down to the docks with him and see Richard's ship at its berth. It would also be an opportunity, he added, to bring Helen up to date with Company news, those items which didn't feature in the Company's monthly report.

Richard's delight at seeing her at the quayside was very obvious. She was shown over his ship with enthusiasm and laughed when she saw the meticulous neatness of his cabin.

"Absolutely essential, my dear Miss Calloway", his brown eyes laughed back at her. "On board all space is limited and one has to make maximum use of it. Everything has its place and must be returned to that place after use. It's because of this that men of the sea make such wonderful husbands. Their tidiness is beyond belief!"

Bidding him goodnight she reflected how different this evening had been compared with the sombre outing two nights earlier. Being with Richard had been fun, something she often longed for when she felt her life to be hemmed in by weighty and sometimes unpleasant matters. How much she had enjoyed hearing his anecdotes about the fascinating places he had visited! She could, of course, be travelling around the world herself, certainly she had sufficient funds to do so. But everything seemed in a state of flux and, like so many others, she felt she was awaiting the advent of war. For two things this week she had been most grateful. One that Iain McNeal's trees had not been on Richard's ship, so there had been no necessity for shared meetings, and secondly that J.C., who at one point seemed about to suggest joining them for dinner, had suddenly made his excuses and left. Looking forward to enjoying Richard's company, unfettered by a third party, she could not help wondering where, and with whom, J.C. would be dining.

Walter stopped abruptly. Sonia must be ill! He moved forward. The sound came again and this time an awful realisation stopped him in his tracks. The sound was not of distress - but ecstasy. Deeper masculine sounds of encouragement roused him to an awareness of his own situation. Turning in the narrow hallway, the bunch of yellow roses fell from his grasp unheeded as he left the flat with all haste. Oblivious to all around him, he hurried down the street, his pace unslackening until the building which housed Sonia's apartment was out of sight.

At the first public house he gruffly ordered a double whisky and, clutching it to him, sank into a corner seat. The bitch! All that teasing, the capricious looks, the provocative clothes and conversation designed to titillate and then the look of demure horror if he attempted anything more than a chaste kiss. How many times had she said, just when he'd thought this time he'd be lucky, "I'm not that kind of a girl Walter. Fond as I am of you, I must save myself for the man I marry." Which was why he was here this evening. Tonight he'd decided he would ask her to marry him, make sure she was his before the war started. She wasn't expecting him until the following day, but changes in the duty roster had meant he could see her a day earlier and get it over with. Finding the door on the latch, he'd just barged in and found, or rather heard, his not-so innocent and demure Sonia having the time of her life in bed with Jim Calloway.

He'd recognised the voice, but in any event he would have known the smell of J.C.'s cheroots, an aroma which now seemed to be lodged in his nostrils. He ordered another drink. No doubt she's been laughing at me these last few weeks. Whilst I've been wining and dining her, she's just been marking time until J.C. arrived, then leapt into bed with him at the first opportunity. But perhaps it wasn't the first time, or for that matter her first lover. What a complete fool he'd been. He should have known, read the signs. Helen's manner that day at the Salon had been cool, as if she disapproved of Sonia. Probably knew a darn sight more about her than he did. Ironical that it should be Helen's father she was with. But of course, realisation suddenly surfaced in his be-fuddled brain, it was the money. He knew only too well her love of the good life, expensive clothes and food. J.C. could give her all these. A gold band on her finger wouldn't be enough for Sonia; it had to be a rich man's gold band.

Twice, money had proved the obstacle on which his happiness had foundered. At least, he thought ruefully, I've now something in common with Helen. She too, was deceived by someone she believed to be in love with her. Like Helen I'll never be so readily deceived again. Illusions shattered, he set out for the Barracks.

J.C. had no illusions whatsoever about Sonia. With him she made no pretence at being demure, knowing he would have laughed in her face. From their first meeting he had known them to be two of a kind, each out to achieve their aims by almost any means. She wanted money of course, who didn't? Of one thing he could be certain she would be the best dressed accessory any man could wish for! She'd been good in bed too and he knew to his cost that this didn't always apply. The most extrovert of females could be amazingly coy once divested of wearing apparel.

He had neither expected nor found a virgin in her bed. When they'd first headed for the bedroom he'd been in a hurry and knew that his early climax was no use to her. There had been no sulking, merely a period of waiting during which by a steady process of unhurried caresses and manipulation she had rekindled his desire, bringing him again to a state of tumescence. Then, their naked bodies blending together seamlessly, moving as one, they had enjoyed each other, until finally they collapsed, satiated and happy. Marriage had been on his mind during the journey south and this evening's events decided him. Within an hour of Walter's hurried departure, Sonia had agreed to be Mrs. Jim Calloway.

In his hotel the next morning, Jim pondered on the fact that his daughter would not be overjoyed at this news. He knew that she and Sonia had once been friends, good friends; now he sensed a coolness between them. Not surprising really, they were such different types. Much as he admired his daughter he would never consider marrying such a woman. There was enough of Mary in her to make him feel always slightly wary, careful of his behaviour. Only recently had Helen told him of Mary's Craybourne connection and for him too, this had been the answer to a number of puzzling questions. Whilst abroad he had been amazed to learn how

Elizabeth Craybourne was caring for his children. Now he knew the full story he was even more amazed that she should have done so for her husband's 'wrong side of the blanket' child and her offspring. The fact that Elizabeth had been kept unaware of this situation until after Oliver's death made her generosity of spirit the more remarkable.

Perhaps Helen's ancestry held the key to the formality in her behaviour which he found difficult to surmount. He'd been a rotten father, he knew that, had admitted as much to her. But still the barriers remained. Or perhaps her failed marriage was responsible. Sonia had told him that Helen had been a quaint little innocent when she first came to London. Initially, introspective and shy, she had gradually gained confidence and blossomed during her success as a model and again during Jai's courtship.

The Indian experiences had created a harder, shrewder Helen. Now she daily became more decisive and spoke with authority. Au fait with Governmental affairs through her contact with James, her interest in the suffrage movement and sorties into the East End with Daphne and Muriel had made her well-versed in social conditions. Experienced in haute couture and its subsidiary branches, she now had further knowledge of commerce, through the shipping line. Add to that the fortune she owned which must be steadily working for her and there was little doubt that Helen was a young lady of stature and a considerable force to be reckoned with.

J.C. was right in assuming Helen would not be overjoyed to learn of his impending marriage to Sonia and Helen's defence mechanisms, those barriers he had so often tried to break down, were well to the fore when she received the news. Inherent good manners prevailed, and she smiled and mouthed her congratulations. Realistically she told herself this marriage would have little effect upon her personally. The couple would be living in the North, so there would be limited social intercourse. But images of Sonia and J.C. troubled her. The Sonia who had flexed her muscles by not turning up at the Salon when required, was quite capable of making her presence felt in the Boardroom, via the bedroom. J.C. was a red-blooded male who had always been fond of the ladies; to what extent he would allow his business acumen to be affected by outside interests Helen could not be certain. Often she told herself that had she anticipated this event she would never have gone into partnership with her father and the fact that it was through her that the two had met was even more galling. But, on the credit side, the Calloway Line was prospering, the month's figures were excellent, and there was the added bonus of seeing Richard Thornton from time to time.

Taking stock of her situation she began to realise, as J.C. had done, that her breadth of knowledge was now considerable and, more importantly, to recognise this knowledge as a source of power. She was excited by the fact that the different strands of her life sometimes worked together to give her an over-view of the mechanism and structures of society. She knew why cotton factories in the North were closing through lack of work. It was because people like herself were purchasing materials directly from abroad, instead of waiting for the raw cotton to be imported and fabricated. Now there was a need to find other work for these factories.

Repeatedly she was made aware of the class system in society, the deep divisions between the poor and the middle and upper classes, whether in rural communities like Craybourne or within big cities. That she had been fortunate enough to bridge that gap she now saw not as mere good fortune, but as a real asset. She knew at first hand that there was a vast body of women who were sick of being penned in their homes, women who had never worked but were ready and indeed anxious to do so. Equally there were those working in the city sweatshops for whom leisure had no meaning, living in appalling conditions. The young were old before their time and life expectancy short.

As she signed the documents which made her the owner of some twenty terraced houses in Islington she acknowledged in herself another trait. She was acquisitive. Not for jewels and furs, but for property. The properties she now owned gave her a feeling of stability which the jewellery sitting in the Asprey vaults could never do. No doubt this was a result of her childhood. In spite of Prinny's love and care and Elizabeth's watchfulness, the small Helen had thought of herself as an orphan without a real home. Even now, having mixed for several years with the 'upper classes', she felt herself to be rootless. She recognised that with the purchase of bricks and mortar she was buying a safety net, in case this amazing bubble in which she now existed should suddenly disintegrate.

Lady Eynsford's letter seemed to indicate that Fate not only approved of Helen's instincts, but was pushing her in the same direction. Eynsford House was to be sold as Lady Eynsford and her brother now felt the house too large for them and that the London winters were becoming increasingly hard. They planned to emigrate to Australia to join their friends. The house had been offered first to James and then to Daphne. The former had felt it too large a town house to maintain in addition to the Yorkshire estate and the latter had declared herself unwilling to perpetuate a system which required a number of people working to ensure their employer's leisure. It had occurred to Lady Eynsford that Helen might be interested in the property. If so, perhaps she would join her for tea on the following day to discuss the matter. For a few minutes Helen did not move as excitement and nervousness washed over her. That beautiful house! It was unthinkable that little Helen Galloway of Piggott's Lane should own such a place; then, as the mature level-headed Helen took over, she picked up the telephone.

A call to her bank manager revealed that such a purchase would not be out of the question. Estimating the sort of figure Lady Eynsford would have in mind, he commented,

"May I remind you, Miss Calloway that the shipping line trading figures are extremely encouraging and your dress salon's order books are full. Whilst your capital is now depleted, your jewellery and the shares you hold will always ensure an adequate loan until your account builds up again."

Thereafter events moved rapidly. The escalation of trouble in the Balkans meant that Lady Eynsford was anxious to complete the deal as quickly as possible and be on her way before the outbreak of war. It was therefore agreed that by the following week she would extract for transportation those items she wished to keep and that Helen would then make an offer for everything which remained. On the day that documents were sent by Sir Edward Grey asking both France and Germany to respect Belgium's neutrality, Helen signed the document making her the owner of a mansion. She loved it! Exploring its vastness she recalled the raw country girl who had first gasped at its size and beauty. Wandering through the bedrooms with their deep carpets and swagged curtains, traversing the huge reception rooms, she revelled in the fact that it was hers, but knew that realism was the order of the day.

Whilst in Bond Street a secretary now dealt with much of the work which had initially been Helen's responsibility, there were nevertheless many occasions when it was necessary for her to be on site. For the time being she must remain there. Besides, this place was so huge the thought of a single female occupant with the necessary staffing would not only offend Daphne, it was ridiculous. James had suggested to his Aunt that he might be interested in renting the property. It was close to the House and would provide greater scope for entertaining than their current apartment. Helen sent a letter by hand, asking if he and Muriel were still interested in such an arrangement.

If the German response to Grey had been non-committal, James's telephone answer was quite definite.

"I have to say no Helen, for the best reason in the world. I'm going to be a father."

"James, that's wonderful- I'm delighted for you both."

"You'll understand I know that now everything has changed. War will probably be declared tomorrow, in which case I'll be enlisting with the Yorkshire Green Howards. We'll relinquish the apartment here, because in any event I'd like Muriel to be at Craybourne for the baby's birth early in February. If they land me with a desk job I could still be around but if not, I'd feel she was safe, tucked away at Craybourne. She's not totally sold on the idea, but I think Daphne and I have almost persuaded her."

"It's several days since I've spoken to Daphne, James, what are her plans?"

"You won't have seen or spoken to her because she's been frantically practising her driving. Says she doesn't feel she has the stomach for nursing, but is happy to tackle almost anything else."

"And she will. Your sister's a competent young lady. Give my love and congratulations to Muriel, James.... you've given me a lot to think about, 1'm not quite sure what my role will be in all this".

"I might have some suggestions to make there Helen. Don't do anything more about Eynsford House for a couple of days."

And with this enigmatic remark James put down the receiver.

The Bank Holiday weekend and those early August days saw the nation holding its breath as the international deliberations spiralled into the vortex from which there was no escape. The commencement of war produced a watershed such as had never before been experienced, as the state of limbo gave way to jingoistic euphoria. Young men recalling the exhortations of headteachers, "If a man cannot be useful to his country, he is better off dead", rushed to enlist. They added months, even years to their ages and proudly donned their uniforms. In order to have 'experienced life to the full' before meeting their Maker, they hurried to the altar. People walked away from relationships of which they were weary and forged newer, more exciting ones. Men over thirty complained that it was unfair and that they too should be allowed to go - at once. War became at the same time a reason and an excuse for all their actions.

Walter and Eddy were with the British Expeditionary Force which finally sailed for France on August 6th. The previous week had been exhausting. With instructions to treble the Regiment's number of horses, they had gone out into the country, travelling to bloodstock sales, farms and racing stables. Suitable animals were requisitioned and army cheques handed over to ease the pain. After five days they had culled together some three hundred horses acceptable to the Army vets and were then given two days of precious leave, with the proviso they remained within contact. These two days enabled Eddy to marry his Betty and Walter to stand as his best man.

Since the Sonia episode, Walter had been glad to be occupied and was anxious to get to the theatre of war. He had not relished the thought of seeing Sonia at the wedding but knew it to be inevitable. She had known of course of his presence on the day of her coupling with Jim Galloway, the yellow roses on the floor of the hall had been evidence of that. Now they warily skirted each other around the room, ensuring that a distance of several feet always separated them. Helen saw Walter's discomfiture and was sad for him. In spite of Sonia's showy demonstrations of her engagement ring she also was ill-at-ease. This was not merely Walter registering disappointment at the announced engagement; something more serious had happened and it was impossible to conjecture what that might have been.

Muriel was looking not so much listless as her early pregnancy might warrant, but decidedly strained. Most unlike her. No doubt she knew only too well that James was in a position to pull sufficient strings to make sure he was amongst the 100,000 troops General Kitchener had called for before Christmas. 3,500 of these would be officers and in spite of any constraints regarding his age, in spite of this much-longed-for baby, Muriel and Helen both knew that James would certainly be one of them.

They had intended a quiet wedding, Helen thought ruefully. That is, as quiet as any wedding involving Betty's family could be! Immediately she chastised herself for her uncharitable thoughts. They were a lovely generous-hearted bunch - if noisy! Fortunately, today their good humour masked to some extent the sombre undercurrent.

Her gaze moved to the bridal couple. Why on earth hadn't they tied the knot before this, she wondered. Enjoyed each other before the war-drums started beating on all sides. Weddings were supposed to be joyous occasions, but this was a totally bizarre situation. The bride determined to cover her anxiety was talking too often and too loudly. Trailing in her wake, the groom looked exhausted, yet in a few short days he would be sailing for France and after that only God knew just what would be in store for these young men.

But, she must put away these maudlin thoughts, it was time to drink a toast, to wish the bridal couple good health, good fortune and a lifetime of happiness.....

Following the declaration of war Rosa telephoned Helen often. She was quite fit she insisted, and always had been. Surely she could now come to London to see how she might assist the war effort. Enquiries to her College suggested that a great many students would not be returning in September, until things 'sorted themselves out' and she wanted to do the same.

"I've no objection to that Rosa. I'd just rather you stayed where you are for a few more days."

"But why?"

"Mainly because rail services are currently in a state of chaos. Think about it. Trains are being used to move troops, sometimes to the docks, sometimes to more strategically placed camps. Nurses are on the move. It just seems sensible to wait until the initial chaos sorts itself out. You could fill in the time with some more driving practice."

"I've been doing that every single day for ages. Simmonds says I am now quite competent and, sister dear, would you believe I am now capable of changing a tyre?"

"That's great. When my new car arrives, there'll be two of us to drive it and you can do all the tyre changing!"

"Your new car? Helen you haven't said... When is it coming and what colour is it?"

"I haven't mentioned it before, because it's only just been arranged. I've thought about it of course, often, now James says I must go ahead and purchase immediately because motor cars, like everything else, might soon be in short supply. So, it will be here by the time you arrive.... everything else I shall keep as a surprise. That is, if you're sure you don't want to consider staying put - after all, Muriel will be at Craybourne soon, for several months."

"I know and she's a sweetie, but I want to be with you please. It just seems we've never had much time together, not since we were grown-up. You're involved in so many things, I'm sure I can be a help."

"And so am I. Stay put for a week and then we'll discuss your travel arrangements. Any other news?"

"As a matter of fact, there is. Iain McNeal's gone, joined the Gordon Highlanders."

"What? How? He's outside the age group and in any case ..."

"I imagine it was a sudden decision. Last week he asked for a few days off to go home. I saw him briefly and he called and said would I tell you that you were right and that you'd be hearing from him. After he'd been in Scotland a couple of days he phoned Elizabeth to apologise for letting her down, but said he'd decided to enlist. I don't know how he wangled the age thing, perhaps he just got in before the official declaration. In any event, it's all a nonsense, people are adding and subtracting bits to and from their ages all over the place."

"Well...as we say in Yorkshire, 'There's nowt so queer as folk!' If anyone had asked me, I would have said that enlisting was the last thought on his mind."

Further curiosity over this sudden volte face was pushed to the back of her mind by the letter which arrived from the War Department. Major General Sinclair wrote to say that James had suggested he should write to her.

"We are currently seeking a number of large properties available for rental to serve as military clubs for officers and other ranks. Men whose homes are some distance away, arriving in London for a few days' leave, often at short notice, may well opt to spend their liberty in the city. This will particularly apply to single men. For many, hotels would prove too expensive, so it is proposed that such clubs have short-term residential facilities, with this Department subsidising charges to serving men.

"Your property, Eynsford House, with its large reception rooms and numerous bedrooms, sounds admirably suitable for our purpose and Lord Craybourne informs me you might be interested in such a scheme.

"The War Department would staff the Club and ensure the property was well-cared for during our tenancy. However, we do advise that all valuable items be securely stored during our occupation.

"If you are interested in considering this proposal please be kind enough to telephone so that we may arrange a meeting."

At the ensuing meeting, it was tentatively suggested that Helen might consider spending time at Eynsford House occasionally, in order to 'oil the wheels'.

"You see Miss Galloway, there are certain tasks not within the remit of our managers and housekeepers. For example a young man arriving at Eynsford might find himself alone amongst strangers. In such circumstances it would be nice to think that someone would be around to make the necessary introductions, suggest a visit to the theatre - that sort of thing. Young men away from home, in an all-male environment. missing their mothers and sisters, often long for some female company.".

He did not add that any young man blessed with Miss Calloway's company would be fortunate indeed. After ten days of being closely closeted in smoke filled conference rooms with worried irritable men, Helen's slim upright figure and the delicate caul of perfume in which she seemed wrapped delighted him. She was rather young for the sort of motherly hostess his Committee had had in mind, but she oozed capability, in fact he found her direct gaze rather daunting, being more accustomed to the wavering glances of young men who seemed so nervous in his presence.

When she spoke he had no doubts as to the wisdom of James's recommendations. She would be happy to agree to the rental terms for Eynsford House, renewable at the end of each six monthly period. Once valuable items had been removed there would be inevitable gaps, certainly more china and cutlery would be needed, extra beds and linen. Presumably the War Department would meet this shortfall in equipment? At his nod of affirmation, she continued.

"I shall be happy to act in the capacity of unofficial hostess, providing any housekeeper or manager is made fully aware of the fact that the house is my property and I must have a final say in any matter of importance concerning it. In the circumstances I think it would be advisable for me to retain a bedroom and a small sitting room so that I can divide my time between Eynsford and the Salon. My younger sister joins me shortly and I know will be happy to help in this or any other way."

She smiled and he was enchanted.

"Rosa is shelving her studies at Oxford until the war is over."

His feeling of enchantment faded.

"I hope for her sake and ours that she hasn't long to wait before resuming them."

Following Helen's receipt of their official communication, the War Department moved swiftly. With the addition of a bed, each of the dressing rooms attached to a main bedroom became an extra bedroom, which meant that they could house 28 guests.

A seemingly endless list of requirements was submitted to the War Department. Settees, arm-chairs, china, cutlery, bed-linen, all were needed and gradually put into place. Helen now found her time totally absorbed and decided that Maj. Gen. Sinclair and his Committee had known exactly what they were doing and had very subtly acquired a general factotum to see the exercise through.

Her apologies to Betty for her continued absence from Bond Street were brushed aside.

"It isn't a problem. We've now got some really good girls in the workroom. Lily's in overall charge, but in fact they need very little supervision. The cutters report to me for their work schedules of course, but my team of trimmers know what they're about and I'm left free much of the day to spend time on design work. It's really so much easier than when we were training people, Helen. Not that I regret one minute of the time spent on that. We set our standards and people who work for us know that we expect the best.

"For Heaven's sake, don't start worrying about not being around. With Eddy away I must keep myself occupied or I'll start to dwell too much on what's happening over there. Besides if my being busy releases you to do other things then I feel I'm doing my bit for the war effort too - indirectly."

"How's the order book?"

"It's not brilliant, but then there was bound to be a levelling off after the launch. Clothes are probably the last thing people have on their minds just now."

Rosa too, was kept busy. When she was not at Eynsford she was in the East End with Daphne, Helen having suggested that she should as quickly as possible take over Muriel's workload. Helen had wondered about the advisability of throwing together two such volatile characters as Daphne and Rosa, but in fact they seemed to disagree quite cheerfully, before finding some basis of agreement. There were occasions when, watching Rosa drive off in the new car, she felt a surge of pride in her young sister, who uncomplainingly tackled any job given and who was already very proficient at negotiating the London streets.

Sonia was now with Jim Calloway in Liverpool. He had telephoned two days after the declaration of war to tell Helen that he had suggested Sonia join him immediately and that they marry in a civic ceremony. Whilst Helen and Rosa would be most welcome on that occasion he and Sonia would understand, in view of the exceptional circumstances, if this were not possible. He added that, provided it met with Sonia's approval, he had now found a house, one more suited to a married couple's requirements than his current bachelor apartment. A solid eight-bedroomed property in a good residential area, he was clearly quite proud of the statement this would make about his community status.

"Nothing like that mansion of yours of course Helen. I'm surprised you let the War Department talk you into such a set-up. If some of those young men have a night out on the town, goodness knows what they might get up to."

"The Manager here is a retired Regimental Segt. Major, I doubt he'll countenance any trouble. In any event, when we start getting people here who've been at the front line, we'll be quite prepared, indeed we'll be expecting them to have a good time."

The edge to her voice suggested this was not a subject to be continued with. Politely she declined his invitation to attend the wedding ceremony, but said she would be in touch with Sonia to convey good wishes etc.

"How's the new ship coming along J.C.?"

"Six to eight weeks to completion, unless we have any hold-ups."

"It's Rosa's twenty-first on October 15th. I wondered...it would be quite a thrill for her if she could christen and launch the "Rosa" on that day."

"It would be quite a thrill for me too. I'm very conscious of the fact that I haven't seen my younger daughter since she was very small. And before you say any more, I know that it's probably my fault, but it just seems that we're always at opposite ends of the country!"

"As soon as it's possible, I'll bring her North, it's about time I attended another Board meeting and checked up on my assets!"

Chapter Twenty Five

The cellar was cool and dark after the intolerable glare of the noonday sun. Thankfully Rob put down his pack, posted guards at the entrance, then signalled to the men to relax. There were things to be done but they could wait. Priority now was that all should have an hour's relaxation, a blessed respite from tramping the pavé, the cobbled roads which were turning ankles and reducing feet to blistered nightmares. Gingerly the men tended their sores, then stretched out, heads on packs, to snatch a short period of oblivion. Rob lay, hands behind his head, looking around him, eyes now accustomed to the gloom.

It was reminiscent of the cellars he'd visited in France and Spain, cellars where wine and sherry matured in giant casks. The smell too was familiar, hinting of apples and the bitter sweetness of rotting fruit. The ceilings were lofty and he could now discern the circles where the large barrels had stood. He grinned. No doubt they'd been determined the Bosch were not getting their precious liquor. What panic there must have been a few days ago! Had they decanted the wine into smaller vessels and burned the casks, or had the huge containers been rolled away somewhere to another hiding place? And it had all been such a waste of their time and energy, for the Germans hadn't been aware that the cellar existed.

The farm itself, more of a manor house really, was a shell, but the barns were intact and underneath one they had found the cellar entrance and sanctuary from the heat. Here was calm and order, above chaos and confusion. It had been the same since their arrival in France four weeks ago. Orders would be sent, then countermanded. Directions given, then contradicted. At Le Havre several of the drafts had been disembarked immediately, but the Green Howards and the Kentish Yeomen had remained on board for a further five hours, awaiting orders. At last the Howards learned they were to join the B.E.F. at Locre, but when they detrained at Baillelul, the guide allocated to Robert's platoon seemed uncertain of the way himself. Then the river came into view and they thought they had regained their bearings but the razed buildings and evidence of sporadic fighting told Rob that something was wrong. They were behind at least one squad of Germans, so had drifted much too far East. Unless of course the Germans were also lost! As soon as they were rested, he would strike North West, across the fields, so that the men's swollen feet were spared further torture on the dreaded pavé.

If their experiences so far were a foretaste of modern warfare, then Heaven help them! Of one thing now he was certain, this was a great bunch of lads for which he was responsible and if that meant disobeying some totally ridiculous order, then so be it. With a brisk, "Time to go lads," he was on his feet and they started to gather up their belongings.

They found the rest of the Regiment already bivouacked to the rear of Baillelul and Rob was told to report with other officers at the H.Q. set up in the town.

He would have passed Walter by unrecognised, had not a voice stopped him in his tracks,

"Captain Craybourne?"

The Lieutenant in front of him saluted, then put out his hand, smiling broadly.

"I doubt you'll remember me. Walter of Hislop's farm?"

"Of course, now I can see who it is! Good thing you stopped me though, that's a good disguise and you have grown a bit! Have you just arrived too?"

"No, I'm with the B.E.F. and we were the first here. I'm just back from the front to make my report and see what the Generals have in store for us next. As fast as we get telephone communication in place it's wiped out again. You've just arrived with the Yorkshire Regiment I take it?"

"Yes, we and the Kentish boys are coming up front. The others on our ship have been deployed North of Paris. Where do I report?"

"Up the stairs and you'll see it. I'm afraid everything's disorganised".

"I did get that impression! Would you believe that our guide into Belgium managed to get us lost?"

"I'll believe anything! I'm convinced some of the German platoons are wandering around not knowing where they are. That's fine until we bump into each other, then the results are disastrous."

"They kept warning us it was going to be bloody, I didn't know they meant bloody disorganised!"

"I wondered...perhaps when you've reported in, if you have half an hour, we could have a quick drink and catch up on the news?" In view of the difference in rank, Walter's request was diffident.

"Great! I could murder a drink... that is, if you don't mind waiting around, with no guarantee that I'll be free?"

They managed their quick drink and found themselves discussing not so much news of friends and family, but the complexities which had led Britain into war. Rob's theory was that the countries' leaders were of the generation entrenched in the mores of the duelling code, that is that no insult must pass without retribution. When that insult had been brought to the attention of the world, as in the case of Sarajevo, then it became essential to reciprocate.

Walter did not see it in such simplistic terms. He was convinced that Germany had been planning a European war for a long time and all events had been master-minded to reach that goal. He now believed the Germans were bent on sweeping across Belgium, encircling and cutting off Paris, before retracing their steps to tackle the Russian forces.

"We've been holding our own - just. Things should improve now you Yorkshire tykes have arrived!"

Like a swarm of locusts the three armies of Germany, France and Britain had come to rest on the small country of Belgium, their grey and khaki devouring towns and villages, schools and houses. They obliterated river banks, bivouacked in woods and farms, slept in haystacks and ditches, settling wherever and whenever they felt the need for cover. As Walter and Rob had quickly learned, communications were at best vague, at worst misleading. Confusion reigned.

In Britain too, confusion was rife. For a time frenzied activity with its formation of endless committees and working parties produced little that was constructive or practical. Officialdom seemed at a loss to know how to deal with the great amorphous tide of assistance which was on offer. Only the army, naval and nursing organisations accustomed to provisioning and deploying their members seemed capable of forward planning.

By contrast, in Eaton Square, Eynsford House peacefully awaited occupants. Here all was calm and ordered. The huge house with its air of permanence and stability seemed like a broody hen, her nest comfortable and comforting, ready to accept her chicks. Cupboards breathing lavender were stacked high with snowy towels and crisp bedlinen. Armchairs in convivial clusters stared vacantly at each other. Smug in their pristine readiness the bedrooms glowered at the delay, whilst staff busied themselves with endless, unnecessary and unsatisfying tasks.

Rafe Sinclair had said the first batch of officers would be due for leave about mid-September, after a six week stint at the front. At the comment, Helen's red-gold eyebrows lifted ominously and her eyes widened.

"So, the class barriers don't come down, even when they are all fighting the same war?"

"I'm afraid it just isn't practical Miss Calloway. The last thing we want is people jumping up and down saluting each other and that's exactly what would happen if we mixed the ranks. I'm sure you'll agree our aim is to provide maximum relaxation and anything which works against that is to be avoided."

Yes, she could see his point but this categorising of people still irritated her. The fact that she had managed to jump those barriers made her feel worse not better, guilty that she was now in such a privileged position. And the privileges increased, the wherewithal sometimes created through her own volition to assist, sometimes stumbled upon by accident.

To Helen's surprise and Muriel's obvious delight, Mr. Asquith was not yet prepared to release James and a chance remark of his made Helen aware of the increasing needs of an ever-growing army. A phone call to J.C. put her in touch with property dealers in Lancashire and within a week she had purchased cheaply two cotton mills, no longer operative.

Accompanied by Rosa she made a three day visit to Liverpool, declining J.C.'s invitation to stay at his home, on the grounds that they would have much to accomplish in a very short time. By the time they boarded the train for home, managers had been appointed at each site, the mills emptied of machinery and fitted with batteries of sewing machines, tables and chairs and contracts agreed with two of James's Halifax mills to supply khaki material for uniforms and greatcoats and lighter weight materials for shirts, vests and pants. So it was with a sigh of satisfaction at a job well done that Helen removed her hat and settled back against the cushions.

Rosa smiled.

"No-one could accuse you of dragging your heels, when speed is of the essence."

"I should hope not. What really delights me is that we've managed to kill two birds with one stone. We'll be producing army supplies and creating jobs in an area which was becoming run down. The jobs will be mainly for women and that too, is a double-edged benefit. With so many men enlisting more women will be needed in the workforce and it won't do any harm to the suffragist movement to know we have factories operated by women. But that's enough talk about work. What did you think of J.C.?"

Rosa laughed, "Well, he's a much smoother, slicker version of what I vaguely remembered. Charming of course, with a touch of the blarney. I hadn't expected him to be quite so debonair, it doesn't quite fit the image I had in mind of a shipping magnate! Although come to think of it, neither do you."

"Well, if it's white whiskers and dark suits you were expecting, I can assure you that those are to be found in abundance at any meeting of the Board. He certainly took a shine to you Rosa. You've got just the sort of bubbly personality he can relate to. 1'm afraid he finds me far too serious minded".

"Thank you very much. So I'm some sort of light-weight flibbertygibbet...is that it?"
They both laughed.

"Hardly. I don't suppose light-weight flibbertygibbets are much in evidence at Oxford. No, it's just that your nature is far more outgoing than mine, like his I suppose. I envy you, wish I could be more like that. Only one person has ever made me feel well, skittish, is I suppose the nearest definition I could give you...."

"And that was...?"

"Well it certainly wasn't Jai, I was far too aware of his changeable moods. You'll be told all in good time sister dear. You haven't told me yet what you thought of Sonia."

"A better friend than an enemy I'd say. Great to be with when everything in the garden is lovely, but I wouldn't want to be around when the going was tough. Canny, but not a lot of depth."

"Ouch! I doubt if she'd welcome your character appraisal. I notice you've refrained from saying 'they deserve each other.' "

"I didn't say it because I didn't think it! I feel J.C. learned some hard lessons as a young man and now he values anything he acquires, whether in business or personal relationships. His heart is in the right place, I'm not so sure about Sonia!"

"What about the house, wasn't it too awful for words?"

"Ghastly! Just too much of everything, frills and furbelows. J.C. probably hates it. It's strange, you always said Sonia had such a good eye for what's right in clothes."

"Yes...although yesterday, I thought she was tending towards the flamboyant. Like the house, too much ruching, too much ribbon and definitely too much lace!"

"Well, that's well and truly taken care of J.C., Sonia and their house! Touching on more serious matters ..."

"Yes?"

"I've been wondering about the large Salon in Bond Street?"

"I'm intrigued, go on..."

"Well, a doctor I met in the East End last week was saying that the Red Cross needs more depots in London - immediately. Places where bandages can be rolled, men's individual kits made up, plus the larger medical packs for ambulances and field hospitals. The salon is so huge it would be ideal and I wondered if we couldn't get some of our Bond Street clientele to assist."

"Rosa, that's a brilliant idea. All those women with too much time on their hands, women who keep on about how much they want to help. Why didn't I think of it?"

"Because you've been busy with a thousand and one other things. If you agree I'll contact the Red Cross and find out the procedure for setting it up. I'm afraid it will mean a lot of people tramping in and out of the premises."

"That's a small price to pay. Alf will be delighted, he's been dying to do something for the war effort and under your scheme I'm sure there'll be dozens of jobs for him to do. I'll check with Betty, make sure she has no objections. You get on to it and make up a list of people prepared to help. If we need more I'm sure Muriel and James can add others. Now I'm going to close my eyes for a moment".

"Sorry Sis, I keep forgetting you're getting on a bit. Feeling our age are we?"

Still smiling, Helen closed her eyes. With luck the Lancashire mills would be operative within the week. Soon now young men would be returning from the front and descending on Eaton Square....

And the young men she knew, what of them? Walter and Eddy were no doubt already in the front lines, though information to date had been sketchy. And Richard somewhere on the high seas, was he too, in danger? News of the build-up of the German navy had been terrifying. If it really was the most powerful in the world then all shipping could be at risk. She hadn't yet received the promised letter from Iain McNeal, a letter which she had hoped might in some way explain his odd behaviour. If, as Rosa had said, he had joined a Scottish regiment, then he too might already be in France, or was even now on his way there.

Iain McNeal was not in transit for France, he was burying his father. Following the coffin, he felt rather than saw the scene around him. The extra bearers to take the weight of the casket's huge occupant, the slight hissing of the summer rain as it struck the thirsty grass, the perfume of the wild flowers growing rampant at the graveyard's edges. The absence of mourners did not surprise him. Who would regret the old man's passing? Certainly not his family. For as long as Iain could remember they had lived in fear of this giant of a man. Six foot five and barrel-chested, his size alone enough to intimidate. Add to that his evangelistic fanaticism and James McNeal was a terrifying figure. Locally known as 'Big Jamie, the tub-thumper' his manner had grown more bizarre as the years progressed. Eight years ago he had been forbidden further access to the pulpit at the local presbyterian church and had taken to speaking in the marketplace, castigating those within ear-shot for their sinful ways, indulgence in demon drink, lewd and lustful behaviour and fornication. All of them he warned, were doomed to burn for ever in Hellfire.

Latterly there had been a change in the attitude of those who heard him. Fear had given way to scorn. Most endeavoured to ignore him whilst some smothered their giggles, knowing that Jamie himself regularly imbibed the juice of the grain he so decried. They spoke of the drunken Jamie who staggered home and beat his wife and daughter and, more covertly, of the times when the sober Jamie dragged either or both into his bed.

Iain was not there to pay his respects. Any such feeling for the man who had died choking on his own vomit, had withered more than twenty years ago. The grief which overwhelmed Iain was not for Jamie McNeal, but for his own failings. As a gawky youth he had made several abortive attempts to protect his mother and sister, never totally recovering from the trauma of the beatings he received. In his early twenties he had left the croft. In what he now saw as a sop to his own conscience he had, intermittently, sent sums of money to his mother, via a neighbour.

There had been little truth in the story of his background as related to Elizabeth Craybourne and Helen. The idyllic picture of the small family living in the croft on the Laird's estate, struggling to send their son to University was entirely fictitious. Iain's mother occasionally helped out in the kitchens of the big house and learning of their eviction from a village house, because of her husband's eccentricities, the Laird had offered Molly a tiny, run-down croft on the perimeter of his land. There they had lived for some fifteen years. Twice the Laird had had Jamie put in prison for a few days to 'cool his heels', but long term punishment for this type of domestic dispute seemed beyond the jurisdiction of any court.

When Iain had left home at twenty he was penniless and the only work he knew was assisting the Laird's gamekeeper. Quick to learn he had gradually built on that knowledge, noting the speech and manners of those he served. An avid reader, he made himself familiar with new techniques in game protection and breeding, studied estate management, until at last he felt ready to apply for a more senior post as Assistant Factor to the Earl of Cleish. This latter strand of his story was authentic. From there the Earl's recommendation had taken him to Craybourne.

Iain watched the coffin lowered into the earth and turned away. This was what he had come for and it was done. Now he could relax, think things through. He should have done more....somehow. But, he now acknowledged, the problem once distanced had dwindled in importance. Last Christmas at Craybourne, included in their family parties, he had known for the first time what it was to feel young.

Enjoying a drink, he had pushed to the back of his mind thoughts that he might have inherited his father's weakness in this respect. Surrounded by articulate young men and women in a delightful setting, he was happy and relaxed. But his problems had not disappeared, merely receded.

Immediately prior to his London visit in July, he had received a note from his sister. She wrote that she feared their father was insane, the drunken bouts and the beatings becoming more frequent and more severe. Now Iain resolved that once the consignment of trees was safely at Craybourne he must go to Scotland and try again to have his father sent away, anywhere, away from his mother and sister. That day he made another resolution, that he would never again touch alcohol, in case he too succumbed to its influence.

What a dreadful companion he must have been that night! What must Helen have thought of him? During the last week in July, he'd managed to get away from Craybourne and during an overnight stay in Hawick decided on his course of action. He would talk to the Laird and ask for help in either evicting Jamie from the estate, or having him admitted to a mental institution. Once that was resolved then he knew he must enlist. He had seen the flicker of disapproval in Helen's eyes during their discussion about Rob. He knew she could not understand why he too had not made a move earlier. But, there was something else, something he had admitted to no-one before, not even himself. He was afraid. The fear he had known at the hands of his father, the remembered pain and discomfort of those beatings sent shock waves through him. Local people he knew, thought him a coward for not making a better job of protecting his mother and sister. Could he face the unknown horrors of war?

He'd intended to take the plunge that first evening as soon as he'd spoken to the Laird, but when his father staggered into the croft, the leather belt already twitching in his hands, all else was forgotten. Jamie's roar sent Mollie and Fiona scrambling for safety and Iain, squaring up to his father with the nearest thing to hand, a large skillet pan. Chairs crashed to the ground as his father reeled towards him, precious utensils shattering as they fell and always the roaring, like some wild demented beast. Iain dodged and weaved, using the pan as both shield and weapon. But the passage of time was beginning to tell on Big Jamie, the years of heavy drinking had taken their toll. No longer agile, tonight liquor blunted his reactions. A few sharp blows with the heavy pan and he stumbled and fell, winded. One more abortive attempt to raise himself and then with a sickening thud he fell backwards, slipping almost immediately into a drunken stupor.

Iain, bleeding from cuts to his face and hand staggered from the croft to find Fiona and his mother. Crouched in the shelter of the low wall which enclosed their livestock, they exclaimed at his appearance, then together they returned to start their usual task of setting right the damage caused by Big Jamie's drunken bouts. But tonight other work awaited them. Jamie McNeal was dead, asphyxiated by vomit. Glassy-eyed and white faced they set to work. He was too large and the table not stout enough to take his weight, so laying-out was done where his body sprawled, on the floor. They stretched out his limbs and washed his naked body, pulled a clean nightshirt over his head, then wrapped him in a blanket, pinning and tying it until he became one large grotesque parcel. The horse was turned out of her small lean-to, fresh straw spread over the ground and together Jamie McNeal's three kinsmen dragged, pushed and lifted him to the place from whence he would be collected by the undertakers. They shed no tears. Felt no remorse at leaving his body unattended. Only relief that they need no longer fear his brutal excesses.

Now, the funeral over, his mother and sister already happily occupied turning the croft into a home, Iain climbed the ridge behind it and sat amidst the blaze of purple heather. Perhaps the war really would be over before his age group was called; perhaps he should remain here for a time to give his mother support. Perhaps …. perhaps, he was a coward! Groaning, he rolled over, beating the hard earth with clenched fists.

Helen had intended that they take a cab directly to Eaton House, telephoning Betty on arrival, but the headlines screaming at them from every news vendor's stand sent them hurrying to Bond Street. "Retreat from Mons" could only mean that the British boys were in trouble and Betty would be in need of moral support. From the cab windows they watched as people scurried down the streets, whey-faced. The unbelievable had happened, their glorious British army had been routed by the Germans and forced to retreat. Jingoistic phrases died suddenly on lips thin and drawn, and 'All over by Christmas' seemed like a sick joke.

Betty was composed. It was too soon for news, she declared, and busied herself making cups of tea. Nevertheless, when Helen said they would spend the night at Bond Street her relief was evident. The next morning, surrounded by her sympathetic staff, they left her.

At Eaton Square Helen and Rosa went immediately to their own rooms, formerly the Eynsford House nursery suite. Consisting of a sitting room, two bedrooms, a bathroom and a tiny kitchen, it had been totally refurbished and was ideal for their needs.

A message from Rafe Sinclair awaited them saying they should expect eighteen personnel on the following day. At the news a wave of relief swept through the house. Now, at last, they would have worthwhile occupation. There was a letter too from Walter, relating his meeting with Rob and commenting briefly on the new style of warfare with which he and Eddy were now confronted. "Most of what we learned in India is useless here," he wrote, adding that, as increased mechanisation took over, the horses' role would soon cease to be and, obviously heartfelt, "Providing several hundred horses with daily fodder is an on-going headache!"

He sounded well and cheerful, but her heart lurched at the thought that by this time he, Rob and Eddy would have all been through the thick of battle, a battle which Britain was now known to have lost.

There was a further letter from India and Helen devoured its contents. The Rani expressed concern at the war in Europe. Was Helen short of food or anything else, because if so, she would find some means to get it to her. She was enjoying her role as Regent and relished being both mother and father to the small Maharajah. "It is, dear Helen, as if I were being given a second chance with my own small son. Now I have the opportunity to school Niaz in all that is brightest and best of our Indian culture and to instil values that are both humane and moderate.

"One day when the war is over you must come again to Jaishalpar and we will enjoy our friendship, unclouded by fear.

"I pray always for your happiness and for the safety of you and your friends." Carefully folding the letter and replacing it in its envelope, Helen realised that for the first time she was able to contemplate the possibility of returning to Jaishalpar. Once the war was over she would do it. She would take Rosa and show her all that had so astonished Betty and herself. With the Rani's guidance there was so much she would like to see and do outside the parameters of the Palace to which she and Betty had been confined. Now she must get to work.

Understandably all lines to the War Department were busy and Helen tried not to think of the desperate parents, wives and sweethearts attempting to get news of their loved ones. After numerous abortive attempts to get through they decided that Rosa should go in person and see if anyone had a list of the personnel expected and their time of arrival.

Busy at her desk some time later, Helen heard Rosa's footsteps and turned to greet her. The girl's stricken expression brought her swiftly to her feet and across the room. Hastily bundling her into the nearest chair she knelt beside her, holding her close.

"What is it darling? What has distressed you?"

"I called at Bond Street to see how Betty was and to get those clients' names I wanted. When I got to Charring Cross station there was a huge crowd, so I stopped to see what was going on". She choked back sobs, "Oh Helen, it was so awful, they were bringing the wounded back from the front, taking them to the hospitals. They all looked so ill. Some were bandaged round the eyes, some had lost limbs and ..." Here the tears welled up and she sobbed uncontrollably. "They were boys, Helen, just boys, they kept trying to smile..but their eyes weren't smiling and they were all so young, younger than me I think...." The words spilled over and were once more engulfed by tears.

Helen left her crying quietly and returned with a small glass of brandy.

"Drink it, Rosa. I think we're going to have to steel ourselves to face all sorts of terrible things. James is very astute, his opinions have always seemed very sensible to me. Whilst we didn't like what he said at Christmas, I get the feeling from Walter's letter that once the two sides achieve some sort of balance over new weaponry, the struggle which seems to be going on now, then it will be exactly as James forecast, a long war with everyone having to sit tight, waiting to see who gives in first. Now, if you feel well enough, let's get back to work. Did you manage to get the information we wanted?"

Wordlessly Rosa produced lists and Helen busied herself allocating rooms, relieved when Rosa eventually started work on her Red Cross project.

It was three o'clock when James telephoned and Helen knew immediately that it was bad news. His voice broke as he told her that Robert had been killed in action during the Mons retreat. Desperately Helen tried to contain her grief, to listen and register his words. In view of Muriel's distress and fearful of a miscarriage, her doctor had said she must stay in bed for at least forty-eight hours. Could they help? He had thought it advisable not to send for Daphne who was herself heartbroken and being looked after by Peter Fairburn. Prinny had telephoned to say that when the telegram arrived at Craybourne, suspecting its contents, she had kept it from Elizabeth until her doctor was contacted and on the premises. The shock had brought on a series of small convulsions, but she had been given an injection and was sleeping. "Thank God for Prinny's common-sense," James had said, adding that as soon as Muriel was well enough they would of course be travelling to Yorkshire.

Helen put aside her own grief, that could be dealt with later. As Prinny had demonstrated, practical help was what was needed now. She assured James that one of them would be with Muriel within the hour and that he and Muriel were in their thoughts. Rosa was crying but composed and insisted that in view of the impending influx of visitors, she must be the one to go to Muriel. By four o'clock she was on her way.

Alone, Helen now grieved for the loss of Rob. They had met as adults on so few occasions, but in that time she had felt his warmth and sensitivity and responded to it. She remembered his understanding at James's wedding when he had so tactfully extricated her from a difficult situation, his boyish sense of fun in the silly games they'd played and his artistic appreciation of all that was beautiful. Why could she no longer picture his face? Only his smiling eyes, crinkling at the corners burned into her vision. And the young men whom Rosa had seen, whose eyes no longer smiled, what of them? They and the others still out there, nervously awaiting the next onslaught, were all going to need love and understanding and in full measure. Sick at heart she picked up her sheaf of papers and went downstairs.

Three days passed before the doctor gave permission for Muriel to travel and during that time the Prime Minister agreed that in view of his family tragedy, James might leave the seat of Government. Muriel, fully aware of James's intentions was now in control of emotions and determined to be as supportive as possible. His mother would need her. James would need her until..... And of course, she must make plans for the baby's arrival at Craybourne.

James had much with which to occupy himself during those three days. Arrangements were put in hand to lease the apartment, office paperwork was filed and stored, urgent matters brought to a conclusion, others less so, entrusted to someone else.

At last they were ready to leave and bidding them farewell at Victoria, Helen thought what a sad little group they were. All in deepest black, their pallid unsmiling faces drew many a sympathetic glance.

"Rob was one of the lucky ones," James had said bitterly, "at least there was something to bury. His body will remain in Belgium with the others who died. One day Helen, when this is over, we'll visit his grave. Now...well, I'll organise the Craybourne memorial service and send you details, as soon as I feel we, that is Mother, Daphne and Muriel, are strong enough to cope with it."

Another matter was troubling Daphne as they journeyed northwards. Peter Fairburn's brother had left the family home in Kent and not returned. His distraught parents, finding the note that told them their fifteen year old son had gone to enlist were doing everything they could to trace him.

Peter raged against the enlisting officers.

"How could he possibly have fooled them? He's a tall lad, but you've only got to look at his face to see he's nothing but a kid. Dad says he's not even shaving yet and I doubt his chest measurement is the regulation thirty four inches."

She let him vent his anger as he strode up and down between the machinery, striking things with his fists in his desire to punish something, or someone. Not knowing exactly where or when Colin had enlisted had not helped, but the War Department's inability to trace him suggested he had not only lied about his age, but had given a false surname.

"This is what comes of their damned publicity campaign. All that "We don't want to lose you, but we think you ought to go" stuff, turning war into some glorious adventure. Youngsters like Colin see it as their chance to be a hero. None of us, apart from those already out there, have any idea what it's really like. I'll fight my corner along with the next man, when I'm asked to do so, but I'd like to see a lot more sense and control coming out of Whitehall, before I agree to rush off to war at the drop of a hat."

The news of Rob's death refuelled the anger he tried now to conceal. But even whilst comforting her, the hard set of his mouth, told her of his inner turmoil. As they sat, his arms around her she felt numb with shock. James had always been the serious and reliable elder brother. Robert was the Will-o'-the-wisp, unpredictable, the one with whom she'd shared escapades and dreams of the adult world. Now he was gone, the golden boy whose charms had enchanted those he met.

Daphne's anger was slower in starting, less violent, but in the north-bound train with the preparations and turmoil of the last few days behind her, she felt it fester and grow until it seeped through to the core of her being. She knew now what she must do. Peter had been dismissive about 'rushing out to the front', and she knew him to be no coward. The fact remained that there were already thousands of young men out there, men like Rob and Walter and they needed all the support they could get. Unfit for nursing she may be, but she could drive and the War Office was crying out for drivers. That was the answer. If, Heaven forbid, she was allocated to ambulances, then she would force herself to do what was necessary, however unpleasant.

An August meeting in London of the National Union of Women's Suffrage Societies had made it plain that for the period of the war, the Pankhursts were to join the recruiting drive; all members had been asked to suspend their actions and assured that in return all sentences would be remitted. Her work there had ceased, albeit temporarily, and any number of people could fill her role as overseer of the two East End Schools. There would be opposition from Peter of course, a great deal of it, but whatever he said, she was now resolved to offer her services.

Her feelings for Peter had undergone a drastic change since her illness. Attracted by Iain McNeal, those weeks of convalescence in Yorkshire had made her aware of a weakness in him she found difficult to identify. Certain subjects had appeared taboo. After a time she had avoided discussing the war, religion and, strangely, alcohol! Gradually she had come to realise he became monosyllabic and downright morose when any of these topics were raised.

There had been several occasions when he had seemed what she could only describe as 'negative', which was totally at variance with his overt masculinity. Helen had been right in suggesting she was never satisfied! She now realised that she did care for Peter in a way she had not thought possible. Often she called at his place of work and, unobserved, stood and watched him for a while. Always she felt a surge of pleasure at seeing his face light up as he turned and saw her. No longer did she make even a token protest when they kissed. Now she was anxious only for him to be more demanding. She was well aware that his natural reticence and the fact that she was a woman of some means didn't help, but was convinced that given the right time and place he might actually ask her to marry him.

His name was so apt she decided, Peter the Rock, the epitome of the good old-fashioned word 'steadfast'. He would go unflinchingly to war when he was called, but now with the younger men away he was running the works with the assistance of a team of women and taking a pride in getting his newspaper out daily and on time. When, this week, the first list of the dead and wounded had reached him for publication, she had seen the slow, heavy tears slide down his face as he started the lengthy business of type-setting each young man's name. Yes, he would oppose her decision, but he knew her to be strong-willed and, she suspected, loved her because of it. However much leaving him hurt, she would go. On this issue she was determined.

She felt relief at having come to a decision and a little colour filtered back into her cheeks. Muriel smiled across at her, as if aware of her thoughts, then together the three of them discussed how best to deal with the unsavoury tasks which lay ahead.

Without hesitation Rosa took over the East End projects, adding these to her Red Cross work, which was progressing well. Helen now felt that she too, must find some worthwhile occupation. Dressing herself up to play the hostess for the young men who arrived at Eaton House was certainly not sufficient, although the challenge of removing that strained look from their young faces was considerable. She felt satisfied on seeing them leave, looking rested and alert, recoiling from the unbidden thoughts which surfaced to remind her that they must now face the horrors of war again. She marvelled at their quick wit and innate good humour, which bubbled so readily to the surface and took pride in the fact that they were able to leave with squared shoulders and heads held high.

Eight weeks had now passed since she had seen Richard Thornton and she longed for his company. To Rosa she had admitted feeling 'skittish' with an unspecified someone. With Richard she felt a young girl again, safe and comfortable. But never too comfortable, for his ready wit allowed no complacency on her part. His teasing forced her to remain alert and lively, the qualities of the young.

J.C. had intimated that Richard would be back by mid September and it was now the 18th. Tomorrow she would telephone Liverpool and find out what news they had of his movements. Helen picked up the phone and dialled Betty's number.

"Helen, thank goodness. I was just going to contact you. I need an opinion and some help. Since that terrible business at Mons, we've been inundated and I do mean inundated with enquiries about mourning clothes. I know it's pretty sickening to make money under these circumstances, but I suppose someone has to meet the need. The stores we have contracts with in London have asked us to send at least quadruple their original orders as soon as possible and we've even had calls from as far afield as Manchester and Leeds, asking if they might act as outlets for the mourning range. If we do so, I'll need to take on more staff, cutters and seamstresses, finishers and probably a packer to help Alf."

"I'll come over right away, Betty. Phone Simmonds and tell him we need some more draft contracts drawn up. Let's aim to get an outlet in say half a dozen of the major cities - Leeds, Manchester, Nottingham, Birmingham, Southampton and Newcastle. And Betty, don't feel bad about this. If the need is there we must meet it. People want to go to funeral and memorial services suitably dressed, it's a mark of respect for their loved ones. We'll talk more when I see you."

By the time Helen left the Bond St. premises terms had been provisionally agreed with six major stores in the designated cities, advertisements drafted and taken by hand to Fleet Street and, most important of all, Betty had been reassured.

Driving back to Eaton Square, Helen reflected on the events of the long, hot summer that was now slipping into autumn. Those few outings to Henley and Wimbledon seemed to have taken place aeons ago. Invitations to Ascot she had refused, doubtful that she would ever be able to face it again. Always whilst the hooves thundered past would be the thought of the day a pathetic bundle had been left behind. Courageous, yes, but had it really benefited the cause of the suffragettes? Most men appeared to have regarded it as a theatrical gesture, typical of the female sex and irrelevant to any serious discussion. Now the War had placed such discussion in limbo; more serious matters were to hand.

She stopped to buy flowers at a street barrow. The last hour had been totally given over to the black, grey and purple of mourning and now she needed colour and the fresh beauty of flora to push back, however temporarily, the darkness of the war clouds gradually impinging on all aspects of their lives. Her spirits lifted as she inhaled the perfume of the huge bunches of roses and carnations, their brilliance enhanced by the misty green fern surrounding them.

And so Richard saw her, descending from the dark blue Renault, arms full of flowers, her brilliant sea-green eyes concealed behind driving goggles. Two strides and she was in his arms, enfolded for the first time in his embrace. And when those first moments of joy subsided he carefully removed her goggles, so that he might see the message in her eyes.

For Helen this meeting on the dusty pavement was confirmation of all that she had hoped for. During the separation her feelings had crystallised and she now saw her own love reflected in Richard's eyes and was content. Hand in hand, laughing, unaware of the curious glances of the Eynsford House 'guests' they made their way to the nursery suite and there, divesting her of flowers and duster coat, he embraced her again, cupping her cheeks with his strong brown hands and drawing her to him to be kissed. She tasted the salt still on his lips and as their breathing quickened, she felt her desire mounting, rushing to meet his own and had to force herself to draw away.

"I'm sorry Richard...it's just that, well Rosa might..."

"Helen my darling, dear God, you don't know how wonderful it is to be able to say that out loud. I've waited for this moment for eight long weeks."

"I do know Richard - you've never been far from my thoughts either, but you've been away so long, much, much longer than I expected - even for the West Indies."

"A seaman's time-table is always unpredictable! There were the usual crop of problems. First, some engineering problems, then one of the crew was ill and we had to change course to get him to hospital. I kept thinking there was bound to be a third thing - perhaps a German U boat popping up."

"Oh don't, don't even joke about it. I've been so worried."

"Well, you needn't worry any more. From now on we're only going out in convoys. Did you know that the local fishermen in Devon have formed a patrol system to keep a constant lookout for mines and U-boats in the Channel? The idea's already catching on in other areas. We shall soon have them all round the coast."

She sat down disconsolately.

"The sea's a big place to protect."

"I know, my darling, but however much we ration supplies and tighten our belts, there are some things we still need and my job is to go out and get them. If I were not doing this, then I'd be at the front, you know that don't you?"

He sat down and took her hand, drinking in her beauty and cool elegance. Her dress was of a dove-grey with matching high-button boots of the softest kid. A purple satin sash banded her waist and was echoed in narrower bands at her wrists and on the tiny buttons which traced a line from throat to waist. As she removed her hat he saw it too, bore a cluster of deep purple violets.

Suddenly the significance of the colour struck him.

"Helen, what an ignorant fool you must take me for. I've just realised - the purple, for the Craybourne boy of course?"

She looked at him enquiringly.

"I had to phone J.C. on arrival and he told me. When will you be travelling North?"

"Next Friday, by rail. All being well we'll be back on the following Monday."

"Good. Selfish of me I know, but I was hoping you'd still be able to attend the launch on October and that we might travel to Liverpool together."

She laughed, "Well of course we have to attend that. After all without Rosa there wouldn't be a launch."

He looked puzzled. "I don't...."

"Come on Richard, the S.S.Rosa launched by Rosa on her twenty first birthday, of course we've got to be there."

Now it was her turn to look puzzled at his grim expression.

"I don't know what's been going on whilst I've been away, but I do know that J.C. invited me to attend the launching, by his wife, of her namesake the S.S.Sonia."

Helen's sharp intake of breath and momentary silence was followed by an explosion such as he'd never heard from her.

"I don't believe it! Two months married and she's already telling him what to do and, no doubt, dictating her terms. How can he do this to his own daughter after making such a promise? And how can he do it to me without consultation? Surely naming a new ship of the line is a Board decision?"

He hesitated, "Well..I suppose it is something that is often within the gift of the Chairman of the Board."

"Much as we would have enjoyed your company, the answer to your invitation Richard is no, we will not be able to travel with you to Liverpool, because Rosa and I will certainly not be attending. I notice J.C. hasn't been in touch with me yet. Nervous of my reaction I suppose, as well he might be!"

"It's very disappointing for you...and for Rosa..." Richard started.

"This isn't just about the launch, Richard, this is just the beginning. I've always suspected that dear Sonia would start to make her presence felt, but I certainly didn't expect it to happen so soon."

"Surely you're over-estimating what she can do. All major decisions will have to be made by the Board."

"Yes, and if I know dear Sonia she will already have been wining and dining those old boys and flirting with them to such an extent that if they were asked they'd say the moon was made of green cheese!"

"We don't know of course, that it isn't!". Richard looked at her quizzically and they both laughed, defusing the situation.

"I know you think I'm over-reacting, but surely I'm allowed a female tantrum once in a while. Besides Rosa will be so disappointed and now I've got to think up an alternative celebration for her twenty-first".

"I like your tantrums. You have my permission to have at least one per week. You're quite the little tigress when those velvet paws are unsheathed". Why did she suddenly look startled he wondered? "Now..this is what I suggest, I'll make my apologies to J.C. and on her birthday I'll escort you and Rosa to wherever you'd like to go."

She had regained her composure. "Richard, I feel better already. The three of us could have lunch together, perhaps by the river at Richmond. Then I could take her to Asprey's. I've had a necklace made for her from..." she hesitated, "my pearls. I'll tell you about those and - about everything else, sometime.. soon. I want her to choose some ear-rings to go with them. If they haven't got what she wants they'll make them up to her design. All this is a surprise of course, so not a word!"

"I'll leave you two ladies to do your birthday shopping, then we could meet in the evening for dinner and dancing. My repertoire is not restricted to the Sailors' Hornpipe you know!"

"If we're dancing, perhaps we might suggest Rosa invites one of the Eynsford House boys to make up a foursome? We're constantly getting invitations from them and it seems so churlish to keep on saying no."

"I like you being churlish, almost as much as your tantrums! Long may it continue."

"You don't think it's wrong to plan this with all the unhappiness around us?"

"Certainly not. Now, where were we my darling, before this matter of the S.S. Sonia reared its ugly head?"

Once again he drew her to him and sighing with pleasure she nestled into the curve of his arm, the flowers crushed by that first embrace and thirsty for water, lying unheeded on the floor.

In retrospect, Rob's memorial service became for Helen a huge collage of snapshots thrown into relief by conflicting emotions. The doleful chiming of the bells led them to church. Was it really only ten short months since they had listened with Rob to that joyful New Year carrillon? Their feet crunched the carpet of copper-coloured leaves until they left the crispness of an early frost and moved into the hushed chill of the church.

Although too frail to attend, Elizabeth's elegant persona seemed to dominate the scene. Lilies were massed on the altar, but it was her small wreath of flowers from the Manor gardens, borne on a velvet cushion of deepest blue which drew all eyes. It seemed to Helen to epitomise the circle of love which started in the womb and bonded the mother/child relationship, a bond which survived the most severe of set-backs. Elizabeth must have been devastated to learn about her son's sexual proclivities, yet she had never turned her back on him, her love had never wavered. Just as the Rani, in spite of all Jai's wickedness, could still say to Helen, "I bore him and I love him."

Her eyes misted and she forced herself to concentrate on Prinny's straight back. Then anger surfaced as the vicar's voice penetrated her grief and she felt a sudden surge of annoyance at his use of the fallen leaves as a metaphor for the war's fatalities. How could he compare the leaves, which had lived out their season's lifespan, to the boys who had been struck from the tree of life before they had even reached their potential? In their black gloves, her hands balled into tight fists.

"Thank God we haven't to go through the ordeal of a funeral wake," Helen confessed to Rosa. "If that man or anyone else comes to me with sanctimonious phrases, I know I shall erupt."

Daphne joined the sisters on their return journey to London the following day. They had much to discuss. The handing over of Iain McNeal's work to the newly appointed Estate Manager was taking James longer than he had anticipated, but they all knew that Muriel was braced ready for the day when he announced that his presence was no longer needed. Then he would enlist.

Michael Featherstone's letter to Prinny, the first in eighteen months, was another talking point. He had just joined the Yorkshire Fusiliers and was under canvas near Ripon for a month's training prior to leaving for the front. Annie Hinton was now his wife. They had a small son with another baby expected. To Rosa and any others who remembered him, he sent his regards. Raw from their loss of Rob, each of them remembered the old butler's words to James, his concern as to what would happen should both the Craybourne boys die. Had Michael known all along who his grandfather was? Was this why he maintained contact with Prinny, in order to glean what family news he could? These questions were not voiced, but each was aware of the frisson of anxiety which passed between them.

Brusquely, Daphne changed the subject, reiterating her own intention of reporting to the War Department on the following day.

"You must ask for Major Gen. Sinclair,"Helen advised, "he knows James, and me too of course. I'm sure he'll be able to help."

Chapter Twenty Six

Just two weeks after Robert's memorial service, James enlisted in the Yorkshire Green Howards and within four days, together with some two hundred officers and men, left for the front. His mother, now in a world where past and present were intermingled, was unaware of his departure. Muriel, six months pregnant, stoically smiled and reassured him that she was in good health and would expect him home for Christmas, or earlier, the set of his jaw telling her that he could not see either as remotely possible.

She had travelled to Leeds to see the troop train leave for the South and now found that the sight of so many other women saying goodbye to husbands, sons and sweethearts was somehow supportive. James and his fellow officers saw the men entrained, returned for their own quick farewells and then, as the regimental band played the new song sweeping the country, the train pulled out of the platform.

Miles, the Craybourne chauffeur, waiting for her at the barrier, was alarmed at her pallor and suggested that she should either take tea at the Queen's Hotel before the drive home or let him escort her to the refreshment bar. At his kindly insistence, she finally opted for the latter, soon finding herself holding a strong cup of tea to which had been added a reviving tot of brandy.

Looking around her she thought once again how the old-fashioned ideas of right and wrong were giving way to a more sensible approach. Groups of women, thrown together by circumstances had now filtered into the room and were thankfully offloading their fears and problems to each other between intermittent gulps of refreshing tea. Watching them, it occurred to Muriel that a few years ago, many of them would not have set foot in such a place without a male escort. If this war continues for long, she thought, there'll no longer be any need for the Women's Suffrage Movement - all the independence we've wanted will just happen.

For the first time she acknowledged just how weary she felt in mind and body and was thankful when she was at last inside the car and it was no longer necessary for her to look or feel brave. Even the weather was depressing with lowering rain clouds which threatened a heavy downpour. Then, just as they left the outskirts of the city, she saw ahead a cloud scored by fissures of gold and then the gradual silvering of its edges. The words of the song she'd just heard throbbed in her mind...'There's a silver lining, thro' the dark clouds shining...' How Rob would have condemned it as trite! Never mind, it still seemed an omen, an indication that all would be well. At the sudden movement inside her womb, she smiled and gave her abdomen a comforting pat.

On October 13th as James and his battalion disembarked at Calais, the British cavalry, Walter and Eddy amongst them, were passing through the Grote Markt at Ypres. Somehow, against all the odds, the B.E.F. had managed to hold their line on one section of the River Yser. Now, the only area where the Allies and the Germans could hope to outflank each other was on the farmland which surrounded this market town. Seven days later, battalions arriving from the Aisne with orders to advance north of Ypres and strengthen the area, met German forces head on. Then began a long drawn out battle with see-sawing victories and defeats for both sides. All their experiences in India had not prepared either Walter or Eddy for the sight of the deaths of the thousands of young Reserve Corps Germans, mostly inexperienced boys, who were poured into this battle.

To assist the flagging Belgian resistance near the coast, Belgian engineers opened the gates of an old lock and let the sea pour into the low-lying areas. This served its immediate purpose, but meant that Germans retreating from the flooding were now forced to concentrate their attacks around Ypres. When the battle was at its height, the Yorkshire Green Howards were moved forward into the trenches.

If Walter and Eddy were horrified by the sheer volume of the young German dead, their service in India had at least schooled them in the art of living rough. James had no such backlog of experience. Short bouts of Territorial training under canvas could never simulate the conditions of trench warfare. James's innate sense of refinement, his sensitivity and privileged upbringing all shrank from the sudden lack of privacy, the crudeness and raw horrors with which he was now surrounded. Brought up to respect death, he now found himself in a world where life was cheap and there was no time for reverence. Indeed, the only way to survive seemed to make light of everything and fervently pray that the nightmare would soon draw to its close.

In the midst of all this mayhem James 'found' Peter Fairburn's young brother Colin. Too late to save his life, James was able to ensure that the boy's real name would appear on his headstone and, a small solace, that Colin's parents would know where he was buried.

His discovery occurred in the early part of November, whilst visiting the field hospital to check on the progress of Green Howards men. Pausing at the bed of a young man, delirious and obviously close to death, something struck a discordant note and James realised that the young man's dialect was not of Yorkshire, but the Kentish burr. Within a few days James's hunch had proved correct. This was indeed Colin Fairburn and before his death, the boy's faint glimmer of pleasure at being addressed by his own name, gave James some satisfaction in a world of disillusionment.

Disillusionment was now Sonia's daily companion. The novelty of a new husband and pride in her new home had waned. With no-one around to envy her status and latest acquisitions pride had withered into resentment and loathing. Resentment at the hours Jim now spent at the Company offices, time he justified by reminding her repeatedly 'We are at war you know.' The loathing directed at Liverpool. How she longed for London's elegant buildings, its beautiful parks. Here all seemed grimy and down-at-heel. Each day she faced acres of unoccupied time. Time in which to brood about Helen and Rosa's visit when their disapproval had hung in the air and lingered long after their departure.

Desperate for company she had now taken to walking to the dock area, ostensibly to meet Jim, or to find what time he would be returning. In reality to bask in the admiration of males, any males who might pass her by. Had he been aware of the area she traversed before arriving at the Company offices, even the broad-minded Jim would have been horrified. But the battery of eyes which flashed appreciation of her trim figure and saucy outfits, were just the balm Sonia needed to ease the irritation of the Calloway sisters' disdain. On one such outing, having stopped to watch a ship of the Calloway Line, the S.S. Marguerita, unloading, she was seen by Henry Gurney.

He knew her immediately. Wasn't the word already out that she was 'a bit of a goer'? Not many women would have the nerve to parade herself around the docks in this fashion. And there was no doubt about it, she was very easy on the eye. Henry Gurney's eye was experienced in this field and he liked what he saw. Jim Calloway must be twenty years her senior, perhaps not quite the man she first thought he was. Perhaps she was already looking for pastures new, in which case

A few quick strides and he was down the gangplank and standing in front of her. With a mock flourish he bowed and said,

"Mrs. Calloway, I presume? Henry Gurney, ma'am, one of the Line's sea captains. May I escort you to wherever you're going?"

Sonia's eyes widened, taking in the rakish air, the weather-beaten, handsome face, the strong jaw-line which seemed at conflict with the full sensuous mouth. Extending a hand in her most lady-like fashion, she endeavoured to appear cool and collected, whilst stifling the urge to say out loud, "My, my, things are looking up!"

Rosa was glad when Richard went back to sea and hated herself for being so. Always he had been kind and courteous to her. Whilst Rosa had not felt so keenly as Helen her father's volte face regarding the shipping launch, it was nevertheless satisfying to feel her birthday had been celebrated in style as Richard had promised.

Lunch at Richmond was followed by the Asprey visit, where she became the owner of a double stranded necklace of exquisite pearls and diamond and tear-drop pearl ear-rings. Tea at Fortnum's, a brief respite and time to change, then to the Music Hall and a late dinner. It had been a lovely, lovely day and yet, always she had been conscious of being the odd one out. She had declined Helen's suggestion of inviting one of the young men staying at Eynsford House. This might have seemed an admission of a special interest, something she certainly did not feel. Nevertheless she had never been so conscious of her single status as on that evening.

It was as if Helen and Richard's delight in their own love unintentionally and unwittingly excluded her. She knew her state of mind to be selfish, uncharitable and, in view of what she now intended, unforgivable, but then, as she ruefully admitted to herself, she had never been as 'good' as Helen.

Daphne's approach to Major Sinclair had resulted in her being appointed as a War Department driver in and around London and Rosa assumed that Daphne's diffidence regarding nursing was the reason for her not being sent further afield. She herself had no such qualms. What she needed now more than anything was time in which she and Helen could sit down alone to discuss at length her own plans. Rosa's lines of argument were ready to meet the expected opposition. The Red Cross unit at the Salon had now an abundance of people well able to cope, indeed plans were afoot to set up another unit in a hotel ballroom. Her own presence at Eynsford House was superfluous. The two adult schools in the East End had fewer applicants as more and more women turned to war work, although many complained they couldn't contemplate this because of young families - the whole situation needed re-thinking.

Helen, saddened by Richard's departure and fearful for his safety did not put forward the opposition Rosa had anticipated. Rob's death and, strangely, that of young Colin Fairburn whom she had never met, the stream of weary young men passing through Eynsford House and the recent reportage of the Massacre of the Innocents at Ypres had crystallised in Helen a state of fatalism. The anger she had felt after Rob's death faded as she recognised her own world and that of those around her to be in complete chaos. Facing facts and making decisions seemed now to be the only sensible and constructive method of dealing with the situation. And so, when Rosa diffidently started upon her well rehearsed brief, a surprisingly brusque Helen dealt efficiently with the points raised. Yes, the Red Cross unit could certainly manage without her, as could Eynsford House. The problem of the East End schools was more complex... Helen thought for a moment, before stating that, realistically, these should be closed for the duration of the war. Enquiries would be made at munitions factories and other essential services and where possible, creches set up.

"I'm quite sure the mothers themselves will be able to organise these, once they know they've the backing of management. Probably pregnant women, or those still nursing their babies could look after other toddlers, say with the help of a few teenage girls. Let's float the idea, see what happens. What we need from management is only a reasonably sized room, with access to a sink and lavatories - and a bit of understanding. We'll get on to it right away.

"Now that seems to be the difficulties out of the way, tell me exactly what you have in mind."

Rosa hesitated   "Well, I've made a few enquiries . . ."

"I rather thought you might have," Helen smiled.

"I don't think I'm squeamish about blood.. .well, let's say I'm determined not to be. I'm going to offer to drive ambulances. Obviously it would be an advantage if I had some knowledge of first aid, so what they recommend is a month's crash course in a London hospital, before I'm sent overseas."

'Overseas', the word dropped like a stone in the quiet room and suddenly the enormity of what Rosa was proposing struck Helen. This was her little sister, a girl who had never yet been abroad and who was now talking of driving vehicles of badly injured men, through an arena of war. For a moment she was unable to speak and Rosa, realising, hurried on.

"I have to go, Helen. I'm young and strong and not doing enough. You and Betty have a business to run. Sad though the reason is, the market for mourning clothes is multiplying daily and, you never know, J.C. might want some assistance with the shipping line, now some have been re-routed to Tilbury. Then there's Eynsford House, they need you there, not every day perhaps but...?"

"Enough, I'm convinced! You must go and I must stay". She turned towards the window, looking out across London's skyline. "I shall hate it though, Rosa. Why must all the people I love, go away?" She shrugged off the innermost echoes which begged the question 'And never come back?' and smiling, said briskly,

"No, I'm not going to go all maudlin on you. Let's be totally practical. You're going to need some really warm sensible clothes, waterproof boots, woollen stockings and underwear. Let's go and see if Helena's Salon has anything even remotely suitable."

Iain McNeal drew the white feather carefully from the envelope, holding it delicately between thumb and forefinger. He laid it on the table before him and extracted the small accompanying card. The bold copper-plate writing glared up at him accusingly,

'Even cowards are needed at the front.' The White Feather Club.

There was a sudden constriction in his chest and his heart thumped. Anticipation had not lessened the pain of the envelope's receipt. Almost three months had passed since his father's death. Three months in which he'd found endless reasons why he shouldn't enlist. With the young men away there'd been plenty of casual work on the farms, though he would never forget the day when a farmhouse door was opened by a woman in black, toddlers at her skirts. Nor was her blazing diatribe as she sent him packing ever far from his mind. In the town where he'd found lodgings, the women had become more and more overt in their disapproval. Eyes would sweep over him, then pointedly look away. Women in clusters whispered at his passing.

He'd read about the White Feather Club and that there were now groups everywhere who styled themselves on its name and sought out likely recipients. Whilst he hated the thought of seeing men killed or maimed, he was beginning to dread this stigma of cowardice almost as much. He knew he could no longer remain where he was or continue to avoid decisive action. Sick at heart, he at last packed his belongings and set out for Inverness and the recruiting office.

It was mid-November before Helen received Iain's letter. In it he apologised for his deception, described his upbringing and outlined the events which had led up to his sombre mood on their evening out. Now, drawing these threads together, she could understand his ambivalent actions and feel sorry for him. Whilst only hinting at his fears, Helen was quick to draw her own conclusions, as did Rosa who after reading his letter, voiced her sympathy.

"Poor devil, if he'd only realise he's not alone in his fear. Even my brief experience with the wounded seems to indicate that they, and all of us for that matter, are scared to death at heart. It's understandable isn't it? We're moving into the unknown and we're afraid of what our reactions will be in situations we can't begin to imagine. When it comes to it, Iain will probably put up a better show than the types who are full of what they're going to do to the Bosche. Let me see, this was written about ten days ago. At least we haven't any other news of him."

"What sort of news?...I don't understand."

"Well....someone was telling me yesterday that on average ten men a week are committing suicide before they even reach the war zone. At home, on the train, on the boat, some in the trenches, they each choose their own place and time".

"Rosa, that's horrible!"

"War is horrible. But don't worry about it, we would have heard if anything was wrong."

Don't worry, Helen thought, easier said than done. Rob lost to them for ever, James, Walter, Eddy and now Iain, facing all sorts of horrors, horrors which Rosa would soon be sharing, and Richard, her dear Richard, God knows where, on the high seas.

She closed the lid of the bureau sharply,

"I'll write to Iain tonight", she said "I must let him know I understand."

Once the matter of the factory creches had been dealt with, Helen, as James had requested, visited his solicitors, to see if there was any possibility of either obtaining an indefinite lease on his flat, or selling it. She found the agents expressing concern that other flats in the same building had now been vacated and making no secret of the fact that they were anxious to dispose of the property. Only one sitting tenant remained, an elderly lady who was happy to be rehoused if a suitable flat was offered. This was speedily dealt with, and as soon as Helen became the owner of the elegant Georgian building, she offered it on a rental basis to the War Office. They accepted with alacrity, its proximity to the Moorfields Eye Hospital making it an ideal recovery centre for post-surgery patients.

To date, Helen's acquisition of property had occurred almost accidentally. Now for the first time she started to look around at what was available. If the properties could earn their keep during the period of the war, she felt sure they must appreciate in value afterwards. When the wounded were brought into London by the boat-train, large numbers were too ill to face immediate onward journeys to other areas and in any event, many had to remain near the facilities offering the optimum treatment. Five other large properties were soon offered to her, approved and purchased. All were speedily adapted to nursing and convalescent needs.

One of these, a building in Grosvenor Square, adjacent to several of the foreign embassies, was particularly handsome. Helen envisaged no difficulty in selling this, once peace was declared - providing she herself could bear to part with it!

Nor were her interests confined to the upper class areas of London. Between Blackfriars and Charing Cross she came across a four storeyed building, previously a workhouse. Here she decided to incorporate the original idea behind the East End schools with that of factory and creche. The top floor became a nursery and creche with the three lower floors a factory for young mothers. Their objective was to meet the growing demand for shirts and underwear for service personnel, with a separate section devoted to making stretchers and tarpaulins.

Personnel for the factory did not prove a problem. Major Sinclair, having soon identified Daphne's usefulness in her large number of contacts amongst both the wealthy and underprivileged, now gave her the task of setting up a clearing house for the many women wishing to find work, or give their services. All places of employment were asked to co-operate and soon Daphne and her staff were busily matching applicants to suitable work. Ruefully she complained to Helen,

"It's not what I had in mind as war work, but I suppose it's useful!"

Daphne was now much more contented. Her relationship with Peter had become the stabilising influence of her life. After Rob's death there had been times when she had felt desperate for comfort. At such times the touch of firm flesh became an affirmation of life and Peter had stayed with her.

At first their lovemaking had been tentative. She, sure of herself in so many ways, was nervous in this new situation. Always more the gamine than the voluptuary, she felt her slender body to be unattractive, too boyish for his robust masculinity. Only his constant assurances that she was all he desired, and his patience in ensuring that she enjoyed the union as much as he, convinced her. Then, finally, she blossomed, her face under the silver blonde of her hair, losing the sharp angles heightened by her illness. Her eyes without their hard brightness became blue-grey pools. Now, as she had once hoped he might, he begged her to marry him. She refused.

"If ... when you go away, you won't want a wife to worry about."

"That's a specious argument. Whether wife or sweetheart, I'm going to worry about you - as well, you know."

"I'll think about it, perhaps next year..."

"Why then and not now? Why wait at all?"

"It's just the uncertainty of everything. All these hurried weddings, with everyone looking unhappy, I don't think I could stand that."

At the touch of his hand on her breast, the subject was again abandoned. Now he delighted in the way she responded to him, the curling and stretching of her slim body, the sounds of pleasure she emitted. They spoke of love and she acknowledged that her own had been slow in developing. He laughingly answering that he'd known from the start that she was his girl, because she was so wilful and outspoken.

With him like this, she could shut out the pain of losing Rob and when on one such occasion at the point of climax, she clung to him passionately, entreating.

"Don't leave me, please don't leave me."

Peter, the hitherto so-careful lover, misunderstanding her plea, drew her closer

216

to him, thrust deep into her welcoming body and relaxed. And in this moment, Oliver Craybourne's fifth grandchild was conceived.

The two officers were in no doubt that Craybourne Manor would make an excellent rehabilitation centre for the shell-shocked and amputees. Mindful of Lady Craybourne's pregnancy and Prinny's age, they proposed sending in a team of men who would, under their supervision, effect the move of 'family' and servants into one wing. At the same time, all valuables would also be moved. The drawing room was to house ten leg and foot amputees, whilst those with injuries, but still able to walk, would have bedrooms on the first floor.

Prinny's cottage, still fully furnished, was ideal for four of the nurses and the three empty cottages in Piggott's Lane would take at least six others. Accommodation for two doctors and two sisters would be found in the House.

By the second week in December all was ready and Muriel, suddenly aware that Christmas was imminent, discussed with the Dennisons at the farm, just what would be available to feed her guests and any of the nursing staff who might arrive before their own full provisioning was effected. Daphne, Peter and Helen were coming to the Manor. Rosa, having already served her month in hospital, was due to leave for the front on December 9th.

There would be no problems this year, Mr. Dennison assured her. Plenty of geese, a brace of pheasants and a pig ready for the killing, plus unlimited milk and cream, their own butter and eggs, vegetables and fruit. The Manor larders were stocked from floor to ceiling with preserves and pickles and Mrs. Waring, with great foresight, had doubled her usual generous quantity of Christmas puddings. In the Butler's Pantry, a new cooker awaited her, so that family cooking and that of the hospital personnel could be kept quite separate.

As part of the re-organisation, Elizabeth's boudoir had been converted into a small dining room for family occasions and it was here that they gathered on Christmas Eve, very conscious of those not present. Only one doctor had taken up residence and Muriel had asked him to join them. It was a double-edged invitation. She could not countenance anyone being alone at Christmas, knowing at the same time that his presence would, hopefully, dispel the inevitable comparisons with Christmas 1913.

"I'm a Welshman with a Scottish Christian name and an English surname!" Bruce Maynard laughingly introduced himself to Helen. "Brought up in a small village in the Rhonda, I can assure you I was at least ten before I realised that in other places people weren't named according to their occupations. It really was Dai the Milk, Gwilm the Post and all that, where I come from!"

He was lively and entertaining and each of them was grateful for Muriel's foresight, which imposed upon them the need to consider their guest and not brood upon their individual problems.

In just three days at Craybourne, Bruce Maynard had learned much about them all. Now, meeting them for the first time, he was able to flesh out the different characters. In one way or another they've all lost someone, he thought, whether temporarily or permanently. Even Prinny. She had felt keenly Rob's death and now her beloved Elizabeth was lost to her, incarcerated in a world of her own.

Deliberately Bruce set about lightening the atmosphere, regaling them with tales of his boyhood, so that they were all surprised to hear the clock strike midnight. And, as they raised their glasses and drank their toast to "Peace, may it come soon", many miles away each of those missing from the circle was uttering the same words.

Chapter Twenty Seven

In the trenches' H.Q., a tiny room reeking of damp and decay, James listened to the strains of 'Stille Nacht' drifting across No Man's Land and joined his fellow officers in the Christmas toast. Eddy, eyes firmly fixed on a sniper's nest, sipped from the enamel mug which Walter passed him, whilst six miles away Iain McNeal, chilled to the bone and feeling the chatter of his teeth against the cup's metal rim, prayed fervently that his courage would not let him down. In the field hospital, Rosa joined the nurses and patients and acted a cheerfulness she was far from feeling. And, as Richard Thornton's ship turned for home, he gazed at the Northern Star and wondered what 1915 would bring to him and the beautiful Helen.

Boxing Day over, Craybourne Manor started to take on its new role with the arrival of different personnel. A second doctor and the two sisters had travelled together from London by car. The first batch of nurses arrived at Leeds, were duly collected by the Craybourne chauffeur and settled in at Orchard Cottage. Maintenance men installed handrails in sections of the gardens and wheel chairs were delivered. Then the roar of a motor-bike announced the arrival of the army cook, speedily followed by his two assistants. Now the kitchen became a powerhouse of activity as these three set about the task of provisioning the nursing home within the allotted forty-eight hours.

Helen, concerned at the amount of work Muriel was still finding to do, delayed her departure until all the patients and staff were installed and a complete night and day roster had been successfully operative. It seemed to her that the shell-shocked were in a far worse condition than the amputees. They followed instructions, their young faces grey and tense, yet never seemed to be wholly present. By contrast, the amputees made light of their injuries, each battling against his own personal set of problems in his own way. Uncharitable as the thought might be, Helen could not help but wonder if they were now experiencing relief that for them the war was over. For the others not only the trauma remained, but always the question of if and when would they be called upon to return.

Not until she was ensconced on the train returning home was she able to contemplate her own situation. Counting the days to Richard's return at the end of the month, she reviewed their relationship. They each believed themselves to be in love, but their time together could be counted in days. What did they really know of each other? And was that knowledge sufficient to support a marriage? She had thought she loved Jai, thought she knew him and yet she couldn't have been more wrong. Richard had not yet even mentioned marriage.... and how on earth would he react when he learned the extent of the Formidable Fortune?

In spite of her property purchases, this continued to increase. On her last visit to the Bank, sensing her concern, her Bank Manager pursed his lips and said somewhat reprovingly,

"It's just what I would have expected, Miss Calloway, indeed hoped for. The shipping line continues to do well. Your father had the foresight to have four new ships in the pipeline when the war started and this has paid dividends. As to the Helena Salon it is, to coin a phrase, 'a little gold mine'. Sales are up by 300% and I think we have your own shrewd planning and marketing to thank for that. With the exception of two or three smaller properties, all your purchases are bringing in sufficient revenue to more than cover their upkeep. I'm afraid, Miss Calloway, like it or not, you are now a very rich young lady."

Within a week of Helen arriving back in London, Prinny phoned to say that Muriel had gone into labour. Vaguely remembered phrases came flooding back; old wives' tales about the difficulties of bearing an eight month baby. Better late, than the month of eight, the village women used to say, heads solemnly nodding. Firmly she told herself it was all nonsense, but her relief was tremendous when a second call brought the news that Muriel had given birth to a little girl and both were well. Olivia, named for the grandfather she would never know, was already according to Prinny, showing every sign of having the Craybourne's ash-blonde hair. Pleasure rippled through the family - some good news at last! Messages were sent to James by a variety of methods, but a month elapsed before Muriel received the letter she'd been waiting for telling her that James now knew of his daughter's existence and was thrilled by it.

He wrote, "You cannot imagine how often I picture the two of you together my darling. You tell me Olivia has the Craybourne hair. That gives me pleasure of course, but my dearest wish is that she also has all her mother's sweetness and intelligence. If so, she will indeed be a most blessed child."

Muriel's joy in her child was infectious and the baby, passed around like a parcel to anyone who asked if they might hold her, thrived on a surfeit of affection and attention. In Elizabeth's dream world she became the tiny Daphne; to Prinny, the child she had never had and the young men coming to terms with their injuries found in the baby Olivia a symbol of stability, of new life and hope, a sweet-scented reminder of the family circle.

Iain carried Helen's letter with him as a talisman. Her understanding of what had happened and its effect on him, her support and encouragement for what he now faced daily, acting as a salve to sores which had festered untended for years. She was so right in saying that having learned to fear his father as a child, the difficulty for him had been to rethink his attitude as an adult. But, she insisted, he had overcome that fear on the night he confronted his father and she had confidence that he would be able to conquer other fears in the same way.

He had told her all. The burning shame of the white feather, the treatment which had made him feel degraded. And he was glad that she knew. During the crossing from Dover to Calais there had been a fresh horror when a young man from the Lancashire Fusiliers was found hanging in one of the maintenance lockers. Rumours were rife, the one common thread being that the young man was terrified at the thought of what lay ahead. Never before had Iain been so close to a suicide, listened to so many details as to the how and why. Now with a terrible certainty he came to realise that he was not capable of taking his own life. Nothing he had to face could be worse than, by his own hand, taking that final step into oblivion.

On the fringe of Ypres, the bitterly cold night had seemed endless. At 3.00 a.m. the temperature lifted slightly, snow started to fall and now the reproachful mounds which littered No Man's Land, were decently clothed in white, the only sounds being the scuffling of the rats about their obscene feasting. With the dawn, snipers on both sides started their 'morning hate' campaign, sending the bloated rats scurrying for shelter, leaving a mosaic of prints across the fresh snow.

As fast as the Highlanders raised the level of the trenches, so the bullets skimmed the uppermost layer of sandbags. Due to be relieved by the Cheshires at 8.00 a.m., the news that this had been postponed for a further three hours sent echoing along the trenches a groan, which rose and fell like a mighty wave. At half past eight the attack started in earnest with heavy shell fire over Ypres. Well short of its target, the first shell to hit the Highlanders was from a Belgian gun. Two men were killed instantly and two others thrown several yards clear of the trench.

Iain, stunned by the blast, peered through the pall of smoke. Now he could see that the leg of the man lying next to him was completely shattered, the virgin snow crimsoning with his blood. Already the protective smoke was clearing. Very soon they would be silhouetted against the surrounding whiteness and form an easy target. Painfully he dragged himself to a half sitting position. His left arm and shoulder felt useless and he guessed them to be broken. There was a searing pain down the right side of his face, probably caused by flash burns, but at least he was conscious. With a mighty effort he staggered to his feet, then grasped the injured man's collar with his right hand. Now the sniper was aware of some activity and the whine of his bullets gave Iain extra momentum. Keeping as low as he could beneath the rapidly dissipating smoke, he clung determinedly to the scruff of the man's neck, grunting aloud with the pain of his own exertions. At last he reached a point where welcoming hands could reach out and drag the man's limp body into the trench. As Iain himself was hauled unceremoniously over the sandbags, toppling onto the men below, a gruff Scottish voice said,

"Couldn't wait to get out there and start making snowballs eh?...Well done Mac!"

Iain's grin became a grimace of pain, until mercifully he blacked out.

Rosa had already made one return journey to the trenches since daybreak. It promised to be a busy day. The early snow had melted and then frozen into treacherous pockets of ice, making driving hazardous. Her regular assistant Bert, a huge Cockney, grunted each time the ambulance veered out of control, then uttered a different sound one she took to be of commendation, when she brought it back into line. En route they passed an ambulance headed for the front line, already off the road. Horses had been brought up from the rear to try and haul it out of a ditch some two feet deep.

Shells screamed overhead as they reached the pick-up point and saw the usual cluster of stretchers and accompanying medical orderlies. The man Iain had brought in was losing a great deal of blood and it took all the expertise Rosa and Bert could muster to staunch the flow. Two men, walking, but with eye injuries were boarded next and it was then that Rosa turned to the man on the second stretcher. His face burned down one side and blackened from the smoking shell, his clothes were caked with blood and snow, now melting into rusty puddles, Iain was completely unrecognisable. Until his eyes met hers.... Dragging himself back to reality, his eyes opened wide at the sight of her. The fixation of his stare, a hand fluttering in a half gesture of greeting, and she realised.

"Iain ...?"

"The very same, but...."

"We'll talk later." Rosa lightly touched his fingers and signalling to the men to lift him into the ambulance, she climbed into the driving seat.

It was to be three days before they were able to do so. Soon after arriving at the hospital, Iain had gone into deep shock and was kept heavily sedated whilst his arm and shoulder were set and his burns treated. Curiously, the fresh snow had proved a benison. Initially sterile, it had not only cooled and kept his facial burns less painful but reduced the possibility of disfigurement. Each evening after finishing her spell of duty, an exhausted Rosa went into his ward, but it was not until two days had passed before she found him sitting up and grinning at her lop-sidedly.

"Sorry," he said, "the bandages are restrictive."

"Don't apologise for heaven's sake! It's just great to see you back in the land of the living again."

"Rosa, no-one has said... The man I brought back, how's he doing?"

"He's gone." Then seeing his alarmed expression, she added hastily, "No, no, I don't mean gone, as in dead. It's just that whilst you've been unconscious he's had surgery and has now left for home - under sedation of course. You would have gone too, if it hadn't been for the delayed shock - worse in your case because you were conscious during most of the incident."

And in answer to his unspoken question,

"I'm afraid his leg couldn't be saved. But we must be positive. Without your help he would have died out there."

He changed the subject.

"I was so amazed to see you, Rosa. How long have you been here?"

"Several weeks - it just seems longer! Every day seems to race by, we're so busy, then the nights seem extra short, because we're so tired. London and comfortable beds seem a million miles away."

"And Helen?"

"She's fine. Muriel and James have a baby daughter, who is apparently quite beautiful."

"Must run in the family!"

"Do I detect a compliment? You must be feeling better, but by the way Sister is looking at me I assume my couple of minutes must be up, so I'm sorry but it's time to say goodnight."

She kissed him lightly on the exposed left side of his face.

"I'll pop in again tomorrow."

And with that she set off briskly down the ward, auburn curls bobbing, to the delight of the watching men.

In that winter of 1915 there were countless acts of heroism on the Western Front. Only the unselfishness of officers who persisted until their commendations brought results, ensured that some of these were recognised. One such list from Iain's C.O. was seen by both James and Walter and whilst James was unable to leave his post during the ensuing days, Walter, whose regiment was only sent into the trenches in a relief capacity, managed to get to the hospital before Iain left. Without divulging any of the reasons leading to his enlistment, Helen's last letter had asked Walter to be on the lookout for Iain. Now Walter was able to pass on up-to-date news about the Salon, the opening of the Blackfriars factory, and of course, Richard Thornton.

"Sounds as if this could be serious..."Walter's voice tailed off and Iain heard the note of anxiety.

Deliberately, he made light of it.

"Oh, I don't know.. A sea captain, that's pretty glamorous to a young woman!"

"Helen's not like that," Walter was emphatic. "Not likely to be taken in by what's on the surface .... at least, not now. She learned the hard way."

There was a small, companionable silence, each aware that his own feelings for Helen made him anxious for her safety and jealous of others.

"We're out of the trenches now, thank God! Did our relief spell over Christmas. Weren't you staggered at meeting up with Rosa? Only made contact with her myself just before Christmas. Wonderful as it is to see her now and again, I'm worried sick about what she's doing - and seeing! You know I've known her since she was a very little girl and still find it difficult to think of her as a woman. James isn't far from here, we've met a couple of times - not a lot of time for socialising! They tell me you'll be back in Blighty in a couple of days, lucky you. Give my love to everyone, especially Helen. She'll never know how much I value her letters."

She was waiting to greet him as the train steamed into Waterloo. The scene was one of apparent confusion. Ambulances, stretchers, service personnel and civilians, all seemed at first to be moving aimlessly. Gradually order emerged and several minutes before Helen located him, he watched her elegant approach along the line of the train. Her wine-coloured coat with its banding of silver-grey velvet, the matching hat with its small dark red aigrette, her erect composure, as always drew attention even in this situation.

223

She smelled so good! For him the odour of the trenches, a blend of dank earth, decomposition and urine had been superseded by that of disinfectant and ether. Now he drank in her fragrance, the touch of her soft skin, her voice. It was all arranged, she told him. He was to stay at Eynsford House as her guest - Rosa's room was empty. She, herself, would take him to the hospital as and when necessary and Major Sinclair would be informed as soon as Iain was judged medically fit to rejoin his regiment. As they drove to Eynsford House he decided that it was more, much more than he could have ever hoped for.

"What the devil's going on? You did this on purpose didn't you?" Richard's eyes were dilated with anger.

"What on earth do you mean? I think, Richard...."

He interrupted her.

"This Iain fellow, you've installed him as some sort of chaperone".

"That's absolutely ridiculous."

"Is it? Both you and I knew that with Rosa away this could have been our own domain, however temporary. We've been patient whilst she was around, but you know how I feel. I thought you felt the same, obviously I was wrong."

"No..that is, I did, I do feel the same but..."

"There's still a but, isn't there? Is it the sex you're afraid of? I don't know what on earth that black husband of yours did to you, but you seem to have a marked reluctance to try it again, with me."

"Don't be coarse and for heaven's sake keep your voice down or Iain will wonder what on earth's going on."

"Sorry, we mustn't forget Iain, must we? As if we could!"

"If you'll calm down I'll explain. Iain's home is in the Scottish Highlands and he's just not well enough to travel so far."

"So why isn't he downstairs with your other boys?"

"Because he's not an officer that's why. Though after what he did a few days ago, he's in line for a field commission."

"Oh, a hero is he? I might have guessed! Been telling you what a wonderful chap he is?"

"He hasn't been telling me anything. Rosa met him at the field hospital and he's brought me a letter from her. She told me what happened."

"So, if he's not quite top-drawer officer material, what does he do, when he's not saving people's lives?"

"He is, or rather he was, the estate manager and game-keeper at Craybourne."

"That explains a lot. Like a bit of the rough stuff do you, dished out by the rough and ready types, gamekeepers and heavy-handed princes?"

"You'd better leave... .Now!"

"Oh, I'm leaving alright. Sonia said I was on to a good thing, but I can see your little hero has beaten me to it."

"Sonia... ? What on earth has Sonia got to do with any of this?"

"Quite a lot! Your new stepmother and I have known each other since we were kids in Tilbury, shared the same mother, would you believe? When the succession of "fathers", and I use the term lightly, started to change too often for my liking, I went as far away as I could, to another seafaring port. Not much choice really, boats being the only thing I knew anything about. Sonia stayed put. But we kept in touch and before you even set foot in Liverpool I knew all about you and the little nest-egg you have tucked away. Let's face it, if I hadn't known about that, I wouldn't be here in the first place. Kept me well primed with what was afoot, dear little Sonia. She was wrong about one thing though, said you were prim and proper and I'd have to watch my manners until I'd got the ring on your finger. I suppose the laugh's on me really, while I'm being the perfect gentleman you're already consoling someone fresh from battle by tucking him up with you in bed."

"Get out!" Helen now white with shock, turned to see the surreal figure of Iain in the doorway. His arm and shoulder encased in plaster, the hair on one side of his head closely cropped revealing the burns to his scalp and one cheek crimson and scabbed.

"So, this is the wonder-boy! Not much to look at is he? Shouldn't think he's much use in bed at the moment either, but no doubt you can always take your pick from the motley collection you have downstairs."

With that Richard was gone, leaving his nastiness to spread like a stain in the quiet room.

Retrospectively, Helen could see it all. Sonia relaying information to Richard regarding her affairs. Giving him advice as to how to approach her. Advice he'd carried out to the letter - polite but firm; attentive, but not deferential. Helen was sickened. Was she really so gullible, so naive? No wonder Sonia had always seemed to interested in her activities and particularly her purchases.

In those early days at Miss Tindall's, Sonia had said little about her own origins, but if Richard and Sonia's mother had lived off a succession of men, then Sonia must have from an early age learned the art of duplicity and opportunism. No wonder too that Richard had seemed so familiar with London's docklands. When she had questioned him about it, he'd laughed it off, saying that one set of docks was much like another. When she'd asked why there wasn't a trace of the Lancashire dialect in his speech, his explanation had seemed reasonable, "Travelling the world, soon removes those."

Helen shuddered at the thought of how close she had been to making another terrible mistake; another liaison with a man of no scruples whatsoever. At what point Sonia had devised her scheme, Helen couldn't be sure, but certainly fate seemed to have ensured that everything went her way - until today. Thank God for the spur of the moment decision to bring Iain to Eynsford. But what of Sonia's marriage to J.C.? How long before she put a foot wrong there, in her endeavour to have the best of all possible worlds?

Sonia had already done just that. Rifling through the pages of the calendar, checking and rechecking her dates she at last hurled it across the room with such force that it struck an occasional table and sent its contents crashing to the floor. The little parlourmaid who came scurrying in to see what was wrong, almost joined the debris, as Sonia pushed her out of the way, stormed up the stairs and in the privacy of her own room, flung herself face down on the bed.

Here was a pretty kettle of fish and no mistake! She'd had scares of this sort before of course, many of them, but this was different. She was now at least three weeks overdue and J.C. hadn't been near her for more than a month. A few days of feeling 'not one hundred per cent' and his doctor had diagnosed angina and advised a period of rest. Whilst the latter had not extended to his daily visits to the office, it had deterred him from entering Sonia's bed, knowing full well the energy which would then be required! Still, she consoled herself, men were notoriously vague about such matters. With a little judicious juggling of dates, it should not be too difficult to convince J.C. that Henry Gurney's child was his own. "Pull yourself together girl," she sternly admonished herself. Rising from the bed she straightened her dress and tidied her hair and, the picture of composure, went downstairs to retrieve her calendar. It was, in fact, a wasted exercise.

It was J.C.'s custom to leave the office at lunchtime for a beer and a sandwich at The Ship and Anchor. Today, feeling drained of all energy and mindful of the doctor's advice, he decided to try and snatch forty winks before the afternoon's business began. Awakening to the sound of voices in the adjacent office, he heard snatches of dialogue which roused him instantly. "One of his own sea captains..." Then, "that wife of his, eyes everywhere." "Could fancy a bit of that myself..." "The boss's own house." And, quite clearly "You know what they say, while the cat's away..." The rest was drowned in laughter, a laughter which, as he moved into the doorway, died on the lips of the two young clerks, their horrified silence and stricken expressions confirming his suspicions.

Leaving the Calloway building, he walked briskly until he came to where the Marguerita lay at anchor on a high running tide. Now his pace quickened and as he started up the steep gangway he started to shout. "Where are you, you bastard? Come out and show yourself." Alerted by the noise, Henry Gurney and several seamen surfaced from below decks, but before J.C. reached the top a massive pain seared up his left arm and seized his chest in a fist of iron. Startled, he stopped and the pain struck again, felling him to a crumpled heap, his groan fading with the final expiration of breath.

Sonia went through the motions of course- beautifully. Was the grieving widow- most of the time. Even managed some tears in remembrance of the good times she had had with J.C.- but barely enough to dampen a handkerchief. In fact she couldn't believe her luck. Now she really was on the winning straight! What a wonderful quirk of fate it had been which had sent her to Helen's flat and her first meeting with J.C.

Henry Gurney was not too thrilled about the child. In his opinion women, without exception, changed when babies came on the scene. However, if it was his child, and the now 'merry widow' assured him this was the case, then he was onto a good thing here. Sonia would inherit J.C.'s half of the business, in shares, of course. The three senior captains held three shares each and as she already had the old boys on the Board eating out of the palm of her hand she would effectively control the business. And as a wife was really part of her husband's goods and chattels... Yes, as soon as it was decently possible, he'd marry the widow. The pregnancy couldn't be announced yet of course, but when it was she'd elicit even more sympathy for her situation, at which time a 'for the sake of her fatherless child' marriage would be seen as a noble gesture. Or would it? No matter! Between them they could control the Line and money talked more than gossip - and was more effective, everywhere!

Sonia's thoughts ran much on the same lines. With a fortune behind her and a handsome young husband, the world would be her oyster, just as soon as this wretchedly inconvenient war was over.

Of necessity Helen travelled alone to Liverpool for her father's funeral. Rosa was in Belgium and there was no question of leave being arranged at such short notice. Even the black veil and mourning clothes could not conceal Sonia's suppressed excitement and Helen guessed at its root cause. She had always felt that there would come a time when she and Sonia would be battling over the control of the shipping line and that time had come much sooner than anticipated. Another factor had now appeared in the equation of the balance of power. As Sonia's half brother, Richard would be lined up with the other captains and the rest of the Directors against her. "Well, I'm ready for them;" she thought, as the train reached the grimy environs of the city, "Let battle commence!"

They assembled for the reading of the will in Sonia's ornate drawing room. Too much plush, too many tassels, too many frills, too awful! Helen thought, but let's be thankful for small mercies, at least Richard's not here, I don't think I'm quite ready yet to be in the same room with him.

As expected, J.C.'s block of shares, amounting to 38%, and the house were left to his widow. For Helen and Rosa 'because it might interest them' there was the record J.C. had kept of his activities after he left Yorkshire, together with a small chest of artefacts acquired during his journeying. Sonia, already tight-lipped, relaxed when the solicitor announced.

"I was instructed by my client, Mr. Calloway, that should he predecease his fifth wedding anniversary, then the item he was keeping for that occasion, should be given to Mrs. Calloway now".

With this he handed a velvet box to Sonia, who gasped with pleasure at the sight of the jade necklace it contained. The solicitor added, "There is an explanatory note inside". J.C.'s card told Sonia that the necklace had been purchased two years after his Liverpool venture had started to prove successful, "from an Oriental gentleman, who assured me it was a family heirloom."

Sonia's pleasure was short-lived, as the solicitor started to read aloud a codicil, "I am aware of the unhappiness and disappointment caused to my daughter Rosa on her twenty first birthday, when she did not christen a ship of the Calloway Line. So that she may now feel fully involved in this enterprise, I bequeath her 6% of the Line's shares. My last request to the Directors is that she be invited to join the Board and that, as soon as may be possible, she launches a ship of the Line bearing her own name. James Calloway."

There was a stunned silence as everyone started mentally doing sums. An astonished Henry Gurney blurted out, "Where were they, these extra shares?"

"Mr. Calloway always had a small percentage in hand", the solicitor answered primly.

"The sly old fox," Helen thought, "Kept them hidden from me and, amazingly, from my bank. But never mind, at least he's made good that business over the launch. Just where it leaves us though in the power stakes, I'm not sure."

As if in answer to her thoughts, the solicitor said, "Mr. Calloway thought you might all like a break-down of the shares situation, as it now stands?"

Without wishing to appear too eager, encouraging murmurs from those present indicated that they would like nothing more.

"Mrs. Sonia Calloway 38%, Miss Helen Calloway 38%, Miss Rosa Calloway 6% and the Directors of the Board - Captains Thornton, Gurney and Sibbick 3% each, Messrs. Grimes, Hayden and Clarke 3% each".

Sonia's face said it all. The old boys on the Board had been cool to the point of rudeness at the funeral. Gossip about her relationship with Henry Gurney and the circumstances of J.C.'s death must have already reached them. If their support could not be counted upon, then even with the help of Richard and Henry's shares, this bequest to Rosa was really going to queer her pitch. Damn you Jim Calloway. Those girls of yours could still rule the roost!

Looks as if your head ruled your heart after all, Helen thought, you always were a shrewd businessman. This isn't about the launch at all, it's about Sonia's greed taking over and perhaps ruining something you've taken years to create. Be assured wherever you are, that Rosa and I will do all in our power to keep the Line secure. Bless you J.C. and from both of us... Thanks Dad!

Chapter Twenty Eight

March 1915

Pewter clouds were encroaching on a March sky of palest primrose as Helen walked in Hyde Park. Fallen leaves picked up by the gusts of wind, swirled and encapsulated the flurries of snow, like a child's toy globe. Warmly wrapped in her furs, Helen welcomed the intermittent onslaught of the elements. Like some purification rite it left her feeling tired, but cleansed of Richard's cruel words.

At first she had pushed them into the recesses of her mind. During J.C.'s funeral and the ensuing days she had deliberately kept herself busy until she felt herself ready to consider reasonably what he had said. Iain's rapid departure the day after the incident had brought nothing but relief. Whilst evidence of his own embarrassment, it removed from her sight a permanent reminder of what had occurred. Now she must consider rationally whether Richard's words contained a nub of truth.

Was she afraid of physical intimacy? She had told Walter that there could never be any question of love between them. Had she been too hasty? Was that evidence of some defence mechanism coming into play? Always at Craybourne she had kept Iain McNeal at arm's length and on many occasions when Richard would have taken their embraces a stage further, it was she who had always found some excuse for not doing so.

It was true that the war had removed all normality, but was she guilty of using it as an excuse? To others her life might seem full, exciting even. In reality she felt herself to be rootless, stumbling through life in an aimless fashion, waiting, but for what?

Always she had felt the Formidable Fortune to be something of a threat. Now having heard Richard say that he wanted to get his hands not so much on her as on the money, her worst fears were confirmed. It was obvious it would prove for some a stumbling block, for others an incentive. Was she always to fall between the two stools?

At such a time as this she longed for James's calm manner, his carefully considered response to each problem. Of all the men she now knew, only with James and Walter was she completely relaxed. With these two who had known her as a young girl she needed no facade, no pretences. Perhaps Walter had found her new role of wealthy widow, property owner, somewhat intimidating but she hoped her letters had erased that once and for all.

Her letters to the Front took a substantial slice out of her week, but she felt them important, some justification for not playing a more active role. Three went every week to Rosa, one each to Walter and Iain and intermittent letters to James and the Rani. Only to the latter had she spoken of Richard, disillusionment and concern. There had been a prompt reply.

"Your time will come dear Helen, perhaps when and from a source you least expect. Love cannot be explained or quantified. It will not be deterred by what you have or by what has happened to you in the past. No obstacle will prove too large to be overcome by it, only what you are and what you feel will be important. Remember dear Helen, that Jai damaged much more than your body. Sadly he made you lose the faith in human nature, the optimistic zest for life, with which most people are born. The healing process cannot yet be complete. Be patient!"

She felt the folds of the letter deep in her pocket and thought affectionately of its author. Here was another whose counsel had always been wise. She would take heed and be patient. As she turned towards the Park gates, there was a new spring in her step.

Craybourne Manor, 5th Jan. 1916

James Darling,

I have been thinking of you so much today, Olivia's first birthday, knowing how dearly you would have loved to be with us. I'm afraid with no other children around, she was spoiled as always by a very attentive retinue of adults! For the young men here she is probably the best tonic they could have. When she prattles away in her 'scribble' talk they laugh so much, more I feel than they have for a very long time.

Looking back on what has occurred since Olivia's birth is a chastening experience. At least you managed a few days' leave for Daphne's wedding and I cherish the memory of the blissful time we spent in London. It was typical of Helen to vacate her flat at Eynsford so that we might have complete privacy.

Daphne is still not fully recovered from her miscarriage. The weeks spent here brought more colour to her cheeks, but little joy to her soul, I feel. Peter has asked her to consider taking over the running of the printing firm when he enlists. (Definitely now a question of 'when' and not 'if'.) Daphne is totally familiar with the processes and the team of women and older men now working with Peter are most efficient, so what is required is editing and administration, both of which she is well capable of. Sadly she feels herself in a cleft stick, knowing that as soon as she agrees he will leave.

Sonia Calloway now has a baby boy, who, rumour has it, looks exactly like Henry Gurney! Helen says it's only a matter of time before they marry. Gossip about Sonia and her sea captain has tipped the support of the older directors well in Helen's favour, but she's sensible enough to know that this won't apply indefinitely - people have such short memories! In view of the age of some of the directors, Helen sees the whole situation as very fluid!

It's difficult to imagine that you, Rosa, Walter and Iain are all within about ten miles of each other, yet rarely meet. Eddy was injured a few weeks ago, had shrapnel embedded in his thigh. I think Betty was hoping it would prove serious enough for him to be sent home and I can't say I blame her.

Olivia will think this is a world of adults! Christmas with Helen, Bruce, Prinny and me and then not a child in sight on her birthday. I haven't mentioned it before but must confess to being intrigued by the Bruce Maynard/Helen situation. There is absolutely nothing yet, other than friendship, but I feel that Bruce is working on it and biding his time. Certainly whenever Helen visits us, we seem to see more of him than at any other time.

Your mother continues with us, but no longer in spirit. She always was and still is, quite beautiful, but her frailty is heart-breaking, our only consolation being that she is in no pain. We are all strangers to her now and I feel the end must come soon. When that happens I know I shall long for your presence even more than usual, not for Olivia and myself, but because of your own need to say goodbye. In this terrible war death has become so commonplace that I fear the expression of such feelings has become a luxury.

Prinny sends you her love and the smudged fingerprint below is Olivia's own! Darling, I miss so much the calm reassurance of your presence, but somehow knowing that the same sun and moon which look down on Craybourne are also with you is comforting. I pray daily for your safety and enclose in this letter more love than you can possibly imagine.

Always yours, dearest James,
  Muriel.

Eynsford House, 9th September 1916

My Dear James,

Your mother's death has left such a void. In my life's shifting fortunes, she has for so long been a constant. When I think of her kindness to me as a child and how she ensured that Rosa and I had a secure home and upbringing with Prinny, I realise I have so much for which to be grateful to her. Who would have blamed her in the circumstances, if her reaction had been very different?

As you can imagine, Muriel made sure that the funeral was exactly as you and Elizabeth would have wished. The hatchment was fixed to the Manor gates and very splendid it looked. All her favourite flowers filled the church and the crowds who gathered spoke of how much she was loved and respected.

Whilst grieving at her loss and not being able to be with us on that day, I am sure you feel as I do, that we did in fact say our goodbyes to her some months ago, before she slipped into a world of her own. For my part, I shall always feel privileged to have known her.

Daphne continues to do splendidly with Peter's printing works. She tells me she has many plans for the future! She has always had an amazing rapport with the East Enders and her workers are totally supportive to all her efforts. From the start they were proud to have a female editor (was she the first ever?), but when the word got around that she was an 'Honourable' to boot, they were quite overwhelmed!

During one of my visits to the North I learned of someone else who is doing a man's job successfully. Forgive me if you've already heard all this from another source. Annie Featherstone (Michael's wife) apparently heard about the creches in other parts of the country and persuaded your mill at Halifax to start one. This enabled her to go back to her old job there, where she soon gained promotion and is now regarded as an under-manager. I find the factories' grape-vine very efficient. One visit to a Yorkshire mill and I'm told what is happening throughout the West Riding.

I am glad you managed to see Rosa recently, if only for a short time. When she was last on leave I was shocked at how thin she was, but she laughed it off and said the diet out there is wonderful for losing weight. She is expecting to be moved soon and I am hopeful that it will be to a quieter area.

I often think about that Christmas when we were all together and you spoke of 'a war of attrition'. How right you have been proved. Like you I'm sickened by the constant loss of life to achieve a few yards' advantage.

On a much happier note, your Olivia is a delight. Probably because she sees so many adults under her own roof, she is not in the least shy, but Mu has seen to it that she is not precocious. I think whilst teaching, your wife saw quite enough precocious children to last a lifetime!

You once told me that if having too much money worried me, I should give some away! I have one or two ideas along those lines, but I think they'll have to wait until the war is over. Meanwhile, I've made some more purchases of which I think you would approve. A dozen acres by the river at Henley, a very desirable residence in Richmond and 25 terraced houses in Tilbury. The Richmond house and the one close to Grosvenor Square have already been snapped up as convalescent homes.

I expect Muriel has told you that we recently averted a serious situation at the Tilbury warehouse. Thank goodness J.C. insisted that there should be day and night supervision once the building was full. The materials there are stored in the dark to avoid fading and things are moved around at least once a month to deter inquisitive moths. The last 'movement' had taken place just three days earlier. The night watchman spotted smoke seeping from under one of the wooden racks and sure enough it was a fire just starting to get established. I dread to think what would have happened if it had not been for his quick thinking. It's still a puzzle as to how it happened, but the watchmen are being extra vigilant.

Dear James, for so long now I've been used to asking for and acting upon your wise counsel. I know others feel exactly the same. We all miss you so much. Take good care of yourself and come home to us soon.

Much love,
Helen

Sonia had not expected to like her child. Sorely taxed by the final weeks of pregnancy, loathing her shapelessness and afraid of what was to come, she focussed the blame for all of this on her unborn child. When he painfully thrust his way into the world she was staggered at her own feelings. The baby was perfect in every way and she, Sonia, had achieved this little miracle.

"Another J.C.," she said quizzically, as he was christened Joseph, hopeful that the thought of J.C.'s son waiting in the wings might temper the attitude of the Directors towards her. But within a few weeks, totally besotted by her son, she was no longer concerned with what happened at the Calloway Line, providing of course that it continued to support her in the style to which she had become accustomed. Now she became the doting mother of Henry Gurney's worst nightmares and he began to have second thoughts. Sonia's slim figure had been enhanced by motherhood, its contours more curvaceous and tantalising. Henry had been prepared to wait the discreet interval society demanded of a widow and then marry her. Until the baby arrived....Now he found that her life and often his was dominated by her son's needs.

"Why is he down here? Shouldn't he be in the nursery? I thought that was what nannies were for." This, sulkily, when on the second occasion in two days he arrived to find her nursing the baby.

"And," he added irritably, "I didn't think ladies in your position did that sort of thing. Surely he could have a bottle?"

He motioned towards her bare breast. The sight which would have at one time excited him, now leaving him with a feeling of revulsion.

"I prefer to feed him myself. My God, Henry, you're surely not embarrassed, after all you've seen? Stop being such a grouch. Look how his dear little head nestles against me. Isn't he too sweet for words?"

There were quite a few words which Henry could have used and 'sweet' did not feature amongst them. Privately he thought the child rather ugly, all arms and legs and so wrinkled and red. No, however tempting the money was, he was not going to be tied down by a wife totally absorbed in a brood of puking infants.

Within three months of Joe's birth, he told Sonia there would be no wedding. He'd decided that he enjoyed his life at sea with 'a girl in every port' too much and had no intention of changing it. Before Joe's birth, Sonia would have ranted and raved, called him 'an ungrateful bastard'! Now a mellower, unperturbed Sonia informed him there were 'plenty of other fish in the sea' . But they both knew only too well that for the time being, Sonia's life was full and the only 'fish' she currently had time for, was her son.

Nov. 1917

Captain Walter Heaton examined the map before him, mentally listing the B.E.F.'s successes during the past year. 1917 had seen the storming of Vimy Ridge and an amazing three and a half mile advance at Arras in April. In June they had captured the Messines Ridge and now they had at last penetrated the Hindenburg Line. In spite of this, the men in his command were low in spirits and in health. The presence of the Australians on their left flank had helped at first, but the plain truth was they had all been out here too long, living in disgusting conditions with death a daily visitor. Only the prospect of a few days' leave kept them going and some of the men in the ranks had waited as long as 18 months for that. Returning to the trenches then became harder and harder. No wonder some of the poor devils couldn't face it and took the other way out.

He looked at his kitbag lying on the bunk. All packed and ready to go. For him a precious week, starting tonight. He was going home! More and more often now he found himself fantasising about home. Watching, as in front of a cinema screen, a youth walking in the Yorkshire moors, the same lad taking two small girls to see a secret carpet of bluebells and a young man striding through the grounds of Craybourne and inhaling the sweet, heavy perfume of the roses.

He missed Rosa. Although they had met infrequently, seeing her had always been such a boost to his morale. She was so colourful! Existing in a world of khaki, grey and brown, he delighted in the rich auburn of her hair and feasted his eyes on her glowing cheeks and the pearly whiteness of her teeth. Her re-assignment to a hospital near Calais meant that contact with her too, would now be by letter. He never underestimated the value of the mail received by the men in his command, knowing that so often it was the letters he received which kept him sane. They came to him from Rosa, Hislop's Farm, India - and Helen.

Through the latter he had at last seen glimpses of the real Helen. An adult Helen, who in the world of business could be shrewd and assertive, but in personal matters was often confused. Rosa had told him of Helen's depression after the incident with Richard. Deceived by Jai and Sonia, let down by J.C. over the launching incident, perplexed by McNeal's odd behaviour and now attempting to come to terms with Richard's duplicity, no wonder she felt unable to trust anyone. Walter thought back to his second meeting with her in Jai's palace, when she was still able to show her affection for him in a spontaneous innocent fashion. And how in a few short weeks all had changed. Cowed by Jai's presence, nervous at putting a foot wrong, she had seemed continually ill-at-ease. And during the escape, her movements had been that of a robot, obeying instructions without question.

He admitted to having been worried by the knowledge of her wealth. Now, her confession that the fortune often troubled her also, brought him relief. He knew of her many property purchases and had realised belatedly, as Helen herself had done, that this was a reaction against her feeling of rootlessness. Her life had been so full of contradictions. The granddaughter of an aristocrat, yet the daughter of a very rough diamond. Admittedly, the said diamond had, with a certain amount of polishing, made good but it was still a bizarre mix. As a child on the Craybourne estate, she had been regarded by most as a poor relation, but within a few short years was wining and dining with the wealthy, until finally she had taken up residence in a palace! Everything had been too extreme, had happened too quickly. Finally toppled from a pinnacle of optimism, where all people were good and to be trusted, she had been unable to see the way forward. Unaware at first that the kindly Rani had provided her with the cushion on which to raise herself up again.

He was in touch with the Rani. It was his secret and hers. To his surprise he had received a reply to his letter thanking her for her part in the palace escape.

"I see in you a true friend of my dear Helen. Whilst your duties will often take you away from her, I feel that should there come a time when she again requires support, you will be more accessible than I. I was grateful for your determination and courage in removing Helen from India and I know I can rely upon you to assist her in finding true happiness."

From that time the Rani had written to him intermittently, with items of news she knew would be of interest; the skirmishes amongst the hill tribes, political infighting about the many reforms she was encouraging and, discreetly, of relations between the British and the Indian Raj.

Strange that distanced by miles, his correspondence with Helen had made him feel closer to her than ever before. Distressed at the loss of friends and colleagues in horrific circumstances, he had often felt the need to unburden himself. Now he felt she knew of his own suffering, whilst he in turn recognised her areas of pain and vulnerability.

Yesterday the successful penetration of the Hindenburg Line had taken its toll and now he had the unenviable task of listing the wounded and dead from his Company. Wearily he pulled the requisite form towards him and started to write. Soon the roar of motor cycles told him of the arrival of similar lists from the regiments on their right flank, the 51st Highland Division and beyond them the Yorkshire Green Howards. The compiled information he was to deliver in person to the War Department. Unfolding the two lists he turned to that of the Yorkshire Regiment. The first entry leapt out at him.

'Killed in action. Captain James Craybourne, Bt.'

***

Early evening at Eynsford House was the time Helen liked best of all. The drawing room with its clusters of settees and armchairs smelled of leather and polish, intermingled with cheroots, pipe tobacco and a hint of whisky. Amber-coloured lamps shed pools of light onto the low tables and were reflected and multiplied. The atmosphere was exactly what Helen and the House Manager had strived for, one of convivial relaxation. When Walter arrived, Helen was enjoying a pre-dinner drink with two young officers who had arrived that morning. Svelte in a dress of deep blue velvet she was stunningly beautiful, a fact obviously appreciated by the young men around her.

Hearing the flurry of movement she turned and saw him in the doorway. Her face alight with pleasure she quickly excused herself and almost ran towards him, but within a few feet her steps faltered to a standstill. He moved towards her, drawing her from the room.

"Walter, what is it....?. Who?..."

"Not here Helen, not here." Her arm drawn firmly through his, he mounted the stairs. Halfway up she again came to a halt.

"Not Rosa, Walter....dear God, tell me it's not Rosa."

Quickly he capped the note of hysteria in her voice.

"Not Rosa," he answered firmly and led her on.

At last her rooms were reached and, the door closed, she turned to him, her eyes dark with anxiety.

"Tell me...."

"It's James, Helen...."

Her half wail, half howl of pain filled the room.

"No, no..Not James, not..." Then hopefully, "Wounded?"

"No my darling...Killed in action. I'm so sorry".

The endearment passed unnoticed as she went into deep shock and started to shake violently, all colour draining rapidly from her face. He ran to the bedroom and dragged an eiderdown from the bed then drew it round her, edging her rigid body towards the settee. Easing her to a sitting position, they sat thus, he with his arms holding the eiderdown in position, rocking her backwards and forwards, all the while murmuring reassuringly.

"There, my darling, it's all right. Don't fret. There, there my love..... You're safe. I'm with you."

At last the shaking subsided and great racking sobs tore through her body. Still her head moved from side to side as if to negate what had occurred and the tears flowed until, spent at last, her head on his shoulder, she relaxed. Gently he released his grip on the coverlet and cupping her face with his hands he lightly brushed away her tears with his lips. As a child receiving comfort after a fall, she stared back at him making no protest, unseeing.

When the telephone rang she started as if roused from slumber and when he made a move to answer it she suddenly clung to him as if reluctant to be separated for even a moment. But he knew this was not a time for self-indulgence. Helen was only one of several grieving for James and others were closer by ties of blood and law.

It was Bruce Maynard on the phone. Quick explanations were required and given as to the other's identity and then decisions made on what was to be done. Muriel had now received the wire which all mothers and wives dreaded. In her anxiety that Olivia should not be upset, she was being very brave, too brave for her own good Bruce felt. Prinny was very shocked and Bruce had administered a sedative and sent her off to bed. Daphne had been informed by telephone but she was alone, so perhaps Walter could contact Betty and ask her to go and stay with Daphne. How was Helen? Bruce knew that she and James had been very close. Walter told him what had occurred and Bruce suggested a sedative for her too, adding that someone in Eynsford would be bound to have something of that nature. After that he advised a quiet period of reflection.

"It's vital that you get her to talk about James as much as possible. Get her to reminisce. Keep reminding her of the good times they all shared, it's the only way for her to come to terms with all this."

When the call was completed and the message to Betty delivered, Walter looked across at Helen huddled on the sofa. The lids of her closed eyes were swollen and red, her hair ruffled and the eiderdown clasped round her like protective armour.

"I'm going to find something to help you sleep. Don't move."

On his return he could see that his last remark had been unnecessary. Deftly he made thick sweet cocoa, making her drink deeply and swallow the pills. Then, removing the eiderdown from her clenched fists, he led her into the bedroom. How often he had dreamed of such an occasion. Of he and his beloved Helen in such a room. But never like this! She stood motionless as he carefully unbuttoned her dress until it slithered into a soft pool at her feet. At his bidding she stepped out of it, then lifted each foot in turn as her shoes were removed. Turning back the sheets he gently eased her down between them, covering her as one might a child. When he turned to go, she spoke for the first time, her voice high-pitched, fearful.

"Don't go, don't leave me stay with me.... oh, please stay. . ."

It was three o'clock in the morning when Walter awoke. He was lying awkwardly on top of the covers and extremely cold. He had slept for six hours. Even in these circumstances, his own exhaustion after the journey, coupled with the softness of the bed, had ensured that he sleep deeply. Now he was hungry and realised that he had missed both dinner and supper on the previous day. He moved carefully, trying not to disturb Helen, but the effect of the pills was wearing off and she stirred. Suddenly, she was awake and trying to make sense of the situation, he in his dishevelled clothing, the rumpled bed and she half undressed. As remembrance came flooding back, she shuddered.

"Walter...oh my dear, you can't have had any sleep...how selfish of me."

Still there remained a slight slurring of the words, a dislocation between thought and speech caused by the drugs. He moved across to her, looked down and grinned.

"I slept alright. Your bed my dear Helen, was slightly more comfortable than the style to which I have grown accustomed. How do you feel? Can I get you anything? Something to drink perhaps?"

"Yes, I'd like a drink, I'm so thirsty...I'm sure you would too. Let me get it..."

He helped her into a robe and together they went into the tiny kitchen, made tea and toast and scrambled eggs. They spoke little, but the normality of the homely tasks was reassuring and gradually Helen's manner became more focussed, more rational. Warming her hands around her cup, she at last said,

"I'm sorry I went to pieces. It's just that all the people I really care about seem to disappear from my life - my mother, Rob, Elizabeth and now James." She hesitated, "There was nothing wrong you know in what I felt for James. For me he was a sheet anchor. I could rely on him totally to give me an honest opinion - on anything. I loved him very much, not of course in the way that Muriel does... did. I think in a way he was the father which J.C. never was."

"And me, Helen? Is there anything left for me? I'm still with you, do I have a part to play in your life?"

She put the cup down and moved so that she was standing beside him.

"Oh yes my darling Walter, you do," she put her arms around him. "I've been so stupid. And it's taken this tragedy to make me realise just how stupid. When I was little and needed you, you were always there and again in India, you never thought of your own safety, always of mine. Last night I needed your strength and your love and you gave me both, not asking anything in return. I think if you had..."

She didn't finish. He was on his feet and folding her in an embrace of almost crushing delight. Unshaven, his skin harsh against hers, he kissed her.

"No...forgive me Walter, but not like this. I want it to be so special and now, well..." she laughed for the first time since his arrival. "I need to get rid of yesterday's underwear, take a bath and do something about my mouth which tastes ghastly after those pills. You probably want to shave. Let's wait just a little while, then... afterwards, we can have a few more hours sleep, together.

He humoured her, though all his senses were urging him to take her there and then. They respected each other's privacy as each bathed. Walter then meticulously folded his rumpled trousers and from the depths of his kit-bag produced a clean shirt which he spread carefully over an armchair. Now, suddenly, he felt nervous. She was waiting for him, but was she really ready for intimacy? How would she react? Would it be too much after last night's shock? And how on earth could he be patient when suddenly he felt as if the world was on fire?

She had tidied the bed and lay between the sheets. As he lifted the top sheet he saw that she was naked and beautiful. His groan was one of ecstasy.

"Helen my love, you're so beautiful."

And she seeing the breadth of his shoulders, the fine blonde hair curling on his chest, his manhood fully erect, drew him towards her.

"You're beautiful too, my darling."

He tried desperately to be patient, to curb his own desire for instant gratification. Delicately, he traced the line of her firm breasts, revelled in the touch of her soft sweet-smelling skin and at last when he felt her to be moist with anticipation he entered her. They moved together in an exquisite bonding and now for both of them it was a speedy conclusion. But to Walter's horror, Helen's orgasm with its soft gasps of pleasure was followed by a swift onrush of tears.

"Helen, what is it? Have I hurt you?"

She smiled, brushing the tears away.

"I'm sorry. I think it's just reaction, one release of emotion causing another. It's certainly nothing you did wrong. It was... well, wonderful is an understatement."

"But over much too quickly! It's been such a long time... .Not that I often...."

"No confessions my love....You can't have been in the army for, what seven or eight years? and lived the life of a monk. Just put me out of my misery on one point though, not with my stepmother?"

"Your stepmother? Oh - dear Sonia! The femme fatale! Good Lord no. I had a narrow escape there. A fine friend she turned out to be for all of us."

"Come back into bed," Helen said. "I'm tired again now and I want to go to sleep with your arms around me." And so she did.

Chapter Twenty Nine

They awoke to new delight in each other's presence, to the joy of making love leisurely, to discovering each other's bodies and making them as familiar as their own. And they talked about anything and everything. Remembering Bruce's advice, Walter encouraged Helen to talk about James. And at last she was able to speak his name easily with affection, rather than recoiling from it as she pondered on the manner of his death.

But at 9.0 a.m. there were other matters to consider. A phone call to Daphne advised them that Betty was still with her. The decision was made that Walter should escort Daphne and Helen to Yorkshire on the mid-day train from Euston. Then Rosa telephoned and Walter explained to Helen that he had contacted Rosa before leaving France, asking her not to speak of James's death, until the official information had been relayed.

Bruce Maynard phoned with the news that Muriel still seemed much too composed for his liking, but that Prinny after a tablet-induced sleep was more in control. They told him of their plans and it was arranged that a car would meet them at Leeds.

Helen was shocked when she saw Daphne. Even allowing for the news of James, there was a dreadful lack-lustre appearance about her which gave rise for concern. Feeling guilty that so occupied with her own concerns she had not seen Daphne for several weeks, Helen now probed her about her health and found that once again the onset of the winter fogs had brought on asthmatic attacks and two bouts of bronchitis. Although the younger of the two, Helen felt responsible for Daphne. She'd had a rotten time when she lost her baby and Helen was well able to empathise with that. Now with her husband away at the Front and the second of her brothers killed she looked shrunken and bereft. Guiltily, Walter and Helen tried to hide their new-found joy in each other, turning all their attention to Daphne and her needs.

If Walter was Helen's mainstay, then Bruce Maynard was certainly Muriel's. It was he who ensured Olivia was happily occupied, that both Mu and Prinny had, in spite of their protestations, sufficient rest. On his instructions the hatchment announcing to the world the death of Craybourne's beloved Lord of the Manor was mounted on the Manor gates. And it was he who put in train the arrangements for James's memorial service. Having convinced Muriel that it was better for all concerned that this not be delayed, the service was held two days after the arrival of the group from London.

It was during the service that the words of Haig, the retired family butler came rushing back. Seeing his sister amongst the mourners, Helen was suddenly reminded of Haig's warning to James that should both the Craybourne boys die during the war, then, if Michael Featherstone knew of his origins and could prove them, as the closest male heir, he would inherit the title.

Looking at Daphne's pallid face, her eyes ringed by purple smudges, her body so painfully thin, Helen tried to blank out the bizarre words of the song ringing inside her head, 'if one green bottle should accidentally fall...' It was unlikely that the question of inheritance would be raised until the war ended. Now with only one girl in the Craybourne fold, it was crucial that Daphne and Peter Fairburn produce a male child.

Declining Mu's pressing invitation that she remain in Yorkshire for a while, Daphne travelled south with Helen and Walter. They separated from her at Euston with an assurance from Helen that she would be in touch very soon, then went straight to the Salon, Walter having promised Eddy that he would give Betty as much news as possible. It was an elated Betty they found awaiting them, Eddy's letter having just arrived with the news that he would be home on leave in three weeks' time.

They spent a happy evening, Helen and Walter making no secret of the fact that they were now lovers. Thank goodness Helen's at last come to her senses, Betty thought, she's realised that the one person who's always cared for her is Walter. He follows her every movement with his eyes as if he's terrified she'll disappear! Somewhat different from the Indian princeling, whose only interest in beauty was as an adjunct to his own wonderful self!

Back at Eynsford, Helen was very aware of what a brief time she and Walter had left together. Two short days in which to love and be loved. Never had she felt so desired, nor so desirable. When they had of necessity to go out and buy food, it was she who felt proud as female eyes assessed Walter with admiration, then flickered over her with envy. This was a Walter, Helen felt she had never known. Blonde and handsome in his immaculate uniform, with a confident spring in his step and eyes only for her. What was it the Rani had said? That her time would come from a source she would least expect. What a wise old bird she was, probably knew all the time this was how it would end! Parting would be very hard indeed, but it seemed that Lady Luck, or the Rani's gods were smiling on her at last, so she must be strong and as Prinny constantly advised, 'Think positively'.

Eynsford House, May 1918

Rosa Darling,

It was so wonderful to see you and with a little more flesh on your bones than a year ago. I have no doubt that that meets with the approval of the latest man in your life!

So much family news to relate. But first things first - Betty is pregnant. I'm so delighted for them, they have been longing to start a family. Already her figure is quite rounded and I've suggested that we might consider designing wear specifically for ladies 'in an interesting condition'. Don't you agree that it's ridiculous that at such a time women should just make do with adapting what is already in their wardrobes?

The Salon is all ready for the end of the War We have on standby a range of new designs and as soon as we have the news we're all longing for, we'll cut the mourning clothes to a minimum and flood the market with ready-to-wear clothes that are bright and innovative. There have got to be radical changes. Women are never going to return to the pre-war days when they stayed at home and there was always cheap servant labour available. Now it's been proved that women can hold down jobs, often very important ones, we must adapt to our new lifestyles and wear clothes that are practical. Sorry about that! Having been on both sides of the fence, I feel qualified to have an unjaundiced view of the situation. Let me know if you think there's any merit in the maternity wear idea.

Muriel and Olivia are well - and so is Bruce. Mu, once said that she thought Bruce was sweet on me. I now think she had it all wrong and he was strongly attracted to her right from the start. He half admitted this to me recently and said the only reason he was more in evidence when I went to visit was both to prevent gossip and to ensure he wouldn't be tempted to overstep the mark if they were alone!

I admire Bruce tremendously. He's very interested in some of the skin-grafting techniques and plastic surgery which have been developed during the war and says he would like to study that branch of medicine. I hope he gets the opportunity, he certainly deserves it. He's leaving for the Front soon, says he's convinced other people older and less fit could cope with what he's doing here. I don't know if I can go along with that. His work at Craybourne has been quite exceptional. Always his primary concern is to get the mental attitude right, believing that without that, all the medicine in the world won't work.

Mu took such a long while to recover from the delayed shock of James's death, but Bruce was always there ensuring she had sufficient rest and creating diversion to arouse her interest. His insistence that she walk every day that the weather was reasonable, achieved a little miracle. She now looks fit and seems extremely well-adjusted. Incidentally Olivia dotes on Bruce. He has, after all been part of her world since she was born. So....let me just say I'm hopeful.

I've kept the most amazing news for the big finish. Sonia telephoned to say she needed to see me and would I be very kind and go to her because of the baby, etc., etc. I thought, here we go again, dear Sonia trying it on. What's she up to this time? When she added that it was most important and concerned the Line, I knew I had no option but to meet her request.

The long and short of it is that when Henry Gurney turned his back on her, she decided she'd had enough of Liverpool. Her first thoughts were to return to London, but one of the captains started extolling the virtues of America, saying life there was wonderful and that it was a young people's country. He convinced her and she decided to sell up lock, stock and barrel and go.

Give the devil his, or in this case, her due, she did give me first option on the shares. Or was it just that she knew I had the money to meet her demands? She drove a hard bargain, said she wanted 50% more than their market value and I was to take it or leave it, no room for discussion. Well, as I told her, I don't do business like that, so I did talk to my adviser at the bank and he said I should definitely go ahead.

So now little sister, a further 35% shares have been added to your 6% and a further 3% to mine, making you and me principal joint shareholders with 41% each. I thought the news might be enough to send the elder Directors into a decline, but they all seem to have taken it well. (I think they were more than a little tired of Sonia's tarnished reputation.) All this begs the question what are your plans for the future? Back to Oxford? Or to pastures new?

If you are interested in being more than a nominal joint head of the Line, there is much we might consider. e.g. We could make Tilbury our home base. (I tend to agree with Sonia about Liverpool). We could also follow P.& O.'s lead and build passenger liners. I doubt very much that a shipping line has been run by two sisters before, so it could be an exciting challenge. Don't forget the situation is open-ended. No pressures at all, entirely your own choice.

Walter will also have some decisions to make. One thing that's come to light since we've become a couple is that he always felt Prinny had educated us out of his class! Only now has he realised that there's a great deal more to it than what can be learned in a schoolroom. He's been involved with so many things, - the farm, assistant Estate Manager at Craybourne, then into the army where his expertise with horses came to the fore. He seems to have totally discounted the qualities of leadership required as an officer and the administration skills involved, not to mention the travelling he's done (an education in itself) and the knowledge he's gained about political situations en route. As I pointed out in no uncertain terms the breadth of his experience is endless. I doubt if he'll want to remain in the army after this. Will anyone? The money isn't a problem, so the opportunities are unlimited.

Sonia's little Joe is an engaging child. Not particularly attractive to look at, but he's so bright and full of fun. Never thought I'd be in a position to envy Sonia anything, but I must admit to the strongest urge to pick him up and hold him tightly. Am I getting broody do you think? If we didn't know differently, I'd swear he was a J.C. in the making. Just shows how wrong one can be!

I've bought some more houses. (Do I hear a groan from across the Channel?) 'Adding to my Empire', Walter calls it. But as I have every intention of being a very responsible landlord it's surely better for me to buy the properties now before they fall into disrepair. Now.....I don't want you to laugh at this, but one property I bought with Mu and Olivia in mind. After all if Michael Featherstone claims Craybourne, Mu has to live somewhere. It's on the borders of London and Surrey and would make a superb small boarding school, with plenty of room for expansion. Well, who knows? There'll be money from James of course and from the mills, but I can't imagine Mu wanting to go into retirement for a very long time and her own school where she could indoctrinate all the little darlings with the right feminist ideas might be the very thing!

I've just had an amazing thought. If Michael inherited the title that would make Annie Hinton the next Lady Craybourne. Can you believe it ?!

I finally got Prinny to London last week. (Bruce had to come down on business for several days so was able to escort her). She's still as quick-witted as ever and has managed to adapt her metaphors to take in modern technology. She told me her motor was running well, but her bodywork was 'in need of repair '.

Delighted you met up with Iain after all this time. It's oddly reassuring to me to think of the people I care about, distanced by the war, seeing each other. Glad to hear he's unscathed and relatively at peace with himself. You probably told him that Walter and I .... Well I've no doubt you told him something! The poor man will probably be most relieved. That ghastly incident with Richard must have cured him once and for all of any feelings he had for me.

I told you I had a great deal of news, quite sufficient for you to digest at one sitting. As always I so look forward to your letters and the news that you are safe and well. I pray that you and everyone else will be coming home very soon.

My love to you always Rosa darling,

Helen.

B.E.F., Belgium, June, 1918

Dearest Helen,

Just a brief note to say that I've now met your Bruce Maynard. The long arm of coincidence has brought him right to my doorstep, or rather to my own particular Clearing Station. What a lovely fellow he is. We have managed to snatch a few moments together on several occasions,(usually at about 9.0 p.m.!) and he has brought me up to date with the news from Craybourne, the farm and what's going on in the village. He makes some of the young men I met at Oxford, and elsewhere, seem like babes-in-arms. Yet he has none of the broodiness of Iain McNeal, thank heavens! I admire so much his positive approach to everything. Long may it continue in this depressing environment.

Yesterday was not a good day. As you know we normally just collect the wounded from the line dressing stations, bringing them back here, where surgery is performed as necessary. Occasionally though a situation arises where immediate surgery is imperative at the first aid dressing post. Yesterday was such a day and I had to stay and assist with an amputation. Whilst I have now seen and learned to cope with many terrible injuries, there is something about amputating a limb which I find particularly horrific. I managed not to faint, but at one point it was a very close call.

Stories of ghosts are once again running rife in the trenches. (We seem to get a resurgence of these about every three months.) Men going 'over the top' claim that they see a dead comrade sometimes running alongside them, sometimes urging them forward. There are two schools of thought about this. One that it's the worst possible luck, as it means you're about to join those who have died, the other that these are protective spirits who will guide you out of danger. I'm keeping an open mind until someone on whom I can rely tells me they've had such an experience. Although if the former is true, then there will never be anyone in a position to tell me....

I'm due for a three day rest period soon and so looking forward to not having to rise at first light when the 'morning hate' firing starts on both sides, indicating we're back in the business of war again.

I haven't seen Walter for a while, they've been doing a spell of relief work in the trenches. Whilst I usually get news of Eddy from Walter, I've not heard anything about Daphne's husband and am not likely to, as I believe the Kents are ten to fifteen miles away to our west.

I sometimes wonder when and if we shall all ever get together again. But that's morbid talk and I must, as Bruce says, think positively.

Much love,

Rosa.

Rosa Darling,

Mu has had an amazing letter from Michael Featherstone answering all, or most, of our questions. The two of them have now met and what I can tell you is that he has been aware for some time that Oliver Craybourne was his grandfather. Apparently he went to see Haig and asked him to put something in writing to that effect As you would expect from a family retainer, Haig declined. His sister had no such scruples. Anxious to keep on the right side of the man who could become the new Lord of the Manor, she craftily wrote down the whole story then asked the doctor to call. Siting that gentleman in the next room behind the bedroom's open door, she read the story aloud and asked her brother if it was an accurate record of what actually happened, as he knew it. Once he'd confirmed it, she and the doctor signed the document It's likely that that paper, together with some items found in the box which Bea Featherstone left for her grandson would be sufficient to convince a court.

Bea had asked that the box be buried with her and Michael felt guilty that in the turmoil of what happened he hadn't done so - let's face it he was only a boy when all this took place. When he went back to retrieve the box from the Vicar's keeping several years later, they examined the contents together and started to draw conclusions. There was the corner of a man's handkerchief with the initials O.C., the family tree torn from the Bible, where Bea had superimposed Oliver's initials over those of her husband. And, wrapped in a piece of soft cloth, a half hunter gold watch. The watch bears the inscription 'To Oliver on his 16th birthday'. No doubt it was filched from his jacket at some point.

Michael is anxious that everything be dealt with as amicably as possible, but equally determined that he should receive what he feels is now rightfully his. Mu has no argument with that. As she says, with James and Elizabeth both gone, Craybourne can never be the same for her again. At heart she is a Southerner, whilst Michael was born in the Yorkshire moors and has his roots here. She says she feels Craybourne is more his than hers. She was obviously impressed by him and tells me that Prinny, thinking back to those early days when she was surreptitiously passing on knowledge, was absolutely delighted with her erstwhile pupil.

I don't think the matter would ever go to court. If James had not told us all about his conversation with Haig it would have been a different story. But knowing that and with this other evidence, Mu is too honourable a person to fight an unjust cause. Nothing is to be done until the war is over. And then, only when Mu has found somewhere she wishes to live. My boarding school idea suddenly sounds less ridiculous, don't you think?

Apparently Michael laughed outright at the idea that he and his family would occupy the whole house. He said he intends continuing along the present system with a family wing. The remainder he hopes to lease as a headquarters cum retreat for Methodists. He wants to continue working but says he'll require more revenue to support the estate so will have to consider different methods of raising this. He was delighted when Mu told him that two large parcels of land to the south and west of the village form part of the estate and that James had intended they should be used for building when the time was ripe. As Mu now owns the Halifax mills, I think she might well install Michael as manager at one or all of them. He can hardly go back and work on the shop floor!

Having received nothing but kindness from the Craybournes, Michael stressed that he would do nothing to hurt the family. But what a diminished family it now is! Daphne will mourn the loss of her beautiful family home but realistically, would never have lived there again, even if the circumstances were different. Your roots and mine are tied to Craybourne and I can't help wondering how we might retain a foothold of some kind there.

Daphne came to Eynsford and dined with me yesterday. As you can imagine we had plenty to talk about. All seems well at the printing works. She misses Peter of course and I do worry about her living alone. Now that our Indian summer is giving way to the first frosts of winter, the fogs are starting to build up and as always these affect her badly.

Betty, after a a sickly few weeks, is now blooming, just wishes that Eddy was around to share each new stage with her.

Rafe Sinclair called yesterday full of doom and gloom about not having enough drivers. I've told him he can put me on the relief roster for three days per week.

Once the war is over, I've decided to convert some of my factories into rehabilitation centres for the men returning. So many of them joined up, not solely because of enlistment euphoria, but just to get away from poorly paid dead-end jobs. I'm sure they won't readily go back to menia tasks with no prospects. If they could be taught other skills or trades, then their horizons would be broadened.

It's now some months since we moved the sewing of the ready-made clothes out to the East Ham factory. I've found two other buildings in that area, so will be ready at any time to expand production. The majority of the work at all three factories will be carried out by women. No-one can say I'm not doing my bit to try and ensure equal opportunity for women!

I really thought the food situation would ease once rationing was brought in in February, on the assumption that if you had coupons for meat, etc., there would be no need to queue. I was wrong. Sometimes I feel the British see queuing as a viruous occupation!

Delighted to hear you met up with Bruce. Do give him my regards.

Much love,

Helen

B.E.F., Belgium

Dearest Helen,

There is not an easy way to say this, so I won't beat about the bush. Meeting Bruce is the most amazing thing that has ever happened to me. There was an instant rapport I've never felt with anyone else. And it was mutual! I know you will be upset on Mu's behalf, but Bruce assures me there has been no firm commitment on either side.

He managed to get a three day pass to coincide with mine and we were taken to the rest centre seven miles behind the lines. Whatever you thought about my relations with Alex, or anyone else, I was still virgo intacto - until last week. Bruce and I found a farmhouse and stayed there as man and wife. I'm being deliberately blunt about this, so that you will realise that we care deeply about each other and when the time is appropriate we shall marry. With every day which passes we see around us the frailty of human life, surely it isn't wrong to seize our own happiness whilst we can?

Helen dear, please write and say you understand.

All my love, Rosa

B.E. F., Belgium

Helen,

Two weeks and no letter. You must be very upset indeed. Perhaps you should ask yourself honestly whether that is because of Mu's feelings, or because your own plans for her future and mine, have been tampered with?

Has it occurred to you that you are in danger of becoming too manipulative? Always you are planning and arranging what you think other people should do with their lives. Mu, Daphne, Betty, me and... soon, no doubt, Walter. Forward planning might be acceptable in business but manipulating people's private lives is not. Since you recovered from that business in India you seem to have been on a whirlwind carousel, dashing here and there, dabbling in this enterprise and that, buying up property. Is it perhaps that you're afraid if you stop rushing around there will be more time to think? Surely now that you know how much Walter cares for you, you can slow down, relax, take each day as it comes?

I feel so wonderfully fortunate to have found Bruce. We are part of the same profession, with common interests. And yes, I know now what I want to do when this is over and Bruce is very much a part of it. I want to study medicine, build on the bedrock of knowledge I've acquired out here. Bruce is set on medical research, so we'll arrange it so that we can be together during our studies. Money will be a problem and it might mean that I have to sell some of the shares I own in a shipping line. Do you know anyone who might be interested?

Please write Helen. Your silence grieves me. Out of your happiness with Walter can you not see a way to appreciate my own feelings for Bruce?

My love always,
Rosa

Eynsford Ho.

Rosa,

If I'm in danger of being manipulative, it is, as far as you are concerned, because at eight years old I was made to feel responsible for you and that feeling has persisted.

I have had to consider the possibility, which you presumably refused to do, that Bruce having learned Mu was to lose Craybourne and the estate, might no longer find her so attractive as before. And the further possibility that he knows you to be part owner of a shipping line, with a rich sister. Not pleasant thoughts? I'm afraid the realistic approach rarely is.

However, I've now resolved all my heart-searching. I have always found Bruce to be a man of integrity, dedicated to his profession and there is no reason for me to revise that opinion. Forgive me. I am overly suspicious of people's motives I know, but I think perhaps with good reason.

I commend your plans for the future even if it means having a partner in name only on the Calloway Line. Perhaps Walter...? There you see, I'm doing it again! Must really cure myself of the habit. Seriously, financing your studies is certainly not a problem. I would prefer you to hang on to the shares, but if Bruce is uneasy about my contributing towards your studies, then of course I would purchase some of them. I ask only that you will always give me first refusal, as I would hate the Line to go out of our family's hands.

Here there is a definite feeling in the air that things are at last going well at the Front. God willing it may be over by Christmas and we can all be together again. If Walter and Bruce are prepared to make honest women of us, what about a double wedding?

Your ever loving, if manipulative, sister.
Helen

Dearest Helen,

What a joy to hear from you and to know that I can count on your support and love.

And how splendid the news from here. We're told that your newspapers and broadcasts have been full of what has happened, so I know I'm not breaking any censorship rules. Of course the Hindenburg Line has been penetrated before, but this time it has been forced back along a distance of some 100 miles! Everyone's spirits have been so lifted by this. There is talk now of going home soon and suddenly Christmas looks as if it might just be a possibility.

So, sister dear, get my bed aired and kill the fatted calf, or whatever else you feel like doing! I could be with you soon.

Much love,

Rosa

P.S. It occurs to me that you might want to spend Christmas at Craybourne as usual and whilst both Bruce and I have been in touch with Mu, I do feel it would be too soon for us to spend any time with her, as a couple. Perhaps you'd think about this - if you agree with me, then I will go with Bruce to Wales during the holiday period. It will be an opportunity to meet his family. We can discuss that joint wedding when we all return to London.

P. P.S. Just think Eynsford will soon be empty of all its personnel. I can't imagine it!

Eynsford House, Nov. 13th 1918

Rosa Darling,

I do so wish this could be the joyful letter I'd expected to write, but all the happiness at the ending of hostilities has been overwhelmed by a dreadful sorrow. Daphne died yesterday, on the evening of Armistice Day. I've always felt older than she and now I can't help a terrible feeling of guilt that I have somehow failed her.

You will have heard that a new virulent strain of influenza has been sweeping the country, causing hundreds of deaths. When Daphne telephoned me on the 8th, she said she felt very poorly and with Rafe's help I managed to get a doctor to go with me to her flat straight away. He was very alarmed at the chronic weakness of her chest and tried to get her into hospital. There was not a bed anywhere. I hired a nurse and together we looked after her, but on the very day that the whole country was bursting with joy, she slipped quietly away from us.

To me Daphne was always the typical 'poor little rich girl', whilst having everything, there was still an aura of sadness about her. It took her a long time to remove the 'spoiled brat' image, the legacy of her nannies. I was delighted for her when she at last found happiness with Peter, but it's been so short-lived. Peter is due home today - he must be devastated.

It's almost beyond comprehension that all the Craybourne children are now gone. But we are not alone in mourning several loved ones and as you'd expect, the widespread joy at the Armistice has been interlaced with the grief that has touched so many hearts and homes.

I know that it's likely to be a while before everything can be wound down over there and your work completed, but yes, your bed is aired and I am so very anxious to see and hug you again.

All love,

Helen

Craybourne Manor, Boxing Day, 1918

Typical of Mu's thoughtfulness, Helen mused, that the Featherstones be invited to afternoon tea so that they and their children might start to feel at ease in what is to be their new home. All the little ones now having been removed to the nursery so that the adults might chat, Helen sat back and allowed the conversation to flow over and around her.

What a motley lot we are, she thought. Prinny, daughter of a clergyman, poor as a church mouse; Mu, daughter of a singing teacher and orphaned at 15; Michael brought up on the moors by a bully of a father; Annie, like me, from Piggott's Lane, with a glutton for a mother and a father with a roving eye. Walter, saved from the Poor House when he was ten, to work at Hislop's Farm and me, motherless at eight, no father around and future prospects pretty bleak. Now look at us!

Mu is the Dowager Lady Craybourne, and with Prinny runs this mansion and all that that entails as if they had always been accustomed to living in such style. Walter is an army officer, with a distinguished career behind him and as for me, well as Rosa pointed out, I'm involved in many disparate enterprises and have that Formidable Fortune lurking in the background. That we should have been drawn together by circumstances into this lovely old house is amazing. And that Michael and I share the same grandfather is even more so.

His face is so serious as he listens to Prinny's remarks. He seems a kind and thoughtful young man, a good successor for James. Oh James, dearest James, I miss you so. Feeling the warm pressure of Walter's hand she knew he sensed her thoughts. But now eyes turned to Annie, knowing that of them all, it was she who had changed beyond all recognition. Reaching only to Michael's shoulder, Annie was smiling and bright-eyed. It was she, Helen noted, who within the bounds of politeness, directed the conversation. This was no shrinking violet likely to be daunted either by surroundings or company. Annie was confident, obviously well-read and articulate. Together the young Lord and Lady Craybourne made a likeable and thoughtful couple. It was as if their adverse childhood experiences had bred in them a compulsion to be both good citizens and good parents. And that's what I want to be, she thought. I have tried to make a start, but there's so much that could and should be done... Again there was the warm pressure of Walter's hand. He's wondering what's wrong with me, Helen thought. I haven't spoken for ages.

At the pressure of his arm under her elbow, she rose with him as he spoke and said, easily,

"I think if you'll excuse us, Helen and I would like to breathe in some good Yorkshire air, before it gets dark."

It had been a bright wintry day with the pale sun appearing intermittently. Now the sky was shading over into deepest lavender, the departing sun defining the clouds with bands of gold. They walked to the point where the Manor grounds stopped and parkland took over and Walter drawing her towards him said,

"Now my love, where have you been for the last half hour?"

"Only as far as Piggott's Lane, but I can't help thinking .."

"Yes?"

"That it's a whole world away from where the new Lord and Lady Craybourne and you and me are today."

"But that's as it should be, as we move onward we improve and progress."

"We've been so lucky."

"Has it all been luck? I tend to think we are what we make of ourselves. The Rani said in one of her letters that there was a flame inside each one of us..."

"I know that quotation! Something about us 'living by an invisible sun within us'. But sometimes I've felt that my own particular sun was almost eclipsed by problems and grief. Can we go back to India one day Walter, just you and me? It would be so wonderful to see the Rani again."

"We can go anywhere you like my darling, just so long as we go together. Now, if you've finished putting the world to rights, perhaps we should rejoin the others. I suppose whilst you were cogitating you didn't decide what to do about the Formidable Fortune?"

"Well... I did have some ideas."

He chuckled and drew her towards him.

"I rather thought you might!"

And as the warm glow of the Manor lights spilled over onto its environs, they turned their backs on the encroaching darkness and laughing together, stepped into the light.